TELL ME A LITTLE ABOUT YOURSELF, MR. MARLOWE

"I'm a licensed private investigator and have been for quite a while. I'm a lone wolf, unmarried, getting middle aged and not rich. I've been in jail more than once and I don't do divorce business. I like liquor and women and chess and a few other things. The cops don't like me too well, but I know a couple I get along with. I'm a native son, both parents dead, no brothers or sisters and when I get knocked off in a dark alley sometime, if it happens, as it could to anyone in my business, nobody will feel that the bottom has dropped out of his or her life.

"I left out one item. I have a portrait of Madison in my pocket.

"A five thousand dollar bill."

By Raymond Chandler
Published by Ballantine Books:

KILLER IN THE RAIN

PLAYBACK

THE LONG GOODBYE

THE SIMPLE ART OF MURDER

PICKUP ON NOON STREET

TROUBLE IS MY BUSINESS

RAYMOND CHANDLER

THE LONG GOODBYE

BALLANTINE BOOKS • NEW YORK

Copyright © 1953 by Raymond Chandler

All rights reserved. Published in the United States by Ballantine Books, a division of Random House, Inc., New York,
and simultaneously in Canada by Random House of Canada
Limited, Toronto.

Library of Congress Catalog Card Number: 54-5278

ISBN 0-345-30582-5

This edition published by arrangement with
Houghton Mifflin Company

Manufactured in the United States of America

First Ballantine Books Edition: October 1971
Tenth Printing: December 1982

THE LONG GOODBYE

1

THE FIRST TIME I laid eyes on Terry Lennox he was drunk in a Rolls-Royce Silver Wraith outside the terrace of The Dancers. The parking lot attendant had brought the car out and he was still holding the door open because Terry Lennox's left foot was still dangling outside, as if he had forgotten he had one. He had a young-looking face but his hair was bone white. You could tell by his eyes that he was plastered to the hairline, but otherwise he looked like any other nice young guy in a dinner jacket who had been spending too much money in a joint that exists for that purpose and for no other.

There was a girl beside him. Her hair was a lovely shade of dark red and she had a distant smile on her lips and over her shoulders she had a blue mink that almost made the Rolls-Royce look like just another automobile. It didn't quite. Nothing can.

The attendant was the usual half-tough character in a white coat with the name of the restaurant stitched across the front of it in red. He was getting fed up.

"Look, mister," he said with an edge to his voice, "would you mind a whole lot pulling your leg into the car so I can kind of shut the door? Or should I open it all the way so you can fall out?"

The girl gave him a look which ought to have stuck at least four inches out of his back. It didn't bother him enough to give him the shakes. At The Dancers they get the sort of people that disillusion you about what a lot of golfing money can do for the personality.

A low-swung foreign speedster with no top drifted into the parking lot and a man got out of it and used the dash lighter on a long cigarette. He was wearing a pullover check shirt, yellow slacks, and riding boots. He strolled off trailing clouds of incense, not even bothering to look towards the Rolls-Royce. He probably thought it was corny.

At the foot of the steps up to the terrace he paused to stick a monocle in his eye.

The girl said with a nice burst of charm: "I have a wonderful idea, darling. Why don't we just take a cab to your place and get your convertible out? It's such a wonderful night for a run up the coast to Montecito. I know some people there who are throwing a dance around the pool."

The white-haired lad said politely: "Awfully sorry, but I don't have it any more. I was compelled to sell it." From his voice and articulation you wouldn't have known he had had anything stronger than orange juice to drink.

"Sold it, darling? How do you mean?" She slid away from him along the seat but her voice slid away a lot farther than that.

"I mean I had to," he said. "For eating money."

"Oh, I see." A slice of spumoni wouldn't have melted on her now.

The attendant had the white-haired boy right where he could reach him—in a low-income bracket. "Look, buster," he said, "I've got to put a car away. See you some more some other time—maybe."

He let the door swing open. The drunk promptly slid off the seat and landed on the blacktop on the seat of his pants. So I went over and dropped my nickel. I guess it's always a mistake to interfere with a drunk. Even if he knows and likes you he is always liable to haul off and poke you in the teeth. I got him under the arms and got him up on his feet.

"Thank you so very much," he said politely.

The girl slid under the wheel. "He gets so goddam English when he's loaded," she said in a stainless-steel voice. "Thanks for catching him."

"I'll get him in the back of the car," I said.

"I'm terribly sorry. I'm late for an engagement." She let the clutch in and the Rolls started to glide. "He's just a lost dog," she added with a cool smile. "Perhaps you can find a home for him. He's housebroken—more or less."

And the Rolls ticked down the entrance driveway onto Sunset Boulevard, made a right turn, and was gone. I was looking after her when the attendant came back. And I was still holding the man up and he was now sound asleep.

"Well, that's one way of doing it," I told the white coat.

"Sure," he said cynically. "Why waste it on a lush? Them curves and all."

"You know him?"

"I heard the dame call him Terry. Otherwise I don't know him from a cow's caboose. But I only been here two weeks."

"Get my car, will you?" I gave him the ticket.

By the time he brought my Olds over I felt as if I was holding up a sack of lead. The white coat helped me get him into the front seat. The customer opened an eye and thanked us and went to sleep again.

"He's the politest drunk I ever met," I said to the white coat.

"They come all sizes and shapes and all kinds of manners," he said. "And they're all bums. Looks like this one had a plastic job one time."

"Yeah." I gave him a dollar and he thanked me. He was right about the plastic job. The right side of my new friend's face was frozen and whitish and seamed with thin fine scars. The skin had a glossy look along the scars. A plastic job and a pretty drastic one.

"Whatcha aim to do with him?"

"Take him home and sober him up enough to tell me where he lives."

The white coat grinned at me. "Okay, sucker. If it was me, I'd just drop him in the gutter and keep going. Them booze hounds just make a man a lot of trouble for no fun. I got a philosophy about them things. The way the competition is nowadays a guy has to save his strength to protect hisself in the clinches."

"I can see you've made a big success out of it," I said.

He looked puzzled and then he started to get mad, but by that time I was in the car and moving.

He was partly right of course. Terry Lennox made me plenty of trouble. But after all that's my line of work.

I was living that year in a house on Yucca Avenue in the Laurel Canyon district. It was a small hillside house on a dead-end street with a long flight of redwood steps to the front door and a grove of eucalyptus trees across the way. It was furnished, and it belonged to a woman who had gone to Idaho to live with her widowed daughter for a while. The rent was low, partly because the owner wanted to be able to come back on short notice, and partly because of the steps. She was getting too old to face them every time she came home.

I got the drunk up them somehow. He was eager to help but his legs were rubber and he kept falling asleep in the middle of an apologetic sentence. I got the door unlocked and dragged him inside and spread him on the long couch, threw a rug over him and let him go back to sleep. He snored like a grampus for an hour. Then he came awake all of a sudden and wanted to go to the bathroom. When he came back he looked at me peeringly, squinting his eyes, and wanted to know where the hell he was. I told him. He said his name was Terry Lennox and that he lived in an apartment in Westwood and no one was waiting up for him. His voice was clear and unslurred.

He said he could handle a cup of black coffee. When I brought it he sipped it carefully holding the saucer close under the cup.

"How come I'm here?" he asked, looking around.

"You squiffed out at The Dancers in a Rolls. Your girl friend ditched you."

"Quite," he said. "No doubt she was entirely justified."

"You English?"

"I've lived there. I wasn't born there. If I might call a taxi, I'll take myself off."

"You've got one waiting."

He made the steps on his own going down. He didn't say much on the way to Westwood, except that it was very kind of me and he was sorry to be such a nuisance. He had probably said it so often and to so many people that it was automatic.

His apartment was small and stuffy and impersonal. He might have moved in that afternoon. On a coffee table in front of a hard green davenport there was a half empty Scotch bottle and melted ice in a bowl and three empty fizzwater bottles and two glasses and a glass ash tray loaded with stubs with and without lipstick. There wasn't a photograph or a personal article of any kind in the place. It might have been a hotel room rented for a meeting or a farewell, for a few drinks and a talk, for a roll in the hay. It didn't look like a place where anyone lived.

He offered me a drink. I said no thanks. I didn't sit down. When I left he thanked me some more, but not as if I had climbed a mountain for him, nor as if it was nothing at all. He was a little shaky and a little shy but polite as hell. He stood in the open door until the automatic elevator came up and I got into it. Whatever he didn't have he had manners.

He hadn't mentioned the girl again. Also, he hadn't mentioned that he had no job and no prospects and that almost his last dollar had gone into paying the check at The Dancers for a bit of high class fluff that couldn't stick around long enough to make sure he didn't get tossed in the sneezer by some prowl car boys, or rolled by a tough hackie and dumped out in a vacant lot.

On the way down in the elevator I had an impulse to go back up and take the Scotch bottle away from him. But it wasn't any of my business and it never does any good anyway. They always find a way to get it if they have to have it.

I drove home chewing my lip. I'm supposed to be tough but there was something about the guy that got me. I didn't know what it was unless it was the white hair and the scarred face and the clear voice and the politeness. Maybe that was enough. There was no reason why I should ever see him again. He was just a lost dog, like the girl said.

2

IT WAS THE WEEK after Thanksgiving when I saw him again. The stores along Hollywood Boulevard were already beginning to fill up with overpriced Christmas junk, and the daily papers were beginning to scream about how terrible it would be if you didn't get your Christmas shopping done early. It would be terrible anyway; it always is.

It was about three blocks from my office building that I saw a cop car double-parked and the two buttons in it staring at something over by a shop window on the sidewalk. The something was Terry Lennox—or what was left of him—and that little was not too attractive.

He was leaning against a store front. He had to lean against something. His shirt was dirty and open at the neck and partly outside his jacket and partly not. He hadn't shaved for four or five days. His nose was pinched. His skin was so pale that the long thin scars hardly showed. And his eyes were like holes poked in a snowbank. It was pretty obvious that the buttons in the prowl car were about ready to drop the hook on him, so I went over there fast and took hold of his arm.

"Straighten up and walk," I said, putting on the tough. I winked at him from the side. "Can you make it? Are you stinko?"

He looked me over vaguely and then smiled his little one-sided smile. "I have been," he breathed. "Right now I guess I'm just a little—empty."

"Okay, but make with the feet. You're halfway into the drunk tank already."

He made the effort and let me walk him through the sidewalk loafers to the edge of the curb. There was a taxi stand there and I yanked open the door.

"He goes first," the hackie said, jerking a thumb at the cab ahead. He swung his head around and saw Terry. "If at all," he added.

"This is an emergency. My friend is sick."

"Yeah," the hackie said. "He could get sick somewheres else."

"Five bucks," I said, "and let's see that beautiful smile."

"Oh well," he said, and stuck a magazine with a Martian on the cover behind his mirror. I reached in and got the door open. I got Terry Lennox in and the shadow of the prowl car blocked the far window. A gray-haired cop got out and came over. I went around the taxi and met him.

"Just a minute, Mac. What have we got here? Is the gentleman in the soiled laundry a real close friend of yours?"

"Close enough for me to know he needs a friend. He's not drunk."

"For financial reasons, no doubt," the cop said. He put his hand out and I put my license in it. He looked at it and handed it back. "Oh-oh," he said. "A P.I. picking up a client." His voice changed and got tough. "That tells a little something about you, Mr. Marlowe. What about him?"

"His name's Terry Lennox. He works in pictures."

"That's nice." He leaned into the taxi and stared at Terry back in the corner. "I'd say he didn't work too lately. I'd say he didn't sleep indoors too lately. I'd even say he was a vag and so maybe we ought to take him in."

"Your arrest record can't be that low," I said. "Not in Hollywood."

He was still looking in at Terry. "What's your friend's name, buddy?"

"Philip Marlowe," Terry said slowly. "He lives on Yucca Avenue, Laurel Canyon."

The cop pulled his head out of the window space. He turned, and made a gesture with his hand. "You could of just told him."

"I could have, but I didn't."

He stared at me for a second or two. "I'll buy it this time," he said. "But get him off the street." He got into the police car and the police car went away.

I got into the taxi and we went the three-odd blocks to my parking lot and shifted to my car. I held out the five-spot to the hackie. He gave me a stiff look and shook his head.

"Just what's on the meter, Jack, or an even buck if you feel like it. I been down and out myself. In Frisco. Nobody picked me up in no taxi either. There's one stony-hearted town."

"San Francisco," I said mechanically.

"I call it Frisco," he said. "The hell with them minority groups. Thanks." He took the dollar and went away.

We went to a drive-in where they made hamburgers that didn't taste like something the dog wouldn't eat. I fed Terry Lennox a couple and a bottle of beer and drove him home. The steps were still tough on him but he grinned and panted and made the climb. An hour later he was shaved and bathed and he looked human again. We sat down over a couple of very mild drinks.

"Lucky you remembered my name," I said.

"I made a point of it," he said. "I looked you up too. Could I do less?"

"So why not give me a ring? I live here all the time. I have an office as well."

"Why should I bother you?"

"Looks like you had to bother somebody. Looks like you don't have many friends."

"Oh I have friends," he said, "of a sort." He turned his glass on the table top. "Asking for help doesn't come easy—especially when it's all your own fault." He looked up with a tired smile. "Maybe I can quit drinking one of these days. They all say that, don't they?"

"It takes about three years."

"Three years?" He looked shocked.

"Usually it does. It's a different world. You have to get used to a paler set of colors, a quieter lot of sounds. You have to allow for relapses. All the people you used to know well will get to be just a little strange. You won't even like most of them, and they won't like you too well."

"That wouldn't be much of a change," he said. He turned and looked at the clock. "I have a two-hundred-dollar suitcase checked at the Hollywood bus station. If I could bail it out I could buy a cheap one and pawn the one that's checked for enough to get to Vegas on the bus. I can get a job there."

I didn't say anything. I just nodded and sat there nursing my drink.

"You're thinking that idea might have come to me a little sooner," he said quietly.

"I'm thinking there's something behind all this that's none of my business. Is the job for sure or just a hope?"

"It's for sure. Fellow I knew very well in the army runs a big club there, the Terrapin Club. He's part racketeer, of course, they all are—but the other part is a nice guy."

"I can manage the bus fare and something over. But I'd just as soon it bought something that would stay bought for a while. Better talk to him on the phone."

"Thank you, but it's not necessary. Randy Starr won't let me down. He never has. And the suitcase will pawn for fifty dollars. I know from experience."

"Look," I said, "I'd put up what you need. I'm no big soft-hearted slob. So you take what's offered and be good. I want you out of my hair because I've got a feeling about you."

"Really?" He looked down into his glass. He was only

sipping the stuff. "We've only met twice and you've been more than white to me both times. What sort of feeling?"

"A feeling that next time I'll find you in worse trouble than I can get you out of. I don't know just why I have the feeling, but I have it."

He touched the right side of his face gently with two fingertips. "Maybe it's this. It does make me look a little sinister, I suppose. But it's an honorable wound—or anyhow the result of one."

"It's not that. That doesn't bother me at all. I'm a private dick. You're a problem that I don't have to solve. But the problem is there. Call it a hunch. If you want to be extra polite, call it a sense of character. Maybe that girl didn't walk out on you at The Dancers just because you were drunk. Maybe she had a feeling too."

He smiled faintly. "I was married to her once. Her name is Sylvia Lennox. I married her for her money."

I stood up scowling at him. "I'll fix you some scrambled eggs. You need food."

"Wait a minute, Marlowe. You're wondering why if I was down and out and Sylvia had plenty I couldn't ask her for a few bucks. Did you ever hear of pride?"

"You're killing me, Lennox."

"Am I? My kind of pride is different. It's the pride of a man who has nothing else. I'm sorry if I annoy you."

I went out to my kitchen and cooked up some Canadian bacon and scrambled eggs and coffee and toast. We ate in the breakfast nook. The house belonged to the period that always had one.

I said I had to go to the office and would pick up his suitcase on the way back. He gave me the check ticket. His face now had a little color and the eyes were not so far back in his head that you had to grope for them.

Before I went out I put the whiskey bottle on the table in front of the couch. "Use your pride on that," I said. "And call Vegas, if only as a favor to me."

He just smiled and shrugged his shoulders. I was still sore going down the steps. I didn't know why, any more than I knew why a man would starve and walk the streets rather than pawn his wardrobe. Whatever his rules were he played by them.

The suitcase was the damndest thing you ever saw. It

was bleached pigskin and when new had been a pale cream color. The fittings were gold. It was English made and if you could buy it here at all, it would cost more·like eight hundred than two.

I planked it down in front of him. I looked at the bottle on the cocktail table. He hadn't touched it. He was as sober as I was. He was smoking, but not liking that very well.

"I called Randy," he said. "He was sore because I hadn't called him before."

"It takes a stranger to help you," I said. "A present from Sylvia?" I pointed at the suitcase.

He looked out of the window. "No. That was given to me in England, long before I met her. Very long ago indeed. I'd like to leave it with you, if you could lend me an old one."

I got five double sawbucks out of my wallet and dropped them in front of him. "I don't need security."

"That wasn't the idea at all. You're no pawnbroker. I just don't want it with me in Vegas. And I don't need this much money."

"Okay. You keep the money and I'll keep the suitcase. But this house is easy to burgle."

"It wouldn't matter," he said indifferently. "It wouldn't matter at all."

He changed his clothes and we ate dinner at Musso's about five-thirty. No drinks. He caught the bus on Cahuenga and I drove home thinking about this and that. His empty suitcase was on my bed where he had unpacked it and put his stuff in a lightweight job of mine. His had a gold key which was in one of the locks. I locked the suitcase up empty and tied the key to the handle and put it on the high shelf on my clothes closet. It didn't feel quite empty, but what was in it was no business of mine.

It was a quiet night and the house seemed emptier than usual. I set out the chessmen and played a French defense against Steinitz. He beat me in forty-four moves, but I had him sweating a couple of times.

The phone rang at nine-thirty and the voice that spoke was one I had heard before.

"Is this Mr. Philip Marlowe?"

"Yeah. I'm Marlowe."

"This is Sylvia Lennox, Mr. Marlowe. We met very

briefly in front of The Dancers one night last month. I heard afterwards that you had been kind enough to see that Terry got home."

"I did that."

"I suppose you know that we are not married any more, but I've been a little worried about him. He gave up the apartment he had in Westwood and nobody seems to know where he is."

"I noticed how worried you were the night we met."

"Look, Mr. Marlowe, I've been married to the man. I'm not very sympathetic to drunks. Perhaps I was a little unfeeling and perhaps I had something rather important to do. You're a private detective and this can be put on a professional basis, if you prefer it."

"It doesn't have to be put on any basis at all, Mrs. Lennox. He's on a bus going to Las Vegas. He has a friend there who will give him a job."

She brightened up very suddenly. "Oh—to Las Vegas? How sentimental of him. That's where we were married."

"I guess he forgot," I said, "or he would have gone somewhere else."

Instead of hanging up on me she laughed. It was a cute little laugh. "Are you always as rude as this to your clients?"

"You're not a client, Mrs. Lennox."

"I might be someday. Who knows? Let's say to your lady friends, then."

"Same answer. The guy was down and out, starving, dirty, without a bean. You could have found him if it had been worth your time. He didn't want anything from you then and he probably doesn't want anything from you now."

"That," she said coolly, "is something you couldn't possibly know anything about. Good night." And she hung up.

She was dead right, of course, and I was dead wrong. But I didn't feel wrong. I just felt sore. If she had called up half an hour earlier I might have been sore enough to beat the hell out of Steinitz—except that he had been dead for fifty years and the chess game was out of a book.

3

THREE DAYS BEFORE CHRISTMAS I got a cashier's check on a Las Vegas bank for $100. A note written on hotel paper came with it. He thanked me, wished me a Merry Christmas and all kinds of luck and said he hoped to see me again soon. The kick was in a postscript. "Sylvia and I are starting a second honeymoon. She says please don't be sore at her for wanting to try again."

I caught the rest of it in one of those snob columns in the society section of the paper. I don't read them often, only when I run out of things to dislike.

"Your correspondent is all fluttery at the news that Terry and Sylvia Lennox have rehitched at Las Vegas, the dears. She's the younger daughter of multimillionaire Harlan Potter of San Francisco and Pebble Beach, of course. Sylvia is having Marcel and Jeanne Duhaux redecorate the entire mansion in Encino from basement to roof in the most *devastatingly* dernier cri. Curt Westerheym, Sylvia's last but one, my dears, gave her the little eighteen-room shack for a wedding present, you may remember. And whatever happened to Curt, you ask? Or do you? St. Tropez has the answer, and permanently I hear. Also a certain very, *very* blue-blooded French duchess with two perfectly adorable children. And what does Harlan Potter think of the remarriage, you may also ask? One can only guess. Mr. Potter is one person who but *never* gives an interview. How exclusive can you get, darlings?"

I threw the paper into the corner and turned on the TV set. After the society page dog vomit even the wrestlers looked good. But the facts were probably right. On the society page they better be.

I had a mental picture of the kind of eighteen-room shack that would go with a few of the Potter millions, not to mention decorations by Duhaux in the last subphallic symbolism. But I had no mental picture at all of Terry Lennox loafing around one of the swimming pools in

12

Bermuda shorts and phoning the butler by R/T to ice the champagne and get the grouse atoasting. There was no reason why I should have. If the guy wanted to be somebody's woolly bear, it was no skin off my teeth. I just didn't want to see him again. But I knew I would—if only on account of his goddamn gold-plated pigskin suitcase.

It was five o'clock of a wet March evening when he walked into my down-at-heels brain emporium. He looked changed. Older, very sober and severe and beautifully calm. He looked like a guy who had learned to roll with a punch. He wore an oyster-white raincoat and gloves and no hat and his white hair was as smooth as a bird's breast.

"Let's go to some quiet bar and have a drink," he said, as if he had been in ten minutes before. "If you have the time, that is."

We didn't shake hands. We never did. Englishmen don't shake hands all the time like Americans and although he wasn't English he had some of the mannerisms.

I said: "Let's go by my place and pick up your fancy suitcase. It kind of worries me."

He shook his head. "It would be kind of you to keep it for me."

"Why?"

"I just feel that way. Do you mind? It's a sort of link with a time when I wasn't a no-good waster."

"Nuts to that," I said. "But it's your business."

"If it bothers you because you think it might be stolen—"

"That's your business too. Let's go get that drink."

We went to Victor's. He drove me in a rust-colored Jupiter-Jowett with a flimsy canvas rain top under which there was only just room for the two of us. It had pale leather upholstery and what looked like silver fittings. I'm not too fussy about cars, but the damn thing did make my mouth water a little. He said it would do sixty-five in second. It had a squatty little gear shift that barely came up to his knee.

"Four speeds," he said. "They haven't invented an automatic shift that will work for one of these jobs yet. You don't really need one. You can start it in third even uphill and that's as high as you can shift in traffic anyway."

"Wedding present?"

"Just a casual 'I happened to see this gadget in a window' sort of present. I'm a very pampered guy."

"Nice," I said. "If there's no price tag."

He glanced at me quickly and then put his eyes back on the wet pavement. Double wipers swished gently over the little windscreen. "Price tag? There's always a price tag, chum. You think I'm not happy maybe?"

"Sorry. I was out of line."

"I'm rich. Who the hell wants to be happy?" There was a bitterness in his voice that was new to me.

"How's your drinking?"

"Perfectly elegant, old top. For some strange reason I seem to be able to handle the stuff. But you never know, do you?"

"Perhaps you were never really a drunk."

We sat in a corner of the bar at Victor's and drank gimlets. "They don't know how to make them here," he said. "What they call a gimlet is just some lime or lemon juice and gin with a dash of sugar and bitters. A real gimlet is half gin and half Rose's Lime Juice and nothing else. It beats martinis hollow."

"I was never fussy about drinks. How did you get on with Randy Starr? Down my street he's called a tough number."

He leaned back and looked thoughtful. "I guess he is. I guess they all are. But it doesn't show on him. I could name you a couple of lads in the same racket in Hollywood that act the part. Randy doesn't bother. In Las Vegas he's a legitimate businessman. You look him up next time you're there. He'll be your pal."

"Not too likely. I don't like hoodlums."

"That's just a word, Marlowe. We have that kind of world. Two wars gave it to us and we are going to keep it. Randy and I and another fellow were in a jam once. It made a sort of bond between us."

"Then why didn't you ask him for help when you needed it?"

He drank up his drink and signaled the waiter. "Because he couldn't refuse."

The waiter brought fresh drinks and I said: "That's just talk to me. If by any chance the guy owed you something, think of *his* end. He'd like a chance to pay something back."

He shook his head slowly. "I know you're right. Of course I did ask him for a job. But I worked at it while I had it. As for asking favors or handouts, no."

"But you'll take them from a stranger."

He looked me straight in the eye. "The stranger can keep going and pretend not to hear."

We had three gimlets, not doubles, and it didn't do a thing to him. That much would just get a real souse started. So I guess maybe he was cured at that.

Then he drove me back to the office.

"We have dinner at eight-fifteen," he said. "Only millionaires can afford it. Only millionaires' servants will stand for it nowadays. Lots of lovely people coming."

From then on it got to be a sort of habit with him to drop in around five o'clock. We didn't always go to the same bar, but oftener to Victor's than anywhere else. It may have had some association for him that I didn't know about. He never drank too much, and that surprised him.

"It must be something like the tertian ague," he said. "When it hits you it's bad. When you don't have it, it's as though you never did have it."

"What I don't get is why a guy with your privileges would want to drink with a private eye."

"Are you being modest?"

"Nope. I'm just puzzled. I'm a reasonably friendly type but we don't live in the same world. I don't even know where you hang out except that it's Encino. I should guess your home life is adequate."

"I don't have any home life."

We were drinking gimlets again. The place was almost empty. There was the usual light scattering of compulsive drinkers getting tuned up at the bar on the stools, the kind that reach very slowly for the first one and watch their hands so they won't knock anything over.

"I don't get that. Am I supposed to?"

"Big production, no story, as they say around the movie lots. I guess Sylvia is happy enough, though not necessarily with me. In our circle that's not too important. There's always something to do if you don't have to work or consider the cost. It's no real fun but the rich don't know that. They never had any. They never want anything very hard except maybe somebody else's wife and that's a pretty pale desire compared with the way a plumber's wife wants new curtains for the living room."

I didn't say anything. I let him carry the ball.

"Mostly I just kill time," he said, "and it dies hard. A little tennis, a little golf, a little swimming and horseback riding, and the exquisite pleasure of watching Sylvia's friends trying to hold out to lunch time before they start killing their hangovers."

"The night you went to Vegas she said she didn't like drunks."

He grinned crookedly. I was getting so used to his scarred face that I only noticed it when some change of expression emphasized its one-sided woodenness.

"She meant drunks without money. With money they are just heavy drinkers. If they vomit in the lanai, that's for the butler to handle."

"You didn't have to have it the way it is."

He finished his drink at a gulp and stood up. "I've got to run, Marlowe. Besides I'm boring you and God knows I'm boring myself."

"You're not boring me. I'm a trained listener. Sooner or later I may figure out why you like being a kept poodle."

He touched his scars gently with a fingertip. He had a remote little smile. "You should wonder why she wants me around, not why I want to be there, waiting patiently on my satin cushion to have my head patted."

"You like satin cushions," I said, as I stood up to leave with him. "You like silk sheets and bells to ring and the butler to come with his deferential smile."

"Could be. I was raised in an orphanage in Salt Lake City."

We went out into the tired evening and he said he wanted to walk. We had come in my car, and for once I had been fast enough to grab the check. I watched him out of sight. The light from a store window caught the gleam of his white hair for a moment as he faded into the light mist.

I liked him better drunk, down and out, hungry and beaten and proud. Or did I? Maybe I just liked being top man. His reasons for things were hard to figure. In my business there's a time to ask questions and a time to let your man simmer until he boils over. Every good cop knows that. It's a good deal like chess or boxing. Some people you have to crowd and keep off balance. Some you just box and they will end up beating themselves.

He would have told me the story of his life if I had asked him. But I never even asked him how he got his face smashed. If I had and he told me, it just possibly might have saved a couple of lives. Just possibly, no more.

4

THE LAST TIME we had a drink in a bar was in May and it was earlier than usual, just after four o'clock. He looked tired and thinner but he looked around with a slow smile of pleasure.

"I like bars just after they open for the evening. When the air inside is still cool and clean and everything is shiny and the barkeep is giving himself that last look in the mirror to see if his tie is straight and his hair is smooth. I like the neat bottles on the bar back and the lovely shining glasses and the anticipation. I like to watch the man mix the first one of the evening and put it down on a crisp mat and put the little folded napkin beside it. I like to taste it slowly. The first quiet drink of the evening in a quiet bar—that's wonderful."

I agreed with him.

"Alcohol is like love," he said. "The first kiss is magic, the second is intimate, the third is routine. After that you take the girl's clothes off."

"Is that bad?" I asked him.

"It's excitement of a high order, but it's an impure emotion—impure in the aesthetic sense. I'm not sneering at sex. It's necessary and it doesn't have to be ugly. But it always has to be managed. Making it glamorous is a billion-dollar industry and it costs every cent of it."

He looked around and yawned. "I haven't been sleeping well. It's nice in here. But after a while the lushes will fill the place up and talk loud and laugh and the goddam women will start waving their hands and screwing up their faces and tinkling their goddam bracelets and making with the packaged charm which will later on in the evening have a slight but unmistakable odor of sweat."

"Take it easy," I said. "So they're human, they sweat, they get dirty, they have to go to the bathroom. What did you expect—golden butterflies hovering in a rosy mist?"

He emptied his glass and held it upside down and watched a slow drop form on the rim and then tremble and fall.

"I'm sorry for her," he said slowly. "She's such an absolute bitch. Could be I'm fond of her too in a remote sort of way. Some day she'll need me and I'll be the only guy around not holding a chisel. Likely enough then I'll flunk out."

I just looked at him. "You do a great job of selling yourself," I said after a moment.

"Yeah, I know. I'm a weak character, without guts or ambition. I caught the brass ring and it shocked me to find out it wasn't gold. A guy like me has one big moment in his life, one perfect swing on the high trapeze. Then he spends the rest of his time trying not to fall off the sidewalk into the gutter."

"What's this in favor of?" I got out a pipe and started to fill it.

"She's scared. She's scared stiff."

"What of?"

"I don't know. We don't talk much any more. Maybe of the old man. Harlan Potter is a coldhearted son of a bitch. All Victorian dignity on the outside. Inside he's as ruthless as a Gestapo thug. Sylvia is a tramp. He knows it and he hates it and there's nothing he can do about it. But he waits and he watches and if Sylvia ever gets into a big mess of scandal he'll break her in half and bury the two halves a thousand miles apart."

"You're her husband."

He lifted the empty glass and brought it down hard on the edge of the table. It smashed with a sharp ping. The barman stared, but didn't say anything.

"Like that, chum. Like that. Oh sure, I'm her husband. That's what the record says. I'm the three white steps and the big green front door and the brass knocker you rap one long and two short and the maid lets you into the hundred-dollar whorehouse."

I stood up and dropped some money on the table. "You

talk too damn much," I said, "and it's too damn much about you. See you later."

I walked out leaving him sitting there shocked and white-faced as well as I could tell by the kind of light they have in bars. He called something after me, but I kept going.

Ten minutes later I was sorry. But ten minutes later I was somewere else. He didn't come to the office any more. Not at all, not once. I had got to him where it hurt.

I didn't see him again for a month. When I did it was five o'clock in the morning and just beginning to get light. The persistent ringing of the doorbell yanked me out of bed. I plowed down the hall and across the living room and opened up. He stood there looking as if he hadn't slept for a week. He had a light topcoat on with the collar turned up and he seemed to be shivering. A dark felt hat was pulled down over his eyes.

He had a gun in his hand.

5

THE GUN WASN'T POINTED at me, he was just holding it. It was a medium-caliber automatic, foreign made, certainly not a Colt or a Savage. With the white tired face and the scars and the turned-up collar and the pulled-down hat and the gun he could have stepped right out of an old fashioned kick-em-in-the-teeth gangster movie.

"You're driving me to Tijuana to get a plane at ten-fifteen," he said. "I have a passport and visa and I'm all set except for transportation. For certain reasons I can't take a train or a bus or a plane from L.A. Would five hundred bucks be a reasonable taxi fare?"

I stood in the doorway and didn't move to let him in. "Five hundred plus the gat?" I asked.

He looked down at it rather absently. Then he dropped it into his pocket.

"It might be a protection," he said, "for you. Not for me."

"Come on in then." I stood to one side and he came in with an exhausted lunge and fell into a chair.

The living room was still dark, because of the heavy growth of shrubbery the owner had allowed to mask the windows. I put a lamp on and mooched a cigarette. I lit it. I stared down at him. I rumpled my hair which was already rumpled. I put the old tired grin on my face.

"What the hell's the matter with me sleeping such a lovely morning away? Ten-fifteen, huh? Well, there's plenty of time. Let's go out to the kitchen and I'll brew some coffee."

"I'm in a great deal of trouble, shamus." Shamus, it was the first time he had called me that. But it kind of went with his style of entry, the way he was dressed, the gun and all.

"It's going to be a peach of a day. Light breeze. You can hear those tough old eucalyptus trees across the street whispering to each other. Talking about old times in Australia when the wallabies hopped about underneath the branches and the koala bears rode piggyback on each other. Yes, I got the general idea you were in some trouble. Let's talk about it after I've had a couple of cups of coffee. I'm always a little lightheaded when I first wake up. Let us confer with Mr. Huggins and Mr. Young."

"Look, Marlowe, this is not the time—"

"Fear nothing, old boy. Mr. Huggins and Mr. Young are two of the best. They make Huggins-Young coffee. It's their life work, their pride and joy. One of these days I'm going to see that they get the recognition they deserve. So far all they're making is money. You couldn't expect that to satisfy them."

I left him with that bright chatter and went out to the kitchen at the back. I turned the hot water on and got the coffee maker down off the shelf. I wet the rod and measured the stuff into the top and by that time the water was steaming. I filled the lower half of the dingus and set it on the flame. I set the upper part on top and gave it a twist so it would bind.

By that time he had come in after me. He leaned in the doorway a moment and then edged across to the breakfast nook and slid into the seat. He was still shaking. I got a bottle of Old Grand-Dad off the shelf and poured him a shot in a big glass. I knew he would need a big glass. Even with that he had to use both hands to get it to his mouth. He swallowed, put the glass down with a thud, and hit the back of the seat with a jar.

"Almost passed out," he muttered. "Seems like I've been up for a week. Didn't sleep at all last night."

The coffee maker was almost ready to bubble. I turned the flame low and watched the water rise. It hung a little at the bottom of the glass tube. I turned the flame up just enough to get it over the hump and then turned it low again quickly. I stirred the coffee and covered it. I set my timer for three minutes. Very methodical guy, Marlowe. Nothing must interfere with his coffee technique. Not even a gun in the hand of a desperate character.

I poured him another slug. "Just sit there," I said. "Don't say a word. Just sit."

He handled the second slug with one hand. I did a fast wash-up in the bathroom and the bell of the timer went just as I got back. I cut the flame and set the coffee maker on a straw mat on the table. Why did I go into such detail? Because the charged atmosphere made every little thing stand out as a performance, a movement distinct and vastly important. It was one of those hypersensitive moments when all your automatic movements, however long established, however habitual, become separate acts of will. You are like a man learning to walk after polio. You take nothing for granted, absolutely nothing at all.

The coffee was all down and the air rushed in with its usual fuss and the coffee bubbled and then became quiet. I removed the top of the maker and set it on the drainboard in the socket of the cover.

I poured two cups and added a slug to his. "Black for you, Terry." I added two lumps of sugar and some cream to mine. I was coming out of it by now. I wasn't conscious of how I opened the Frig and got the cream carton.

I sat down across from him. He hadn't moved. He was propped in the corner of the nook, rigid. Then without warning his head came down on the table and he was sobbing.

He didn't pay any attention when I reached across and dug the gun out of his pocket. It was a Mauser 7.65, a beauty. I sniffed it. I sprang the magazine loose. It was full. Nothing in the breach.

He lifted his head and saw the coffee and drank some

slowly, not looking at me. "I didn't shoot anybody," he said.

"Well—not recently anyhow. And the gun would have had to be cleaned. I hardly think you shot anybody with this."

"I'll tell you about it," he said.

"Wait just a minute." I drank my coffee as quickly as the heat would let me. I refilled my cup. "It's like this," I said. "Be very careful what you tell me. If you really want me to ride you down to Tijuana, there are two things I must not be told. One—are you listening?"

He nodded very slightly. He was looking blank-eyed at the wall over my head. The scars were very livid this morning. His skin was almost dead white but the scars seemed to shine out of it just the same.

"One," I repeated slowly, "if you have committed a crime or anything the law calls a crime—a serious crime, I mean—I can't be told about it. Two, if you have essential knowledge that such a crime has been committed, I can't be told about that either. Not if you want me to drive you to Tijuana. That clear?"

He looked me in the eye. His eyes focused, but they were lifeless. He had the coffee inside him. He had no color, but he was steady. I poured him some more and loaded it the same way.

"I told you I was in a jam," he said.

"I heard you. I don't want to know what kind of jam. I have a living to earn, a license to protect."

"I could hold the gun on you," he said.

I grinned and pushed the gun across the table. He looked down at it but didn't touch it.

"Not to Tijuana you couldn't hold it on me, Terry. Not across the border, not up the steps into a plane. I'm a man who occasionally has business with guns. We'll forget about the gun. I'd look great telling the cops I was so scared I just had to do what you told me to. Supposing, of course, which I don't know, that there was anything to tell the cops."

"Listen," he said, "it will be noon or even later before anybody knocks at the door. The help knows better than to disturb her when she sleeps late. But by about noon her maid would knock and go in. She wouldn't be in her room."

I sipped my coffee and said nothing.

"The maid would see that her bed hadn't been slept in," he went on. "Then she would think of another place to look. There's a big guest house pretty far back from the main house. It has its own driveway and garage and so on. Sylvia spent the night there. The maid would eventually find her there."

I frowned. "I've got to be very careful what questions I ask you, Terry. Couldn't she have spent the night away from home?"

"Her clothes would be thrown all over her room. She never hangs anything up. The maid would know she had put a robe over her pajamas and gone out that way. So it would only be to the guest house."

"Not necessarily," I said.

"It would be to the guest house. Hell, do you think they don't know what goes on in the guest house? Servants always know."

"Pass it," I said.

He ran a finger down the side of his good cheek hard enough to leave a red streak. "And in the guest house," he went on slowly, "the maid would find—"

"Sylvia dead drunk, paralyzed, spifflicated, iced to the eyebrows," I said harshly.

"Oh." He thought about it. Big think. "Of course," he added, "that's how it would be. Sylvia is not a souse. When she does get over the edge it's pretty drastic."

"That's the end of the story," I said. "Or almost. Let me improvise. The last time we drank together I was a bit rough with you, walked out if you recall. You irritated the hell out of me. Thinking it over afterwards I could see that you were just trying to sneer yourself out of a feeling of disaster. You say you have a passport and a visa. It takes a little time to get a visa to Mexico. They don't let just anybody in. So you've been planning to blow for some time. I was wondering how long you would stick."

"I guess I felt some vague kind of obligation to be around, some idea she might need me for something more than a front to keep the old man from nosing around too hard. By the way, I tried to call you in the middle of the night."

"I sleep hard. I didn't hear."

"Then I went to a Turkish bath place. I stayed a couple

of hours, had a steam bath, a plunge, a needle shower, a rubdown and made a couple of phone calls from there. I left the car at La Brea and Fountain. I walked from there. Nobody saw me turn into your street."

"Do these phone calls concern me?"

"One was to Harlan Potter. The old man flew down to Pasadena yesterday, some business. He hadn't been to the house. I had a lot of trouble getting him. But he finally talked to me. I told him I was sorry, but I was leaving." He was looking a little sideways when he said this, towards the window over the sink and the tecoma bush that fretted against the screen.

"How did he take it?"

"He was sorry. He wished me luck. Asked if I needed any money." Terry laughed harshly. "Money. Those are the first five letters of his alphabet. I said I had plenty. Then I called Sylvia's sister. Much the same story there. That's all."

"I want to ask this," I said. "Did you ever find her with a man in that guest house?"

He shook his head. "I never tried. It would not have been difficult. It never has been."

"Your coffee's getting cold."

"I don't want any more."

"Lots of men, huh? But you went back and married her again. I realize that she's quite a dish, but all the same—"

"I told you I was no good. Hell, why did I leave her the first time? Why after that did I get stinking every time I saw her? Why did I roll in the gutter rather than ask her for money? She's been married five times, not including me. Any one of them would go back at the crook of her finger. And not just for a million bucks."

"She's quite a dish," I said. I looked at my watch. "Just why does it have to be the ten-fifteen at Tijuana?"

"There's always space on that flight. Nobody from L.A. wants to ride a DC-3 over mountains when he can take a Connie and make it in seven hours to Mexico City. And the Connies don't stop where I want to go."

I stood up and leaned against the sink. "Now let's add it up and don't interrupt me. You came to me this morning in a highly emotional condition and wanted to be driven to Tijuana to catch an early plane. You had a gun in your pocket, but I needn't have seen it. You told me you had stood things as long as you could but last night you blew up. You found your wife dead drunk and a man had been with her. You got out and went to a Turkish bath to pass the time until morning and you phoned your wife's two closest relatives and told them what you were doing. Where you went was none of my business. You had the necessary documents to enter Mexico. How you went was none of my business either. We are friends and I did what you asked me without much thought. Why wouldn't I? You're not paying me anything. You had your car but you felt too upset to drive yourself. That's your business too. You're an emotional guy and you got yourself a bad wound in the war. I think I ought to pick up your car and shove it in a garage somewhere for storage."

He reached into his clothes and pushed a leather key-holder across the table.

"How does it sound?" he asked.

"Depends who's listening. I haven't finished. You took nothing but the clothes you stood up in and some money you had from your father-in-law. You left everything she had given you including that beautiful piece of machinery you parked at La Brea and Fountain. You wanted to go away as clean as it was possible for you to go and still go. All right. I'll buy it. Now I shave and get dressed."

"Why are you doing it, Marlowe?"

"Buy yourself a drink while I shave."

I walked out and left him sitting there hunched in the corner of the nook. He still had his hat and light topcoat on. But he looked a lot more alive.

I went into the bathroom and shaved. I was back in the bedroom knotting my tie when he came and stood in the doorway. "I washed the cups just in case," he said. "But I got thinking. Maybe it would be better if you called the police."

"Call them yourself. I haven't anything to tell them."

"You want me to?"

I turned around sharply and gave him a hard stare. "God damn it!" I almost yelled at him. "Can't you for Chrissake just leave it lay?"

"I'm sorry."

"Sure you're sorry. Guys like you are always sorry, and always too late."

He turned and walked back along the hall to the living room.

I finished dressing and locked up the back part of the house. When I got to the living room he had fallen asleep in a chair, his head on one side, his face drained of color, his whole body slack with exhaustion. He looked pitiful. When I touched his shoulder he came awake slowly as if it was a long way from where he was to where I was.

When I had his attention I said, "What about a suitcase? I still got that white pigskin job on the top shelf in my closet."

"It's empty," he said without interest. "Also it's too conspicuous."

"You'd be more conspicuous without any baggage."

I walked back to the bedroom and stood up on the steps in the clothes closet and pulled the white pigskin job down off the high shelf. The square ceiling trap was right over my head, so I pushed that up and reached in as far as I could and dropped his leather keyholder behind one of the dusty tie beams or whatever they were.

I climbed down with the suitcase, dusted it off, and shoved some things into it, a pair of pajamas never worn, toothpaste, an extra toothbrush, a couple of cheap towels and washcloths, a package of cotton handkerchiefs, a fifteen-cent tube of shaving cream, and one of the razors they give away with a package of blades. Nothing used, nothing marked, nothing conspicuous, except that his own stuff would be better. I added a pint of bourbon still in its wrapping paper. I locked the suitcase and left the key in one of the locks and carried it up front. He had gone to sleep again. I opened the door without waking him and carried the suitcase down to the garage and put it in the convertible behind the front seat. I got the car out and locked the garage and went back up the steps to wake him. I finished locking up and we left.

I drove fast but not fast enough to get tagged. We hardly spoke on the way down. We didn't stop to eat either. There wasn't that much time.

The border people had nothing to say to us. Up on the windy mesa where the Tijuana Airport is I parked close to the office and just sat while Terry got his ticket. The propellers of the DC-3 were already turning over slowly, just enough to keep warm. A tall dreamboat of a pilot in a gray uniform was chatting with a group of four people. One was about six feet four and carried a gun case. There was a girl in slacks beside him, and a smallish middle-aged man and a gray-haired woman so tall that she made him look puny. Three or four obvious Mexicans were standing around as well. That seemed to be the load. The steps were at the door but nobody seemed anxious to get in. Then a Mexican flight steward came down the steps and stood waiting. There didn't seem to be any loudspeaker equipment. The Mexicans climbed into the plane but the pilot was still chatting with the Americans.

There was a big Packard parked next to me. I got out and took a gander at the license on the post. Maybe someday I'll learn to mind my own business. As I pulled my head out I saw the tall woman staring in my direction.

Then Terry came across the dusty gravel.

"I'm all set," he said. "This is where I say goodbye."

He put his hand out. I shook it. He looked pretty good now, just tired, just tired as all hell.

I lifted the pigskin suitcase out of the Olds and put it down on the gravel. He stared at it angrily.

"I told you I didn't want it," he said snappishly.

"There's a nice pint of hooch in it, Terry. Also some pajamas and stuff. And it's all anonymous. If you don't want it, check it. Or throw it away."

"I have reasons," he said stiffly.

"So have I."

He smiled suddenly. He picked up the suitcase and squeezed my arm with his free hand. "Okay, pal. You're the boss. And remember, if things get tough, you have a blank check. You don't owe me a thing. We had a few drinks together and got to be friendly and I talked too much about me. I left five C notes in your coffee can. Don't be sore at me."

"I'd rather you hadn't."

"I'll never spend half of what I have."

"Good luck, Terry."

The two Americans were going up the steps into the plane. A squatty guy with a wide dark face came out of the door of the office building and waved and pointed.

"Climb aboard," I said. "I know you didn't kill her. That's why I'm here."

He braced himself. His whole body got stiff. He turned slowly, then looked back.

"I'm sorry," he said quietly. "But you're wrong about that. I'm going to walk quite slowly to the plane. You have plenty of time to stop me."

He walked. I watched him. The guy in the doorway of the office was waiting, but not too impatient. Mexicans seldom are. He reached down and patted the pigskin suitcase and grinned at Terry. Then he stood aside and Terry went through the door. In a little while Terry came out through the door on the other side, where the customs people are when you're coming in. He walked, still slowly, across the gravel to the steps. He stopped there and looked towards me. He didn't signal or wave. Neither did I. Then he went up into the plane, and the steps were pulled back.

I got into the Olds and started it and backed and turned and moved halfway across the parking space. The tall woman and the short man were still out on the field. The woman had a handkerchief out to wave. The plane began to taxi down to the end of the field raising plenty of dust. It turned at the far end and the motors revved up in a thundering roar. It began to move forward picking up speed slowly.

The dust rose in clouds behind it. Then it was airborne. I watched it lift slowly into the gusty air and fade off into the naked blue sky to the southeast.

Then I left. Nobody at the border gate looked at me as if my face meant as much as the hands on a clock.

6

IT'S A LONG DRAG back from Tijuana and one of the dullest drives in the state. Tijuana is nothing; all they want there is the buck. The kid who sidles over to your car and looks at you with big wistful eyes and says, "One dime, please, mister," will try to sell you his sister in the next sentence. Tijuana is not Mexico. No border town is anything but a border town, just as no waterfront is anything but a waterfront. San Diego? One of the most beautiful harbors in the world and nothing in it but navy and a few fishing boats. At night it is fairyland. The swell is as gentle as an old lady singing hymns. But Marlowe has to get home and count the spoons.

The road north is as monotonous as a sailor's chantey. You go through a town, down a hill, along a stretch of beach, through a town, down a hill, along a stretch of beach.

It was two o'clock when I got back and they were waiting for me in a dark sedan with no police tags, no red light, only the double antenna, and not only police cars have those. I was halfway up the steps before they came out of it and yelled at me, the usual couple in the usual suits, with the usual stony leisure of movement, as if the world was waiting hushed and silent for them to tell it what to do.

"Your name Marlowe? We want to talk to you."

He let me see the glint of a badge. For all I caught of it he might have been Pest Control. He was gray blond and looked sticky. His partner was tall, good-looking, neat, and had a precise nastiness about him, a goon with an education. They had watching and waiting eyes, patient and careful eyes, cool disdainful eyes, cops' eyes. They get them at the passing-out parade at the police school.

"Sergeant Green, Central Homicide. This is Detective Dayton."

I went on up and unlocked the door. You don't shake hands with big city cops. That close is too close.

They sat in the living room. I opened the windows and the breeze whispered. Green did the talking.

"Man named Terry Lennox. Know him, huh?"

"We have a drink together once in a while. He lives in Encino, married money. I've never been where he lives."

"Once in a while," Green said. "How often would that be?"

"It's a vague expression. I meant it that way. It could be once a week or once in two months."

"Met his wife?"

"Once, very briefly, before they were married."

"You saw him last when and where?"

I took a pipe off the end table and filled it. Green

leaned forward close to me. The tall lad sat farther back holding a ballpoint poised over a red-edged pad.

"This is where I say, 'What's this all about?' and you say, 'We ask the questions.' "

"So you just answer them, huh?"

I lit the pipe. The tobacco was a little too moist. It took me some time to light it properly and three matches.

"I got time," Green said, "but I already used up a lot of it waiting around. So snap it up, mister. We know who you are. And you know we ain't here to work up an appetite."

"I was just thinking," I said. "We used to go to Victor's fairly often, and not so often to The Green Lantern and The Bull and Bear—that's the place down at the end of the Strip that tries to look like an English inn—"

"Quit stalling."

"Who's dead?" I asked.

Detective Dayton spoke up. He had a hard, mature, don't-try-to-fool-with-me voice. "Just answer the questions, Marlowe. We are conducting a routine investigation. That's all you need to know."

Maybe I was tired and irritable. Maybe I felt a little guilty. I could learn to hate this guy without even knowing him. I could just look at him across the width of a cafeteria and want to kick his teeth in.

"Shove it, Jack," I said. "Keep that guff for the juvenile bureau. It's a horse laugh even to them."

Green chuckled. Nothing changed in Dayton's face that you could put a finger on but he suddenly looked ten years older and twenty years nastier. The breath going through his nose whistled faintly.

"He passed the bar examination," Green said. "You can't fool around with Dayton."

I got up slowly and went over to the bookshelves. I took down the bound copy of the California Penal Code. I held it out to Dayton.

"Would you kindly find me the section that says I have to answer the questions?"

He was holding himself very still. He was going to slug me and we both knew it. But he was going to wait for the break. Which meant that he didn't trust Green to back him up if he got out of line.

He said: "Every citizen has to co-operate with the police. In all ways, even by physical action, and especially by answering any questions of a non-incriminating nature the police think it necessary to ask." His voice saying this was hard and bright and smooth.

"It works out that way," I said. "Mostly by a process of direct or indirect intimidation. In law no such obligation exists. Nobody has to tell the police anything, any time, anywhere."

"Aw shut up," Green said impatiently. "You're crawfishing and you know it. Sit down. Lennox's wife has been murdered. In a guest house at their place in Encino. Lennox has skipped out. Anyway he can't be found. So we're looking for a suspect in a murder case. That satisfy you?"

I threw the book in a chair and went back to the couch across the table from Green. "So why come to me?" I asked. "I've never been near the house. I told you that."

Green patted his thighs, up and down, up and down. He grinned at me quietly. Dayton was motionless in the chair. His eyes ate me.

"On account of your phone number was written on a pad in his room during the past twenty-four hours," Green said. "It's a date pad and yesterday was torn off but you could see the impression on today's page. We don't know when he called you up. We don't know where he went or why or when. But we got to ask, natch."

"Why in the guest house?" I asked, not expecting him to answer, but he did.

He blushed a little. "Seems she went there pretty often. At night. Had visitors. The help can see down through the trees where the lights show. Cars come and go, sometimes late, sometimes very late. Too much is enough, huh? Don't kid yourself. Lennox is our boy. He went down that way about one in the A.M. The butler happened to see. He come back alone, maybe twenty minutes later. After that nothing. The lights stayed on. This morning no Lennox. The butler goes down by the guest house. The dame is as naked as a mermaid on the bed and let me tell you he don't recognize her by her face. She practically ain't got one. Beat to pieces with a bronze statuette of a monkey."

"Terry Lennox wouldn't do anything like that," I said. "Sure she cheated on him. Old stuff. She always had. They'd been divorced and remarried. I don't suppose it made him happy but why should he go crazy over it now?"

"Nobody knows that answer," Green said patiently. "It happens all the time. Men and women both. A guy takes it and takes it and takes it. Then he don't. He probably don't know why himself, why at that particular instant he goes berserk. Only he does, and somebody's dead. So we got business to do. So we ask you one simple question. So quit horsing around or we take you in."

"He's not going to tell you, Sergeant," Dayton said acidly. "He read that law book. Like a lot of people that read a law book he thinks the law is in it."

"You make the notes," Green said, "and leave your brains alone. If you're real good we'll let you sing 'Mother Machree' at the police smoker."

"The hell with you, Sarge, if I may say so with proper respect for your rank."

"Let's you and him fight," I said to Green. "I'll catch him when he drops."

Dayton laid his note pad and ball-point aside very carefully. He stood up with a bright gleam in his eyes. He walked over and stood in front of me.

"On your feet, bright boy. Just because I went to college don't make me take any guff from a nit like you."

I started to get up. I was still off balance when he hit me. He hooked me with a neat left and crossed it. Bells rang, but not for dinner. I sat down hard and shook my head. Dayton was still there. He was smiling now.

"Let's try again," he said. "You weren't set that time. It wasn't really kosher."

I looked at Green. He was looking at his thumb as if studying a hangnail. I didn't move or speak, waiting for him to look up. If I stood up again, Dayton would slug me again. He might slug me again anyhow. But if I stood up and he slugged me, I would take him to pieces, because the blows proved he was strictly a boxer. He put them in the right place but it would take a lot of them to wear me down.

Green said almost absently: "Smart work, Billy boy. You gave the man exactly what he wanted. Clam juice."

Then he looked up and said mildly: "Once more, for the record, Marlowe. Last time you saw Terry Lennox, where and how and what was talked about, and where did you come from just now. Yes—or no?"

Dayton was standing loosely, nicely balanced. There was a soft sweet sheen in his eyes.

"How about the other guy?" I asked, ignoring him.

"What other guy was that?"

"In the hay, in the guest house. No clothes on. You're not saying she had to go down there to play solitaire."

"That comes later—when we get the husband."

"Fine. If it's not too much trouble when you already have a patsy."

"You don't talk, we take you in, Marlowe."

"As a material witness?"

"As a material my foot. As a suspect. Suspicion of accessory after the fact of murder. Helping a suspect escape. My guess is you took the guy somewhere. And right now a guess is all I need. The skipper is tough these days. He knows the rule book but he gets absent-minded. This could be a misery for you. One way or another we get a statement from you. The harder it is to get, the surer we are we need it."

"That's a lot of crap to him," Dayton said. "He knows the book."

"It's a lot of crap to everybody," Green said calmly. "But it still works. Come on, Marlowe. I'm blowing the whistle on you."

"Okay," I said. "Blow it. Terry Lennox was my friend. I've got a reasonable amount of sentiment invested in him. Enough not to spoil it just because a cop says come through. You've got a case against him, maybe far more than I hear from you. Motive, opportunity, and the fact that he skipped out. The motive is old stuff, long neutralized, almost part of the deal. I don't admire that kind of deal, but that's the kind of guy he is—a little weak and very gentle. The rest of it means nothing except that if he knew she was dead he knew he was a sitting duck for you. At the inquest if they have one and if they call me, I'll have to answer questions. I don't have to answer yours. I can see you're a nice guy, Green. Just as I can see your partner is just another goddam badge flasher with a power complex. If you want to get me in a real jam, let him hit me again. I'll break his goddam pencil for him."

Green stood up and looked at me sadly. Dayton hadn't moved. He was a one-shot tough guy. He had to have time out to pat his back.

"I'll use the phone," Green said. "But I know what answer I'll get. You're a sick chicken, Marlowe. A very sick chicken. Get the hell outa my way." This last to Dayton. Dayton turned and went back and picked up his pad.

Green crossed to the phone and lifted it slowly, his plain face creased with the long slow thankless grind. That's the trouble with cops. You're all set to hate their guts and then you meet one that goes human on you.

The Captain said to bring me in, and rough.

They put handcuffs on me. They didn't search the house, which seemed careless of them. Possibly they figured I would be too experienced to have anything there that could be dangerous to me. In which they were wrong. Because if they had made any kind of job of it they would have found Terry Lennox's car keys. And when the car was found, as it would be sooner or later, they would fit the keys to it and know he had been in my company.

Actually, as it turned out, that meant nothing. The car was never found by any police. It was stolen sometime in the night, driven most probably to El Paso, fitted with new keys and forged papers, and put on the market eventually in Mexico City. The procedure is routine. Mostly the money comes back in the form of heroin. Part of the good-neighbor policy, as the hoodlums see it.

7

THE HOMICIDE SKIPPER that year was a Captain Gregorius, a type of copper that is getting rarer but by no means extinct, the kind that solves crimes with the bright light, the soft sap, the kick to the kidneys, the knee to the groin, the fist to the solar plexus, the night stick to the base of the spine. Six months later he was indicted for perjury before a grand jury, booted without trial, and later stamped to death by a big stallion on his ranch in Wyoming.

Right now I was his raw meat. He sat behind his desk with his coat off and his sleeves rolled almost to his shoulders. He was as bald as a brick and getting heavy around the waist like all hard-muscled men in middle age. His eyes were fish gray. His big nose was a network of burst capillaries. He was drinking coffee and not quietly. His blunt strong hands had hairs thick on their backs. Grizzled tufts stuck out of his ears. He pawed something on his desk and looked at Green.

Green said: "All we got on him is he won't tell us nothing, skipper. The phone number makes us look him up. He's out riding and don't say where. He knows Lennox pretty well and don't say when he saw him last."

"Thinks he's tough," Gregorius said indifferently. "We could change that." He said it as if he didn't care one way or another. He probably didn't. Nobody was tough to him. "Point is the D.A. smells a lot of headlines on this one. Can't blame him, seeing who the girl's old man is. I guess we better pick this fellow's nose for him."

He looked at me as if I was a cigarette stub, or an empty chair. Just something in his line of vision, without interest for him.

Dayton said respectfully: "It's pretty obvious that his whole attitude was designed to create a situation where he could refuse to talk. He quoted law at us and needles me into socking him. I was out of line there, Captain."

Gregorius eyed him bleakly. "You must needle easy if this punk can do it. Who took the cuffs off?"

Green said he did. "Put them back on," Gregorius said. "Tight. Give him something to brace him up."

Green put the cuffs back on or started to. "Behind the back," Gregorius barked. Green cuffed my hands behind my back. I was sitting in a hard chair.

"Tighter," Gregorius said. "Make them bite."

Green made them tighter. My hands started to feel numb.

Gregorius looked at me finally. "You can talk now. Make it snappy."

I didn't answer him. He leaned back and grinned. His hand went out slowly for his coffee cup and went around it. He leaned forward a little. The cup jerked but I beat it by going sideways out of the chair. I landed hard on my shoulder, rolled over and got up slowly. My hands were quite numb now. They didn't feel anything. The arms above the cuffs were beginning to ache.

Green helped me back into the chair. The wet smear of

the coffee was over the back and some of the seat, but most of it was on the floor.

"He don't like coffee," Gregorius said. "He's a swifty. He moves fast. Good reflexes."

Nobody said anything. Gregorius looked me over with fish eyes.

"In here, mister, a dick license don't mean any more than a calling card. Now let's have your statement, verbal at first. We'll take it down later. Make it complete. Let's have, say, a full account of your movements since ten P.M. last night. I mean full. This office is investigating a murder and the prime suspect is missing. You connect with him. Guy catches his wife cheating and beats her head to raw flesh and bone and bloodsoaked hair. Our old friend the bronze statuette. Not original but it works. You think any goddam private eye is going to quote law at me over this, mister, you got a hell of a tough time coming your way. There ain't a police force in the country could do its job with a law book. You got information and I want it. You could of said no and I could of not believed you. But you didn't even say no. You're not dummying up on me, my friend. Not six cents worth. Let's go."

"Would you take the cuffs off, Captain?" I asked. "I mean if I made a statement?"

"I might. Make it short."

"If I told you I hadn't seen Lennox within the last twenty-four hours, hadn't talked to him and had no idea where he might be—would that satisfy you, Captain?"

"It might—if I believed it."

"If I told you I had seen him and where and when, but had no idea he had murdered anyone or that any crime had been committed, and further had no idea where he might be at this moment, that wouldn't satisfy you at all, would it?"

"With more detail I might listen. Things like where, when, what he looked like, what was talked about, where he was headed. It might grow into something."

"With your treatment," I said, "it would probably grow into making me an accessory."

His jaw muscles bulged. His eyes were dirty ice. "So?"

"I don't know," I said. "I need legal advice. I'd like to co-operate. How would it be if we had somebody from the D.A.'s office here?"

He let out a short raucous laugh. It was over very soon. He got up slowly and walked around the desk. He leaned down close to me, one big hand on the wood, and smiled. Then without change of expression he hit me on the side of the neck with a fist like a piece of iron.

The blow traveled eight or ten inches, no more. It nearly took my head off. Bile seeped into my mouth. I tasted blood mixed with it. I heard nothing but a roaring in my head. He leaned over me still smiling, his left hand still on the desk. His voice seemed to come from a long way off.

"I used to be tough but I'm getting old. You take a good punch, mister, and that's all you get from me. We got boys over at the City Jail that ought to be working in the stockyards. Maybe we hadn't ought to have them because they ain't nice clean powderpuff punchers like Dayton here. They don't have four kids and a rose garden like Green. They live for different amusements. It takes all kinds and labor's scarce. You got any more funny little ideas about what you might say, if you bothered to say it?"

"Not with the cuffs on, Captain." It hurt even to say that much.

He leaned farther towards me and I smelled his sweat and the gas of corruption. Then he straightened and went back around the desk and planted his solid buttocks in his chair. He picked up a three-cornered ruler and ran his thumb along one edge as if it was a knife. He looked at Green.

"What are you waiting for, Sergeant?"

"Orders." Green ground out the word as if he hated the sound of his own voice.

"You got to be told? You're an experienced man, it says in the records. I want a detailed statement of this man's movements for the past twenty-four hours. Maybe longer, but that much at first. I want to know what he did every minute of the time. I want it signed and witnessed and checked. I want it in two hours. Then I want him back here clean, tidy, and unmarked. And one thing more, Sergeant."

He paused and gave Green a stare that would have frozen a fresh-baked potato.

"—next time I ask a suspect a few civil questions I don't want you standing there looking as if I had torn his ear off."

"Yes, sir." Green turned to me. "Let's go," he said gruffly.

Gregorius bared his teeth at me. They needed cleaning—badly. "Let's have the exit line, chum."

"Yes, sir," I said politely. "You probably didn't intend it, but you've done me a favor. With an assist from Detective Dayton. You've solved a problem for me. No man likes to betray a friend but I wouldn't betray an enemy into your hands. You're not only a gorilla, you're an incompetent. You don't know how to operate a simple investigation. I was balanced on a knife edge and you could have swung me either way. But you had to abuse me, throw coffee in my face, and use your fists on me when I was in a spot where all I could do was take it. From now on I wouldn't tell you the time by the clock on your own wall."

For some strange reason he sat there perfectly still and let me say it. Then he grinned. "You're just a little old cop-hater, friend. That's all you are, shamus, just a little old cop-hater."

"There are places where cops are not hated, Captain. But in those places you wouldn't be a cop."

He took that too. I guess he could afford it. He'd probably taken worse many times. Then the phone rang on his desk. He looked at it and gestured. Dayton stepped smartly around the desk and lifted the receiver.

"Captain Gregorius' office. Detective Dayton speaking."

He listened. A tiny frown drew his handsome eyebrows together. He said softly: "One moment, please, sir."

He held the phone out to Gregorius. "Commissioner Allbright, sir."

Gregorius scowled. "Yeah? What's that snotty bastard want?" He took the phone, held it a moment and smoothed his face out. "Gregorius, Commissioner."

He listened. "Yeah, he's here in my office, Commissioner. I been asking him a few questions. Not co-operative. Not co-operative at all ... How's that again?" A sudden ferocious scowl twisted his face into dark knots. The blood darkened his forehead. But his voice didn't change in tone by a fraction. "If that's a direct order, it ought to come through the Chief of Detectives, Commissioner ... Sure, I'll act on it until it's confirmed. Sure ... Hell, no. Nobody laid a glove on him ... Yes, sir. Right away."

He put the phone back in its cradle. I thought his hand

shook a little. His eyes moved up and across my face and then to Green. "Take the cuffs off," he said tonelessly.

Green unlocked the cuffs. I rubbed my hands together, waiting for the pins and needles of circulation.

"Book him in the county jail," Gregorius said slowly. "Suspicion of murder. The D.A. has glommed the case right out of our hands. Lovely system we got around here."

Nobody moved. Green was close to me, breathing hard. Gregorius looked up at Dayton."

"Whatcha waiting for, cream puff? An ice-cream cone maybe?"

Dayton almost choked. "You didn't give me any orders, skipper."

"Say sir to me, damn you! I'm skipper to sergeants and better. Not to you, kiddo. Not to you. Out."

"Yes, sir." Dayton walked quickly to the door and went out. Gregorius heaved himself to his feet and moved to the window and stood with his back to the room.

"Come on, let's drift," Green muttered in my ear.

"Get him out of here before I kick his face in," Gregorius said to the window.

Green went to the door and opened it. I started through. Gregorius barked suddenly: "Hold it! Shut that door!"

Green shut it and leaned his back to it.

"Come here, you!" Gregorius barked at me.

I didn't move. I stood and looked at him. Green didn't move either. There was a grim pause. Then very slowly Gregorius walked across the room and stood facing me toe to toe. He put his big hard hands in his pockets. He rocked on his heels.

"Never laid a glove on him," he said under his breath, as if talking to himself. His eyes were remote and expressionless. His mouth worked convulsively.

Then he spat in my face.

He stepped back. "That will be all, thank you."

He turned and went back to the window. Green opened the door again.

I went through it reaching for my handkerchief.

8

CELL No. 3 in the felony tank has two bunks, Pullman style, but the tank was not very full and I had the cell to myself. In the felony tank they treat you pretty well. You get two blankets, neither dirty nor clean, and a lumpy mattress two inches thick which goes over crisscrossed metal slats. There is a flush toilet, a washbasin, paper towels and gritty gray soap. The cell block is clean and doesn't smell of disinfectant. The trusties do the work. The supply of trusties is always ample.

The jail deputies look you over and they have wise eyes. Unless you are a drunk or a psycho or act like one you get to keep your matches and cigarettes. Until preliminary you wear your own clothes. After that you wear the jail denim, no tie, no belt, no shoelaces. You sit on the bunk and wait. There is nothing else to do.

In the drunk tank it is not so good. No bunk, no chair, no blankets, no nothing. You lie on the concrete floor. You sit on the toilet and vomit in your own lap. That is the depth of misery. I've seen it.

Although it was still daylight the lights were on in the ceiling. Inside the steel door of the cell block was a basket of steel bars around the Judas window. The lights were controlled from outside the steel door. They went out at nine P.M. Nobody came through the door or said anything. You might be in the middle of a sentence in a newspaper or magazine. Without any sound of a click or any warning—darkness. And there you were until the summer dawn with nothing to do but sleep if you could, smoke if you had anything to smoke, and think if you had anything to think about that didn't make you feel worse than not thinking at all.

In jail a man has no personality. He is a minor disposal problem and a few entries on reports. Nobody cares who loves or hates him, what he looks like, what he did with his life. Nobody reacts to him unless he gives trouble. Nobody abuses him. All that is asked of him is that he go quietly to the right cell and remain quiet when he gets there. There is nothing to fight against, nothing to be mad at. The jailers are quiet men without animosity or sadism. All this stuff you read about men yelling and screaming, beating against the bars, running spoons along them, guards rushing in with clubs—all that is for the big house. A good jail is one of the quietest places in the world. You could walk through the average cell block at night and look in through the bars and see a huddle of brown blanket, or a head of hair, or a pair of eyes looking at nothing. You might hear a snore. Once in a long while you might hear a nightmare. The life in a jail is in suspension, without purpose or meaning. In another cell you might see a man who cannot sleep or even try to sleep. He is sitting on the edge of his bunk doing nothing. He looks at you or doesn't. You look at him. He says nothing and you say nothing. There is nothing to communicate.

In the corner of the cell block there may be a second steel door that leads to the show-up box. One of its walls is wire mesh painted black. On the back wall are ruled lines for height. Overhead are floodlights. You go in there in the morning as a rule, just before the night captain goes off duty. You stand against the measuring lines and the lights glare at you and there is no light behind the wire mesh. But plenty of people are out there: cops, detectives, citizens who have been robbed or assaulted or swindled or kicked out of their cars at gun point or conned out of their life savings. You don't see or hear them. You hear the voice of the night captain. You receive him loud and clear. He puts you through your paces as if you were a performing dog. He is tired and cynical and competent. He is the stage manager of a play that has had the longest run in history, but it no longer interests him.

"All right, you. Stand straight. Pull your belly in. Pull your chin in. Keep your shoulders back. Hold your head level. Look straight front. Turn left. Turn right. Face front again and hold your hands out. Palms up. Palms down. Pull your sleeves back. No visible scars. Hair dark brown, some gray. Eyes brown. Height six feet, one half inch. Weight about one ninety. Name, Philip Marlowe. Occupation private detective. Well, well, nice to see you, Marlowe. That's all. Next man."

Much obliged, Captain. Thanks for the time. You forgot to have me open my mouth. I have some nice inlays and one very high-class porcelain jacket crown. Eighty-seven dollars worth of porcelain jacket crown. You forgot to look inside my nose too, Captain. A lot of scar tissue in there for you. Septum operation and was that guy a butcher! Two hours of it in those days. I hear they do it in twenty minutes now. I got it playing football, Captain, a slight miscalculation in an attempt to block a punt. I blocked the guy's foot instead—after he kicked the ball. Fifteen yards penalty, and that's about how much stiff bloody tape they pulled out of my nose an inch at a time the day after the operation. I'm not bragging, Captain. I'm just telling you. It's the little things that count.

On the third day a deputy unlocked my cell in the middle of the morning.

"Your lawyer's here. Kill the butt—and not on the floor."

I flushed it down the toilet. He took me to the conference room. A tall pale dark-haired man was standing there looking out of the window. There was a fat brown briefcase on the table. He turned. He waited for the door to close. Then he sat down near his briefcase on the far side of a scarred oak table that came out of the Ark. Noah bought it secondhand. The lawyer opened a hammered silver cigarette case and put it in front of him and looked me over.

"Sit down, Marlowe. Care for a cigarette? My name is Endicott. Sewell Endicott. I've been instructed to represent you without cost or expense to you. I guess you'd like to get out of here, wouldn't you?"

I sat down and took one of the cigarettes. He held a lighter for me.

"Nice to see you again, Mr. Endicott. We've met before—while you were D.A."

He nodded. "I don't remember, but it's quite possible." He smiled faintly. "That position was not quite in my line. I guess I don't have enough tiger in me."

"Who sent you?"

"I'm not at liberty to say. If you accept me as your attorney, the fee will be taken care of."

"I guess that means they've got him."

He just stared at me. I puffed at the cigarette. It was one

of those things with filters in them. It tasted like a high fog strained through cotton wool.

"If you mean Lennox," he said, "and of course you do, no—they haven't got him."

"Why the mystery, Mr. Endicott? About who sent you."

"My principal wishes to remain anonymous. That is the privilege of my principal. Do you accept me?"

"I don't know," I said. "If they haven't got Terry, why are they holding me? Nobody has asked me anything, nobody has been near me."

He frowned and looked down at his long white delicate fingers. "District Attorney Springer has taken personal charge of this matter. He may have been too busy to question you yet. But you are entitled to arraignment and a preliminary hearing. I can get you out on bail on a habeas corpus proceeding. You probably know what the law is."

"I'm booked on suspicion of murder."

He shrugged impatiently. "That's just a catch-all. You could have been booked in transit to Pittsburgh, or any one of a dozen charges. What they probably mean is accessory after the fact. You took Lennox somewhere, didn't you?"

I didn't answer. I dropped the tasteless cigarette on the floor and stepped on it. Endicott shrugged again and frowned.

"Assume you did then, just for the sake of argument. To make you an accessory they have to prove intent. In this case that would mean knowledge that a crime had been committed and that Lennox was a fugitive. It's bailable in any case. Of course what you really are is a material witness. But a man can't be held in prison as a material witness in this state except by court order. He's not a material witness unless a judge so declares. But the law enforcement people can always find a way to do what they want to do."

"Yeah," I said. "A detective named Dayton slugged me. A homicide captain named Gregorius threw a cup of coffee at me, hit me in the neck hard enough to bust an artery—you can see it's still swollen, and when a call from Police Commissioner Allbright kept him from turning me over to the wrecking crew, he spat in my face. You're quite right,

Mr. Endicott. The law boys can always do what they want to do."

He looked at his wrist watch rather pointedly. "You want out on bail or don't you?"

"Thanks. I don't think I do. A guy out on bail is already half guilty in the public mind. If he gets off later on, he had a smart lawyer."

"That's silly," he said impatiently.

"Okay, it's silly. I'm silly. Otherwise I wouldn't be here. If you're in touch with Lennox, tell him to quit bothering about me. I'm not in here for him. I'm in here for me. No complaints. It's part of the deal. I'm in a business where people come to me with troubles. Big troubles, little troubles, but always troubles they don't want to take to the cops. How long would they come if any bruiser with a police shield could hold me upside down and drain my guts?"

"I see your point," he said slowly. "But let me correct you on one thing. I am not in touch with Lennox. I scarcely know him. I'm an officer of the court, as all lawyers are. If I knew where Lennox was, I couldn't conceal the information from the District Attorney. The most I could do would be to agree to surrender him at a specified time and place after I had had an interview with him."

"Nobody else would bother to send you here to help me."

"Are you calling me a liar?" He reached down to rub out his cigarette stub on the underside of the table.

"I seem to remember that you're a Virginian, Mr. Endicott. In this country we have a sort of historical fixation about Virginians. We think of them as the flower of southern chivalry and honor."

He smiled. "That was nicely said. I only wish it was true. But we're wasting time. If you had had a grain of sense you'd have told the police you hadn't seen Lennox for a week. It didn't have to be true. Under oath you could always have told the real story. There's no law against lying to the cops. They expect it. They feel much happier when you lie to them than when you refuse to talk to them. That's a direct challenge to their authority. What do you expect to gain by it?"

I didn't answer. I didn't really have an answer. He stood up and reached for his hat and snapped his cigarette case shut and put it in his pocket.

"You had to play the big scene," he said coldly. "Stand on your rights, talk about the law. How ingenuous can a man get, Marlowe? A man like you who is supposed to know his way around. The law isn't justice. It's a very imperfect mechanism. If you press exactly the right buttons and are also lucky, justice may show up in the answer. A mechanism is all the law was ever intended to be. I guess you're not in any mood to be helped. So I'll take myself off. You can reach me if you change your mind."

"I'll stick it out for a day or two longer. If they catch Terry they won't care how he got away. All they'll care about is the circus they can make of the trial. The murder of Mr. Harlan Potter's daughter is headline material all over the country. A crowd-pleaser like Springer could ride himself right into Attorney General on that show, and from there into the governor's chair and from there—"I stopped talking and let the rest of it float in the air.

Endicott smiled a slow derisive smile. "I don't think you know very much about Mr. Harlan Potter," he said.

"And if they don't get Lennox, they won't *want* to know how he got away, Mr. Endicott. They'll just want to forget the whole thing fast."

"Got it all figured out, haven't you, Marlowe?"

"I've had the time. All I know about Mr. Harlan Potter is that he is supposed to be worth a hundred million bucks, and that he owns nine or ten newspapers. How's the publicity going?"

"The publicity?" His voice was ice cold saying it.

"Yeah. Nobody's interviewed me from the press. I expected to make a big noise in the papers out of this. Get lots of business. Private eye goes to jail rather than split on a pal."

He walked to the door and turned with his hand on the knob. "You amuse me, Marlowe. You're childish in some ways. True, a hundred million dollars can buy a great deal of publicity. It can also, my friend, if shrewdly employed, buy a great deal of silence."

He opened the door and went out. Then a deputy came in and took me back to Cell No. 3 in the felony block.

"Guess you won't be with us long, if you've got Endi-cott," he said pleasantly as he locked me in. I said I hoped he was right.

9

THE DEPUTY on the early night shift was a big blond guy with meaty shoulders and a friendly grin. He was middle-aged and had long since outlived both pity and anger. He wanted to put in eight easy hours and he looked as if almost anything would be easy down his street. He un-locked my door.

"Company for you. Guy from the D.A.'s office. No sleep, huh?"

"It's a little early for me. What time is it?"

"Ten-fourteen." He stood in the doorway and looked over the cell. One blanket was spread on the lower bunk, one was folded for a pillow. There were a couple of used paper towels in the trash bucket and a small wad of toilet paper on the edge of the washbasin. He nodded approval. "Anything personal in here?"

"Just me."

He left the cell door open. We walked along a quiet corridor to the elevator and rode down to the booking desk. A fat man in a gray suit stood by the desk smoking a corncob. His fingernails were dirty and he smelled.

"I'm Spranklin from the D.A.'s office," he told me in a tough voice. "Mr. Grenz wants you upstairs." He reached behind his hip and came up with a pair of bracelets. "Let's try these for size."

The jail deputy and the booking clerk grinned at him with deep enjoyment. "What's the matter, Sprank? Afraid he'll mug you in the elevator?"

"I don't want no trouble," he growled. "Had a guy break from me once. They ate my ass off. Let's go, boy."

The booking clerk pushed a form at him and he signed it with a flourish. "I never take no unnecessary chances," he said. "Man never knows what he's up against in this town."

A prowl car cop brought in a drunk with a bloody ear. We went towards the elevator. "You're in trouble, boy," Spranklin told me in the elevator. "Heap bad trouble." It seemed to give him a vague satisfaction. "A guy can get hisself in a lot of trouble in this town."

The elevator man turned his head and winked at me. I grinned.

"Don't try nothing, boy," Spranklin told me severely. "I shot a man once. Tried to break. They ate my ass off."

"You get it coming and going, don't you?"

He thought it over. "Yeah," he said. "Either way they eat your ass off. It's a tough town. No respect."

We got out and went in through the double doors of the D.A.'s office. The switchboard was dead, with lines plugged in for the night. There was nobody in the waiting chairs. Lights were on in a couple of offices. Spranklin opened the door of a small lighted room which contained a desk, a filing case, a hard chair or two, and a thick-set man with a hard chin and stupid eyes. His face was red and he was just pushing something into the drawer of his desk.

"You could knock," he barked at Spranklin.

"Sorry, Mr. Grenz," Spranklin bumbled. "I was thinkin' about the prisoner."

He pushed me into the office. "Should I take the cuffs off, Mr. Grenz?"

"I don't know what the hell you put them on for," Grenz said sourly. He watched Spranklin unlock the cuffs on my wrist. He had the key on a bunch the size of a grapefruit and it troubled him to find it.

"Okay, scram," Grenz said. "Wait outside to take him back."

"I'm kind of off duty, Mr. Grenz."

"You're off duty when I say you're off duty."

Spranklin flushed and edged his fat bottom out through the door. Grenz looked after him savagely, then when the door closed he moved the same look to me. I pulled a chair over and sat down.

"I didn't tell you to sit down," Grenz barked.

I got a loose cigarette out of my pocket and stuck it in my mouth. "And I didn't say you could smoke," Grenz roared.

"I'm allowed to smoke in the cell block. Why not here?"

"Because this is my office. *I* make the rules here." A raw smell of whiskey floated across the desk.

"Take another quick one," I said. "It'll calm you down. You got kind of interrupted when we came in."

His back hit the back of the chair hard. His face went dark red. I struck a match and lit my cigarette.

After a long minute Grenz said softly. "Okay, tough boy. Quite a man, aren't you? You know something? They're all sizes and shapes when they come in here, but they all go out the same size—small. And the same shape—bent."

"What did you want to see me about, Mr. Grenz? And don't mind me if you feel like hitting that bottle. I'm a fellow that will take a snort myself, if I'm tired and nervous and overworked."

"You don't seem much impressed by the jam you're in."

"I don't figure I'm in any jam."

"We'll see about that. Meantime I want a very full statement from you." He flicked a finger at a recording set on a stand beside his desk. "We'll take it now and have it transcribed tomorrow. If the Chief Deputy is satisfied with your statement, he may release you on your own undertaking not to leave town. Let's go." He switched on the recorder. His voice was cold, decisive, and as nasty as he knew how to make it. But his right hand kept edging towards the desk drawer. He was too young to have veins in his nose, but he had them, and the whites of his eyes were a bad color.

"I get so tired of it," I said.

"Tired of what?" he snapped.

"Hard little men in hard little offices talking hard little words that don't mean a goddam thing. I've had fifty-six hours in the felony block. Nobody pushed me around, nobody tried to prove he was tough. They didn't have to. They had it on ice for when they needed it. And why was I in there? I was booked on suspicion. What the hell kind of legal system lets a man be shoved in a felony tank because some cop didn't get an answer to some questions? What evidence did he have? A telephone number on a pad. And what was he trying to prove by locking me up? Not a damn thing except that he had the power to do it. Now you're on the same pitch—trying to make me feel what a lot of power you generate in this cigar box you call your office. You send this scared baby sitter over late at night to bring me in here. You think maybe sitting alone with my thoughts for fifty-six hours has made gruel out of my brains? You think I'm going to cry in your lap and ask you to stroke my head because I'm so awful goddam lonely in the great big jail? Come off it, Grenz. Take your drink and get human; I'm willing to assume you are just doing your job. But take the brass knuckles off before you start. If you're big enough you don't need them, and if you need them you're not big enough to push me around."

He sat there and listened and looked at me. Then he grinned sourly. "Nice speech," he said. "Now you've got the crap out of your system, let's get that statement. You want to answer specific questions or just tell it your own way?"

"I was talking to the birds," I said. "Just to hear the breeze blow. I'm not making any statement. You're a lawyer and you know I don't have to."

"That's right," he said coolly. "I know the law. I know police work. I'm offering you a chance to clear yourself. If you don't want it, that's jake with me too. I can arraign you tomorrow morning at ten A.M and have you set for a preliminary hearing. You may get bail, although I'll fight it, but if you do, it will be stiff. It'll cost you plenty. That's one way we can do it."

He looked down at a paper on his desk, read it, and turned it face down.

"On what charge?" I asked him.

"Section thirty-two. Accessory after the fact. A felony. It rates up to a five-spot in Quentin."

"Better catch Lennox first," I said carefully. Grenz had something and I sensed it in his manner. I didn't know how much, but he had something all right.

He leaned back in his chair and picked up a pen and twirled it slowly between his palms. Then he smiled. He was enjoying himself.

"Lennox is a hard man to hide, Marlowe. With most people you need a photo and a good clear photo. Not with a guy that has scars all over one side of his face. Not to mention white hair, and not over thirty-five years old. We got four witnesses, maybe more."

"Witnesses to what?" I was tasting something bitter in my mouth, like the bile I had tasted after Captain Gregorius slugged me. That reminded me that my neck was still sore and swollen. I rubbed it gently.

"Don't be a chump, Marlowe. A San Diego superior court judge and his wife happened to be seeing their son and daughter-in-law off on that plane. All four saw Lennox and the judge's wife saw the car he came in and who came with him. You don't have a prayer."

"That's nice," I said. "How did you get to them?"

"Special bulletin on radio and TV. A full description was all it took. The judge called in."

"Sounds good," I said judicially. "But it takes a little more than that, Grenz. You have to catch him and prove he committed a murder. Then you have to prove I knew it."

He snapped a finger at the back of the telegram. "I think I will take that drink," he said. "Been working nights too much." He opened the drawer and put a bottle and a shot glass on the desk. He poured it full to the brim and knocked it back in a lump. "Better," he said. "Much better. Sorry I can't offer you one while you're in custody." He corked the bottle and pushed it away from him, but not out of reach. "Oh yeah, we got to prove something, you said. Well, it could be we already got a confession, chum. Too bad, huh?"

A small but very cold finger moved the whole length of my spine, like an icy insect crawling.

"So why do you need a statement from me?"

He grinned. "We like a tidy record. Lennox will be brought back and tried. We need everything we can get. It's not so much what we want from you as what we might be willing to let you get away with—if you co-operate."

I stared at him. He did a little paper-fiddling. He moved around in his chair, looked at his bottle, and had to use up a lot of will power not grabbing for it. "Maybe you'd like the whole libretto," he said suddenly with an off-key leer. "Well, smart guy, just to show you I'm not kidding, here it is."

I leaned across his desk and he thought I was reaching for his bottle. He grabbed it away and put it back in the drawer. I just wanted to drop a stub in his ash tray. I leaned back again and lit another pill. He spoke rapidly.

"Lennox got off the plane at Mazatlán, an airline junction point and a town of about thirty-five thousand.

He disappeared for two or three hours. Then a tall man with black hair and a dark skin and what might have been a lot of knife scars booked to Torreón under the name of Silvano Rodriguez. His Spanish was good but not good enough for a man of his name. He was too tall for a Mexican with such dark skin. The pilot turned in a report on him. The cops were too slow at Torreón. Mex cops are no balls of fire. What they do best is shoot people. By the time they got going the man had chartered a plane and gone on to a little mountain town called Otatoclán, a small time summer resort with a lake. The pilot of the charter plane had trained as a combat pilot in Texas. He spoke good English. Lennox pretended not to catch what he said."

"If it *was* Lennox," I put in.

"Wait a while, chum. It was Lennox all right. Okay, he gets off at Otatoclán and registers at the hotel there, this time as Mario de Cerva. He was wearing a gun, a Mauser 7.65, which doesn't mean too much in Mexico, of course. But the charter pilot thought the guy didn't seem kosher, so he had a word with the local law. They put Lennox under surveillance. They did some checking with Mexico City and then they moved in."

Grenz picked up a ruler and sighted along it, a meaningless gesture which kept him from looking at me.

I said, "Uh-huh. Smart boy, your charter pilot, and nice to his customers. The story stinks."

He looked up at me suddenly. "What we want," he said dryly, "is a quick trial, a plea of second degree which we will accept. There are some angles we'd rather not go into. After all, the family is pretty influential."

"Meaning Harlan Potter."

He nodded briefly. "For my money the whole idea is all wet. Springer could have a field day with it. It's got everything. Sex, scandal, money, beautiful unfaithful wife, wounded war hero husband—I suppose that's where he got the scars—hell, it would be front page stuff for weeks. Every rag in the country would eat it up. So we shuffle it off to a fast fade." He shrugged. "Okay, if the chief wants it that way, it's up to him. Do I get that statement?" He turned to the recording machine which had been humming away softly all this time, with the light showing in front.

"Turn it off," I said.

He swung around and gave me a vicious look. "You like it in jail?"

"It's not too bad. You don't meet the best people, but who the hell wants to? Be reasonable, Grenz. You're trying to make a fink out of me. Maybe I'm obstinate, or even sentimental, but I'm practical too. Suppose you had to hire a private eye—yeah, yeah, I know how you would hate the idea—but just suppose you were where it was your only out. Would you want one that finked on his friends?"

He stared at me with hate.

"A couple more points. Doesn't it strike you that Lennox's evasion tactics were just a little too transparent? If he wanted to be caught, he didn't have to go to all that trouble. If he didn't want to be caught, he had brains enough not to disguise himself as a Mexican in Mexico."

"Meaning what?" Grenz was snarling at me now.

"Meaning you could just be filling me up with a lot of hooey you made up, that there wasn't any Rodriguez with dyed hair and there wasn't any Mario de Cerva at Otatoclán, and you don't know any more about where Lennox is than where Black Beard the Pirate buried his treasure."

He got his bottle out again. He poured himself a shot and drank it down quickly, as before. He relaxed slowly. He turned in his chair and switched off the recording machine.

"I'd like to have tried you," he said gratingly. "You're the kind of wise guy I like to work over. This rap will be hanging over you for a long long time, cutie. You'll walk with it and eat with it and sleep with it. And next time you step out of line we'll murder you with it. Right now I got to do something that turns my guts inside out."

He pawed on his desk and pulled the face-down paper to him, turned it over and signed it. You can always tell when a man is writing his own name. He has a special way of moving. Then he stood up and marched around the desk and threw the door of his shoe box open and yelled for Spranklin.

The fat man came in with his B.O. Grenz gave him the paper.

"I've just signed your release order," he said. "I'm a public servant and sometimes I have unpleasant duties. Would you care to know why I signed it?"

I stood up. "If you want to tell me."

"The Lennox case is closed, mister. There ain't any Lennox case. He wrote out a full confession this afternoon in his hotel room and shot himself. In Otatoclán, just like I said."

I stood there looking at nothing. Out of the corner of my eye I saw Grenz back away slowly as if he thought I might be going to slug him. I must have looked pretty nasty for a moment. Then he was behind his desk again and Spranklin had grabbed onto my arm.

"Come on, move," he said in a whining kind of voice. "Man likes to get to home nights once in a while."

I went out with him and closed the door. I closed it quietly as if on a room where someone had just died.

10

I DUG OUT THE CARBON of my property slip and turned it over and receipted on the original. I put my belongings back in my pockets. There was a man draped over the end of the booking desk and as I turned away he straightened up and spoke to me. He was about six feet four inches tall and as thin as a wire.

"Need a ride home?"

In the bleak light he looked young-old, tired and cynical, but he didn't look like a grifter. "For how much?"

"For free. I'm Lonnie Morgan of the *Journal*. I'm knocking off."

"Oh, police beat," I said.

"Just this week. The City Hall is my regular beat."

We walked out of the building and found his car in the parking lot. I looked up at the sky. There were stars but there was too much glare. It was a cool pleasant night. I breathed it in. Then I got into his car and he drove away from there.

"I live way out in Laurel Canyon," I said. "Just drop me anywhere."

"They ride you in," he said, "but they don't worry how

you get home. This case interests me, in a repulsive sort of way."

"It seems there isn't any case," I said. "Terry Lennox shot himself this afternoon. So they say. So they say."

"Very convenient," Lonnie Morgan said, staring ahead through the windshield. His car drifted quietly along quiet streets. "It helps them build their wall."

"What wall?"

"Somebody's building a wall around the Lennox case, Marlowe. You're smart enough to see that, aren't you? It's not getting the kind of play it rates. The D.A. left town tonight for Washington. Some kind of convention. He walked out on the sweetest hunk of publicity he's had in years. Why?"

"No use to ask me. I've been in cold storage."

"Because somebody made it worth his while, that's why. I don't mean anything crude like a wad of dough. Somebody promised him something important to him and there's only one man connected with the case in a position to do that. The girl's father."

I leaned my head back in a corner of the car. "Sounds a little unlikely," I said. "What about the press? Harlan Potter owns a few papers, but what about the competition?"

He gave me a brief amused glance and then concentrated on his driving. "Ever been a newspaperman?"

"No."

"Newspapers are owned and published by rich men. Rich men all belong to the same club. Sure, there's competition—hard tough competition for circulation, for newsbeats, for exclusive stories. Just so long as it doesn't damage the prestige and privilege and position of the owners. If it does, down comes the lid. The lid, my friend, is down on the Lennox case. The Lennox case, my friend, properly built up, could have sold a hell of a lot of papers. It has everything. The trial would have drawn feature writers from all over the country. But there ain't going to be no trial. On account of Lennox checked out before it could get moving. Like I said—very convenient—for Harlan Potter and his family."

I straightened up and gave him a hard stare.

"You calling the whole thing a fix?"

He twisted his mouth sardonically. "Could just be Lennox had some help committing suicide. Resisting arrest a little. Mexican cops have very itchy trigger fingers. If you want to lay a little bet, I'll give you nice odds that nobody gets to count the bullet holes."

"I think you're wrong," I said. "I knew Terry Lennox pretty well. He wrote himself off a long time ago. If they brought him back alive, he would have let them have it their way. He'd have copped a manslaughter plea."

Lonnie Morgan shook his head. I knew what he was going to say and he said it. "Not a chance. If he had shot her or cracked her skull, maybe yes. But there was too much brutality. Her face was beaten to a pulp. Second degree murder would be the best he could get, and even that would raise a stink."

I said: "You could be right."

He looked at me again. "You say you knew the guy. Do you go for the setup?"

"I'm tired. I'm not in a thinking mood tonight."

There was a long pause. Then Lonnie Morgan said quietly: "If I was a real bright guy instead of a hack newspaperman, I'd think maybe he didn't kill her at all."

"It's a thought."

He stuck a cigarette in his mouth and lit it by scratching a match on the dashboard. He smoked silently with a fixed frown on his thin face. We reached Laurel Canyon and I told him where to turn off the boulevard and where to turn into my street. His car churned up the hill and stopped at the foot of my redwood steps.

I got out. "Thanks for the ride, Morgan. Care for a drink?"

"I'll take a rain check. I figure you'd rather be alone."

"I've got lots of time to be alone. Too damn much."

"You've got a friend to say goodbye to," he said. "He must have been that if you let them toss you into the can on his account."

"Who said I did that?"

He smiled faintly. "Just because I can't print it don't mean I didn't know it, chum. So long. See you around."

I shut the car door and he turned and drove off down the hill. When his tail lights vanished around the corner I climbed the steps, picked up newspapers, and let myself into the empty house. I put all the lamps on and opened all the windows. The place was stuffy.

I made some coffee and drank it and took the five C notes out of the coffee can. They were rolled tight and pushed down into the coffee at the side. I walked up and down with a cup of coffee in my hand, turned the TV on, turned it off, sat, stood, and sat again. I read through the papers that had piled up on the front steps. The Lennox case started out big, but by that morning it was a Part Two item. There was a photo of Sylvia, but none of Terry. There was a snap of me that I didn't know existed. "L.A. Private Detective Held for Questioning." There was a large photo of the Lennox home in Encino. It was pseudo English with a lot of peaked roof and it would have cost a hundred bucks to wash the windows. It stood on a knoll in a big two acres, which is a lot of real estate for the Los Angeles area. There was a photo of the guest house, which was a miniature of the main building. It was hedged in with trees. Both photos had obviously been taken from some distance off and then blown up and trimmed. There was no photo of what the papers called the "death room."

I had seen all this stuff before, in jail, but I read it and looked at it again with different eyes. It told me nothing except that a rich and beautiful girl had been murdered and the press had been pretty thoroughly excluded. So the influence had started to work very early. The crime beat boys must have gnashed their teeth and gnashed them in vain. It figured. If Terry talked to his father-in-law in Pasadena the very night she was killed, there would have been a dozen guards on the estate before the police were even notified.

But there was something that didn't figure at all—the way she had been beaten up. Nobody could sell me that Terry had done that.

I put the lamps out and sat by an open window. Outside in a bush a mockingbird ran through a few trills and admired himself before settling down for the night. My neck itched, so I shaved and showered and went to bed and lay on my back listening, as if far off in the dark I might hear a voice, the kind of calm and patient voice that makes everything clear. I didn't hear it and I knew I wasn't going to. Nobody was going to explain the Lennox case to me. No explanation was necessary. The murderer had confessed and he was dead. There wouldn't even be an inquest.

As Lonnie Morgan of the *Journal* had remarked—very

convenient. If Terry Lennox had killed his wife, that was fine. There was no need to try him and bring out all the unpleasant details. If he hadn't killed her, that was fine too. A dead man is the best fall guy in the world. He never talks back.

11

IN THE MORNING I shaved again and dressed and drove downtown in the usual way and parked in the usual place and if the parking lot attendant happened to know that I I was an important public character he did a top job in hiding it. I went upstairs and along the corridor and got keys out to unlock my door. A dark smooth-looking guy watched me.

"You Marlowe?"

"So?"

"Stick around," he said. "A guy wants to see you." He unplastered his back from the wall and strolled off languidly.

I stepped inside the office and picked up the mail. There was more of it on the desk where the night cleaning woman had put it. I slit the envelopes after I opened windows, and threw away what I didn't want, which was practically all of it. I switched on the buzzer to the other door and filled a pipe and lit it and then just sat there waiting for somebody to scream for help.

I thought about Terry Lennox in a detached sort of way. He was already receding into the distance, white hair and scarred face and weak charm and his peculiar brand of pride. I didn't judge him or analyze him, just as I had never asked him questions about how he got wounded or how he ever happened to get himself married to anyone like Sylvia. He was like somebody you meet on board ship and get to know very well and never really know at all. He was gone like the same fellow when he says goodbye at the pier and let's keep in touch, old man, and you know you won't and he won't. Likely enough you'll never even see the guy again. If you do he will be an entirely different person, just another Rotarian in a club car. How's business? Oh, not too bad. You look good. So do you. I've put on too much weight. Don't we all? Remember that trip in the *Franconia* (or whatever it was)? Oh sure, swell trip, wasn't it?

The hell it was a swell trip. You were bored stiff. You only talked to the guy because there wasn't anybody around that interested you. Maybe it was like that with Terry Lennox and me. No, not quite. I owned a piece of him. I had invested time and money in him, and three days in the icehouse, not to mention a slug on the jaw and a punch in the neck that I felt every time I swallowed. Now he was dead and I couldn't even give him back his five hundred bucks. That made me sore. It is always the little things that make you sore.

The door buzzer and the telephone rang at the same time. I answered the phone first because the buzzer meant only that somebody had walked into my pint-size waiting room.

"Is this Mr. Marlowe? Mr. Endicott is calling you. One moment please."

He came on the line. "This is Sewell Endicott," he said, as if he didn't know his goddam secretary had already fed me his name.

"Good morning, Mr. Endicott."

"Glad to hear they turned you loose. I think possibly you had the right idea not to build any resistance."

"It wasn't an idea. It was just mulishness."

"I doubt if you'll hear any more about it. But if you do and need help, let me hear from you."

"Why would I? The man is dead. They'd have a hell of a time proving he ever came near me. Then they'd have to prove I had guilty knowledge. And then they'd have to prove he had committed a crime or was a fugitive."

He cleared his throat. "Perhaps," he said carefully, "you haven't been told he left a full confession."

"I was told, Mr. Endicott. I'm talking to a lawyer. Would I be out of line in suggesting that the confession would have to be proved too, both as to genuineness and as to veracity?"

"I'm afraid I have no time for a legal discussion," he

said sharply. "I'm flying to Mexico with a rather melancholy duty to perform. You can probably guess what it is?"

"Uh-huh. Depends who you're representing. You didn't tell me, remember."

"I remember very well. Well, goodbye, Marlowe. My offer of help is still good. But let me also offer you a little advice. Don't be too certain you're in the clear. You're in a pretty vulnerable business."

He hung up. I put the phone back in its cradle carefully. I sat for a moment with my hand on it, scowling. Then I wiped the scowl off my face and got up to open the communicating door into my waiting room.

A man was sitting by the window ruffling a magazine. He wore a bluish-gray suit with an almost invisible pale blue check. On his crossed feet were black moccasin-type ties, the kind with two eyelets that are almost as comfortable as strollers and don't wear your socks out every time you walk a block. His white handkerchief was folded square and the end of a pair of sunglasses showed behind it. He had thick dark wavy hair. He was tanned very dark. He looked up with bird-bright eyes and smiled under a hairline mustache. His tie was a dark maroon tied in a pointed bow over a sparkling white shirt.

He threw the magazine aside. "The crap these rags go for," he said. "I been reading a piece about Costello. Yeah, they know all about Costello. Like I know all about Helen of Troy."

"What can I do for you?"

He looked me over unhurriedly. "Tarzan on a big red scooter," he said.

"What?"

"You. Marlowe. Tarzan on a big red scooter. They rough you up much?"

"Here and there. What makes it your business?"

"After Allbright talked to Gregorius?"

"No. Not after that."

He nodded shortly. "You got a crust asking Allbright to use ammunition on that slob."

"I asked you what made it your business. Incidentally I don't know Commissioner Allbright and I didn't ask him to do anything. Why would he do anything for me?"

He stared at me morosely. He stood up slowly, graceful as a panther. He walked across the room and looked into my office. He jerked his head at me and went in. He was a guy who owned the place where he happened to be. I went in after him and shut the door. He stood by the desk looking around, amused.

"You're small time," he said. "Very small time."

I went behind my desk and waited.

"How much you make in a month, Marlowe?"

I let it ride, and lit my pipe.

"Seven-fifty would be tops," he said.

I dropped a burnt match into a tray and puffed tobacco smoke.

"You're a piker, Marlowe. You're a peanut grifter. You're so little it takes a magnifying glass to see you."

I didn't say anything at all.

"You got cheap emotions. You're cheap all over. You pal around with a guy, eat a few drinks, talk a few gags, slip him a little dough when he's strapped, and you're sold out to him. Just like some school kid that read *Frank Merriwell*. You got no guts, no brains, no connections, no savvy, so you throw out a phony attitude and expect people to cry over you. Tarzan on a big red scooter." He smiled a small weary smile. "In my book you're a nickel's worth of nothing."

He leaned across the desk and flicked me across the face back-handed, casually and contemptuously, not meaning to hurt me, and the small smile stayed on his face. Then when I didn't even move for that he sat down slowly and leaned an elbow on the desk and cupped his brown chin in his brown hand. The bird-bright eyes stared at me without anything in them but brightness.

"Know who I am, cheapie?"

"Your name's Menendez. The boys call you Mendy. You operate on the Strip."

"Yeah? How did I get so big?"

"I wouldn't know. You probably started out as a pimp in a Mexican whorehouse."

He took a gold cigarette case out of his pocket and lit a brown cigarette with a gold lighter. He blew acrid smoke and nodded. He put the gold cigarette case on the desk and caressed it with his fingertips.

"I'm a big bad man, Marlowe. I make lots of dough. I got to make lots of dough to juice the guys I got to juice in order to make lots of dough to juice the guys I got to juice.

I got a place in Bel-Air that cost ninety grand and I already spent more than that to fix it up. I got a lovely platinum-blond wife and two kids in private schools back east. My wife's got a hundred and fifty grand in rocks and another seventy-five in furs and clothes. I got a butler, two maids, a cook, a chauffeur, not counting the monkey that walks behind me. Everywhere I go I'm a darling. The best of everything, the best food, the best drinks, the best hotel suites. I got a place in Florida and a seagoing yacht with a crew of five men. I got a Bentley, two Cadillacs, a Chrysler station wagon, and an MG for my boy. Couple of years my girl gets one too. What you got?"

"Not much," I said. "This year I have a house to live in—all to myself."

"No woman?"

"Just me. In addition to that I have what you see here and twelve hundred dollars in the bank and a few thousand in bonds. That answer your question?"

"What's the most you ever made on a single job?"

"Eight-fifty."

"Jesus, how cheap can a guy get?"

"Stop hamming and tell me what you want."

He killed his cigarette half smoked and immediately lit another. He leaned back in his chair. His lip curled at me.

"We were three guys in a foxhole eating," he said. "It was cold as hell, snow all around. We eat out of cans. Cold food. A little shelling, more mortar fire. We are blue with the cold, and I mean blue, Randy Starr and me and this Terry Lennox. A mortar shell plops right in the middle of us and for some reason it don't go off. Those jerries have a lot of tricks. They got a twisted sense of humor. Sometimes you think it's a dud and three seconds later it ain't a dud. Terry grabs it and he's out of the foxhole before Randy and me can even start to get unstuck. But I mean quick, brother. Like a good ball handler. He throws himself face down and throws the thing away from him and it goes off in the air. Most of it goes over his head but a hunk gets the side of his face. Right then the krauts mount an attack and the next thing we know we ain't there any more."

Menendez stopped talking and gave me the bright steady glare of his dark eyes.

"Thanks for telling me," I said.

"You take a good ribbing, Marlowe. You're okay. Randy

and me talked things over and we decided that what happened to Terry Lennox was enough to screw up any guy's brains. For a long time we figured he was dead but he wasn't. The krauts got him. They worked him over for about a year and a half. They did a good job but they hurt him too much. It cost us money to find out, and it cost us money to find him. But we made plenty in the black market after the war. We could afford it. All Terry gets out of saving our lives is half of a new face, white hair, and a bad case of nerves. Back east he hits the bottle, gets picked up here and there, kind of goes to pieces. There's something on his mind but we never know what. The next thing we know he's married to this rich dame and riding high. He unmarries her, hits bottom again, marries her again, and she gets dead. Randy and me can't do a thing for him. He won't let us except for that short job in Vegas. And when he gets in a real jam he don't come to us, he goes to a cheapie like you, a guy that cops can push around. So then *he* gets dead, and without telling us goodbye, and without giving us a chance to pay off. I could have got him out of the country faster than a card sharp can stack a deck. But he goes crying to you. It makes me sore. A cheapie, a guy cops can push around."

"The cops can push anybody around. What do you want me to do about it?"

"Just lay off," Menendez said tightly.

"Lay off what?"

"Trying to make yourself dough or publicity out of the Lennox case. It's finished, wrapped up. Terry's dead and we don't want him bothered any more. The guy suffered too much."

"A hoodlum with sentiment," I said. "That slays me."

"Watch your lip, cheapie. Watch your lip. Mendy Menendez don't argue with guys. He tells them. Find yourself another way to grab a buck. Get me?"

He stood up. The interview was finished. He picked up his gloves. They were snow-white pigskin. They didn't look as if he ever had them on. A dressy type, Mr. Menendez. But very tough behind it all.

"I'm not looking for publicity," I said. "And nobody's offered me any dough. Why would they and for what?"

"Don't kid me, Marlowe. You didn't spend three days in the freezer just because you're a sweetheart. You got paid off. I ain't saying who by but I got a notion. And the party I'm thinking about has plenty more of the stuff. The Lennox case is closed and it stays closed even if—" He stopped dead and flipped his gloves at the desk edge.

"Even if Terry didn't kill her," I said.

His surprise was as thin as the gold on a weekend wedding ring. "I'd like to go along with you on that, cheapie. But it don't make any sense. But if it did make sense—and Terry wanted it the way it is—then that's how it stays."

I didn't say anything. After a moment he grinned slowly. "Tarzan on a big red scooter," he drawled. "A tough guy. Lets me come in here and walk all over him. A guy that gets hired for nickels and dimes and gets pushed around by anybody. No dough, no family, no prospects, no nothing. See you around, cheapie."

I sat still with my jaws clamped, staring at the glitter of his gold cigarette case on the desk corner. I felt old and tired. I got up slowly and reached for the case.

"You forgot this," I said, going around the desk.

"I got half a dozen of them," he sneered.

When I was near enough to him I held it out. His hand reached for it casually. "How about half a dozen of these?" I asked him and hit him as hard as I could in the middle of his belly.

He doubled up mewling. The cigarette case fell to the floor. He backed against the wall and his hands jerked back and forth convulsively. His breath fought to get into his lungs. He was sweating. Very slowly and with an intense effort he straightened up and we were eye to eye again. I reached out and ran a finger along the bone of his jaw. He held still for it. Finally he worked a smile onto his brown face.

"I didn't think you had it in you," he said.

"Next time bring a gun—or don't call me cheapie."

"I got a guy to carry the gun."

"Bring him with you. You'll need him."

"You're a hard guy to get sore, Marlowe."

I moved the gold cigarette case to one side with my foot and bent and picked it up and handed it to him. He took it and dropped it into his pocket.

"I couldn't figure you," I said. "Why it was worth your time to come up here and ride me. Then it got monotonous. All tough guys are monotonous. Like playing cards with a deck that's all aces. You've got everything and you've got nothing. You're just sitting there looking at yourself. No wonder Terry didn't come to you for help. It would be like borrowing money from a whore."

He pressed delicately on his stomach with two fingers. "I'm sorry you said that, cheapie. You could crack wise once too often."

He walked to the door and opened it. Outside the bodyguard straightened from the opposite wall and turned. Menendez jerked his head. The bodyguard came into the office and stood there looking me over without expression.

"Take a good look at him, Chick," Menendez said. "Make sure you know him just in case. You and him might have business one of these days."

"I already saw him, Chief," the smooth dark tight-lipped guy said in the tight-lipped voice they all affect. "He wouldn't bother me none."

"Don't let him hit you in the guts," Menendez said with a sour grin. "His right hook ain't funny."

The bodyguard just sneered at me. "He wouldn't get that close."

"Well, so long, cheapie," Menendez told me and went out.

"See you around," the bodyguard told me coolly. "The name's Chick Agostino. I guess you'll know me."

"Like a dirty newspaper," I said. "Remind me not to step on your face."

His jaw muscles bulged. Then he turned suddenly and went out after his boss.

The door closed slowly on the pneumatic gadget. I listened but I didn't hear their steps going down the hall. They walked as softly as cats. Just to make sure, I opened the door again after a minute and looked out. But the hall was quite empty.

I went back to my desk and sat down and spent a little time wondering why a fairly important local racketeer like Menendez would think it worth his time to come in person to my office and warn me to keep my nose clean, just minutes after I had received a similiar though differently expressed warning from Sewell Endicott.

I didn't get anywhere with that, so I thought I might as well make it a perfect score. I lifted the phone and put in a call to the Terrapin Club at Las Vegas, person to person, Philip Marlowe calling Mr. Randy Starr. No soap. Mr. Starr was out of town, and would I talk to anyone else? I would not. I didn't even want to talk to Starr very badly. It was just a passing fancy. He was too far away to hit me.

After that nothing happened for three days. Nobody slugged me or shot at me or called me up on the phone and warned me to keep my nose clean. Nobody hired me to find the wandering daughter, the erring wife, the lost pearl necklace, or the missing will. I just sat there and looked at the wall. The Lennox case died almost as suddenly as it had been born. There was a brief inquest to which I was not summoned. It was held at an odd hour, without previous announcement and without a jury. The coroner entered his own verdict, which was that the death of Sylvia Potter Westerheym di Giorgio Lennox had been caused with homicidal intent by her husband, Terence William Lennox, since deceased outside the jurisdiction of the coroner's office. Presumably a confession was read into the record. Presumably it was verified enough to satisfy the coroner.

The body was released for burial. It was flown north and buried in the family vault. The press was not invited. Nobody gave any interviews, least of all Mr. Harlan Potter, who never gave interviews. He was about as hard to see as the Dalai Lama. Guys with a hundred million dollars live a peculiar life, behind a screen of servants, bodyguards, secretaries, lawyers, and tame executives. Presumably they eat, sleep, get their hair cut, and wear clothes. But you never know for sure. Everything you read or hear about them has been processed by a public relations gang of guys who are paid big money to create and maintain a usable personality, something simple and clean and sharp, like a sterilized needle. It doesn't have to be true. It just has to be consistent with the known facts, and the known facts you could count on your fingers.

Late afternoon of the third day the telephone rang and I was talking to a man who said his name was Howard Spencer, that he was a representative of a New York publishing house in California on a brief business trip, that he had a problem he would like to discuss with me and would I meet him in the bar of the Ritz-Beverly Hotel at eleven A.M. the next morning.

I asked him what sort of problem.

"Rather a delicate one," he said, "but entirely ethical. If we don't agree, I shall expect to pay you for your time, naturally."

"Thank you, Mr. Spencer, but that won't be necessary. Did someone I know recommend me to you?"

"Someone who knows about you—including your recent brush with the law, Mr. Marlowe. I might say that that was what interested me. My business, however, has nothing to do with that tragic affair. It's just that—well, let's discuss it over a drink, rather than over the telephone."

"You sure you want to mix it with a guy who has been in the cooler?"

He laughed. His laugh and his voice were both pleasant. He talked the way New Yorkers used to talk before they learned to talk Flatbush.

"From my point of view, Mr. Marlowe, that is a recommendation. Not, let me add, the fact that you were, as you put it, in the cooler, but the fact, shall I say, that you appear to be extremely reticent, even under pressure."

He was a guy who talked with commas, like a heavy novel. Over the phone anyway.

"Okay, Mr. Spencer, I'll be there in the morning."

He thanked me and hung up. I wondered who could have given me the plug. I thought it might be Sewell Endicott and called him to find out. But he had been out of town all week, and still was. It didn't matter much. Even in my business you occasionally get a satisfied customer. And I needed a job because I needed the money—or thought I did, until I got home that night and found the letter with a portrait of Madison in it.

12

THE LETTER was in the red and white birdhouse mailbox at the foot of my steps. A woodpecker on top of the box attached to the swing arm was raised and even at that I might not have looked inside because I never got mail at the house. But the woodpecker had lost the point of his beak quite recently. The wood was fresh broken. Some smart kid shooting off his atom gun.

The letter had Correo Aéreo on it and a flock of Mexican stamps and writing that I might or might not have recognized if Mexico hadn't been on my mind pretty constantly lately. I couldn't read the postmark. It was hand-stamped and the ink pad was pretty far gone. The letter was thick. I climbed my steps and sat down in the living room to read it. The evening seemed very silent. Perhaps a letter from a dead man brings its own silence with it.

It began without date and without preamble.

I'm sitting beside a second-floor window in a room in a not too clean hotel in a town called Otatoclán, a mountain town with a lake. There's a mailbox just below the window and when the mozo comes in with some coffee I've ordered he is going to mail the letter for me and hold it up so that I can see it before he puts it in the slot. When he does that he gets a hundred-peso note, which is a hell of a lot of money for him.

Why all the finagling? There's a swarthy character with pointed shoes and a dirty shirt outside the door watching it. He's waiting for something, I don't know what, but he won't let me out. It doesn't matter too much as long as the letter gets posted. I want you to have this money because I don't need it and the local gendarmerie would swipe it for sure. It is not intended to buy anything. Call it an apology for making you so much trouble and a token of esteem for a pretty decent guy. I've done everything wrong as usual, but I still have the gun. My hunch is that you have probably made up your mind on a certain point. I might have killed her and perhaps I did, but I never could have done the other thing. That kind of brutality is not in my line. So something is very sour. But it doesn't matter, not in the least. The main thing now is to save an unnecessary and useless scandal. Her father and her sister never did me any harm. They have their lives to live and I'm up to here in disgust with mine. Sylvia didn't make a bum out of me, I was one already. I can't give you any very clean answer about why she married me. I suppose it was just a whim. At least she died young and beautiful. They say lust makes a man old, but keeps a woman young. They say a lot of nonsense. They say the rich can always protect themselves and that in their world it is always summer. I've lived with them and they are bored and lonely people.

I have written a confession. I feel a little sick and more than a little scared. You read about these situations in books, but you don't read the truth. When it happens to you, when all you have left is the gun in your pocket, when you are cornered in a dirty little hotel in a strange country, and have only one way out—believe me, pal, there is nothing elevating or dramatic about it. It is just plain nasty and sordid and gray and grim.

So forget it and me. But first drink a gimlet for me at Victor's. And the next time you make coffee, pour me a cup and put some bourbon in it and light me a cigarette and put it beside the cup. And after that forget the whole thing. Terry Lennox over and out. And so goodbye.

A knock at the door. I guess it will be the mozo with the coffee. If it isn't, there will be some shooting. I like Mexicans, as a rule, but I don't like their jails. So long.

TERRY

That was all. I refolded the letter and put it back in the envelope. It had been the mozo with the coffee all right. Otherwise I would never have had the letter. Not with a portrait of Madison in it. A portrait of Madison is a $5000 bill.

It lay in front of me green and crisp on the table top. I had never even seen one before. Lots of people who work in banks haven't either. Very likely characters like Randy Starr and Menendez wear them for folding money. If you went to a bank and asked for one, they wouldn't have it. They'd have to get it for you from the Federal Reserve. It might take several days. There are only about a thousand of them in circulation in the whole U.S.A. Mine had a nice glow around it. It created a little private sunshine all its own.

I sat there and looked at it for a long time. At last I put

it away in my letter case and went out to the kitchen to make that coffee. I did what he asked me to, sentimental or not. I poured two cups and added some bourbon to his and set it down on the side of the table where he had sat the morning I took him to the plane. I lit a cigarette for him and set it in an ash tray beside the cup. I watched the steam rise from the coffee and the thin thread of smoke rise from the cigarette. Outside in the tecoma a bird was gussing around, talking to himself in low chirps, with an occasional brief flutter of wings.

Then the coffee didn't steam any more and the cigarette stopped smoking and was just a dead butt on the edge of an ash tray. I dropped it into the garbage can under the sink. I poured the coffee out and washed the cup and put it away.

That was that. It didn't seem quite enough to do for five thousand dollars.

I went to a late movie after a while. It meant nothing. I hardly saw what went on. It was just noise and big faces. When I got home again I set out a very dull Ruy Lopez and that didn't mean anything either. So I went to bed.

But not to sleep. At three A.M. I was walking the floor and listening to Khachaturyan working in a tractor factory. He called it a violin concerto. I called it a loose fan belt and the hell with it.

A white night for me is as rare as a fat postman. If it hadn't been for Mr. Howard Spencer at the Ritz-Beverly I would have killed a bottle and knocked myself out. And the next time I saw a polite character drunk in a Rolls-Royce Silver Wraith, I would depart rapidly in several directions. There is no trap so deadly as the trap you set for yourself.

13

At eleven o'clock I was sitting in the third booth on the right-hand side as you go in from the dining-room annex. I had my back against the wall and I could see anyone who came in or went out. It was a clear morning, no smog, no high fog even, and the sun dazzled the surface of the swimming pool which began just outside the plateglass wall of the bar and stretched to the far end of the dining room. A girl in a white sharkskin suit and a luscious figure was climbing the ladder to the high board. I watched the band of white that showed between the tan of her thighs and the suit. I watched it carnally. Then she was out of sight, cut off by the deep overhang of the roof. A moment later I saw her flash down in a one and a half. Spray came high enough to catch the sun and make rainbows that were almost as pretty as the girl. Then she came up the ladder and unstrapped her white helmet and shook her bleach job loose. She wobbled her bottom over to a small white table and sat down beside a lumberjack in white drill pants and dark glasses and a tan so evenly dark that he couldn't have been anything but the hired man around the pool. He reached over and patted her thigh. She opened a mouth like a firebucket and laughed. That terminated my interest in her. I couldn't hear the laugh but the hole in her face when she unzippered her teeth was all I needed.

The bar was pretty empty. Three booths down a couple of sharpies were selling each other pieces of Twentieth Century-Fox, using double-arm gestures instead of money. They had a telephone on the table between them and every two or three minutes they would play the match game to see who called Zanuck with a hot idea. They were young, dark, eager and full of vitality. They put as much muscular activity into a telephone conversation as I would put into carrying a fat man up four flights of stairs. There was a sad fellow over on a bar stool talking to the bartender, who was polishing a glass and listening with that plastic smile people wear when they are trying not to scream. The customer was middle-aged, handsomely dressed, and drunk. He wanted to talk and he couldn't have stopped even if he hadn't really wanted to talk. He was polite and friendly and when I heard him he didn't seem to slur his words much, but you knew that he got up on the bottle and only let go of it when he fell asleep at night. He would be like that for the rest of his life and that was what his life was. You would never know how he got that way because even if he told you it would not be the truth. At the very best a distorted memory of the truth as he knew it. There is a sad man like that in every quiet bar in the world.

I looked at my watch and this high-powered publisher man was already twenty minutes late. I would wait half an hour and then I would leave. It never pays to let the customer make all the rules. If he can push you around, he will assume other people can too, and that is not what he hires you for. And right now I didn't need the work badly enough to let some fathead from back east use me for a horse-holder, some executive character in a paneled office on the eighty-fifth floor, with a row of pushbuttons and an intercom and a secretary in a Hattie Carnegie Career Girl's Special and a pair of those big beautiful promising eyes. This was the kind of operator who would tell you to be there at nine sharp and if you weren't sitting quietly with a pleased smile on your pan when he floated in two hours later on a double Gibson, he would have a paroxysm of outraged executive ability which would necessitate five weeks at Acapulco before he got back the hop on his high hard one.

The old bar waiter came drifting by and glanced softly at my weak Scotch and water. I shook my head and he bobbed his white thatch, and right then a dream walked in. It seemed to me for an instant that there was no sound in the bar, that the sharpies stopped sharping and the drunk on the stool stopped burbling away, and it was like just after the conductor taps on his music stand and raises his arms and holds them poised.

She was slim and quite tall in a white linen tailormade with a black and white polka-dotted scarf around her throat. Her hair was the pale gold of a fairy princess. There was a small hat on it into which the pale gold hair nestled like a bird in its nest. Her eyes were cornflower blue, a rare color, and the lashes were long and almost too pale. She reached the table across the way and was pulling off a white gauntleted glove and the old waiter had the table pulled out in a way no waiter ever will pull a table out for me. She sat down and slipped the gloves under the strap of her bag and thanked him with a smile so gentle, so exquisitely pure, that he was damn near paralyzed by it. She said something to him in a very low voice. He hurried away, bending forward. There was a guy who really had a mission in life.

I stared. She caught me staring. She lifted her glance half an inch and I wasn't there any more. But wherever I was I was holding my breath.

There are blondes and blondes and it is almost a joke word nowadays. All blondes have their points, except perhaps the metallic ones who are as blond as a Zulu under the bleach and as to disposition as soft as a sidewalk. There is the small cute blonde who cheeps and twitters, and the big statuesque blonde who straight-arms you with an ice-blue glare. There is the blonde who gives you the up-from-under look and smells lovely and shimmers and hangs on your arm and is always very very tired when you take her home. She makes that helpless gesture and has that god-damned headache and you would like to slug her except that you are glad you found out about the headache before you invested too much time and money and hope in her. Because the headache will always be there, a weapon that never wears out and is as deadly as the bravo's rapier or Lucrezia's poison vial.

There is the soft and willing and alcoholic blonde who doesn't care what she wears as long as it is mink or where she goes as long as it is the Starlight Roof and there is plenty of dry champagne. There is the small perky blonde who is a little pal and wants to pay her own way and is full of sunshine and common sense and knows judo from the ground up and can toss a truck driver over her shoulder without missing more than one sentence out of the editorial in the *Saturday Review*. There is the pale, pale blonde with anemia of some non-fatal but incurable type. She is very languid and very shadowy and she speaks softly out of nowhere and you can't lay a finger on her because in the first place you don't want to and in the second place she is reading *The Waste Land* or Dante in the original, or Kafka or Kierkegaard or studying Provençal. She adores music and when the New York Philharmonic is playing Hindemith she can tell you which one of the six bass viols came in a quarter of a beat too late. I hear Toscanini can also. That makes two of them.

And lastly there is the gorgeous show piece who will outlast three kingpin racketeers and then marry a couple of millionaires at a million a head and end up with a pale rose villa at Cap Antibes, an Alfa-Romeo town car complete with pilot and co-pilot, and a stable of shopworn aristocrats, all of whom she will treat with the affectionate absent-mindedness of an elderly duke saying goodnight to his butler.

The dream across the way was none of these, not even of that kind of world. She was unclassifiable, as remote and clear as mountain water, as elusive as its color. I was still staring when a voice close to my elbow said:

"I'm shockingly late. I apologize. You must blame it on this. My name's Howard Spencer. You're Marlowe, of course."

I turned my head and looked at him. He was middle-aged, rather plump, dressed as if he didn't give any thought to it, but well shaved and with thin hair smoothed back carefully over a head that was wide between the ears. He wore a flashy double-breasted vest, the sort of thing you hardly ever see in California except perhaps on a visiting Bostonian. His glasses were rimless and he was patting a shabby old dog of a briefcase which was evidently the "this."

"Three brand new book-length manuscripts. Fiction. It would be embarrassing to lose them before we have a chance to reject them." He made a signal to the old waiter who had just stepped back from placing a tall green something or other in front of the dream. "I have a weakness for gin and orange. A silly sort of drink really. Will you join me? Good."

I nodded and the old waiter drifted away.

Pointing to the briefcase I said: "How do you know you are going to reject them?"

"If they were any good, they wouldn't be dropped at my hotel by the writers in person. Some New York agent would have them."

"Then why take them at all?"

"Partly not to hurt feelings. Partly the thousand-to-one chance all publishers live for. But mostly you're at a cocktail party and get introduced to all sorts of people, and some of them have novels written and you are just liquored up enough to be benevolent and full of love for the human race, so you say you'd love to see the script. It is then dropped at your hotel with such sickening speed that you are forced to go through the motions of reading it. But I don't suppose you are much interested in publishers and their problems."

The waiter brought the drinks. Spencer grabbed for his and took a healthy swig. He wasn't noticing the golden girl across the way. I had all his attention. He was a good contact man.

"If it's part of the job," I said. "I can read a book once in a while."

"One of our most important authors lives around here," he said casually. "Maybe you've read his stuff. Roger Wade."

"Uh-huh."

"I see your point." He smiled sadly. "You don't care for historical romances. But they sell brutally."

"I don't have any point, Mr. Spencer. I looked at one of his books once. I thought it was tripe. Is that the wrong thing for me to say?"

He grinned. "Oh no. There are many people who agree with you. But the point is at the moment that he's an automatic best seller. And every publisher has to have a couple with the way costs are now."

I looked across at the golden girl. She had finished her limeade or whatever it was and was glancing at a microscopic wrist watch. The bar was filling up a little, but not yet noisy. The two sharpies were still waving their hands and the solo drinker on the bar stool had a couple of pals with him. I looked back at Howard Spencer.

"Something to do with your problem?" I asked him. "This fellow Wade, I mean."

He nodded. He was giving me a careful once over. "Tell me a little about yourself, Mr. Marlowe. That is, if you don't find the request objectionable."

"What sort of thing? I'm a licensed private investigator and have been for quite a while. I'm a lone wolf, unmarried, getting middle-aged, and not rich. I've been in jail more than once and I don't do divorce business. I like liquor and women and chess and a few other things. The cops don't like me too well, but I know a couple I get along with. I'm a native son, born in Santa Rosa, both parents dead, no brothers or sisters, and when I get knocked off in a dark alley sometime, if it happens, as it could to anyone in my business, and to plenty of people in any business or no business at all these days, nobody will feel that the bottom has dropped out of his or her life."

"I see," he said. "But all that doesn't exactly tell me what I want to know."

I finished the gin and orange. I didn't like it. I grinned at him. "I left out one item, Mr. Spencer. I have a portrait of Madison in my pocket."

"A portrait of Madison? I'm afraid I don't—"

"A five-thousand-dollar bill," I said. "Always carry it. My lucky piece."

"Good God," he said in a hushed voice. "Isn't that terribly dangerous?"

"Who was it said that beyond a certain point all dangers are equal?"

"I think it was Walter Bagehot. He was talking about a steeplejack." Then he grinned. "Sorry, but I *am* a publisher. You're all right, Marlowe. I'll take a chance on you. If I didn't you would tell me to go to hell. Right?"

I grinned back at him. He called the waiter and ordered another pair of drinks.

"Here it is," he said carefully. "We are in bad trouble over Roger Wade. He can't finish a book. He's losing his grip and there's something behind it. The man seems to be going to pieces. Wild fits of drinking and temper. Every once in a while he disappears for days on end. Not very long ago he threw his wife downstairs and put her in the hospital with five broken ribs. There's no trouble between them in the usual sense, none at all. The man just goes nuts when he drinks." Spencer leaned back and looked at me gloomily. "We have to have that book finished. We need it badly. To a certain extent my job depends on it. But we need more than that. We want to save a very able writer who is capable of much better things than he has ever done. Something is very wrong. This trip he won't even see me. I realize this sounds like a job for a psychiatrist. Mrs. Wade disagrees. She is convinced that he is perfectly sane but that something is worrying him to death. A blackmailer, for instance. The Wades have been married five years. Something from his past may have caught up with him. It might even be—just as a wild guess—a fatal hit-and-run accident and someone has the goods on him. We don't know what it is. We want to know. And we are willing to pay well to correct the trouble. If it turns out to be a medical matter, well—that's that. If not, there has to be an answer. And in the meantime Mrs. Wade has to be protected. He might kill her the next time. You never know."

The second round of drinks came. I left mine untouched and watched him gobble half of his in one swallow. I lit a cigarette and just stared at him.

"You don't want a detective," I said. "You want a magician. What the hell could I do? If I happened to be there at exactly the right time, and if he isn't too tough for me to handle, I might knock him out and put him to bed. But I'd have to *be* there. It's a hundred to one against. You know that."

"He's about your size," Spencer said, "but he's not in your condition. And you could be there all the time."

"Hardly. And drunks are cunning. He'd be certain to pick a time when I wasn't around to throw his wingding. I'm not in the market for a job as a male nurse."

"A male nurse wouldn't be any use. Roger Wade is not the kind of man to accept one. He is a very talented guy who has been jarred loose from his self-control. He has made too much money writing junk for halfwits. But the only salvation for a writer is to write. If there is anything good in him, it will come out."

"Okay, I'm sold on him," I said wearily. "He's terrific. Also he's damn dangerous. He has a guilty secret and he tries to drown it in alcohol. It's not my kind of problem, Mr. Spencer."

"I see." He looked at his wrist watch with a worried frown that knotted his face and made it look older and smaller. "Well, you can't blame me for trying."

He reached for his fat briefcase. I looked across at the golden girl. She was getting ready to leave. The white-haired waiter was hovering over her with the check. She gave him some money and a lovely smile and he looked as if he had shaken hands with God. She touched up her lips and put her white gauntlets on and the waiter pulled the table halfway across the room for her to stroll out.

I glanced at Spencer. He was frowning down at the empty glass on the table edge. He had the briefcase on his knees.

"Look," I said. "I'll go see the man and try to size him up, if you want me to. I'll talk to his wife. But my guess is he'll throw me out of the house."

A voice that was not Spencer's said: "No, Mr. Marlowe,

I don't think he would do that. On the contrary I think he might like you."

I looked up into the pair of violet eyes. She was standing at the end of the table. I got up and canted myself against the back of the booth in that awkward way you have to stand when you can't slide out.

"Please don't get up," she said in a voice like the stuff they use to line summer clouds with. "I know I owe you an apology, but it seemed important for me to have a chance to observe you before I introduced myself. I am Eileen Wade."

Spencer said grumpily: "He's not interested, Eileen."

She smiled gently. "I disagree."

I pulled myself together. I had been standing there off balance with my mouth open and me breathing through it like a sweet girl graduate. This was really a dish. Seen close up she was almost paralyzing.

"I didn't say I wasn't interested, Mrs. Wade. What I said or meant to say was that I didn't think I could do any good, and it might be a hell of a mistake for me to try. It might do a lot of harm."

She was very serious now. The smile had gone. "You are deciding too soon. You can't judge people by what they do. If you judge them at all, it must be by what they are."

I nodded vaguely. Because that was exactly the way I had thought about Terry Lennox. On the facts he was no bargain, except for that one brief flash of glory in the foxhole—if Menendez told the truth about that—but the facts didn't tell the whole story by any means. He had been a man it was impossible to dislike. How many do you meet in a lifetime that you can say that about?

"And you have to know them for that," she added gently. "Goodbye, Mr. Marlowe. If you should change your mind—" She opened her bag quickly and gave me a card —"and thank you for being here."

She nodded to Spencer and walked away. I watched her out of the bar, down the glassed-in annex to the dining room. She carried herself beautifully. I watched her turn under the archway that led to the lobby. I saw the last flicker of her white linen skirt as she turned the corner. Then I eased myself down into the booth and grabbed the gin and orange.

Spencer was watching me. There was something hard in his eyes.

"Nice work," I said, "but you ought to have looked at her once in a while. A dream like that doesn't sit across the room from you for twenty minutes without your even noticing."

"Stupid of me, wasn't it?" He was trying to smile, but he didn't really want to. He didn't like the way I had looked at her. "People have such queer ideas about private detectives. When you think of having one in your home—"

"Don't think of having this one in your home," I said. "Anyhow, think up another story first. You can do better than trying to make me believe anybody, drunk or sober, would throw that gorgeous downstairs and break five ribs for her."

He reddened. His hands tightened on the briefcase. "You think I'm a liar?"

"What's the difference? You've made your play. You're a little hot for the lady yourself, maybe."

He stood up suddenly. "I don't like your tone," he said. "I'm not sure I like *you*. Do me a favor and forget the whole idea. I think this ought to pay you for your time."

He threw a twenty on the table, and then added some ones for the waiter. He stood a moment staring down at me. His eyes were bright and his face was still red. "I'm married and have four children," he said abruptly.

"Congratulations."

He made a swift noise in his throat and turned and went. He went pretty fast. I watched him for a while and then I didn't. I drank the rest of my drink and got out my cigarettes and shook one loose and stuck it in my mouth and lit it. The old waiter came up and looked at the money.

"Can I get you anything else, sir?"

"Nope. The dough is all yours."

He picked it up slowly. "This is a twenty-dollar bill, sir. The gentleman made a mistake."

"He can read. The dough is all yours, I said."

"I'm sure I'm very grateful. If you are quite sure, sir—"

"Quite sure."

He bobbed his head and went away, still looking worried. The bar was filling up. A couple of streamlined demi-virgins went by caroling and waving. They knew the two hotshots in the booth farther on. The air began to be spattered with darlings and crimson fingernails.

I smoked half of my cigarette, scowling at nothing, and then got up to leave. I turned to reach back for my cigarettes and something bumped into me hard from behind. It was just what I needed. I swung around and I was looking at the profile of a broad-beamed crowd-pleaser in an overdraped oxford flannel. He had the outstretched arm of the popular character and the two-by-six grin of the guy who never loses a sale.

I took hold of the outstretched arm and spun him around. "What's the matter, Jack? Don't they make the aisles wide enough for your personality?"

He shook his arm loose and got tough. "Don't get fancy, buster. I might loosen your jaw for you."

"Ha, ha," I said. "You might play center field for the Yankees and hit a home run with a breadstick."

He doubled a meaty fist.

"Darling, think of your manicure," I told him.

He controlled his emotions. "Nuts to you, wise guy," he sneered. "Some other time, when I have less on my mind."

"Could there be less?"

"G'wan, beat it," he snarled. "One more crack and you'll need new bridgework."

I grinned at him. "Call me up, Jack. But with better dialogue."

His expression changed. He laughed. "You in pictures, chum?"

"Only the kind they pin up in the post office."

"See you in the mug book," he said, and walked away, still grinning.

It was all very silly, but it got rid of the feeling. I went along the annex and across the lobby of the hotel to the main entrance. I paused inside to put on my sunglasses. It wasn't until I got into my car that I remembered to look at the card Eileen Wade had given me. It was an engraved card, but not a formal calling card, because it had an address and a telephone number on it. Mrs. Roger Stearns Wade, 1247 Idle Valley Road. Tel. Idle Valley 5-6324.

I knew a good deal about Idle Valley, and I knew it had changed a great deal from the days when they had the gatehouse at the entrance and the private police force, and the gambling casino on the lake, and the fifty-dollar joy girls. Quiet money had taken over the tract after the casino was closed out. Quiet money had made it a subdivider's dream. A club owned the lake and the lake frontage and if they didn't want you in the club, you didn't get to play in the water. It was exclusive in the only remaining sense of the word that doesn't mean merely expensive.

I belonged in Idle Valley like a pearl onion on a banana split.

Howard Spencer called me up late in the afternoon. He had got over his mad and wanted to say he was sorry and he hadn't handled the situation very well, and had I perhaps any second thoughts.

"I'll go see him if he asks me to. Not otherwise."

"I see. There would be a substantial bonus—"

"Look, Mr. Spencer," I said impatiently, "you can't hire destiny. If Mrs. Wade is afraid of the guy, she can move out. That's *her* problem. Nobody could protect her twenty-four hours a day from her own husband. There isn't that much protection in the world. But that's not all you want. You want to know why and how and when the guy jumped the rails, and then fix it so that he doesn't do it again—at least until he finishes the book. And that's up to him. If he wants to write the damn book bad enough, he'll lay off the hooch until he does it. You want too damn much."

"They all go together," he said. "It's all one problem. But I guess I understand. It's a little oversubtle for your kind of operation. Well, goodbye. I'm flying back to New York tonight."

"Have a smooth trip."

He thanked me and hung up. I forgot to tell him I had given his twenty to the waiter. I thought of calling back to tell him, then I thought he was miserable enough already.

I closed the office and started off in the direction of Victor's to drink a gimlet, as Terry had asked me to in his letter. I changed my mind. I wasn't feeling sentimental enough. I went to Lowry's and had a martini and some prime ribs and Yorkshire pudding instead.

When I got home I turned on the TV set and looked at the fights. They were no good, just a bunch of dancing masters who ought to have been working for Arthur Murray. All they did was jab and bob up and down and feint one another off balance. Not one of them could hit hard enough to wake his grandmother out of a light doze. The crowd was booing and the referee kept clapping his hands for action, but they went right on swaying and jittering and jabbing long lefts. I turned to another channel and looked at a crime show. The action took place in a clothes closet and the faces were tired and over familiar and not beautiful. The dialogue was stuff even Monogram wouldn't have used. The dick had a colored houseboy for comic relief. He didn't need it, he was plenty comical all by himself. And the commercials would have sickened a goat raised on barbed wire and broken beer bottles.

I cut it off and smoked a long cool tightly packed cigarette. It was kind to my throat. It was made of fine tobacco. I forgot to notice what brand it was. I was about ready to hit the hay when Detective-Sergeant Green of homicide called me up.

"Thought you might like to know they buried your friend Lennox a couple of days ago right in that Mexican town where he died. A lawyer representing the family went down there and attended to it. You were pretty lucky this time, Marlowe. Next time you think of helping a pal skip the country, don't."

"How many bullet holes did he have in him?"

"What's that?" he barked. Then he was silent for a space. Then he said rather too carefully: "One, I should say. It's usually enough when it blows a guy's head off. The lawyer is bringing back a set of prints and whatever was in his pockets. Anything more you'd like to know?"

"Yeah, but you can't tell me. I'd like to know who killed Lennox's wife."

"Cripes, didn't Grenz tell you he left a full confession? It was in the papers, anyway. Don't you read the papers any more?"

"Thanks for calling me, Sergeant. It was real kind of you."

"Look, Marlowe," he said raspingly. "You got any funny ideas about this case, you could buy yourself a lot of grief talking about them. The case is closed, finalized, and laid away in mothballs. Damn lucky for you it is. Accessory after the fact is good for five years in this state. And let me tell you something else. I've been a cop a long time and one thing I've learned for sure is it ain't always what you do that gets you sent up. It's what it can be made to look like when it comes in to court. Goodnight."

He hung up in my ear. I replaced the phone thinking that an honest cop with a bad conscience always acts tough. So does a dishonest cop. So does almost anyone, including me.

14

NEXT MORNING THE BELL RANG as I was wiping the talcum off an earlobe. When I got to the door and opened up I looked into a pair of violet-blue eyes. She was in brown linen this time, with a pimento-colored scarf, and no earrings or hat. She looked a little pale, but not as though anyone had been throwing her downstairs. She gave me a hesitant little smile.

"I know I shouldn't have come here to bother you, Mr. Marlowe. You probably haven't even had breakfast. But I had a reluctance to go to your office and I hate telephoning about personal matters."

"Sure. Come in, Mrs. Wade. Would you go for a cup of coffee?"

She came into the living room and sat on the davenport without looking at anything. She balanced her bag on her lap and sat with her feet close together. She looked rather prim. I opened windows and pulled up venetian blinds and lifted a dirty ash tray off the cocktail table in front of her.

"Thank you. Black coffee, please. No sugar."

I went out to the kitchen and spread a paper napkin on a green metal tray. It looked as cheesy as a celluloid collar. I crumpled it up and got out one of those fringed things that come in sets with little triangular napkins. They came with the house, like most of the furniture. I set out two Desert Rose coffee cups and filled them and carried the tray in.

She sipped. "This is very nice," she said. "You make good coffee."

"Last time anyone drank coffee with me was just before

I went to jail," I said. "I guess you knew I'd been in the cooler, Mrs. Wade."

She nodded. "Of course. You were suspected of having helped him escape, wasn't it?"

"They didn't say. They found my telephone number on a pad in his room. They asked me questions I didn't answer—mostly because of the way they were asked. But I don't suppose you are interested in that."

She put her cup down carefully and leaned back and smiled at me. I offered her a cigarette.

"I don't smoke, thank you. Of course I'm interested. A neighbor of ours knew the Lennoxes. He must have been insane. He doesn't sound at all like that kind of man."

I filled a bulldog pipe and lit it. "I guess so," I said. "He must have been. He was badly wounded in the war. But he's dead and it's all done with. And I don't think you came here to talk about that."

She shook her head slowly. "He was a friend of yours, Mr. Marlowe. You must have a pretty strong opinion. And I think you are a pretty determined man."

I tamped the tobacco in my pipe and lit it again. I took my time and stared at her over the pipe bowl while I was doing it.

"Look, Mrs. Wade," I said finally. "My opinion means nothing. It happens every day. The most unlikely people commit the most unlikely crimes. Nice old ladies poison whole families. Clean-cut kids commit multiple holdups and shootings. Bank managers with spotless records going back twenty years are found out to be long-term embezzlers. And successful and popular and supposedly happy novelists get drunk and put their wives in the hospital. We know damn little about what makes even our best friends tick."

I thought it would burn her up, but she didn't do much more than press her lips together and narrow her eyes.

"Howard Spencer shouldn't have told you that," she said. "It was my own fault. I didn't know enough to keep away from him. I've learned since that the one thing you can never do to a man who is drinking too much is to try to stop him. You probably know that much better than I do."

"You certainly can't stop him with words," I said. "If you're lucky, and *if* you have the strength, you can sometimes keep him from hurting himself or someone else. Even that takes luck."

She reached quietly for her coffee cup and saucer. Her hands were lovely, like the rest of her. The nails were beautifully shaped and polished and only very slightly tinted.

"Did Howard tell you he hadn't seen my husband this time?"

"Yeah."

She finished her coffee and put the cup carefully back on the tray. She fiddled with the spoon for a few seconds. Then she spoke without looking up at me.

"He didn't tell you why, because he didn't know. I am very fond of Howard but he is the managing type, wants to take charge of everything. He thinks he is very executive."

I waited, not saying anything. There was another silence. She looked at me quickly then looked away again. Very softly she said: "My husband has been missing for three days. I don't know where he is. I came here to ask you to find him and bring him home. Oh, it has happened before. One time he drove himself all the way to Portland and got sick in a hotel there and had to get a doctor to sober him up. It's a wonder how he ever got that far without getting into trouble. He hadn't eaten anything for three days. Another time he was in a Turkish bath in Long Beach, one of those Swedish places where they give high colonics. And the last time it was some sort of small private and probably not very reputable sanitarium. This was less than three weeks ago. He wouldn't tell me the name of it or where it was, just said he had been taking a cure and was all right. But he looked deadly pale and weak. I got a brief glimpse of the man who brought him home. A tall young man dressed in the sort of overelaborate cowboy outfit you would only see on the stage or in a technicolor musical film. He let Roger out in the driveway and backed out and drove away at once."

"Could have been a dude ranch," I said. "Some of these tame cowpunchers spend every dime they make on a fancy outfit like that. The women go crazy over them. That's what they're there for."

She opened her bag and took out a folded paper. "I've brought you a check for five hundred dollars, Mr. Marlowe. Will you accept it as a retainer?"

She put the folded check down on the table. I looked at it, but didn't touch it. "Why?" I asked her. "You say he has been gone three days. It takes three or four to sober a man up and get some food into him. Won't he come back the way he did before? Or does something make this time different?"

"He can't stand much more of it, Mr. Marlowe. It will kill him. The intervals are getting shorter. I'm badly worried. I'm more than worried, I'm scared. It's unnatural. We've been married for five years. Roger was always a drinker, but not a psychopathic drinker. Something is all wrong. I want him found. I didn't sleep more than an hour last night."

"Any idea *why* he drinks?"

The violet eyes were looking at me steadily. She seemed a bit fragile this morning, but certainly not helpless. She bit her lower lip and shook her head. "Unless it's me," she said at last, almost in a whisper. "Men fall out of love with their wives."

"I'm only an amateur psychologist, Mrs. Wade. A man in my racket has to be a little of that. I'd say it's more likely he has fallen out of love with the kind of stuff he writes."

"It's quite possible," she said quietly. "I imagine all writers have spells like that. It's true that he can't seem to finish a book he is working on. But it isn't as if he had to finish it for the rent money. I don't think that is quite enough reason."

"What sort of guy is he sober?"

She smiled. "Well, I'm rather prejudiced. *I* think he is a very nice guy indeed."

"And how is he drunk?"

"Horrible. Bright and hard and cruel. He thinks he is being witty when he is only being nasty."

"You left out violent."

She raised her tawny eyebrows. "Just once, Mr. Marlowe. And too much has been made of that. I'd never have told Howard Spencer. Roger told him himself."

I got up and walked around in the room. It was going to be a hot day. It already was hot. I turned the blinds on one of the windows to keep the sun out. Then I gave it to her straight.

"I looked him up in *Who's Who* yesterday afternoon. He's forty-two years old, yours is his only marriage, no

children. His people are New Englanders, he went to
Andover and Princeton. He has a war record and a good
one. He has written twelve of these fat sex-and-swordplay
historical novels and every damn one of them has been on
the best-seller lists. He must have made plenty of the
folding. If he had fallen out of love with his wife, he
sounds like the type who would say so and get a divorce. If
he was haring around with another woman, you would
probably know about it, and anyway he wouldn't have to
get drunk just to prove he felt bad. If you've been married
five years, then he was thirty-seven when that happened. I'd
say he knew most of what there is to know about women
by that time. I say most, because nobody ever knows all of
it."

I stopped and looked at her and she smiled at me. I
wasn't hurting her feelings. I went on.

"Howard Spencer suggested—on what grounds I have no
idea—that what's the matter with Roger Wade is something
that happened a long time ago before you were married
and that it has caught up with him now, and is hitting him
harder than he can take. Spencer thought of blackmail.
Would you know?"

She shook her head slowly. "If you mean would I know
if Roger had been paying out a lot of money to someone—
no, I wouldn't know that. I don't meddle with his book-
keeping affairs. He could give away a lot of money without
my knowing it."

"Okay then. Not knowing Mr. Wade I can't have much
idea how he would react to having the bite put on him. If
he has a violent temper, he might break somebody's neck.
If the secret, whatever it is, might damage his social or
professional standing or even, to take an extreme case,
made the law boys drop around, he might pay off—for a
while anyhow. But none of this gets us anywhere. You want
him found, you're worried, you're more than worried. So
how do I go about finding him? I don't want your money,
Mrs. Wade. Not now anyway."

She reached into her bag again and came up with a
couple of pieces of yellow paper. They looked like second
sheets, folded, and one of them looked crumpled. She
smoothed them out and handed them to me.

"One I found on his desk," she said. "It was very late, or
rather early in the morning. I knew he had been drinking

and I knew he hadn't come upstairs. About two o'clock I went down to see if he was all right—or comparatively all right, passed out on the floor or the couch or something. He was gone. The other paper was in the wastebasket or rather caught on the edge, so that it hadn't fallen in."

I looked at the first piece, the one not crumpled. There was a short typewritten paragraph on it, no more. It read: "I do not care to be in love with myself and there is no longer anyone else for me to be in love with. Signed: Roger (F. Scott Fitzgerald) Wade. P.S. This is why I never finished *The Last Tycoon*."

"That mean anything to you, Mrs. Wade?"

"Just attitudinizing. He has always been a great admirer of Scott Fitzgerald. He says Fitzgerald is the best drunken writer since Coleridge, who took dope. Notice the typing, Mr. Marlowe. Clear, even, and no mistakes."

"I did. Most people can't even write their names properly when soused." I opened the crumpled paper. More typing, also without any errors or unevenness. This one read: "I do not like you, Dr. V. But right now you're the man for me."

She spoke while I was still looking at it. "I have no idea who Dr. V. is. We don't know any doctor with a name beginning that way. I suppose he is the one who has that place where Roger was the last time."

"When the cowpoke brought him home? Your husband didn't mention any names at all—even place names?"

She shook her head. "Nothing. I've looked in the directory. There are dozens of doctors of one sort or another whose names begin with V. Also, it may not be his surname."

"Quite likely he's not even a doctor," I said. "That brings up the question of ready cash. A legitimate man would take a check, but a quack wouldn't. It might turn into evidence. And a guy like that wouldn't be cheap. Room and board at his house would come high. Not to mention the needle."

She looked puzzled. "The needle?"

"All the shady ones use dope on their clients. Easiest way to handle them. Knock them out for ten or twelve hours and when they come out of it, they're good boys. But using narcotics without a license can get you room and board with Uncle Sam. And that comes very high indeed."

"I see. Roger probably would have several hundred dollars. He always keeps that much in his desk. I don't know why. I suppose it's just a whim. There's none there now."

"Okay," I said. "I'll try to find Dr. V. I don't know just how, but I'll do my best. Take the check with you, Mrs. Wade."

"But why? Aren't you entitled—"

"Later on, thanks. And I'd rather have it from Mr. Wade. He's not going to like what I do in any case."

"But if he's sick and helpless—"

"He could have called his own doctor or asked you to. He didn't. That means he didn't want to."

She put the check back in her bag and stood up. She looked very forlorn. "Our doctor refused to treat him," she said bitterly.

"There are hundreds of doctors, Mrs. Wade. Any one of them would handle him once. Most of them would stay with him for some time. Medicine is a pretty competitive affair nowadays."

"I see. Of course you must be right." She walked slowly to the door and I walked with her. I opened it.

"You could have called a doctor on your own. Why didn't you?"

She faced me squarely. Her eyes were bright. There might have been a hint of tears in them. A lovely dish and no mistake.

"Because I love my husband, Mr. Marlowe. I'd do anything in the world to help him. But I know what sort of man he is too. If I called a doctor every time he took too many drinks, I wouldn't have a husband very long. You can't treat a grown man like a child with a sore throat."

"You can if he's a drunk. Often you damn well have to."

She was standing close to me. I smelled her perfume. Or thought I did. It hadn't been put on with a spray gun. Perhaps it was just the summer day.

"Suppose there *is* something shameful in his past," she said, dragging the words out one by one as if each of them had a bitter taste. "Even something criminal. It would make no difference to me. But I'm not going to be the means of its being found out."

"But it's all right if Howard Spencer hires me to find out?"

She smiled very slowly. "Do you really think I expected you to give Howard any answer but the one you did—a man who went to jail rather than betray a friend?"

"Thanks for the plug, but that wasn't why I got jugged."

She nodded after a moment of silence, said goodbye, and started down the redwood steps. I watched her get into her car, a slim gray Jaguar, very new looking. She drove it up to the end of the street and swung around in the turning circle there. Her glove waved at me as she went by down the hill. The little car whisked around the corner and was gone.

There was a red oleander bush against part of the front wall of the house. I heard a flutter in it and a baby mockingbird started cheeping anxiously. I spotted him hanging on to one of the top branches, flapping his wings as if he was having trouble keeping his balance. From the cypress trees at the corner of the wall there was a single harsh warning chirp. The cheeping stopped at once and the little fat bird was silent.

I went inside and shut the door and left him to his flying lesson. Birds have to learn too.

15

No matter how smart you think you are, you have to have a place to start from: a name, an address, a neighborhood, a background, an atmosphere, a point of reference of some sort. All I had was typing on a crumpled yellow page that said, "I do not like you, Dr. V. But right now you're the man for me." With that I could pinpoint the Pacific Ocean, spend a month wading through the lists of half a dozen county medical associations, and end up with the big round 0. In our town quacks breed like guinea pigs. There are eight counties within a hundred miles of the City Hall and in every town in every single one of them there are doctors, some genuine medical men, some just mail-order mechanics with a license to cut corns or jump up and down on your spine. Of the real doctors some are prosperous and some poor, some ethical, others not sure they can afford it. A well-heeled patient with incipient D.T.'s could be money from home to plenty of old geezers who have fallen behind in the vitamin and antibiotic trade. But without a clue there was no place to start. I didn't have the clue and Eileen Wade either didn't have it or didn't know she had it. And even if I found somebody that fitted and had the right initial, he might turn out to be a myth, so far as Roger Wade was concerned. The jingle might be something that just happened to run through his head while he was getting himself stewed up. Just as the Scott Fitzgerald allusion might be merely an off-beat way of saying goodbye.

In a situation like that the small man tries to pick the big man's brains. So I called up a man I knew in The Carne Organization, a flossy agency in Beverly Hills that specialized in protection for the carriage trade—protection meaning almost anything with one foot inside the law. The man's name was George Peters and he said he could give me ten minutes if I made it fast.

They had half the second floor of one of these candy-pink four-storied buildings where the elevator doors open all by themselves with an electric eye, where the corridors are cool and quiet, and the parking lot has a name on every stall, and the druggist off the front lobby has a sprained wrist from filling bottles of sleeping pills.

The door was French gray outside with raised metal lettering, as clean and sharp as a new knife. THE CARNE ORGANIZATION, INC. GERALD C. CARNE, PRESIDENT. Below and smaller: *Entrance*. It might have been an investment trust.

Inside was a small and ugly reception room, but the ugliness was deliberate and expensive. The furniture was scarlet and dark green, the walls were a flat Brunswick green, and the pictures hung on them were framed in a green about three shades darker than that. The pictures were guys in red coats on big horses that were just crazy to jump over high fences. There were two frameless mirrors tinted a slight but disgusting shade of rose pink. The magazines on the table of polished primavera were of the latest issue and each one was enclosed in a clear plastic cover. The fellow who decorated that room was not a man to let colors scare him. He probably wore a pimento shirt, mulberry slacks, zebra shoes, and vermilion drawers with his initials on them in a nice Mandarin orange.

The whole thing was just window-dressing. The clients of The Carne Organization were charged a minimum of one hundred fish *per diem* and they expected service in their homes. They didn't go sit in no waiting rooms. Carne was an ex-colonel of military police, a big pink and white guy as hard as a board. He had offered me a job once, but I never got desperate enough to take it. There are one hundred and ninety ways of being a bastard and Carne knew all of them.

A rubbed glass partition slid open and a receptionist looked out at me. She had an iron smile and eyes that could count the money in your hip wallet.

"Good morning. May I help you?"

"George Peters, please. My name is Marlowe."

She put a green leather book on the ledge. "Is he expecting you, Mr. Marlowe? I don't see your name on the appointment list."

"It's a personal matter. I just talked to him on the phone."

"I see. How do you spell your name, Mr. Marlowe? And your first name, please?"

I told her. She wrote it down on a long narrow form, then slipped the edge under a clock punch.

"Who's that supposed to impress?" I asked her.

"We are very particular about details here," she said coldly. "Colonel Carne says you never know when the most trivial fact may turn out to be vital."

"Or the other way around," I said, but she didn't get it. When she had finished her book work she looked up and said:

"I will announce you to Mr. Peters."

I told her that made me very happy. A minute later a door in the paneling opened and Peters beckoned me into a battleship-gray corridor lined with little offices that looked like cells. His office had soundproofing on the ceiling, a gray steel desk with two matching chairs, a gray dictating machine on a gray stand, a telephone and pen set of the same color as the walls and floor. There were a couple of framed photographs on the walls, one of Carne in uniform, with his snowdrop helmet on, and one of Carne as a civilian seated behind a desk and looking inscrutable. Also framed on the wall was a small inspirational legend in steely letters on a gray background. It read:

A CARNE OPERATIVE DRESSES, SPEAKS AND BEHAVES LIKE A GENTLEMAN AT ALL TIMES AND IN ALL PLACES. THERE ARE NO EXCEPTIONS TO THIS RULE.

Peters crossed the room in two long steps and pushed one of the pictures aside. Set into the gray wall behind it was a gray microphone pickup. He pulled it out, unclipped a wire, and pushed it back in place. He moved the picture in front of it again.

"Right now I'd be out of a job," he said, "except that the son of a bitch is out fixing a drunk-driving rap for some actor. All the mike switches are in his office. He has the whole joint wired. The other morning I suggested to him that he have a microfilm camera installed with infra red light behind a diaphanous mirror in the reception room. He didn't like the idea too well. Maybe because somebody else had it."

He sat down in one of the hard gray chairs. I stared at him. He was a gawky long-legged man with a bony face and receding hair. His skin had the worn weathered look of a man who has been out of doors a great deal, in all kinds of weather. He had deep-set eyes and an upper lip almost as long as his nose. When he grinned the bottom half of his face disappeared into two enormous ditches that ran from his nostrils to the ends of his wide mouth.

"How can you take it?" I asked him.

"Sit down, pal. Breathe quietly, keep your voice down, and remember that a Carne operative is to a cheap shamus like you what Toscanini is to an organ grinder's monkey." He paused and grinned. "I take it because I don't give a damn. It's good money and any time Carne starts acting like he thought I was doing time in that maximum-security prison he ran in England during the war, I'll pick up my check and blow. What's your trouble? I hear you had it rough a while back."

"No complaints about that. I'd like to look at your file on the barred-window boys. I know you have one. Eddie Dowst told me after he quit here."

He nodded. "Eddie was just a mite too sensitive for The

Carne Organization. The file you mention is top secret. In no circumstances must any confidential information be disclosed to outsiders. I'll get it at once."

He went out and I stared at the gray wastebasket and the gray linoleum and the gray leather corners of the desk blotter. Peters came back with a gray cardboard file in his hand. He put it down and opened it.

"For Chrissake, haven't you got anything in this place that isn't gray?"

"The school colors, my lad. The spirit of the organization. Yeah, I have something that isn't gray."

He pulled a desk drawer open and took out a cigar about eight inches long.

"An Upman Thirty," he said. "Presented to me by an elderly gent from England who has been forty years in California and still says 'wireless.' Sober he is just an old swish with a good deal of superficial charm, which is all right with me, because most people don't have any, superficial or otherwise, including Carne. He has as much charm as a steel puddler's underpants. Not sober, the client has a strange habit of writing checks on banks which never heard of him. He always makes good and with my fond help he has so far stayed out of the icebox. He gave me this. Should we smoke it together, like a couple of Indian chiefs planning a massacre?"

"I can't smoke cigars."

Peters looked at the huge cigar sadly. "Same here," he said. "I thought of giving it to Carne. But it's not really a one-man cigar, even when the one man is Carne." He frowned. "You know something? I'm talking too much about Carne. I must be edgy." He dropped the cigar back in the drawer and looked at the open file. "Just what do we want from this?"

"I'm looking for a well-heeled alcoholic with expensive tastes and money to gratify them. So far he hasn't gone in for check-bouncing. I haven't heard so anyway. He has a streak of violence and his wife is worried about him. She thinks he's hid out in some sobering-up joint but she can't be sure. The only clue we have is a jingle mentioning a Dr. V. Just the initial. My man is gone three days now."

Peters stared at me thoughtfully. "That's not too long," he said. "What's to worry about?"

"If I find him first, I get paid."

He looked at me some more and shook his head. "I don't get it, but that's okay. We'll see." He began to turn the pages of the file. "It's not too easy," he said. "These people come and go. A single letter ain't much of a lead." He pulled a page out of the folder, turned some more pages, pulled another, and finally a third. "Three of them here," he said. "Dr. Amos Varley, an osteopath. Big place in Altadena. Makes or used to make night calls for fifty bucks. Two registered nurses. Was in a hassle with the State Narcotics people a couple of years back, and turned in his prescription book. This information is not really up to date."

I wrote down the name and address in Altadena.

"Then we have Dr. Lester Vukanich. Ear, Nose, and Throat, Stockwell Building, on Hollywood Boulevard. This one's a dilly. Office practice mostly, and seems to sort of specialize in chronic sinus infections. Rather a neat routine. You go in and complain of a sinus headache and he washes out your antrums for you. First of course he has to anesthetize with Novocain. But if he likes your looks it don't have to be Novocain. Catch?"

"Sure." I wrote that one down.

"This is good," Peters went on, reading some more. "Obviously his trouble would be supplies. So our Dr. Vukanich does a lot of fishing off Ensenada and flies down in his own plane."

"I wouldn't think he'd last long if he brings the dope in himself," I said.

Peters thought about that and shook his head. "I don't think I agree. He could last forever if he's not too greedy. His only real danger is a discontented customer—pardon me, I mean patient—but he probably knows how to handle that. He's had fifteen years in the same office."

"Where the hell do you get this stuff?" I asked him.

"We're an organization, my boy. Not a lone wolf like you. Some we get from the clients themselves, some we get from the inside. Carne's not afraid to spend money. He's a good mixer when he wants to be."

"He'd love this conversation."

"Screw him. Our last offering today is a man named Verringer. The operative who filed on him is long gone. Seems a lady poet suicided at Verringer's ranch in Sepulveda Canyon one time. He runs a sort of art colony for writers and such who want seclusion and a congenial atmosphere. Rates moderate. He sounds legit. He calls himself doctor, but doesn't practice medicine. Could be a Ph.D. Frankly, I don't know why he's in here. Unless there was something about this suicide." He picked up a newspaper clipping pasted to a blank sheet. "Yeah, overdose of morphine. No suggestion Verringer knew anything about it."

"I like Verringer," I said. "I like him very much."

Peters closed the file and slapped it. "You haven't seen this," he said. He got up and left the room. When he came back I was standing up to leave. I started to thank him, but he shook it off.

"Look," he said, "there must be hundreds of places where your man could be."

I said I knew that.

"And by the way, I heard something about your friend Lennox that might interest you. One of our boys ran across a fellow in New York five or six years ago that answers the description exactly. But the guy's name was not Lennox, he says. It was Marston. Of course he could be wrong. The guy was drunk all the time, so you couldn't really be sure."

I said: "I doubt if it was the same man. Why would he change his name? He had a war record that could be checked."

"I didn't know that. Our man's in Seattle right now. You can talk to him when he gets back, if it means anything to you. His name is Ashterfelt."

"Thanks for everything, George. It was a pretty long ten minutes."

"I might need *your* help some day."

"The Carne Organization," I said, "never needs anything from anybody."

He made a rude gesture with his thumb. I left him in his metallic gray cell and departed through the waiting room. It looked fine now. The loud colors made sense after the cell block.

16

BACK FROM THE HIGHWAY at the bottom of Sepulveda
Canyon were two square yellow gateposts. A five-barred
gate hung open from one of them. Over the entrance was a
sign hung on wire: PRIVATE ROAD. NO ADMITTANCE. The
air was warm and quiet and full of the tomcat smell of
eucalyptus trees.

I turned in and followed a graveled road around the
shoulder of a hill, up a gentle slope, over a ridge and down
the other side into a shallow valley. It was hot in the
valley, ten or fifteen degrees hotter than on the highway. I
could see now that the graveled road ended in a loop
around some grass edged with stones that had been lime-
washed. Off to my left there was an empty swimming pool,
and nothing ever looks emptier than an empty swimming
pool. Around three sides of it there was what remained of
a lawn dotted with redwood lounging chairs with badly
faded pads on them. The pads had been of many colors,
blue, green, yellow, orange, rust red. Their edge bindings
had come loose in spots, the buttons had popped, and the
pads were bloated where this had happened. On the fourth
side there was the high wire fence of a tennis court. The
diving board over the empty pool looked knee-sprung and
tired. Its matting covering hung in shreds and its metal
fittings were flaked with rust.

I came to the turning loop and stopped in front of a
redwood building with a shake roof and a wide front
porch. The entrance had double screen doors. Large black
flies dozed on the screens. Paths led off among the ever
green and always dusty California oaks and among the oaks
there were rustic cabins scattered loosely over the side of
the hill, some almost completely hidden. Those I could see
had that desolate out-of-season look. Their doors were shut,
their windows were blanked by drawn curtains of monk's
cloth or something on that order. You could almost feel the
thick dust on their sills.

I switched off the ignition and sat there with my hands on the wheel listening. There was no sound. The place seemed to be as dead as Pharaoh, except that the doors behind the double screens were open and something moved in the dimness of the room beyond. Then I heard a light accurate whistling and a man's figure showed against the screen, pushed it open and strolled down the steps. He was something to see.

He wore a flat black gaucho hat with the woven strap under his chin. He wore a white silk shirt, spotlessly clean, open at the throat, with tight wristlets and loose puffed sleeves above. Around his neck a black fringed scarf was knotted unevenly so that one end was short and the other dropped almost to his waist. He wore a wide black sash and black pants, skin-tight at the hips, coal black, and stitched with gold thread down the side to where they were slashed and belled out loosely with gold buttons along both sides of the slash. On his feet he wore patent-leather dancing pumps.

He stopped at the foot of the steps and looked at me, still whistling. He was as lithe as a whip. He had the largest and emptiest smoke-colored eyes I had ever seen, under long silky lashes. His features were delicate and perfect without being weak. His nose was straight and almost but not quite thin, his mouth was a handsome pout, there was a dimple in his chin, and his small ears nestled gracefully against his head. His skin had that heavy pallor which the sun never touches.

He struck an attitude with his left hand on a hip and his right hand made a graceful curve in the air.

"Greetings," he said. "Lovely day, isn't it?"

"Pretty hot in here for me."

"I like it hot." The statement was flat and final and closed the discussion. What I liked was beneath his notice. He sat down on a step, produced a long file from somewhere, and began to file his fingernails. "You from the bank?" he asked without looking up.

"I'm looking for Dr. Verringer."

He stopped working with the file and looked off into the warm distance. "Who's he?" he asked with no possible interest.

"He owns the place. Laconic as hell, aren't you? As if you didn't know."

He went back to his file and fingernails. "You got told wrong, sweetie. The bank owns the place. They done foreclosed it or it's in escrow or something. I forget the details."

He looked up at me with the expression of a man to whom details mean nothing. I got out of the Olds and leaned against the hot door, then I moved away from that to where there was some air.

"Which bank would that be?"

"You don't know, you don't come from there. You don't come from there, you don't have any business here. Hit the trail, sweetie. Buzz off but fast."

"I have to find Dr. Verringer."

"The joint's not operating, sweetie. Like it says on the sign, this is a private road. Some gopher forgot to lock the gate."

"You the caretaker?"

"Sort of. Don't ask any more questions, sweetie. My temper's not reliable."

"What do you do when you get mad—dance a tango with a ground squirrel?"

He stood up suddenly and gracefully. He smiled a minute, an empty smile. "Looks like I got to toss you back in your little old convertible," he said.

"Later. Where would I find Dr. Verringer about now?"

He pocketed his file in his shirt and something else took its place in his right hand. A brief motion and he had a fist with shining brass knuckles on it. The skin over his cheekbones was tighter and there was a flame deep in his large smoky eyes.

He strolled towards me. I stepped back to get more room. He went on whistling but the whistle was high and shrill.

"We don't have to fight," I told him. "We don't have anything to fight about. And you might split those lovely britches."

He was as quick as a flash. He came at me with a smooth leap and his left hand snaked out very fast. I expected a jab and moved my head well enough but what he wanted was my right wrist and he got it. He had a grip too. He jerked me off balance and the hand with the brass knucks came around in a looping bolo punch. A crack on the back of the head with those and I would be a sick man. If I pulled he would catch me on the side of the face or on the upper arm below the point of the shoulder. It would have been a dead arm or a dead face, whichever it happened to be. In a spot like that there is only one thing to do.

I went with the pull. In passing I blocked his left foot from behind, grabbed his shirt and heard it tear. Something hit me on the back of the neck, but it wasn't the metal. I spun to the left and he went over sideways and landed catlike and was on his feet again before I had any kind of balance. He was grinning now. He was delighted with everything. He loved his work. He came for me fast.

A strong beefy voice yelled from somewhere: "Earl! Stop that at once! At once, do you hear me?"

The gaucho boy stopped. There was a sort of sick grin on his face. He made a quick motion and the brass knucks disappeared into the wide sash around the top of his pants.

I turned and looked at a solid chunk of man in a Hawaiian shirt hurrying towards us down one of the paths waving his arms. He came up breathing a little fast.

"Are you crazy, Earl?"

"Don't ever say that, Doc," Earl said softly. Then he smiled, turned away, and went to sit on the steps of the house. He took off the flat-crowned hat, produced a comb, and began to comb his thick dark hair with an absent expression. In a second or two he started to whistle softly.

The heavy man in the loud shirt stood and looked at me. I stood and looked at him.

"What's going on here?" he growled. "Who are you, sir?"

"Name's Marlowe. I was asking for Dr. Verringer. The lad you call Earl wanted to play games. I figure it's too hot."

"I am Dr. Verringer," he said with dignity. He turned his head. "Go in the house, Earl."

Earl stood up slowly. He gave Dr. Verringer a thoughtful studying look, his large smoky eyes blank of expression. Then he went up the steps and pulled the screen door open. A cloud of flies buzzed angrily and then settled on the screen again as the door closed.

"Marlowe?" Dr. Verringer gave me his attention again. "And what can I do for you, Mr. Marlowe?"

"Earl says you are out of business here."

"That is correct. I am just waiting for certain legal formalities before moving out. Earl and I are alone here."

"I'm disappointed," I said, looking disappointed. "I thought you had a man named Wade staying with you."

He hoisted a couple of eyebrows that would have interested a Fuller Brush man. "Wade? I might possibly know somebody of that name—it's a common enough name—but why should he be staying with me?"

"Taking the cure."

He frowned. When a guy has eyebrows like that he can really do you a frown. "I am a medical man, sir, but no longer in practice. What sort of cure did you have in mind?"

"The guy's a wino. He goes off his rocker from time to time and disappears. Sometimes he comes home under his own power, sometimes he gets brought home, and sometimes he takes a bit of finding." I got a business card out and handed it to him.

He read it with no pleasure.

"What goes with Earl?" I asked him. "He think he's Valentino or something?"

He made with the eyebrows again. They fascinated me. Parts of them curled off all by themselves as much as an inch and a half. He shrugged his meaty shoulders.

"Earl is quite harmless, Mr. Marlowe. He is—at times—a little dreamy. Lives in a play world, shall we say?"

"You say it, Doc. From where I stand he plays rough."

"Tut, tut, Mr. Marlowe. You exaggerate surely. Earl likes to dress himself up. He is childlike in that respect."

"You mean he's a nut," I said. "This place some kind of sanitarium, isn't it? Or was?"

"Certainly not. When it was in operation it was an artists' colony. I provided meals, lodging, facilities for exercise and entertainment, and above all seclusion. And for moderate fees. Artists, as you probably know, are seldom wealthy people. In the term artists I of course include writers, musicians, and so on. It was a rewarding occupation for me—while it lasted."

He looked sad when he said this. The eyebrows drooped at the outer corners to match his mouth. Give them a little more growth and they would be *in* his mouth.

"I know that," I said. "It's in the file. Also the suicide you had here a while back. A dope case, wasn't it?"

He stopped drooping and bristled. "What file?" he asked sharply.

"We've got a file on what we call the barred-window boys, Doctor. Places where you can't jump out of when the French fits take over. Small private sanitariums or what have you that treat alcoholics and dopers and mild cases of mania."

"Such places must be licensed by law," Dr. Verringer said harshly.

"Yeah. In theory anyway. Sometimes they kind of forget about that."

He drew himself up stiffly. The guy had a kind of dignity, at that. "The suggestion is insulting, Mr. Marlowe. I have no knowledge of why my name should be on any such list as you mention. I must ask you to leave."

"Let's get back to Wade. Could he be here under another name, maybe?"

"There is no one here but Earl and myself. We are quite alone. Now if you will excuse me—"

"I'd like to look around."

Sometimes you can get them mad enough to say something off key. But not Dr. Verringer. He remained dignified. His eyebrows went all the way with him. I looked towards the house. From inside there came a sound of music, dance music. And very faintly the snapping of fingers.

"I bet he's in there dancing," I said. "That's a tango. I bet you he's dancing all by himself in there. Some kid."

"Are you going to leave, Mr. Marlowe? Or shall I have to ask Earl to assist me in putting you off my property?"

"Okay, I'll leave. No hard feelings, Doctor. There were only three names beginning with V and you seemed the most promising of them. That's the only real clue we had—Dr. V. He scrawled it on a piece of paper before he left: Dr. V."

"There must be dozens," Dr. Verringer said evenly.

"Oh sure. But not dozens in our file of the barred-window boys. Thanks for the time, Doctor. Earl bothers me a little."

I turned and went over to my car and got into it. By the time I had the door shut Dr. Verringer was beside me. He leaned in with a pleasant expression.

"We need not quarrel, Mr. Marlowe. I realize that in your occupation you often have to be rather intrusive. Just what bothers you about Earl?"

"He's so obviously a phony. Where you find one thing phony you're apt to expect others. The guy's a manic-depressive, isn't he? Right now he's on the upswing."

He stared at me in silence. He looked grave and polite. "Many interesting and talented people have stayed with me, Mr. Marlowe. Not all of them were as level-headed as you may be. Talented people are often neurotic. But I have no facilities for the care of lunatics or alcoholics, even if I had the taste for that sort of work. I have no staff except Earl, and he is hardly the type to care for the sick."

"Just what would you say he is the type for, Doctor? Apart from bubble-dancing and stuff?"

He leaned on the door. His voice got low and confidential. "Earl's parents were dear friends of mine, Mr. Marlowe. Someone has to look after Earl and they are no longer with us. Earl has to live a quiet life, away from the noise and temptations of the city. He is unstable but fundamentally harmless. I control him with absolute ease, as you saw."

"You've got a lot of courage," I said.

He sighed. His eyebrows waved gently, like the antennae of some suspicious insect. "It has been a sacrifice," he said. "A rather heavy one. I thought Earl could help me with my work here. He plays beautiful tennis, swims and dives like a champion, and can dance all night. Almost always he is amiability itself. But from time to time there were—incidents." He waved a broad hand as if pushing painful memories into the background. "In the end it was either give up Earl or give up my place here."

He held both hands palms up, spread them apart, turned them over and let them fall to his sides. His eyes looked moist with unshed tears.

"I sold out," he said. "This peaceful little valley will become a real estate development. There will be sidewalks and lampposts and children with scooters and blatting radios. There will even"—he heaved a forlorn sigh—"be Television." He waved his hand in a sweeping gesture. "I hope they will spare the trees," he said, "but I'm afraid they won't. Along the ridges there will be television aerials instead. But Earl and I will be far away, I trust."

"Goodbye, Doctor. My heart bleeds for you."

He put out his hand. It was moist but very firm. "I appreciate your sympathy and understanding, Mr. Marlowe. And I regret I am unable to help you in your quest for Mr. Slade."

"Wade," I said.

"Pardon me, Wade, of course. Goodbye and good luck, sir."

I started up and drove back along the graveled road by the way I had come. I felt sad, but not quite as sad as Dr. Verringer would have liked me to feel.

I came out through the gates and drove far enough around the curve of the highway to park out of sight of the entrance. I got out and walked back along the edge of the paving to where I could just see the gates from the barbed-wire boundary fence. I stood there under a eucalyptus and waited.

Five minutes or so passed. Then a car came down the private road churning gravel. It stopped out of sight from where I was. I pulled back still farther into the brush. I heard a creaking noise, then the click of a heavy catch and the rattle of a chain. The car motor revved up and the car went back up the road.

When the sound of it had died I went back to my Olds and did a U turn to face back towards town. As I drove past the entrance to Dr. Verringer's private road I saw that the gate was fastened with a padlocked chain. No more visitors today, thank you.

17

I DROVE THE TWENTY-ODD MILES back to town and ate lunch. While I ate I felt more and more silly over the whole deal. You just don't find people the way I was going about it. You meet interesting characters like Earl and Dr. Verringer, but you don't meet the man you are looking for. You waste tires, gasoline, words, and nervous energy in a game with no pay-off. You're not even betting table limit four ways on Black 28. With three names that started with V, I had as much chance of paging my man as I had of breaking Nick the Greek in a crap game.

Anyway the first one is always wrong, a dead end, a promising lead that blows up in your face with no music. But he shouldn't have said Slade instead of Wade. He was an intelligent man. He wouldn't forget that easy, and if he did he would just forget.

Maybe, and maybe not. It had not been a long acquaintance. Over my coffee I thought about Drs. Vukanich and Varley. Yes or no? They would kill most of the afternoon. By then I could call the Wade mansion in Idle Valley and be told the head of the household had returned to his domicile and all was gleaming bright for the time being.

Dr. Vukanich was easy. He was only half a dozen blocks down the line. But Dr. Varley was away to hell and gone in the Altadena hills, a long, hot, boring drive. Yes or no?

The final answer was yes. For three good reasons. One was that you can never know too much about the shadow line and the people who walk it. The second was that anything I could add to the file Peters had got out for me was just that much thanks and goodwill. The third reason was that I didn't have anything else to do.

I paid my check, left my car where it was, and walked the north side of the street to the Stockwell Building. It was an antique with a cigar counter in the entrance and a manually operated elevator that lurched and hated to level off. The corridor of the sixth floor was narrow and the doors had frosted glass panels. It was older and much dirtier than my own building. It was loaded with doctors, dentists, Christian Science practitioners not doing too good, the kind of lawyers you hope the other fellow has, the kind of doctors and dentists who just scrape along. Not too skillful, not too clean, not too much on the ball, three dollars and please pay the nurse; tired, discouraged men who know just exactly where they stand, what kind of patients they can get and how much money they can be squeezed into paying. Please Do Not Ask For Credit. Doctor is In, Doctor is Out. That's a pretty shaky molar you have there, Mrs. Kazinski. Now if you want this new acrylic filling, every bit as good as a gold inlay, I can do it for you for $14. Novocain will be two dollars extra, if you wish it. Doctor is In, Doctor is Out. That will be Three Dollars. Please Pay the Nurse.

In a building like that there will always be a few guys making real money, but they don't look it. They fit into the shabby background, which is protective coloring for them. Shyster lawyers who are partners in a bail-bond racket on the side (only about two per cent of all forfeited bail bonds are ever collected). Abortionists posing as anything you like that explains their furnishings. Dope pushers posing as urologists, dermatologists, or any branch of medicine in which the treatment can be frequent, and the regular use of local anesthetics is normal.

Dr. Lester Vukanich had a small and ill-furnished waiting room in which there were a dozen people, all uncomfortable. They looked like anybody else. They had no signs on them. Anyway you can't tell a doper well under control from a vegetarian bookkeeper. I had to wait three quarters of an hour. The patients went in through two doors. An active ear, nose, and throat man can handle four sufferers at once, if he has enough room.

Finally I got in. I got to sit in a brown leather chair beside a table covered with a white towel on which was a set of tools. A sterilizing cabinet bubbled against the wall. Dr. Vukanich came in briskly with his white smock and his round mirror strapped to his forehead. He sat down in front of me on a stool.

"A sinus headache, is it? Very severe?" He looked at a folder the nurse had given him.

I said it was awful. Blinding. Especially when I first got up in the morning. He nodded sagely.

"Characteristic," he said, and fitted a glass cap over a thing that looked like a fountain pen.

He pushed it into my mouth. "Close the lips but not the teeth, please." While he said it he reached out and switched off the light. There was no window. A ventilating fan purred somewhere.

Dr. Vukanich withdrew his glass tube and put the lights back up. He looked at me carefully.

"No congestion at all, Mr. Marlowe. If you have a headache, it is not from a sinus condition. I'd hazard a guess that you never had sinus trouble in your life. You had a septum operation sometime in the past, I see."

"Yes, Doctor. Got a kick playing football."

He nodded. "There is a slight shelf of bone which should have been cut away. Hardly enough to interfere with breathing, however."

He leaned back on the stool and held his knee. "Just

what did you expect me to do for you?" he asked. He was a thin-faced man with an uninteresting pallor. He looked like a tubercular white rat.

"I wanted to talk to you about a friend of mine. He's in bad shape. He's a writer. Plenty of dough, but bad nerves. Needs help. He lives on the sauce for days on end. He needs that little extra something. His own doctor won't co-operate any more."

"Exactly what do you mean by co-operate?" Dr Vukanich asked.

"All the guy needs is an occasional shot to calm him down. I thought maybe we could work something out. The money would be solid."

"Sorry, Mr. Marlowe. It is not my sort of problem." He stood up. "Rather a crude approach, if I may say so. Your friend may consult me, if he chooses. But he'd better have something wrong with him that requires treatment. That will be ten dollars, Mr. Marlowe."

"Come off it, Doc. You're on the list."

Dr. Vukanich leaned against the wall and lit a cigarette. He was giving me time. He blew smoke and looked at it. I gave him one of my cards to look at instead. He looked at it.

"What list would that be?" he inquired.

"The barred-window boys. I figure you might know my friend already. His name's Wade. I figure you might have him stashed away somewhere in a little white room. The guy is missing from home."

"You are an ass," Dr. Vukanich told me. "I don't go in for penny ante stuff like four-day liquor cures. They cure nothing in any case. I have no little white rooms and I am not acquainted with the friend you mention—even if he exists. That will be ten dollars—cash—right now. Or would you rather I called the police and make a complaint that you solicited me for narcotics?"

"That would be dandy," I said. "Let's."

"Get out of here, you cheap grifter."

I stood up off the chair. "I guess I made a mistake, Doctor. The last time the guy broke parole he holed up with a doctor whose name began with V. It was strictly an undercover operation. They fetched him late at night and brought him back the same way when he was over the jumps. Didn't even wait long enough to see him go in the house. So when he hops the coop again and don't come back for quite a piece, naturally we check over our files for a lead. We come up with three doctors whose names begin with V."

"Interesting," he said with a bleak smile. He was still giving me time. "What is the basis of your selection?"

I stared at him. His right hand was moving softly up and down the upper part of his left arm on the inside of it. His face was covered with a light sweat.

"Sorry, Doctor. We operate very confidential."

"Excuse me a moment. I have another patient that—"

He left the rest of it hanging in the air and went out. While he was gone a nurse poked her head through the doorway, looked at me briefly and withdrew.

Then Dr. Vukanich came back in strolling happily. He was smiling and relaxed. His eyes were bright.

"What? Are you still here?" He looked very surprised or pretended to. "I thought our little visit had been brought to an end."

"I'm leaving. I thought you wanted me to wait."

He chuckled. "You know something, Mr. Marlowe? We live in extraordinary times. For a mere five hundred dollars I could have you put in the hospital with several broken bones. Comical, isn't it?"

"Hilarious," I said. "Shoot yourself in the vein, don't you, Doc? Boy, do you brighten up!"

I started out. "Hasta luego, amigo," he chirped. "Don't forget my ten bucks. Pay the nurse."

He moved to an intercom and was speaking into it as I left. In the waiting room the same twelve people or twelve just like them were being uncomfortable. The nurse was right on the job.

"That will be ten dollars, please, Mr. Marlowe. This office requires immediate cash payment."

I stepped among the crowded feet to the door. She bounded out of her chair and ran around the desk. I pulled the door open.

"What happens when you don't get it?" I asked her.

"You'll find out what happens," she said angrily.

"Sure. You're just doing your job. So am I. Take a gander at the card I left and you'll see what my job is."

I went on out. The waiting patients looked at me with disapproving eyes. That was no way to treat Doctor.

18

DR. AMOS VARLEY was a very different proposition. He had a big old house in a big old garden with big old oak trees shading it. It was a massive frame structure with elaborate scrollwork along the overhang of the porches and the white porch railings had turned and fluted uprights like the legs of an old-fashioned grand piano. A few frail elderly people sat in long chairs on the porches with rugs tucked around them.

The entrance doors were double and had stained-glass panels. The hall inside was wide and cool and the parquetry floor was polished and without a single rug. Altadena is a hot place in summer. It is pushed back against the hills and the breeze jumps clear over it. Eighty years ago people knew how to build houses for this climate.

A nurse in crisp white took my card and after a wait Dr. Amos Varley condescended to see me. He was a big bald-headed guy with a cheery smile. His long white coat was spotless, he walked noiselessly on crepe rubber soles.

"What can I do for you, Mr. Marlowe?" He had a rich soft voice to soothe the pain and comfort the anxious heart. Doctor is here, there is nothing to worry about, everything will be fine. He had that bedside manner, thick, honeyed layers of it. He was wonderful—and he was as tough as armor plate.

"Doctor, I am looking for a man named Wade, a well-to-do alcoholic who has disappeared from his home. His past history suggests that he is holed up in some discreet joint that can handle him with skill. My only lead is a reference to a Dr. V. You're my third Dr. V. and I'm getting discouraged."

He smiled benignly. "Only your third, Mr. Marlowe? Surely there must be a hundred doctors in and around the Los Angeles area whose names begin with V."

"Sure, but not many of them would have rooms with

barred windows. I noticed a few upstairs here, on the side of the house."

"Old people," Dr. Varley said sadly, but it was a rich full sadness. "Lonely old people, depressed and unhappy old people, Mr. Marlowe. Sometimes—" He made an expressive gesture with his hand, a curving motion outwards, a pause, then a gentle falling, like a dead leaf fluttering to the ground. "I don't treat alcoholics here," he added precisely. "Now if you will excuse me—"

"Sorry, Doctor. You just happened to be on our list. Probably a mistake. Something about a run-in with the narcotics people a couple of years ago."

"Is that so?" He looked puzzled, then the light broke. "Ah, yes, an assistant I was unwise enough to employ. For a very short time. He abused my confidence badly. Yes, indeed."

"Not the way I heard it," I said. "I guess I heard it wrong."

"And how did you hear it, Mr. Marlowe?" He was still giving me the full treatment with his smile and his mellow tones.

"That you had to turn in your narcotic prescription book."

That got to him a little. He didn't quite scowl but he peeled off a few layers of the charm. His blue eyes had a chilly glint. "And the source of this fantastic information?"

"A large detective agency that has facilities for building files on that sort of thing."

"A collection of cheap blackmailers, no doubt."

"Not cheap, Doctor. Their base rate is a hundred dollars a day. It's run by a former colonel of military police. No nickel grabber, Doctor. He rates way up."

"I shall give him a piece of my mind," Dr. Varley said with cool distaste. "His name?" The sun had set in Dr. Varley's manner. It was getting to be a chilly evening.

"Confidential, Doctor. But don't give it a thought. All in the day's work. Name of Wade doesn't ring a bell at all, huh?"

"I believe you know your way out, Mr. Marlowe."

The door of a small elevator opened behind him. A nurse pushed a wheel chair out. The chair contained what was left of a broken old man. His eyes were closed, his skin had a bluish tinge. He was well wrapped up. The nurse wheeled him silently across the polished floor and out of a side door. Dr. Varley said softly:

"Old people. Sick old people. Lonely old people. Do not come back, Mr. Marlowe. You might annoy me. When annoyed I can be rather unpleasant. I might even say *very* unpleasant."

"Okay by me, Doctor. Thanks for the time. Nice little dying-in home you got here."

"What was that?" He took a step towards me and peeled off the remaining layers of honey. The soft lines of his face set themselves into hard ridges.

"What's the matter?" I asked him. "I can see my man wouldn't be here. I wouldn't look for anybody here that wasn't too frail to fight back. Sick old people. Lonely old people. You said it yourself, Doctor. Unwanted old people, but with money and hungry heirs. Most of them probably judged incompetent by the court."

"I am getting annoyed," Dr. Varley said.

"Light food, light sedation, firm treatment. Put them out in the sun, put them back in the bed. Bar some of the windows in case there's a little spunk left. They love you, Doctor, one and all. They die holding your hand and seeing the sadness in your eyes. It's genuine too."

"It certainly is," he said in a low throaty growl. His hands were fists now. I ought to knock it off. But he had begun to nauseate me.

"Sure it is," I said. "Nobody likes to lose a good paying customer. Especially one you don't even have to please."

"Somebody has to do it," he said. "Somebody has to care for these sad old people, Mr. Marlowe."

"Somebody has to clean out cesspools. Come to think of it that's a clean honest job. So long, Dr. Varley. When my job makes me feel dirty I'll think of you. It will cheer me up no end."

"You filthy louse," Dr. Varley said between his wide white teeth. "I ought to break your back. Mine is an honorable branch of an honorable profession."

"Yeah." I looked at him wearily. "I know it is. Only it smells of death."

He didn't slug me, so I walked away from him and out. I looked back from the wide double doors. He hadn't moved. He had a job to do, putting back the layers of honey.

19

I DROVE BACK TO HOLLYWOOD feeling like a short length of chewed string. It was too early to eat, and too hot. I turned on the fan in my office. It didn't make the air any cooler, just a little more lively. Outside on the boulevard the traffic brawled endlessly. Inside my head thoughts stuck together like flies on flypaper.

Three shots, three misses. All I had been doing was seeing too many doctors.

I called the Wade home. A Mexican sort of accent answered and said that Mrs. Wade was not at home. I asked for Mr. Wade. The voice said Mr. Wade was not home either. I left my name. He seemed to catch it without any trouble. He said he was the houseboy.

I called George Peters at The Carne Organization. Maybe he knew some more doctors. He wasn't in. I left a phony name and a right telephone number. An hour crawled by like a sick cockroach. I was a grain of sand on the desert of oblivion. I was a two-gun cowpoke fresh out of bullets. Three shots, three misses. I hate it when they come in threes. You call on Mr. A. Nothing. You call on Mr. B. Nothing. You call on Mr. C. More of the same. A week later you find out it should have been Mr. D. Only you didn't know he existed and by the time you found out, the client had changed his mind and killed the investigation.

Drs. Vukanich and Varley were scratched. Varley had it too rich to fool with hooch cases. Vukanich was a punk, a high-wire performer who hit the main line in his own office. The help must know. At least some of the patients must know. All it took to finish him was one sorehead and one telephone call. Wade wouldn't have gone within blocks of him, drunk or sober. He might not be the brightest guy in the world—plenty of successful people are far from mental giants—but he couldn't be dumb enough to fool with Vukanich.

The only possible was Dr. Verringer. He had the space and the seclusion. He probably had the patience. But Sepulveda Canyon was a long way from Idle Valley. Where was the point of contact, how did they know each other, and if Verringer owned that property and had a buyer for it, he was halfway to being pretty well heeled. That gave me an idea. I called a man I knew in a title company to find out the status of the property. No answer. The title company had closed for the day.

I closed for the day too, and drove over to La Cienaga to Rudy's Bar-B-Q, gave my name to the master of ceremonies, and waited for the big moment on a bar stool with a whiskey sour in front of me and Marek Weber's waltz music in my ears. After a while I got in past the velvet rope and ate one of Rudy's "world-famous" Salisbury steaks, which is hamburger on a slab of burnt wood, ringed with browned-over mashed potato, supported by fried onion rings and one of those mixed up salads which men will eat with complete docility in restaurants, although they would probably start yelling if their wives tried to feed them one at home.

After that I drove home. As I opened the front door the phone started to ring.

"This is Eileen Wade, Mr. Marlowe. You wanted me to call you."

"Just to find out if anything had happened at your end. I have been seeing doctors all day and have made no friends."

"No, I'm sorry. He still hasn't showed up. I can't help being rather anxious. Then you have nothing to tell me, I suppose." Her voice was low and dispirited.

"It's a big crowded county, Mrs. Wade."

"It will be four whole days tonight."

"Sure, but that's not too long."

"For me it is." She was silent for a while. "I've been doing a lot of thinking, trying to remember something," she went on. "There must be something, some kind of hint or memory. Roger talks a great deal about all sorts of things."

"Does the name Verringer mean anything to you, Mrs. Wade?"

"No, I'm afraid not. Should it?"

"You mentioned that Mr. Wade was brought home one

time by a tall young man dressed in a cowboy outfit. Would you recognize this tall young man if you saw him again, Mrs. Wade?"

"I suppose I might," she said hesitantly, "if the conditions were the same. But I only caught the merest glimpse of him. Was his name Verringer?"

"No, Mrs. Wade. Verringer is a heavily built, middle-aged man who runs, or more accurately has run, some kind of guest ranch in Sepulveda Canyon. He has a dressed up fancy boy named Earl working for him. And Verringer calls himself a doctor."

"That's wonderful," she said warmly. "Don't you feel that you're on the right track?"

"I could be wetter than a drowned kitten. I'll call you when I know. I just wanted to make sure Roger hadn't come home and that you hadn't recalled anything definite."

"I'm afraid I haven't been of much help to you," she said sadly. "Please call me at any time, no matter how late it is."

I said I would do that and we hung up. I took a gun and a three-cell flashlight with me this time. The gun was a tough little short-barreled .32 with flat-point cartridges. Dr. Verringer's boy Earl might have other toys than brass knuckles. If he had, he was plenty goofy enough to play with them.

I hit the highway again and drove as fast as I dared. It was a moonless night, and would be getting dark by the time I reached the entrance to Dr. Verringer's estate. Darkness was what I needed.

The gates were still locked with the chain and padlock. I drove on past and parked well off the highway. There was still some light under the trees but it wouldn't last long. I climbed the gate and went up the side of the hill looking for a hiking path. Far back in the valley I thought I heard a quail. A mourning dove exclaimed against the miseries of life. There wasn't any hiking path or I couldn't find one, so I went back to the road and walked along the edge of the gravel. The eucalyptus trees gave way to the oaks and I crossed the ridge and far off I could see a few lights. It took me three quarters of an hour to work up behind the swimming pool and the tennis courts to a spot where I could look down on the main building at the end of the road. It was lighted up and I could hear music coming from it. And farther off in the trees another cabin showed light. There were small dark cabins dotted all over the place in the trees. I went along a path now and suddenly a floodlight went on at the back of the main cabin. I stopped dead. The floodlight was not looking for anything. It pointed straight down and made a wide pool of light on the back porch and the ground beyond. Then a door banged open and Earl came out. Then I knew I was in the right place.

Earl was a cowpoke tonight, and it had been a cowpoke who brought Roger Wade home the time before. Earl was spinning a rope. He wore a dark shirt stitched with white and a polka-dot scarf knotted loosely around his neck. He wore a wide leather belt with a load of silver on it and a pair of tooled leather holsters with ivory-handled guns in them. He wore elegant riding pants and boots cross-stitched in white and glistening new. On the back of his head was a white sombrero and what looked like a woven silver cord hanging loosely down his shirt, the ends not fastened.

He stood there alone under the white floodlight, spinning his rope around him, stepping in and out of it, an actor without an audience, a tall, slender, handsome dude wrangler putting on a show all by himself and loving every minute of it. Two-Gun Earl, the Terror of Cochise County. He belonged on one of those guest ranches that are so all-fired horsy the telephone girl wears riding boots to work.

All at once he heard a sound, or pretended to. The rope dropped, his hands swept the two guns from the holsters, and the crook of his thumbs was over the hammers as they came level. He peered into the darkness. I didn't dare move. The damn guns could be loaded. But the floodlight had blinded him and he didn't see anything. He slipped his guns back in the holsters, picked up the rope and gathered it loosely, went back into the house. The light went off, and so did I.

I moved around through the trees and got close to the small lighted cabin on the slope. No sound came from it. I reached a screened window and looked in. The light came from a lamp on a night table beside a bed. A man lay flat on his back in the bed, his body relaxed, his arms in pajama sleeves outside the covers, his eyes wide open and staring at the ceiling. He looked big. His face was partly shadowed, but I could see that he was pale and that he needed a shave and had needed one for just about the right length of time. The spread fingers of his hands lay motionless on the outside of the bed. He looked as if he hadn't moved for hours.

I heard steps coming along the path at the far side of the cabin. A screen door creaked and then the solid shape of Dr. Verringer showed in the doorway. He was carrying what looked like a large glass of tomato juice. He switched on a standing lamp. His Hawaiian shirt gleamed yellowly. The man in the bed didn't even look at him.

Dr. Verringer put the glass down on the night table and pulled a chair close and sat down. He reached for one of the wrists and felt a pulse. "How are you feeling now, Mr. Wade?" His voice was kindly and solicitous.

The man on the bed didn't answer him or look at him. He went on staring at the ceiling.

"Come, come, Mr. Wade. Let us not be moody. Your pulse is only slightly faster than normal. You are weak, but otherwise—"

"Tejjy," the man on the bed said suddenly, "tell the man that if he knows how I am, the son of a bitch needn't bother to ask me." He had a nice clear voice, but the tone was bitter.

"Who is Tejjy?" Dr. Verringer said patiently.

"My mouthpiece. She's up there in the corner."

Dr. Verringer looked up. "I see a small spider," he said. "Stop acting, Mr. Wade. It is not necessary with me."

"*Tegenaria domestica*, the common jumping spider, pal. I like spiders. They practically never wear Hawaiian shirts."

Dr. Verringer moistened his lips. "I have no time for playfulness, Mr. Wade."

"Nothing playful about Tejjy." Wade turned his head slowly, as if it weighed very heavy, and stared at Dr. Verringer contemptuously. "Tejjy is dead serious. She creeps up on you. When you're not looking she makes a quick silent hop. After a while she's near enough. She makes the last jump. You get sucked dry, Doctor. Very dry. Tejjy doesn't eat you. She just sucks the juice until there's nothing left but the skin. If you plan to wear that shirt much longer, Doctor, I'd say it couldn't happen too soon."

Dr. Verringer leaned back in the chair. "I need five thousand dollars," he said calmly. "How soon could that happen?"

"You got six hundred and fifty bucks," Wade said nastily. "As well as my loose change. How the hell much does it cost in this bordello?"

"Chicken feed," Dr. Verringer said. "I told you my rates had gone up."

"You didn't say they had moved to Mount Wilson."

"Don't fence with me, Wade," Dr. Verringer said curtly. "You are in no position to get funny. Also you have betrayed my confidence."

"I didn't know you had any."

Dr. Verringer tapped slowly on the arms of the chair. "You called me up in the middle of the night," he said. "You were in a desperate condition. You said you would kill yourself if I didn't come. I didn't want to do it and you know why. I have no license to practice medicine in this state. I am trying to get rid of this property without losing it all. I have Earl to look after and he was about due for a bad spell. I told you it would cost you a lot of money. You still insisted and I went. I want five thousand dollars."

"I was foul with strong drink," Wade said. "You can't hold a man to that kind of bargain. You're damn well paid already."

"Also," Dr. Verringer said slowly, "you mentioned my name to your wife. You told her I was coming for you."

Wade looked surprised. "I didn't do anything of the sort," he said. "I didn't even see her. She was asleep."

"Some other time then. A private detective has been here asking about you. He couldn't possibly have known where to come, unless he was told. I stalled him off, but he may come back. You have to go home, Mr. Wade. But first I want my five thousand dollars."

"You're not the brightest guy in the world, are you, Doc? If my wife knew where I was, why would she need a detective? She could have come herself—supposing she cared that much. She could have brought Candy, our houseboy. Candy would cut your Blue Boy into thin strips while Blue Boy was making up his mind what picture he was starring in today."

"You have a nasty tongue, Wade. And a nasty mind."

"I have a nasty five thousand bucks too, Doc. Try and get it."

"You will write me a check," Dr. Verringer said firmly. "Now, at once. Then you will get dressed and Earl will take you home."

"A check?" Wade was almost laughing. "Sure I'll give you a check. Fine. How will you cash it?"

Dr. Verringer smiled quietly. "You think you will stop payment, Mr. Wade. But you won't. I assure you that you won't."

"You fat crook!" Wade yelled at him.

Dr. Verringer shook his head. "In some things, yes. Not in all. I am a mixed character like most people. Earl will drive you home."

"Nix. That lad makes my skin crawl," Wade said.

Dr. Verringer stood up gently and reached over and patted the shoulder of the man on the bed. "To me Earl is quite harmless, Mr. Wade. I have ways of controlling him."

"Name one," a new voice said, and Earl came through the door in his Roy Rogers outfit. Dr. Verringer turned smiling.

"Keep that psycho away from me," Wade yelled, showing fear for the first time.

Earl put his hands on his ornamented belt. His face was deadpan. A light whistling noise came from between his teeth. He moved slowly into the room.

"You shouldn't have said that," Dr. Verringer said quickly, and turned towards Earl. "All right, Earl. I'll handle Mr. Wade myself. I'll help him get dressed while you bring the car up here as close to the cabin as possible. Mr. Wade is quite weak."

"And he's going to be a lot weaker," Earl said in a whistling kind of voice. "Out of my way, fatso."

"Now, Earl—" he reached out and grabbed the handsome young man's arm—"you don't want to go back to Camarillo, do you? One word from me and—"

That was as far as he got. Earl jerked his arm loose and his right hand came up with a flash of metal. The armored fist crashed against Dr. Verringer's jaw. He went down as if shot through the heart. The fall shook the cabin. I started running.

I reached the door and yanked it open. Earl spun around, leaning forward a little, staring at me without recognition. There was a bubbling sound behind his lips. He started for me fast.

I jerked the gun out and showed it to him. It meant nothing. Either his own guns were not loaded or he had forgotten all about them. The brass knuckles were all he needed. He kept coming.

I fired through the open window across the bed. The crash of the gun in the small room seemed much louder than it should have been. Earl stopped dead. His head slewed around and he looked at the hole in the window screen. He looked back at me. Slowly his face came alive and he grinned.

"Wha' happen?" he asked brightly.

"Get rid of the knucks," I said, watching his eyes.

He looked surprisingly down at his hand. He slipped the mauler off and threw it casually in the corner.

"Now the gun belt," I said. "Don't touch the guns, just the buckle."

"They're not loaded," he said smiling. "Hell, they're not even guns, just stage money."

"The belt. Hurry it."

He looked at the short-barreled .32. "That a real one? Oh sure it is. The screen. Yeah, the screen."

The man on the bed wasn't on the bed any more. He was behind Earl. He reached swiftly and pulled one of the bright guns loose. Earl didn't like this. His face showed it.

"Lay off him," I said angrily. "Put that back where you got it."

"He's right," Wade said. "They're cap guns." He backed away and put the shiny pistol on the table. "Christ, I'm as weak as a broken arm."

"Take the belt off," I said for the third time. When you start something with a type like Earl you have to finish it. Keep it simple and don't change your mind.

He did it at last, quite amiably. Then, holding the belt, he walked over to the table and got his other gun and put it in the holster and put the belt right back on again. I let him do it. It wasn't until then that he saw Dr. Verringer crumpled on the floor against the wall. He made a sound of concern, went quickly across the room into the bathroom, and came back with a glass jug of water. He dumped the water on Dr. Verringer's head. Dr. Verringer sputtered and rolled over. Then he groaned. Then he clapped a hand to his jaw. Then he started to get up. Earl helped him.

"Sorry, Doc. I must have just let fly without seeing who it was."

"It's all right, nothing broken," Verringer said, waving him away. "Get the car up here, Earl. And don't forget the key for the padlock down below."

"Car up here, sure. Right away. Key for the padlock. I got it. Right away, Doc."

He went out of the room whistling.

Wade was sitting on the side of the bed, looking shaky. "You the dick he was talking about?" he asked me. "How did you find me?"

"Just asking around from people who know about these things," I said. "If you want to get home, you might get clothes on."

Dr. Verringer was leaning against the wall, massaging his jaw. "I'll help him," he said thickly. "All I do is help people and all they do is kick me in the teeth."

"I know just how you feel," I said.

I went out and left them to work at it.

20

THE CAR WAS CLOSE BY when they came out, but Earl was gone. He had stopped the car, cut the lights, and walked back towards the big cabin without saying anything to me. He was still whistling, groping for some half-remembered tune.

Wade climbed carefully into the back seat and I got in beside him. Dr. Verringer drove. If his jaw hurt badly and his head ached, he didn't show it or mention it. We went over the ridge and down to the end of the graveled drive. Earl had already been down and unlocked the gate and pulled it open. I told Verringer where my car was and he pulled up close to it. Wade got into it and sat silent, staring at nothing. Verringer got out and went round beside him. He spoke to Wade gently.

"About my five thousand dollars, Mr. Wade. The check you promised me."

Wade slid down and rested his head on the back of the seat. "I'll think about it."

"You promised it. I need it."

"Duress, the word is, Verringer, a threat of harm. I have protection now."

"I fed and washed you," Verringer persisted. "I came in the night. I protected you, I cured you—for the time being, at least."

"Not five grand worth," Wade sneered. "You got plenty out of my pockets."

Verringer wouldn't let go. "I have a promise of a connection in Cuba, Mr. Wade. You are a rich man. You should help others in their need. I have Earl to look after. To avail myself of this opportunity I need the money. I will pay it back in full."

I began to squirm. I wanted to smoke, but I was afraid it would make Wade sick.

"Like hell you'd pay it back," Wade said wearily. "You won't live long enough. One of these nights Blue Boy will kill you in your sleep."

Verringer stepped back. I couldn't see his expression, but his voice hardened. "There are more unpleasant ways to die," he said. "I think yours will be one of them."

He walked back to his car and got into it. He drove in through his gates and was gone. I backed and turned and headed towards the city. After a mile or two Wade muttered: "Why should I give that fat slob five thousand dollars?"

"No reason at all."

"Then why do I feel like a bastard for not giving it to him?"

"No reason at all."

He turned his head just enough to look at me. "He handled me like a baby," Wade said. "He hardly left me alone for fear Earl would come in and beat me up. He took every dime I had in my pockets."

"You probably told him to."

"You on his side?"

"Skip it," I said. "This is just a job to me."

Silence for a couple of miles more. We went past the fringe of one of the outlying suburbs. Wade spoke again.

"Maybe I'll give it to him. He's broke. The property is foreclosed. He won't get a dime out of it. All on account of that psycho. Why does he do it?"

"I wouldn't know."

"I'm a writer," Wade said. "I'm supposed to understand what makes people tick. I don't understand one damn thing about anybody."

I turned over the pass and after a climb the lights of the valley spread out endlessly in front of us. We dipped down to the highway north and west that goes to Ventura. After a while we passed through Encino. I stopped for a light and looked up towards the lights high on the hill where the big houses were. In one of them the Lennoxes had lived. We went on.

"The turn-off is pretty close now," Wade said. "Or do you know it?"

"I know it."

"By the way, you haven't told me your name."

"Philip Marlowe."

"Nice name." His voice changed sharply, saying: "Wait a minute. You the guy that was mixed up with Lennox?"

"Yeah."

He was staring at me in the darkness of the car. We passed the last buildings on the main drag of Encino.

"I knew her," Wade said. "A little. Him I never saw. Queer business, that. The law boys gave you the rough edge, didn't they?"

I didn't answer him.

"Maybe you don't like to talk about it," he said.

"Could be. Why would it interest you?"

"Hell, I'm a writer. It must be quite a story."

"Take tonight off. You must be feeling pretty weak."

"Okay, Marlowe. Okay. You don't like me. I get it."

We reached the turn-off and I swung the car into it and towards the low hills and the gap between them that was Idle Valley.

"I don't either like you or dislike you," I said. "I don't know you. Your wife asked me to find you and bring you home. When I deliver you at your house I'm through. Why she picked on me I couldn't say. Like I said, it's just a job."

We turned the flank of a hill and hit a wider, more firmly paved road. He said his house was a mile farther on, on the right side. He told me the number, which I already knew. For a guy in his shape he was a pretty persistent talker.

"How much is she paying you?" he asked.

"We didn't discuss it."

"Whatever it is, it's not enough. I owe you a lot of thanks. You did a great job, chum. I wasn't worth the trouble."

"That's just the way you feel tonight."

He laughed. "You know something, Marlowe? I could get to like you. You're a bit of a bastard—like me."

We reached the house. It was a two-story over-all shingle house with a small pillared portico and a long lawn from the entrance to a thick row of shrubs inside the white fence. There was a light in the portico. I pulled into the driveway and stopped close to the garage.

"Can you make it without help?"

"Of course." He got out of the car. "Aren't you coming in for a drink or something?"

"Not tonight, thanks; I'll wait here until you're in the house."

He stood there breathing hard. "Okay," he said shortly.

He turned and walked carefully along a flagged path to the front door. He held on to a white pillar for a moment, then tried the door. It opened, he went in. The door stayed open and light washed across the green lawn. There was a sudden flutter of voices. I started backing from the driveway, following the back-up light. Somebody called out.

I looked and saw Eileen Wade standing in the open doorway. I kept going and she started to run. So I had to stop. I cut the lights and got out of the car. When she came up I said:

"I ought to have called you, but I was afraid to leave him."

"Of course. Did you have a lot of trouble?"

"Well—a little more than ringing a doorbell."

"Please come in the house and tell me all about it."

"He should be in bed. By tomorrow he'll be as good as new."

"Candy will put him to bed," she said. "He won't drink tonight, if that's what you are thinking of."

"Never occurred to me. Goodnight, Mrs. Wade."

"You must be tired. Don't you want a drink yourself?"

I lit a cigarette. It seemed like a couple of weeks since I had tasted tobacco. I drank in the smoke.

"May I have just one puff?"

She came close to me and I handed her the cigarette. She drew on it and coughed. She handed it back laughing. "Strictly an amateur, as you see."

"So you knew Sylvia Lennox," I said. "Was that why you wanted to hire me?"

"I knew who?" She sounded puzzled.

"Sylvia Lennox." I had the cigarette back now. I was eating it pretty fast.

"Oh," she said, startled. "That girl that was—murdered. No, I didn't know her personally. I knew who she was. Didn't I tell you that?"

"Sorry, I'd forgotten just what you did tell me."

She was still standing there quietly, close to me, slim and tall in a white dress of some sort. The light from the open door touched the fringe of her hair and made it glow softly.

"Why did you ask me if that had anything to do with my wanting to, as you put it, hire you?" When I didn't answer at once she added, "Did Roger tell you he knew her?"

"He said something about the case when I told him my name. He didn't connect me with it immediately, then he did. He talked so damn much I don't remember half of what he said."

"I see. I must go in, Mr. Marlowe, and see if my husband needs anything. And if you won't come in—"

"I'll leave this with you," I said.

I took hold of her and pulled her towards me and tilted her head back. I kissed her hard on the lips. She didn't fight me and she didn't respond. She pulled herself away quietly and stood there looking at me.

"You shouldn't have done that," she said. "That was wrong. You're too nice a person."

"Sure. Very wrong," I agreed. "But I've been such a nice faithful well-behaved gun dog all day long, I got charmed into one of the silliest ventures I ever tackled, and damned if it didn't turn out just as though somebody had written a script for it. You know something? I believe you knew where he was all along—or at least knew the name of Dr. Verringer. You just wanted to get me involved with him, tangled up with him so I'd feel a sense of responsibility to look after him. Or am I crazy?"

"Of course you're crazy," she said coldly. "That is the most outrageous nonsense I ever listened to." She started to turn away.

"Wait a minute," I said. "That kiss won't leave a scar. You just think it will. And don't tell me I'm too nice a person. I'd rather be a heel."

She looked back. "Why?"

"If I hadn't been a nice guy to Terry Lennox, he would still be alive."

"Yes?" she said quietly. "How can you be so sure? Goodnight, Mr. Marlowe. And thank you so very much for almost everything."

She walked back along the edge of the grass. I watched her into the house. The door closed. The porch light went off. I waved at nothing and drove away.

21

NEXT MORNING I GOT UP LATE on account of the big fee I had earned the night before. I drank an extra cup of coffee, smoked an extra cigarette, ate an extra slice of Canadian bacon, and for the three hundredth time I swore I would never again use an electric razor. That made the day normal. I hit the office about ten, picked up some odds and ends of mail, slit the envelopes and let the stuff lie on the desk. I opened the windows wide to let out the smell of dust and dinginess that collected in the night and hung in the still air, in the corners of the room, in the slats of the venetian blinds. A dead moth was spread-eagled on a corner of the desk. On the window sill a bee with tattered wings was crawling along the woodwork, buzzing in a tired remote sort of way, as if she knew it wasn't any use, she was finished, she had flown too many missions and would never get back to the hive again.

I knew it was going to be one of those crazy days. Everyone has them. Days when nobody rolls in but the loose wheels, the dingoes who park their brains with their gum, the squirrels who can't find their nuts, the mechanics who always have a gear wheel left over.

The first was a big blond roughneck named Kuissenen or something Finnish like that. He jammed his massive bottom in the customer's chair and planted two wide horny hands on my desk and said he was a power-shovel operator, that he lived in Culver City, and the goddam woman who lived next door to him was trying to poison his dog. Every morning before he let the dog out for a run in the back yard he had to search the place from fence to fence for meatballs thrown over the potato vine from next door. He'd found nine of them so far and they were loaded with a greenish powder he knew was an arsenic weed killer.

"How much to watch out and catch her at it?" He stared at me as unblinkingly as a fish in a tank.

"Why not do it yourself?"

"I got to work for a living, mister. I'm losing four twentyfive an hour just coming up here to ask."

"Try the police?"

"I try the police. They might get around to it some time next year. Right now they're busy sucking up to MGM."

"S.P.C.A.? The Tailwaggers?"

"What's them?"

I told him about the Tailwaggers. He was far from interested. He knew about the S.P.C.A. The S.P.C.A. could take a running jump. They couldn't see nothing smaller than a horse.

"It says on the door you're an investigator," he said truculently. "Okay, go the hell out and investigate. Fifty bucks if you catch her."

"Sorry," I said. "I'm tied up. Spending a couple of weeks hiding in a gopher hole in your back yard would be out of my line anyway—even for fifty bucks."

He stood up glowering. "Big shot," he said. "Don't need the dough, huh? Can't be bothered saving the life of a itty-bitty dog. Nuts to you, big shot."

"I've got troubles too, Mr. Kuissenen."

"I'll twist her goddam neck if I catch her," he said, and I didn't doubt he could have done it. He could have twisted the hind leg off of an elephant. "That's what makes it I want somebody else. Just because the little tike barks when a car goes by the house. Sour-faced old bitch."

He started for the door. "Are you sure it's the dog she's trying to poison?" I asked his back.

"Sure I'm sure." He was halfway to the door before the nickel dropped. He swung around fast then. "Say that again, buster."

I just shook my head. I didn't want to fight him. He might hit me on the head with my desk. He snorted and went out, almost taking the door with him.

The next cookie in the dish was a woman, not old, not young, not clean, not too dirty, obviously poor, shabby, querulous and stupid. The girl she roomed with—in her set any woman who works out is a girl—was taking money out of her purse. A dollar here, four bits there, but it added up. She figured she was out close to twenty dollars in all. She couldn't afford it. She couldn't afford to move either. She couldn't afford a detective. She thought I ought to be willing to throw a scare into the roommate just on the telephone like, not mentioning any names.

It took her twenty minutes or more to tell me this. She kneaded her bag incessantly while telling it.

"Anybody you know could do that," I said.

"Yeah, but you bein' a dick and all."

"I don't have a license to threaten people I know nothing about."

"I'm goin' to tell her I been in to see you. I don't have to say it's her. Just that you're workin' on it."

"I wouldn't if I were you. If you mention my name she may call me up. If she does that, I'll tell her the facts."

She stood up and slammed her shabby bag against her stomach. "You're no gentleman," she said shrilly.

"Where does it say I have to be?"

She went out mumbling.

After lunch I had Mr. Simpson W. Edelweiss. He had a card to prove it. He was manager of a sewing machine agency. He was a small tired-looking man about forty-eight to fifty, small hands and feet, wearing a brown suit with sleeves too long, and a stiff white collar behind a purple tie with black diamonds on it. He sat on the edge of the chair without fidgeting and looked at me out of sad black eyes. His hair was black too and thick and rough without a sign of gray in it that I could see. He had a clipped mustache with a reddish tone. He could have passed for thirty-five if you didn't look at the backs of his hands.

"Call me Simp," he said. "Everybody else does. I got it coming. I'm a Jewish man married to a Gentile woman, twenty-four years of age, beautiful. She run away a couple of times before."

He got out a photo of her and showed it to me. She might have been beautiful to him. To me she was a big sloppy-looking cow of a woman with a weak mouth.

"What's your trouble, Mr. Edelweiss? I don't do divorce business." I tried to give him back the photo. He waved it away. "The client is always mister to me," I added. "Until he has told me a few dozen lies anyway."

He smiled. "Lies I got no use for. It's not a divorce matter. I just want Mabel back again. But she don't come back until I find her. Maybe it's a kind of game with her."

He told me about her, patiently, without rancor. She drank, she played around, she wasn't a very good wife by his standards, but he could have been brought up too strict. She had a heart as big as a house, he said, and he loved her. He didn't kid himself he was any dreamboat, just a steady worker bringing home the pay check. They had a joint bank account. She had drawn it all out, but he was prepared for that. He had a pretty good idea who she had lit out with, and if he was right the man would clean her out and leave her stranded.

"Name of Kerrigan," he said. "Monroe Kerrigan. I don't aim to knock the Catholics. There is plenty of bad Jews too. This Kerrigan is a barber when he works. I ain't knocking barbers either. But a lot of them are drifters and horse players. Not real steady."

"Won't you hear from her when she is cleaned out?"

"She gets awful ashamed. She might hurt herself."

"It's a Missing Persons job, Mr. Edelweiss. You should go down and make a report."

"No. I'm not knocking the police, but I don't want it that way. Mabel would be humiliated."

The world seemed to be full of people Mr. Edelweiss was not knocking. He put some money on the desk.

"Two hundred dollars," he said. "Down payment. I'd rather do it my way."

"It will happen again," I said.

"Sure." He shrugged and spread his hands gently. "But twenty-four years old and me almost fifty. How could it be different? She'll settle down after a while. Trouble is, no kids. She can't have kids. A Jew likes to have a family. So Mabel knows that. She's humiliated."

"You're a very forgiving man, Mr. Edelweiss."

"Well I ain't a Christian," he said. "And I'm not knocking Christians, you understand. But with me it's real. I don't just say it. I do it. Oh, I almost forgot the most important."

He got out a picture postcard and pushed it across the desk after the money. "From Honolulu she sends it. Money goes fast in Honolulu. One of my uncles had a jewelry business there. Retired now. Lives in Seattle."

I picked the photo up again. "I'll have to farm this one out," I told him. "And I'll have to have this copied."

"I could hear you saying that, Mr. Marlowe, before I got here. So I come prepared." He took out an envelope and it contained five more prints. "I got Kerrigan too, but only a snapshot." He went into another pocket and gave me another envelope. I looked at Kerrigan. He had a smooth dishonest face that did not surprise me. Three copies of Kerrigan.

Mr. Simpson W. Edelweiss gave me another card which had on it his name, his residence, his telephone number. He said he hoped it would not cost too much but that he would respond at once to any demand for further funds and he hoped to hear from me.

"Two hundred ought to pretty near do it if she's still in Honolulu," I said. "What I need now is a detailed physical description of both parties that I can put into a telegram. Height, weight, age, coloring, any noticeable scars or other identifying marks, what clothes she was wearing and had with her, and how much money was in the account she cleaned out. If you've been through this before, Mr. Edelweiss, you will know what I want."

"I got a peculiar feeling about this Kerrigan. Uneasy."

I spent another half hour milking him and writing things down. Then he stood up quietly, shook hands quietly, bowed and left the office quietly.

"Tell Mabel everything is fine," he said as he went out.

It turned out to be routine. I sent a wire to an agency in Honolulu and followed it with an airmail containing the photos and whatever information I had left out of the wire. They found her working as a chambermaid's helper in a luxury hotel, scrubbing bathtubs and bathroom floors and so on. Kerrigan had done just what Mr. Edelweiss expected, cleaned her out while she was asleep and skipped, leaving her stuck with the hotel bill. She pawned a ring which Kerrigan couldn't have taken without violence, and got enough out of it to pay the hotel but not enough to buy her way home. So Edelweiss hopped a plane and went after her.

He was too good for her. I sent him a bill for twenty dollars and the cost of a long telegram. The Honolulu agency grabbed the two hundred. With a portrait of Madison in my office safe I could afford to be underpriced.

So passed a day in the life of a P.I. Not exactly a typical day but not totally untypical either. What makes a man stay with it nobody knows. You don't get rich, you don't often have much fun. Sometimes you get beaten up or shot at or tossed into the jailhouse. Once in a long while you get dead. Every other month you decide to give it up and find some sensible occupation while you can still walk without shaking your head. Then the door buzzer rings and you open the inner door to the waiting room and there stands a new face with a new problem, a new load of grief, and a small piece of money.

"Come in, Mr. Thingummy. What can I do for you?"

There must be a reason.

Three days later in the shank of the afternoon Eileen Wade called me up, and asked me to come around to the house for a drink the next evening. They were having a few friends in for cocktails. Roger would like to see me and thank me adequately. And would I please send in a bill?

"You don't owe me anything, Mrs. Wade. What little I did I got paid for."

"I must have looked very silly acting Victorian about it," she said. "A kiss doesn't seem to mean much nowadays. You will come, won't you?"

"I guess so. Against my better judgment."

"Roger is quite well again. He's working."

"Good."

"You sound very solemn today. I guess you take life pretty seriously."

"Now and then. Why?"

She laughed very gently and said goodbye and hung up. I sat there for a while taking life seriously. Then I tried to think of something funny so that I could have a great big laugh. Neither way worked, so I got Terry Lennox's letter of farewell out of the safe and reread it. It reminded me that I had never gone to Victor's for that gimlet he asked me to drink for him. It was just about the right time of day for the bar to be quiet, the way he would have liked it himself, if he had been around to go with me. I thought of him with a vague sadness and with a puckering bitterness too. When I got to Victor's I almost kept going. Almost, but not quite. I had too much of his money. He had made a fool of me but he had paid well for the privilege.

22

IT WAS SO QUIET IN VICTOR'S that you almost heard the temperature drop as you came in at the door. On a bar stool a woman in a black tailormade, which couldn't at that time of year have been anything but some synthetic fabric like orlon, was sitting alone with a pale greenish-colored drink in front of her and smoking a cigarette in a long jade holder. She had that fine-drawn intense look that is sometimes neurotic, sometimes sex-hungry, and sometimes just the result of drastic dieting.

I sat down two stools away and the barkeep nodded to me, but didn't smile.

"A gimlet," I said. "No bitters."

He put the little napkin in front of me and kept looking at me. "You know something," he said in a pleased voice. "I heard you and your friend talking one night and I got me in a bottle of that Rose's Lime Juice. Then you didn't come back any more and I only opened it tonight."

"My friend left town," I said. "A double if it's all right with you. And thanks for taking the trouble."

He went away. The woman in black gave me a quick glance, then looked down into her glass. "So few people drink them around here," she said so quietly that I didn't realize at first that she was speaking to me. Then she looked my way again. She had very large dark eyes. She had the reddest fingernails I had ever seen. But she didn't look like a pickup and there was no trace of come-on in her voice. "Gimlets I mean."

"A fellow taught me to like them," I said.

"He must be English."

"Why?"

"The lime juice. It's as English as boiled fish with that awful anchovy sauce that looks as if the cook had bled into it. That's how they got called limeys. The English—not the fish."

"I thought it was more a tropical drink, hot weather stuff. Malaya or some place like that."

"You may be right." She turned away again.

The bartender set the drink in front of me. With the lime juice it has a sort of pale greenish yellowish misty look. I tasted it. It was both sweet and sharp at the same time. The woman in black watched me. Then she lifted her own glass towards me. We both drank. Then I knew hers was the same drink.

The next move was routine, so I didn't make it. I just sat there. "He wasn't English," I said after a moment. "I guess maybe he had been there during the war. We used to come in here once in a while, early like now. Before the mob started boiling."

"It's a pleasant hour," she said. "In a bar almost the only pleasant hour." She emptied her glass. "Perhaps I knew your friend," she said. "What was his name?"

I didn't answer her right away. I lit a cigarette and watched her tap the stub of hers out of the jade holder and fit another in its place. I reached across with a lighter. "Lennox," I said.

She thanked me for the light and gave me a brief searching glance. Then she nodded. "Yes, I knew him very well. Perhaps a little too well."

The barkeep drifted over and glanced at my glass. "A couple more of the same," I said. "In a booth."

I got down off the stool and stood waiting. She might or might not blow me down. I didn't particularly care. Once in a while in this much too sex-conscious country a man and a woman can meet and talk without dragging bedrooms into it. This could be it, or she could just think I was on the make. If so, the hell with her.

She hesitated, but not for long. She gathered up a pair of

black gloves and a black suede bag with a gold frame and clasp and walked across into a corner booth and sat down without a word. I sat down across the small table.

"My name is Marlowe."

"Mine is Linda Loring," she said calmly. "A bit of a sentimentalist, aren't you, Mr. Marlowe?"

"Because I came in here to drink a gimlet? How about yourself?"

"I might have a taste for them."

"So might I. But it would be a little too much coincidence."

She smiled at me vaguely. She had emerald earrings and an emerald lapel pin. They looked like real stones because of the way they were cut—flat with beveled edges. And even in the dim light of a bar they had an inner glow.

"So you're the man," she said.

The bar waiter brought the drinks over and set them down. When he went away I said: "I'm a fellow who knew Terry Lennox, liked him, and had an occasional drink with him. It was kind of a side deal, an accidental friendship. I never went to his home or knew his wife. I saw her once in a parking lot."

"There was a little more to it than that, wasn't there?"

She reached for her glass. She had an emerald ring set in a nest of diamonds. Beside it a thin platinum band said she was married. I put her in the second half of the thirties, early in the second half.

"Maybe," I said. "The guy bothered me. He still does. How about you?"

She leaned on an elbow and looked up at me without any particular expression. "I said I knew him rather too well. Too well to think it mattered much what happened to him. He had a rich wife who gave him all the luxuries. All she asked in return was to be let alone."

"Seems reasonable," I said.

"Don't be sarcastic, Mr. Marlowe. Some women are like that. They can't help it. It wasn't as if he didn't know in the beginning. If he had to get proud, the door was open. He didn't have to kill her."

"I agree with you."

She straightened up and looked hard at me. Her lip curled. "So he ran away and, if what I hear is true, you helped him. I suppose you feel proud about that."

"Not me," I said. "I just did it for the money."

"That is not amusing, Mr. Marlowe. Frankly I don't know why I sit here drinking with you."

"That's easily changed, Mrs. Loring." I reached for my glass and dropped the contents down the hatch. "I thought perhaps you could tell me something about Terry that I didn't know. I'm not interested in speculating why Terry Lennox beat his wife's face to a bloody sponge."

"That's a pretty brutal way to put it," she said angrily.

"You don't like the words? Neither do I. And I wouldn't be here drinking a gimlet if I believed he did anything of the sort."

She stared. After a moment she said slowly: "He killed himself and left a full confession. What more do you want?"

"He had a gun," I said. "In Mexico that might be enough excuse for some jittery cop to pour lead into him. Plenty of American police have done their killings the same way—some of them through doors that didn't open fast enough to suit them. As for the confession, I haven't seen it."

"No doubt the Mexican police faked it," she said tartly.

"They wouldn't know how, not in a little place like Otatoclán. No, the confession is probably real enough, but it doesn't prove he killed his wife. Not to me anyway. All it proves to me is that he didn't see any way out. In a spot like that a certain sort of man—you can call him weak or soft or sentimental if it amuses you—might decide to save some other people from a lot of very painful publicity."

"That's fantastic," she said. "A man doesn't kill himself or deliberately get himself killed to save a little scandal. Sylvia was already dead. As for her sister and her father—they could take care of themselves very efficiently. People with enough money, Mr. Marlowe, can always protect themselves."

"Okay, I'm wrong about the motive. Maybe I'm wrong all down the line. A minute ago you were mad at me. You want me to leave now—so you can drink *your* gimlet?"

Suddenly she smiled. "I'm sorry. I'm beginning to think you are sincere. What I thought then was that you were trying to justify yourself, far more than Terry. I don't think you are, somehow."

"I'm not. I did something foolish and I got the works for

it. Up to a point anyway. I don't deny that his confession saved me a lot worse. If they had brought him back and tried him, I guess they would have hung one on me too. The least it would have cost me would have been far more money than I could afford."

"Not to mention your license," she said dryly.

"Maybe. There was a time when any cop with a hangover could get me busted. It's a little different now. You get a hearing before a commission of the state licensing authority. Those people are not too crazy about the city police."

She tasted her drink and said slowly: "All things considered, don't you think it was best the way it was? No trial, no sensational headlines, no mud-slinging just to sell newspapers without the slightest regard for truth or fairplay or for the feelings of innocent people."

"Didn't I just say so? And you said it was fantastic."

She leaned back and put her head against the upper curve of the padding on the back of the booth. "Fantastic that Terry Lennox should have killed himself just to achieve that. Not fantastic that it was better for all parties that there should be no trial."

"I need another drink," I said, and waved at the waiter. "I feel an icy breath on the back of my neck. Could you by any chance be related to the Potter family, Mrs. Loring?"

"Sylvia Lennox was my sister," she said simply. "I thought you would know."

The waiter drifted over and I gave him an urgent message. Mrs. Loring shook her head and said she didn't want anything more. When the waiter took off I said:

"With the hush old man Potter—excuse me, Mr. Harlan Potter—put on this affair, I would be lucky to know for sure that Terry's wife even had a sister."

"Surely you exaggerate. My father is hardly that powerful, Mr. Marlowe—and certainly not that ruthless. I'll admit he does have very old-fashioned ideas about his personal privacy. He never gives interviews even to his own newspapers. He is never photographed, he never makes speeches, he travels mostly by car or in his own plane with his own crew. But he is quite human for all that. He liked Terry. He said Terry was a gentleman twenty-four hours a day instead of for the fifteen minutes between the time the guests arrive and the time they feel their first cocktail."

"He slipped a little at the end. Terry did."

The waiter trotted up with my third gimlet. I tried it for flavor and then sat there with a finger on the edge of the round base of the glass.

"Terry's death was quite a blow to him, Mr. Marlowe. And you're getting sarcastic again. Please don't. Father knew it would all look far too neat to some people. He would much rather Terry had just disappeared. If Terry had asked him for help, I think he would have given it."

"Oh no, Mrs. Loring. His own daughter had been murdered."

She made an irritable motion and eyed me coldly.

"This is going to sound pretty blunt, I'm afraid. Father had written my sister off long ago. When they met he barely spoke to her. If he expressed himself, which he hasn't and won't, I feel sure he would be just as doubtful about Terry as you are. But once Terry was dead, what did it matter? They could have been killed in a plane crash or a fire or a highway accident. If she had to die, it was the best possible time for her to die. In another ten years she would have been a sex-ridden hag like some of these frightful women you see at Hollywood parties, or used to a few years back. The dregs of the international set."

All of a sudden I got mad, for no good reason. I stood up and looked over the booth. The next one was still empty. In the one beyond a guy was reading a paper all by himself, quietly. I sat down with a bump, pushed my glass out of the way, and leaned across the table. I had sense enough to keep my voice down.

"For hell's sake, Mrs. Loring, what are you trying to sell me? That Harlan Potter is such a sweet lovely character he wouldn't dream of using his influence on a political D.A. to drop the blanket on a murder investigation so that the murder was never really investigated at all? That he had doubts about Terry's guilt but didn't let anyone lift a finger to find out who was really the killer? That he didn't use the political power of his newspapers and his bank account and the nine hundred guys who would trip over their chins trying to guess what he wanted done before he knew himself? That he didn't arrange it so that a tame lawyer and nobody else, nobody from the D.A.'s office or the city cops, went down to Mexico to make sure Terry actually had put a slug in his head instead of being knocked off by some Indian with a hot gun just for kicks? Your old man is worth a hundred million bucks, Mrs. Loring. I wouldn't know just how he got it, but I know damn well he didn't get it without building himself a pretty far-reaching organization. He's no softie. He's a hard tough man. You've got to be in these days to make that kind of money. And you do business with some funny people. You may not meet them or shake hands with them, but they are there on the fringe doing business with you."

"You're a fool," she said angrily. "I've had enough of you."

"Oh sure. I don't make the kind of music you like to hear. Let me tell you something. Terry talked to your old man the night Sylvia died. What about? What did your old man say to him? 'Just run on down to Mexico and shoot yourself, old boy. Let's keep this in the family. I know my daughter is a tramp and that any one of a dozen drunken bastards might have blown his top and pushed her pretty face down her throat for her. But that's incidental, old boy. The guy will be sorry when he sobers up. You've had it soft and now is the time you pay back. What we want is to keep the fair Potter name as sweet as mountain lilac. She married you because she needed a front. She needs it worse than ever now she's dead. And you're it. If you can get lost and stay lost, fine. But if you get found, you check out. See you in the morgue.' "

"Do you really think," the woman in black asked with dry ice in her voice, "that my father talks like that?"

I leaned back and laughed unpleasantly. "We could polish up the dialogue a little if that helps."

She gathered her stuff together and slid along the seat. "I'd like to give you a word of warning," she said slowly and very carefully, "a very simple word of warning. If you think my father is that kind of man and if you go around broadcasting the kind of thoughts you have just expressed to me, your career in this city in your business or in any business is apt to be extremely short and terminated very suddenly."

"Perfect, Mrs. Loring. Perfect. I get it from the law, I get it from the hoodlum element, I get it from the carriage trade. The words change, but the meaning is the same. Lay off. I came in here to drink a gimlet because a man asked me to. Now look at me. I'm practically in the boneyard."

She stood up and nodded briefly. "Three gimlets. Doubles. Perhaps you're drunk."

I dropped too much money on the table and stood up beside her. "You had one and a half, Mrs. Loring. Why even that much? Did a man ask you too, or was it all your own idea? Your own tongue got a little loose."

"Who knows, Mr. Marlowe? Who knows? Who really knows anything? There's a man over there at the bar watching us. Would it be anyone you know?"

I looked around, surprised that she had noticed. A lean dark character sat on the end stool nearest the door.

"His name is Chick Agostino," I said. "He's a gun toter for a gambling boy named Menendez. Let's knock him down and jump on him."

"You certainly are drunk," she said quickly and started to walk. I went after her. The man on the stool swung around and looked to his front. When I came abreast I stepped up behind him and reached in under both his arms quickly. Maybe I *was* a little drunk.

He swung around angrily and slid off the stool. "Watch it, kiddo," he snarled. Out of the corner of my eye I saw that she had stopped just inside the door to glance back.

"No guns, Mr. Agostino? How reckless of you. It's almost dark. What if you should run into a tough midget?"

"Scram!" he said savagely.

"Aw, you stole that line from the *New Yorker*."

His mouth worked but he didn't move. I left him and followed Mrs. Loring out through the door into the space under the awning. A gray-haired colored chauffeur stood there talking to the kid from the parking lot. He touched his cap and went off and came back with a flossy Cadillac limousine. He opened the door and Mrs. Loring got in. He shut the door as though he was putting down the lid of a jewel box. He went around the car to the driver's seat.

She ran the window down and looked out at me, half smiling.

"Goodnight, Mr. Marlowe. It's been nice—or has it?"

"We had quite a fight."

"You mean you had—and mostly with yourself."

"It usually is. Goodnight, Mrs. Loring. You don't live around here, do you?"

"Not exactly. I live in Idle Valley. At the far end of the lake. My husband is a doctor."

"Would you happen to know any people named Wade?"

She frowned. "Yes, I know the Wades. Why?"

"Why do I ask? They're the only people in Idle Valley that I know."

"I see. Well, goodnight again, Mr. Marlowe."

She leaned back in the seat and the Cadillac purred politely and slid away into the traffic along the Strip.

Turning I almost bumped into Chick Agostino.

"Who's the doll?" he sneered. "And next time you crack wise, be missing."

"Nobody that would want to know you," I said.

"Okay, bright boy. I got the license number. Mendy likes to know little things like that."

The door of a car banged open and a man about seven feet high and four feet wide jumped out of it, took one look at Agostino, then one long stride, and grabbed him by the throat with one hand.

"How many times I gotta tell you cheap hoods not to hang around where I eat?" he roared.

He shook Agostino and hurled him across the sidewalk against the wall. Chick crumpled up coughing.

"Next time," the enormous man yelled, "I sure as hell put the blast on you, and believe me, boy, you'll be holding a gun when they pick you up."

Chick shook his head and said nothing. The big man gave me a raking glance and grinned. "Nice night," he said, and strolled into Victor's.

I watched Chick straighten himself out and regain some of his composure. "Who's your buddy?" I asked him.

"Big Willie Magoon," he said thickly. "A vice squad bimbo. He thinks he's tough."

"You mean he isn't sure?" I asked him politely.

He looked at me emptily and walked away. I got my car out of the lot and drove home. In Hollywood anything can happen, anything at all.

23

A LOW-SWUNG JAGUAR swept around the hill in front of me and slowed down so as not to bathe me in the granite dust from the half mile of neglected paving at the entrance to Idle Valley. It seemed they wanted it left that way to discourage the Sunday drivers spoiled by drifting along on superhighways. I caught a glimpse of a bright scarf and a pair of sun goggles. A hand waved at me casually, neighbor to neighbor. Then the dust slid across the road and added itself to the white film already well spread over the scrub and the sunbaked grass. Then I was around the outcrop and the paving started up in proper shape and everything was smooth and cared for. Live oaks clustered towards the road, as if they were curious to see who went by, and sparrows with rosy heads hopped about pecking at things only a sparrow would think worth pecking at.

Then there were a few cottonwoods but no eucalyptus. Then a thick growth of Carolina poplars screening a white house. Then a girl walking a horse along the shoulder of the road. She had levis on and a loud shirt and she was chewing on a twig. The horse looked hot but not lathered and the girl was crooning to him gently. Beyond a field-stone wall a gardener was guiding a power lawnmower over a huge undulating lawn that ended far back in the portico of a Williamsburg Colonial mansion, the large de luxe size. Somewhere someone was playing left-handed exercises on a grand piano.

Then all this wheeled away and the glisten of the lake showed hot and bright and I began to watch numbers on gateposts. I had seen the Wades' house only once and in the dark. It wasn't as big as it had looked by night. The driveway was full of cars, so I parked on the side of the road and walked in. A Mexican butler in a white coat opened the door for me. He was a slender neat good-looking Mexican and his coat fitted him elegantly and he looked like a Mexican who was getting fifty a week and not killing himself with hard work.

He said: 'Buenas tardes, señor," and grinned as if he had put one over. "Su nombre de Usted, por favor?"

"Marlowe," I said, "and who are you trying to upstage, Candy? We talked on the phone, remember?"

He grinned and I went in. It was the same old cocktail party, everybody talking too loud, nobody listening, everybody hanging on for dear life to a mug of the juice, eyes very bright, cheeks flushed or pale and sweaty according to the amount of alcohol consumed and the capacity of the individual to handle it. Then Eileen Wade materialized beside me in a pale blue something which did her no harm. She had a glass in her hand but it didn't look as if it was more than a prop.

"I'm so glad you could come," she said gravely. "Roger wants to see you in his study. He hates cocktail parties. He's working."

"With this racket going on?"

"It never seems to bother him. Candy will get you a drink—or if you'd rather go to the bar—"

"I'll do that," I said. "Sorry about the other night."

She smiled. "I think you apologized already. It was nothing."

"The hell it was nothing."

She kept the smile long enough to nod and turn and walk away. I spotted the bar over in the corner by some very large french windows. It was one of those things you push around. I was halfway across the room, trying not to bump anybody, when a voice said: "Oh, Mr. Marlowe."

I turned and saw Mrs. Loring on a couch beside a prissy-looking man in rimless cheaters with a smear on his chin that might have been a goatee. She had a drink in her hand and looked bored. He sat still with his arms folded and scowled.

I went over there. She smiled at me and gave me her hand. "This is my husband, Dr. Loring. Mr. Philip Marlowe, Edward."

The guy with the goatee gave me a brief look and a still briefer nod. He didn't move otherwise. He seemed to be saving his energy for better things.

"Edward is very tired," Linda Loring said. "Edward is always very tired."

"Doctors often are," I said. "Can I get you a drink, Mrs. Loring? Or you, Doctor?"

"She's had enough," the man said without looking at either of us. "I don't drink. The more I see of people who do, the more glad I am that I don't."

"Come back, little Sheba," Mrs. Loring said dreamily.

He swung around and did a take. I got away from there and made it to the bar. In the company of her husband Linda Loring seemed like a different person. There was an edge to her voice and a sneer in her expression which she hadn't used on me even when she was angry.

Candy was behind the bar. He asked me what I would drink.

"Nothing right now, thanks. Mr. Wade wants to see me."

"Es muy occupado, señor. Very busy."

I didn't think I was going to like Candy. When I just looked at him he added: "But I go see. De pronto, señor."

He threaded his way delicately through the mob and was back in no time at all. "Okay, chum, let's go," he said cheerfully.

I followed him across the room the long way of the house. He opened a door, I went through, he shut it behind me, and a lot of the noise was dimmed. It was a corner room, big and cool and quiet, with french windows and roses outside and an airconditioner set in a window to one side. I could see the lake, and I could see Wade lying flat out on a long blond leather couch. A big bleached wood desk had a typewriter on it and there was a pile of yellow paper beside the typewriter.

"Good of you to come, Marlowe," he said lazily. "Park yourself. Did you have a drink or two?"

"Not yet." I sat down and looked at him. He still looked a bit pale and pinched. "How's the work going?"

"Fine, except that I get tired too quick. Pity a four-day drunk is so painful to get over. I often do my best work after one. In my racket it's so easy to tighten up and get all stiff and wooden. Then the stuff is no good. When it's good it comes easy. Anything you have read or heard to the contrary is a lot of mishmash."

"Depends who the writer is, maybe," I said. "It didn't come easy to Flaubert, and his stuff is good."

"Okay," Wade said, sitting up. "So you have read Flaubert, so that makes you an intellectual, a critic, a savant of the literary world." He rubbed his forehead. "I'm on the wagon and I hate it. I hate everybody with a drink in his hand. I've got to go out there and smile at those creeps. Every damn one of them knows I'm an alcoholic. So they wonder what I'm running away from. Some Freudian bastard has made that a commonplace. Every ten-year-old kid knows it by now. If I had a ten-year-old kid, which God forbid, the brat would be asking me, 'What are you running away from when you get drunk, Daddy?' "

"The way I got it, all this was rather recent," I said.

"It's got worse, but I was always a hard man with a bottle. When you're young and in hard condition you can absorb a lot of punishment. When you are pushing forty you don't snap back the same way."

I leaned back and lit a cigarette. "What did you want to see me about?"

"What do *you* think I'm running away from, Marlowe?"

"No idea. I don't have enough information. Besides, everybody is running away from something."

"Not everybody gets drunk. What are *you* running away from? Your youth or a guilty conscience or the knowledge that you're a small time operator in a small time business?"

"I get it," I said. "You need somebody to insult. Fire away, chum. When it begins to hurt I'll let you know."

He grinned and rumpled his thick curly hair. He speared his chest with a forefinger. "You're looking right at a small time operator in a small time business, Marlowe. All writers are punks and I am one of the punkest. I've written twelve best sellers, and if I ever finish that stack of magoozlum on the desk there I may possibly have written thirteen. And not a damn one of them worth the powder to blow it to hell. I have a lovely home in a highly restricted residential neighborhood that belongs to a highly restricted multimillionaire. I have a lovely wife who loves me and a lovely publisher who loves me and I love me the best of all. I'm an egotistical son of a bitch, a literary prostitute or pimp—choose your own word—and an all-round heel. So what can you do for me?"

"Well, what?"

"Why don't you get sore?"

"Nothing to get sore about. I'm just listening to you hate yourself. It's boring but it doesn't hurt my feelings."

He laughed roughly. "I like you," he said. "Let's have a drink."

"Not in here, chum. Not you and me alone. I don't care to watch you take the first one. Nobody can stop you and I don't guess anyone would try. But I don't have to help."

He stood up. "We don't have to drink in here. Let's go outside and glance at a choice selection of the sort of people you get to know when you make enough lousy money to live where they live."

"Look," I said. "Shove it. Knock it off. They're no different from anybody else."

"Yeah," he said tightly, "but they ought to be. If they're not, what use are they? They're the class of the county and they're no better than a bunch of truckdrivers full of cheap whiskey. Not as good."

"Knock it off," I said again. "You want to get boiled, get boiled. But don't take it out on a crowd that can get boiled without having to lie up with Dr. Verringer or get loose in the head and throw their wives down the stairs."

"Yeah," he said, and he was suddenly calm and thoughtful. "You pass the test, chum. How about coming to live here for a while? You could do me a lot of good just being here."

"I don't see how."

"But I do. Just by being here. Would a thousand a month interest you? I'm dangerous when I'm drunk. I don't want to be dangerous and I don't want to be drunk."

"I couldn't stop you."

"Try it for three months. I'd finish the damn book and then go far off for a while. Lie up some place in the Swiss mountains and get clean."

"The book, huh? Do you have to have the money?"

"No. I just have to finish something I started. If I don't I'm through. I'm asking you as a friend. You did more than that for Lennox."

I stood up and walked over close to him and gave him a hard stare. "I got Lennox killed, mister. I got him killed."

"Phooey. Don't go soft on me, Marlowe." He put the edge of his hand against his throat. "I'm up to here in the soft babies."

"Soft?" I asked. "Or just kind?"

He stepped back and stumbled against the edge of the couch, but didn't lose his balance.

"The hell with you," he said smoothly. "No deal. I don't blame you, of course. There's something I want to know, that I have to know. You don't know what it is and I'm not sure I know myself. All I'm positive of is that there is something, and I have to know it."

"About who? Your wife?"

He moved his lips one over the other. "I think it's about me," he said. "Let's go get that drink."

He walked to the door and threw it open and we went out.

If he had been trying to make me uncomfortable, he had done a first class job.

24

WHEN HE OPENED THE DOOR the buzz from the living room exploded into our faces. It seemed louder than before, if possible. About two drinks louder. Wade said hello here and there and people seemed glad to see him. But by that time they would have been glad to see Pittsburgh Phil with his custom-built icepick. Life was just one great big vaudeville show.

On the way to the bar we came face to face with Dr. Loring and his wife. The doctor stood up and stepped forward to face Wade. He had a look on his face that was almost sick with hatred.

"Nice to see you, Doctor," Wade said amiably. "Hi, Linda. Where have you been keeping yourself lately? No, I guess that was a stupid question. I—"

"Mr. Wade," Loring said in a voice that had a tremor to it, "I have something to say to you. Something very simple, and I hope very conclusive. Stay away from my wife."

Wade looked at him curiously. "Doctor, you're tired. And you don't have a drink. Let me get you one."

"I don't drink, Mr. Wade. As you very well know. I am here for one purpose and I have expressed that purpose."

"Well, I guess I get your point," Wade said, still amiable. "And since you are a guest in my house, I have nothing to say except that I think you are a little off the beam."

There had been a drop in the talk near by. The boys and girls were all ears. Big production. Dr. Loring took a pair of gloves out of his pocket, straightened them, took hold of one by the finger end, and swung it hard against Wade's face.

Wade didn't bat an eye. "Pistols and coffee at dawn?" he asked quietly.

I looked at Linda Loring. She was flushed with anger. She stood up slowly and faced the doctor.

"Dear God, what a ham you are, darling. Stop acting like a damn fool, will you, darling? Or would you rather stick around until somebody slaps *your* face?"

Loring swung around to her and raised the gloves. Wade stepped in front of him. "Take it easy, Doc. Around here we only hit our wives in private."

"If you are speaking for yourself, I am well aware of it," Loring sneered. "And I don't need lessons in manners from you."

"I only take promising pupils," Wade said. "Sorry you have to leave so soon." He raised his voice. "Candy! Que el Doctor Loring salga de aqui en el acto!" He swung back to Loring. "In case you don't know Spanish, Doctor, that means the door is over there." He pointed.

Loring stared at him without moving. "I have warned you, Mr. Wade," he said icily. "And a number of people have heard me. I shall not warn you again."

"Don't," Wade said curtly. "But if you do, make it on neutral territory. Gives me a little more freedom of action. Sorry, Linda. But you married him." He rubbed his cheek gently where the heavy end of the glove had hit him. Linda Loring was smiling bitterly. She shrugged.

"We are leaving," Loring said. "Come, Linda."

She sat down again and reached for her glass. She gave her husband a glance of quiet contempt. "You are," she said. "You have a number of calls to make, remember."

"You are leaving with me," he said furiously.

She turned her back on him. He reached suddenly and took hold of her arm. Wade took him by the shoulder and spun him around.

"Take it easy, Doc. You can't win them all."

"Take your hand off me!"

"Sure, just relax," Wade said. "I have a good idea, Doctor. Why don't you see a good doctor?"

Somebody laughed loudly. Loring tensed like an animal all set to spring. Wade sensed it and neatly turned his back and moved away. Which left Dr. Loring holding the bag. If he went after Wade, he would look sillier than he looked now. There was nothing for him to do but leave, and he did it. He marched quickly across the room staring straight in front of him to where Candy was holding the door open. He went out. Candy shut the door, wooden-faced, and went back to the bar. I went over there and asked for some Scotch. I didn't see where Wade went. He just disappeared. I didn't see Eileen either. I turned my back on the room and let them sizzle while I drank my Scotch.

A small girl with mud-colored hair and a band around her forehead popped up beside me and put a glass on the bar and bleated. Candy nodded and made her another drink.

The small girl turned to me. "Are you interested in Communism?" she asked me. She was glassy-eyed and she was running a small red tongue along her lips as if looking for a crumb of chocolate. "I think everyone ought to be," she went on. "But when you ask any of the men here they just want to paw you."

I nodded and looked over my glass at her snub nose and sun-coarsened skin.

"Not that I mind too much if it's done nicely," she told me, reaching for the fresh drink. She showed me her molars while she inhaled half of it.

"Don't rely on me," I said.

"What's your name?"

"Marlowe."

"With an 'e' or not?"

"With."

"Ah, Marlowe," she intoned. "Such a sad beautiful name." She put her glass down damn nearly empty and closed her eyes and threw her head back and her arms out, almost hitting me in the eye. Her voice throbbed with emotion, saying:

> *"Was this the face that launch'd a thousand ships*
> *And burnt the topless towers of Ilium?*
> *Sweet Helen, make me immortal with a kiss."*

She opened her eyes, grabbed her glass, and winked at me. "You were pretty good in there, chum. Been writing any poetry lately?"

"Not very much."

"You can kiss me if you like," she said coyly.

A guy in a shantung jacket and an open neck shirt came up behind her and grinned at me over the top of her head. He had short red hair and a face like a collapsed lung. He was as ugly a guy as I ever saw. He patted the top of the little girl's head.

"Come on kitten. Time to go home."

She rounded on him furiously. "You mean you got to water those goddamned tuberous begonias again?" she yelled.

"Aw listen, kitten—"

"Take your hands off me, you goddamned rapist," she screamed, and threw the rest of her drink in his face. The rest wasn't more than a teaspoonful and two lumps of ice.

"For Chrissake, baby, I'm your husband," he yelled back, grabbing for a handkerchief and mopping his face. "Get it? Your husband."

She sobbed violently and threw herself into his arms. I stepped around them and got out of there. Every cocktail party is the same, even the dialogue.

The house was leaking guests out into the evening air now. Voices were fading, cars were starting, goodbyes were bouncing around like rubber balls. I went to the french windows and out onto a flagged terrace. The ground sloped towards the lake which was as motionless as a sleeping cat. There was a short wooden pier down there with a rowboat tied to it by a white painter. Towards the far shore, which wasn't very far, a black waterhen was doing lazy curves, like a skater. They didn't seem to cause as much as a shallow ripple.

I stretched out on a padded aluminum chaise and lit a pipe and smoked peacefully and wondered what the hell I was doing there. Roger Wade seemed to have enough control to handle himself if he really wanted to. He had done all right with Loring. I wouldn't have been too surprised if he had hung one on Loring's sharp little chin. He would have been out of line by the rules, but Loring was much farther out of line.

If the rules mean anything at all any more, they mean

...at you don't pick a roomful of people as the spot to threaten a man and hit him across the face with a glove when your wife is standing right beside you and you are practically accusing her of a little double time. For a man still shaky from a hard bout with the hard stuff Wade had done all right. He had done more than all right. Of course I hadn't seen him drunk. I didn't know what he would be like drunk. I didn't even know that he was an alcoholic. There's a big difference. A man who drinks too much on occasion is still the same man as he was sober. An alcoholic, a real alcoholic, is not the same man at all. You can't predict anything about him for sure except that he will be someone you never met before.

Light steps sounded behind me and Eileen Wade came across the terrace and sat down beside me on the edge of a chaise.

"Well, what did you think?" she asked quietly.

"About the gentleman with the loose gloves?"

"Oh no." She frowned. Then she laughed. "I hate people who make stagy scenes like that. Not that he isn't a fine doctor. He has played that scene with half the men in the valley. Linda Loring is no tramp. She doesn't look like one, talk like one, or behave like one. I don't know what makes Dr. Loring behave as if she was."

"Maybe he's a reformed drunk," I said. "A lot of them grow pretty puritanical."

"It's possible," she said, and looked towards the lake. "This is a very peaceful place. One would think a writer would be happy here—if a writer is ever happy anywhere." She turned to look at me. "So you won't be persuaded to do what Roger asked."

"There's no point in it, Mrs. Wade. Nothing I could do. I've said all this before. I couldn't be sure of being around at the right time. I'd have to be around *all* the time. That's impossible, even if I had nothing else to do. If he went wild, for example, it would happen in a flash. And I haven't seen any indications that he does get wild. He seems pretty solid to me."

She looked down at her hands. "If he could finish his book, I think things would be much better."

"I can't help him do that."

She looked up and put her hands on the edge of the chaise beside her. She leaned forward a little. "You can if he thinks you can. That's the whole point. Is it that you would find it distasteful to be a guest in our house and be paid for it?"

"He needs a psychiatrist, Mrs. Wade. If you know one that isn't a quack."

She looked startled "A psychiatrist? Why?"

I knocked the ashes out of my pipe and sat holding it, waiting for the bowl to get cooler before I put it away.

"You want an amateur opinion, here it is. He thinks he has a secret buried in his mind and he can't get `at it. It may be a guilty secret about himself, it may be about someone else. He thinks that's what makes him drink, because he can't get at this thing. He probably thinks that whatever happened, happened while he was drunk and he ought to find it wherever people go when they're drunk—really bad drunk, the way he gets. That's a job for a psychiatrist. So far, so good. If that is wrong, then he gets drunk because he wants to or can't help it, and the idea about the secret is just his excuse. He can't write his book, or anyway can't finish it. Because he gets drunk. That is, the assumption seems to be that he can't finish his book because he knocks himself out by drinking. It could be the other way around."

"Oh no," she said. "No. Roger has a great deal of talent. I feel quite sure that his best work is still to come."

"I told you it was an amateur opinion. You said the other morning that he might have fallen out of love with his wife. That's something else that could go the other way around."

She looked towards the house, then turned so that she had her back to it. I looked the same way. Wade was standing inside the doors, looking out at us. As I watched he moved behind the bar and reached for a bottle.

"There's no use interfering," she said quickly. "I never do. Never. I suppose you're right, Mr. Marlowe. There just isn't anything to do but let him work it out of his system."

The pipe was cool now and I put it away. "Since we're groping around in the back of the drawer, how about that other way around?"

"I love my husband," she said simply. "Not as a young girl loves, perhaps. But I love him. A woman is only a young girl once. The man I loved then is dead. He died in the war. His name, strangely enough, had the same initials as yours. It doesn't matter now—except that sometimes I can't quite believe that he is dead. His body was never found. But that happened to many men."

She gave me a long searching look. "Sometimes—not often, of course—when I go into a quiet cocktail lounge or the lobby of a good hotel at a dead hour, or along the deck of a liner early in the morning or very late at night, I think I may see him waiting for me in some shadowy corner." She paused and dropped her eyes. "It's very silly. I'm ashamed of it. We were very much in love—the wild, mysterious, improbable kind of love that never comes but once."

She stopped talking and sat there half in a trance looking out over the lake. I looked back at the house again. Wade was standing just inside the open french windows with a glass in his hand. I looked back at Eileen. For her I wasn't there any more. I got up and went into the house. Wade stood there with the drink and the drink looked pretty heavy. And his eyes looked wrong.

"How you making out with my wife, Marlowe?" It was said with a twist of the mouth.

"No passes, if you mean it that way."

"That's exactly the way I mean it. You got to kiss her the other night. Probably fancy yourself as a fast worker, but you're wasting your time, bud. Even if you had the right kind of polish."

I tried to move around him but he blocked me with a solid shoulder. "Don't hurry away, old man. We like you around. We get so few private dicks in our house."

"I'm the one too many," I said.

He hoisted the glass and drank from it. When he lowered it he leered at me.

"You ought to give yourself a little more time to build resistance," I told him. "Empty words, huh?"

"Okay, coach. Some little character builder, aren't you? You ought to have more sense than to try educating a drunk. Drunks don't educate, my friend. They disintegrate. And part of the process is a lot of fun." He drank from the glass again, leaving it nearly empty. "And part of it is damned awful. But if I may quote the scintillating words of the good Dr. Loring, a bastardly bastard with a little black bag, stay away from my wife, Marlowe. Sure you go for her. They all do. You'd like to sleep with her. They all would. You'd like to share her dreams and sniff the rose of her memories. Maybe I would too. But there is nothing to share, chum—nothing, nothing, nothing. You're all alone in the dark."

He finished his drink and turned the glass upside down.

"Empty like that, Marlowe. Nothing there at all. I'm the guy that knows."

He put the glass on the edge of the bar and walked stiffly to the foot of the stairs. He made about a dozen steps up, holding on to the rail, and stopped and leaned against it. He looked down at me with a sour grin.

"Forgive the corny sarcasm, Marlowe. You're a nice guy. I wouldn't want anything to happen to you."

"Anything like what?"

"Perhaps she didn't get around yet to that haunting magic of her first love, the guy that went missing in Norway. You wouldn't want to be missing, would you, chum? You're my own special private eye. You find me when I'm lost in the savage splendor of Sepulveda Canyon." He moved the palm of his hand in a circular motion on the polished wood banister. "It would hurt me to the quick if you got lost yourself. Like that character who hitched up with the limeys. He got so lost a man sometimes wonders if he ever existed. You figure she could have maybe just invented him to have a toy to play with?"

"How would I know?"

He looked down at me. There were deep lines between his eyes now and his mouth was twisted with bitterness.

"How would anybody know? Maybe she don't know herself. Baby's tired. Baby been playing too long with broken toys. Baby wants to go bye-bye."

He went on up the stairs.

I stood there until Candy came in and started tidying up around the bar, putting glasses on a tray, examining bottles to see what was left, paying no attention to me. Or so I thought. Then he said: "Señor. One good drink left. Pity to waste him." He held up a bottle.

"You drink it."

"Gracias, señor, no me gusta. Un vaso de Cerveza, no más. A glass of beer is my limit."

"Wise man."

"One lush in the house is enough," he said, staring at me. "I speak good English, not?"

"Sure, fine."

"But I think Spanish. Sometimes I think with a knife. The boss is my guy. He don't need any help, hombre. I take care of him, see."

"A great job you're doing, punk."

"Hijo de la flauta," he said between his white teeth. He picked up a loaded tray and swung it up on the edge of his shoulder and the flat of his hand, bus boy style.

I walked to the door and let myself out, wondering how an expression meaning 'son of a flute' had come to be an insult in Spanish. I didn't wonder very long. I had too many other things to wonder about. Something more than alcohol was the matter with the Wade family. Alcohol was no more than a disguised reaction.

Later that night, between nine-thirty and ten, I called the Wades' number. After eight rings I hung up, but I had only just taken my hand off the instrument when it started to ring me. It was Eileen Wade.

"Someone just rang here," she said. "I had a sort of hunch it might be you. I was just getting ready to take a shower."

"It was me, but it wasn't important, Mrs. Wade. He seemed a little woolly-headed when I left—Roger did. I guess maybe I feel a little responsibility for him by now."

"He's quite all right," she said. "Fast asleep in bed. I think Dr. Loring upset him more than he showed. No doubt he talked a lot of nonsense to you."

"He said he was tired and wanted to go to bed. Pretty sensible, I thought."

"If that is all he said, yes. Well, goodnight and thank you for calling, Mr. Marlowe."

"I didn't say it was all he said. I said he said it."

There was a pause, then: "Everyone gets fantastic ideas once in a while. Don't take Roger too seriously, Mr. Marlowe. After all, his imagination is rather highly developed. Naturally it would be. He shouldn't have had anything to drink so soon after the last time. Please try to forget all about it. I suppose he was rude to you among other things."

"He wasn't rude to me. He made quite a lot of sense. Your husband is a guy who can take a long hard look at himself and see what is there. It's not a very common gift. Most people go through life using up half their energy trying to protect a dignity they never had. Goodnight, Mrs. Wade."

She hung up and I set out the chess board. I filled a pipe, paraded the chessmen and inspected them for French shaves and loose buttons, and played a championship tournament game between Gortchakoff and Meninkin, seventy-two moves to a draw, a prize specimen of the irresistible force meeting the immovable object, a battle without armor, a war without blood, and as elaborate a waste of human intelligence as you could find anywhere outside an advertising agency.

25

NOTHING HAPPENED FOR A WEEK except that I went about my business which just then didn't happen to be very much business. One morning George Peters of The Carne Organization called me up and told me he had happened to be down Sepulveda Canyon way and had looked in on Dr. Verringer's place just out of curiosity. But Dr. Verringer was no longer there. Half a dozen teams of surveyors were mapping the tract for a subdivision. Those he spoke to had never even heard of Dr. Verringer.

"The poor sucker got closed out on a trust deed," Peters said. "I checked. They gave him a grand for a quitclaim just to save time and expense, and now somebody is going to make a million bucks clear, out of cutting the place up for residential property. That's the difference between crime and business. For business you gotta have capital. Sometimes I think it's the only difference."

"A properly cynical remark," I said, "but big time crime takes capital too."

"And where does it come from, chum? Not from guys that hold up liquor stores. So long. See you soon."

It was ten minutes to eleven on a Thursday night when Wade called me up. His voice was thick, almost gurgling, but I recognized it somehow. And I could hear short hard rapid breathing over the telephone.

"I'm in bad shape, Marlowe. Very bad. I'm slipping my anchor. Could you make it out here in a hurry?"

"Sure—but let me talk to Mrs. Wade a minute."

He didn't answer. There was a crashing sound, then a dead silence, then in a short while a kind of banging around. I yelled something into the phone without getting any answer. Time passed. Finally the light click of the receiver being replaced and the buzz of an open line.

In five minutes I was on the way. I made it in slightly over half an hour and I still don't know how. I went over the pass on wings and hit Ventura Boulevard with the light against me and made a left turn anyhow and dodged between trucks and generally made a damn fool of myself. I went through Encino at close to sixty with a spotlight on the outer edge of the parked cars so that it would freeze anyone with a notion to step out suddenly. I had the kind of luck you only get when you don't care. No cops, no sirens, no red flashers. Just visions of what might be happening in the Wade residence and not very pleasant visions. She was alone in the house with a drunken maniac, she was lying at the bottom of the stairs with her neck broken, she was behind a locked door and somebody was howling outside and trying to break it in, she was running down a moonlit road barefoot and a big buck Negro with a meat cleaver was chasing her.

It wasn't like that at all. When I swung the Olds into their driveway lights were on all over the house and she was standing in the open doorway with a cigarette in her mouth. I got out and walked over the flagstones to her. She had slacks on and a shirt with an open collar. She looked at me calmly. If there was any excitement around there I had brought it with me.

The first thing I said was as loony as the rest of my behavior. "I thought you didn't smoke."

"What? No, I don't usually." She took the cigarette out and looked at it and dropped it and stepped on it. "Once in a long while. He called Dr. Verringer."

It was a remote placid voice, a voice heard at night over water. Completely relaxed.

"He couldn't," I said. "Dr. Verringer doesn't live there any more. He called me."

"Oh really? I just heard him telephoning and asking

someone to come in a hurry. I thought it must be Dr. Verringer."

"Where is he now?"

"He fell down," she said. "He must have tipped the chair too far back. He's done it before. He cut his head on something. There's a little blood, not much."

"Well, that's fine," I said. "We wouldn't want a whole lot of blood. Where is he now, I asked you."

She looked at me solemnly. Then she pointed. "Out there somewhere. By the edge of the road or in the bushes along the fence."

I leaned forward and peered at her. "Chrissake, didn't you look?" I decided by this time that she was in shock. Then I looked back across the lawn. I didn't see anything but there was heavy shadow near the fence.

"No, I didn't look," she said quite calmly. "You find him. I've had all of it I can take. I've had more than I can take. You find him."

She turned and walked back into the house, leaving the door open. She didn't walk very far. About a yard inside the door she just crumpled to the floor and lay there. I scooped her up and spread her out on one of the two big davenports that faced each other across a long blond cocktail table. I felt her pulse. It didn't seem very weak or unsteady. Her eyes were closed and the lids were blue. I left her there and went back out.

He was there all right, just as she had said. He was lying on his side in the shadow of the hibiscus. He had a fast thumping pulse and his breathing was unnatural. Something on the back of his head was sticky. I spoke to him and shook him a little. I slapped his face a couple of times. He mumbled but didn't come to. I dragged him up into a sitting position and dragged one of his arms over my shoulder and heaved him up with my back turned to him and grabbed for a leg. I lost. He was as heavy as a block of cement. We both sat down on the grass and I took a short breather and tried again. Finally I got him hoisted into a fireman's lift position and plowed across the lawn in the direction of the open front door. It seemed about the same distance as a round trip to Siam. The two steps of the porch were ten feet high. I staggered over to the couch and went down on my knees and rolled him off. When I straightened up again my spine felt as if it had cracked in at least three places.

Eileen Wade wasn't there any more. I had the room to myself. I was too bushed at the moment to care where anybody was. I sat down and looked at him and waited for some breath. Then I looked at his head. It was smeared with blood. His hair was sticky with it. It didn't look very bad but you never know with a head wound.

Then Eileen Wade was standing beside me, quietly looking down at him with that same remote expression.

"I'm sorry I fainted," she said. "I don't know why."

"I guess we'd better call a doctor."

"I telephoned Dr. Loring. He is my doctor, you know. He didn't want to come."

"Try somebody else then."

"Oh he's coming," she said. "He didn't want to. But he's coming as soon as he can manage."

"Where's Candy?"

"This is his day off. Thursday. The cook and Candy have Thursdays off. It's the usual thing around here. Can you get him up to bed?"

"Not without help. Better get a rug or blanket. It's a warm night, but cases like this get pneumonia very easily."

She said she would get a rug. I thought it was damn nice of her. But I wasn't thinking very intelligently. I was too bushed from carrying him.

We spread a steamer rug over him and in fifteen minutes Dr. Loring came, complete with starched collar and rimless cheaters and the expression of a man who has been asked to clean up after the dog got sick.

He examined Wade's head. "A superficial cut and bruise," he said. "No chance of concussion. I should say his breath would indicate his condition rather obviously."

He reached for his hat. He picked up his bag.

"Keep him warm," he said. "You might bathe his head gently and get rid of the blood. He'll sleep it off."

"I can't get him upstairs alone, Doctor," I said.

"Then leave him where he is." He looked at me without interest. "Goodnight, Mrs. Wade. As you know I don't treat alcoholics. Even if I did, your husband would not be one of my patients. I'm sure you understand that."

"Nobody's asking you to treat him," I said. "I'm asking

for some help to get him into his bedroom so that I can undress him."

"And just who are you?" Dr. Loring asked me freezingly.

"My name's Marlowe. I was here a week ago. Your wife introduced me."

"Interesting," he said. "In what connection do you know my wife?"

"What the hell does that matter? All I want is—"

"I'm not interested in what you want," he cut in on me. He turned to Eileen, nodded briefly, and started out. I got between him and the door and put my back to it.

"Just a minute, Doc. Must be a long time since you glanced at that little piece of prose called the Hippocratic Oath. This man called me on the phone and I live some way off. He sounded bad and I broke every traffic law in the state getting over here. I found him lying on the ground and I carried him in here and believe me he isn't any bunch of feathers. The houseboy is away and there's nobody here to help me upstairs with Wade. How does it look to you?"

"Get out of my way," he said between his teeth. "Or I shall call the sheriff's substation and have them send over a deputy. As a professional man—"

"As a professional man you're a handful of flea dirt," I said, and moved out of his way.

He turned red—slowly but distinctly. He choked on his own bile. Then he opened the door and went out. He shut it carefully. As he pulled it shut he looked in at me. It was as nasty a look as I ever got and on as nasty a face as I ever saw.

When I turned away from the door Eileen was smiling.

"What's funny?" I snarled.

"You. You don't care what you say to people, do you? Don't you know who Dr. Loring is?"

"Yeah—and I know what he is."

She glanced at her wrist watch. "Candy ought to be home by now," she said. "I'll go see. He has a room behind the garage."

She went out through an archway and I sat down and looked at Wade. The great big writer man went on snoring. His face was sweaty but I left the rug over him. In a minute or two Eileen came back and she had Candy with her.

26

THE MEX HAD a black and white checked sport shirt, heavily pleated black slacks without a belt, two-tone black and white buckskin shoes, spotlessly clean. His thick black hair was brushed straight back and shining with some kind of hair oil or cream.

"Señor," he said, and sketched a brief sarcastic bow.

"Help Mr. Marlowe carry my husband upstairs, Candy. He fell and hurt himself a little. I'm sorry to trouble you."

"De nada, señora," Candy said smiling.

"I think I'll say goodnight," she said to me. "I'm tired out. Candy will get you anything you want."

She went slowly up the stairs. Candy and I watched her.

"Some doll," he said confidentially. "You stay the night?"

"Hardly."

"Es lástima. She is very lonely, that one."

"Get that gleam out of your eyes, kid. Let's put this to bed."

He looked sadly at Wade snoring on the couch. "Pobrecito," he murmured as if he meant it. "Borracho como una cuba."

"He may be drunk as a sow but he sure ain't little," I said. "You take the feet."

We carried him and even for two he was as heavy as a lead coffin. At the top of the stairs we went along an open balcony past a closed door. Candy pointed to it with his chin.

"La señora," he whispered. "You knock very light maybe she let you in."

I didn't say anything because I needed him. We went on with the carcass and turned in at another door and dumped him on the bed. Then I took hold of Candy's arm high up near the shoulder where dug-in fingers can hurt. I made mine hurt him. He winced a little and then his face set hard.

"What's your name, cholo?"

"Take your hand off me," he snapped. "And don't call me a cholo. I'm no wetback. My name is Juan García de Soto yo Soto-mayor. I am Chileno."

"Okay, Don Juan. Just don't get out of line around here. Keep your nose and mouth clean when you talk about the people you work for."

He jerked loose and stepped back, his black eyes hot with anger. His hand slipped inside his shirt and came out with a long thin knife. He balanced it by the point on the heel of his hand, hardly even glancing at it. Then he dropped the hand and caught the handle of the knife while it hung in the air. It was done very fast and without any apparent effort. His hand went up to shoulder height, then snapped forward and the knife sailed through the air and hung quivering in the wood of the window frame.

"Cuidado, señor!" he said with a sharp sneer. "And keep your paws to yourself. Nobody fools with me."

He walked lithely across the room and plucked the knife out of the wood, tossed it in the air, spun on his toes and caught it behind him. With a snap it disappeared under his shirt.

"Neat," I said, "but just a little on the gaudy side."

He strolled up to me smiling derisively.

"And it might get you a broken elbow," I said. "Like this."

I took hold of his right wrist, jerked him off balance, swung to one side and a little behind him, and brought my bent forearm up under the back of his elbow joint. I bore down on it, using my forearm as a fulcrum.

"One hard jerk," I said, "and your elbow joint cracks. A crack is enough. You'd be out of commission as a knife thrower for several months. Make the jerk a little harder and you'd be through permanently. Take Mr. Wade's shoes off."

I let go of him and he grinned at me. "Good trick," he said. "I will remember."

He turned to Wade and reached for one of his shoes, then stopped. There was a smear of blood on the pillow.

"Who cut the boss?"

"Not me, chum. He fell and cut his head on something. It's only a shallow cut. The doctor has been here."

Candy let his breath out slowly. "You see him fall?"

"Before I got here. You like this guy, don't you?"

He didn't answer me. He took the shoes off. We got Wade undressed little by little and Candy dug out a pair of green and silver pajamas. We got Wade into those and got him inside the bed and well covered up. He was still sweaty and still snoring. Candy looked down at him sadly, shaking his sleek head from side to side, slowly.

"Somebody's got to take care of him," he said. "I go change my clothes."

"Get some sleep. I'll take care of him. I can call you if I need you."

He faced me. "You better take care of him good," he said in a quiet voice. "Very good."

He went out of the room. I went into the bathroom and got a wet washcloth and a heavy towel. I turned Wade over a little and spread the towel on the pillow and washed the blood off his head gently so as not to start the bleeding again. Then I could see a sharp shallow cut about two inches long. It was nothing. Dr. Loring had been right that much. It wouldn't have hurt to stitch it but it probably was not really necessary. I found a pair of scissors and cut the hair away enough so that I could put on a strip of adhesive. Then I turned him on his back and washed his face. I guess that was a mistake.

He opened his eyes. They were vague and unfocused at first, then they cleared and he saw me standing beside the bed. His hand moved and went up to his head and felt the adhesive. His lips mumbled something, then his voice cleared up also.

"Who hit me? You?" His hand felt for the adhesive.

"Nobody hit you. You took a fall."

"Took a fall? When? Where?"

"Wherever you telephoned from. You called me. I heard you fall. Over the wire."

"I called you?" He grinned slowly. "Always available, aren't you, fella? What time is it?"

"After one A.M."

"Where's Eileen?"

"Gone to bed. She had it rough."

He thought that over silently. His eyes were full of pain. "Did I—" He stopped and winced.

"You didn't touch her as far as I know. If that's what you mean. You just wandered outdoors and passed out near the fence. Quit talking. Go to sleep."

"Sleep," he said quietly and slowly, like a child reciting its lesson. "What would that be?"

"Maybe a pill would help. Got any?"

"In the drawer. Night table."

I opened it and found a plastic bottle with red capsules in it. Seconal, 1½ grains. Prescription by Dr. Loring. That nice Dr. Loring. Mrs. Roger Wade's prescription.

I shook two of them loose and put the bottle back and poured a glass of water from a thermos jug on the night table. He said one capsule would be enough. He took it and drank some water and lay back and stared at the ceiling again. Time passed. I sat in a chair and watched him. He didn't seem to get sleepy. Then he said slowly:

"I remember something. Do me a favor, Marlowe. I wrote some crazy stuff I don't want Eileen to see. It's on top of the typewriter under the cover. Tear it up for me.

"Sure. That all you remember?"

"Eileen is all right? Positive about that?"

"Yes. She's just tired. Let it ride, Wade. Stop thinking. I shouldn't have asked you."

"Stop thinking, the man says." His voice was a little drowsy now. He was talking as if to himself. "Stop thinking, stop dreaming, stop loving, stop hating. Goodnight, sweet prince. I'll take that other pill."

I gave it to him with some more water. He lay back again, this time with his head turned so that he could see me. "Look, Marlowe, I wrote some stuff I don't want Eileen—"

"You told me already. I'll attend to it when you go to sleep."

"Oh. Thanks. Nice to have you around. Very nice."

Another longish pause. His eyelids were getting heavy.

"Ever kill a man, Marlowe?"

"Yes."

"Nasty feeling, isn't it?"

"Some people like it."

His eyes went shut all the way. Then they opened again, but they looked vague. "How could they?"

I didn't answer. The eyelids came down again, very gradually, like a slow curtain in the theater. He began to snore. I waited a little longer. Then I dimmed the light in the room and went out.

27

I STOPPED OUTSIDE Eileen's door and listened. I didn't
hear any sound of movement inside, so I didn't knock. If
she wanted to know how he was, it was up to her.
Downstairs the living room looked bright and empty. I put
out some of the lights. From over near the front door I
looked up at the balcony. The middle part of the living
room rose to the full height of the house walls and was
crossed by open beams that also supported the balcony.
The balcony was wide and edged on two sides by a solid
railing which looked to be about three and a half feet high.
The top and the uprights were cut square to match the
cross beams. The dining room was through a square arch
closed off by double louvered doors. Above it I guessed
there were servants' quarters. This part of the second floor
was walled off so there would be another stairway reaching
it from the kitchen part of the house. Wade's room was in
the corner over his study. I could see the light from his
open door reflected against the high ceiling and I could see
the top foot of his doorway.

I cut all the lights except in one standing lamp and
crossed to the study. The door was shut but two lamps
were lit, a standing lamp at the end of the leather couch
and a cowled desk lamp. The typewriter was on a heavy
stand under this and beside it on the desk there was a
disorderly mess of yellow paper. I sat in a padded chair
and studied the layout. What I wanted to know was how
he had cut his head. I sat in his desk chair with the phone
at my left hand. The spring was set very weak. If I tilted
back and went over, my head might have caught the corner
of the desk. I moistened my handkerchief and rubbed the
wood. No blood, nothing there. There was a lot of stuff on
the desk, including a row of books between bronze ele-
phants, and an old-fashioned square glass inkwell. I tried
that without result. Not much point to it anyway, because
if someone else had slugged him, the weapon didn't have to

be in the room. And there wasn't anyone else to do it. I stood up and switched on the cornice lights. They reached into the shadowy corners and of course the answer was simple enough after all. A square metal wastebasket was lying on its side over against the wall, with paper spilled. It couldn't have walked there, so it had been thrown or kicked. I tried its sharp corners with my moistened handkerchief. I got the red-brown smear of blood this time. No mystery at all. Wade had fallen over and struck his head on the sharp corner of the wastebasket—a glancing blow most likely—picked himself up and booted the damn thing across the room. Easy.

Then he would have another quick drink. The drinking liquor was on the cocktail table in front of the couch. An empty bottle, another three quarters full, a thermos jug of water and a silver bowl containing water which had been ice cubes. There was only one glass and it was the large economy size.

Having taken his drink he felt a little better. He noticed the phone off the hook in a bleary sort of way and very likely didn't remember any more what he had been doing with it. So he just walked across and put it back in its cradle. The time had been just about right. There is something compulsive about a telephone. The gadget-ridden man of our age loves it, loathes it, and is afraid of it. But he always treats it with respect, even when he is drunk. The telephone is a fetish.

Any normal man would have said hello into the mouth-piece before hanging up, just to be sure. But not necessarily a man who was bleary with drink and had just taken a fall. It didn't matter anyhow. His wife might have done it, she might have heard the fall and the bang as the wastebasket bounced against the wall and come into the study. About that time the last drink would kick him in the face and he would stagger out of the house and across the front lawn and pass out where I had found him. Somebody was coming for him. By this time he didn't know who it was. Maybe the good Dr. Verringer.

So far, so good. So what would his wife do? She couldn't handle him or reason with him and she might well be afraid to try. So she would call somebody to come and help. The servants were out, so it would have to be by the telephone. Well, she *had* called somebody. She had called that nice Dr. Loring. I'd just assumed she called him after I got there. She hadn't said so.

From here on it didn't quite add up. You'd expect her to look for him and find him and make sure he wasn't hurt. It wouldn't hurt him to lie out on the ground on a warm summer night for a while. She couldn't move him. It had taken all I had to do that. But you wouldn't quite expect to find her standing in the open doorway smoking a cigarette, not knowing except very vaguely where he was. Or would you? I didn't know what she had been through with him, how dangerous he was in that condition, how much afraid she might be to go near him. "I've had all of it I can take," she had said to me when I arrived. "You find him." Then she had gone inside and pulled a faint.

It still bothered me, but I had to leave it at that. I had to assume that when she had been up against the situation often enough to know there was nothing she could do about it except to let it ride, then that would be what she would do. Just that. Let it ride. Let him lie out thère on the ground until somebody came around with the physical equipment to handle him.

It still bothered me. It bothered me also that she had checked out and gone into her own room while Candy and I got him upstairs to bed. She said she loved the guy. He was her husband, they had been married for five years, he was a very nice guy indeed when sober—those were her own words. Drunk, he was something else, something to stay away from because he was dangerous. All right, forget it. But somehow it still bothered me. If she was really scared, she wouldn't have been standing there in the open door smoking a cigarette. If she was just bitter and withdrawn and disgusted, she wouldn't have fainted.

There was something else. Another woman, perhaps. Then she had only just found out. Linda Loring? Maybe. Dr. Loring thought so and said so in a very public manner.

I stopped thinking about it and took the cover off the typewriter. The stuff was there, several loose sheets of typed yellow paper that I was supposed to destroy so Eileen wouldn't see them. I took them over to the couch and decided I deserved a drink to go with the reading matter. There was a half bath off the study. I rinsed the tall glass out and poured a libation and sat down with it to read. And what I read was really wild. Like this:

28

The moon's four days off the full and there's a square patch of moonlight on the wall and it's looking at me like a big blind milky eye, a wall eye. Joke. Goddam silly simile. Writers. Everything has to be like something else. My head is as fluffy as whipped cream but not as sweet. More similes. I could vomit just thinking about the lousy racket. I could vomit anyway. I probably will. Don't push me. Give me time. The worms in my solar plexus crawl and crawl and crawl. I would be better off in bed but there would be a dark animal underneath the bed and the dark animal would crawl around rustling and hump himself and bump the underside of the bed, then I would let out a yell that wouldn't make any sound except to me. A dream yell, a yell in a nightmare. There is nothing to be afraid of and I am not afraid because there is nothing to be afraid of, but just the same I was lying like that once in bed and the dark animal was doing it to me, bumping himself against the underside of the bed, and I had an orgasm. That disgusted me more than any other of the nasty things I have done.

I'm dirty. I need a shave. My hands are shaking. I'm sweating. I smell foul to myself. The shirt under my arms is wet and on the chest and back. The sleeves are wet in the folds of the elbows. The glass on the table is empty. It would take both hands to pour the stuff now. I could get one out of the bottle maybe to brace me. The taste of the stuff is sickening. And it wouldn't get me anywhere. In the end I won't be able to sleep even and the whole world will moan in the horror of tortured nerves. Good stuff, huh, Wade? More.

It's all right for the first two or three days and then it is negative. You suffer and you take a drink and for a little while it is better, but the price keeps getting higher and higher and what you get for it is less and less and then there is always the point where you get nothing but nausea. Then you call Verringer. All right, Verringer, here I come. There isn't any Verringer any more. He's gone to Cuba or he is dead. The queen has killed him. Poor old Verringer, what a fate, to die in bed with a queen—that kind of queen. Come on, Wade, let's get up and go places. Places where we haven't ever been and aren't ever going back to when we have been. Does this sentence make sense? No. Okay, I'm not asking any money for it. A short pause here for a long commercial.

Well, I did it. I got up. What a man. I went over to the couch and here I am kneeling beside the couch with my hands down on it and my face in my hands, crying. Then I prayed and despised myself for praying. Grade Three drunk despising himself. What the hell are you praying to, you fool? If a well man prays, that's faith. A sick man prays and he is just scared. Nuts to prayer. This is the world you made and you make it all by yourself and what little outside help you got—well you made that too. Stop praying, you jerk. Get up on your feet and take that drink. It's too late for anything else now.

Well, I took it. Both hands. Poured it in the glass too. Hardly spilled a drop. Now if I can hold it without vomiting. Better add some water. Now lift it slow. Easy, not too much at a time. It gets warm. It gets hot. If I could stop sweating. The glass is empty. It's down on the table again.

There's a haze over the moonlight but I set that glass down in spite of it, carefully, carefully, like a spray of roses in a tall vase. The roses nod their heads with dew. Maybe I'm a rose. Brother, have I got dew. Now to get upstairs. Maybe a short one straight for the journey. No? Okay, whatever you say. Take it upstairs when I get there. If I get there, something to look forward to. If I make it upstairs I am entitled to compensation. A token of regard from me to me. I have such a beautiful love for myself—and the sweet part of it—no rivals.

Double space. Been up and came down. Didn't like it upstairs. The altitude makes my heart flutter. But I keep hitting these typewriter keys. What a magician is the subconscious. If only it would work regular hours. There was moonlight upstairs too. Probably the same moon. No variety about the moon. It comes and goes like the milkman and the moon's milk is always the same. The milk's moon is always—hold it, chum. You've got your feet crossed. This is no time to get involved in the case history of the moon. You got enough case history to take care of the whole damn valley.

She was sleeping on her side without sound. Her knees drawn up. Too still I thought. You always make some sound when you sleep. Maybe not asleep, maybe just trying to sleep. If I went closer I would know. Might fall down too. One of her eyes opened—or did it? She looked at me or did she? No. Would have sat up and said, Are you sick, darling? Yes, I am sick, darling. But don't give it a thought, darling, because this sick is my sick and not your sick, and let you sleep still and lovely and never remember and no slime from me to you and nothing come near you that is grim and gray and ugly.

You're a louse, Wade. Three adjectives, you lousy writer. Can't you even stream-of-consciousness you louse without getting it in three adjectives for Chrissake? I came downstairs again holding on to the rail. My guts lurched with the steps and I held them together with a promise. I made the main floor and I made the study and I made the couch and I waited for my heart to slow down. The bottle is handy. One thing you can say about Wade's arrangements the bottle is always handy. Nobody hides it, nobody locks it up. Nobody says, Don't you think you've had enough, darling? You'll make yourself sick, darling. Nobody says that. Just sleep on side softly like roses.

I gave Candy too much money. Mistake. Should have started him with a bag of peanuts and worked up to a banana. Then a little real change, slow and easy, always keep him eager. You give him a big slug of the stuff to begin with and pretty soon he has a stake. He can live in Mexico for a month, live high wide and nasty, on what it costs here for a day. So when he gets that stake, what does he do? Well, does a man ever have enough money, if he thinks he can get more? Maybe it's all right. Maybe I ought to kill the shiny-

eyed bastard. A good man died for me once, why not a
cockroach in a white jacket?

Forget Candy. There's always a way to blunt a
needle. The other I shall never forget. It's carved on
my liver in green fire.

Better telephone. Losing control. Feel them
jumping, jumping, jumping. Better call someone quick
before the pink things crawl on my face. Better call,
call, call. Call Sioux City Sue. Hello, Operator, give
me Long Distance. Hello, Long Distance, get me Sioux
City Sue. What's her number? No have number, just
name, Operator. You'll find her walking along Tenth
Street, on the shady side, under the tall corn trees with
their spreading ears. ... All right, Operator, all right.
Just cancel the whole program and let me tell you
something, I mean, ask you something. Who's going to
pay for all those snazzy parties Gifford is throwing in
London, if you cancel my long distance call? Yeah, you
think your job is solid. You think. Here, I better talk
to Gifford direct. Get him on the line. His valet just
brought in his tea. If he can't talk we'll send over
somebody that can.

Now what did I write that for? What was I trying
not to think about? Telephone. Better telephone now.
Getting very bad, very, very ...

That was all. I folded the sheets up small and pushed
them down into my inside breast pocket behind the note
case. I went over to the french windows and opened them
wide and stepped out onto the terrace. The moonlight was
a little spoiled. But it was summer in Idle Valley and
summer is never quite spoiled. I stood there looking at
the motionless colorless lake and thought and wondered.
Then I heard a shot.

29

ON THE BALCONY two lighted doors were open now—
Eileen's and his. Her room was empty. There was a sound

of struggling from his and I came through the door in a jump to find her bending over the bed wrestling with him. The black gleam of a gun shot up into the air, two hands, a large male hand and a woman's small hand were both holding it, neither by the butt. Roger was sitting up in bed and leaning forward pushing. She was in a pale blue house coat, one of those quilted things, her hair was all over her face and now she had both hands on the gun and with a quick jerk she got it away from him. I was surprised that she had the strength, even dopey as he was. He fell back glaring and panting and she stepped away and bumped into me.

She stood there leaning against me, holding the gun with both hands pressed hard against her body. She was racked with panting sobs. I reached around her body and put my hand on the gun.

She spun around as if it took that to make her realize I was there. Her eyes widened and her body sagged against me. She let go of the gun. It was a heavy clumsy weapon, a Webley double-action hammerless. The barrel was warm. I held her with one arm, dropped the gun in my pocket, and looked past her head at him. Nobody said anything.

Then he opened his eyes and that weary smile played on his lips. "Nobody hurt," he muttered. "Just a wild shot into the ceiling."

I felt her go stiff. Then she pulled away. Her eyes were focused and clear. I let her go.

"Roger," she said in a voice not much more than a sick whisper, "did it have to be that?"

He stared owlishly, licked his lip and said nothing. She went and leaned against the dressing table. Her hand moved mechanically and threw the hair back from her face. She shuddered once from head to foot, shaking her head from side to side. "Roger," she whispered again. "Poor Roger. Poor miserable Roger."

He was staring straight up at the ceiling now. "I had a nightmare," he said slowly. "Somebody with a knife was leaning over the bed. I don't know who. Looked a little like Candy. Couldn't of been Candy."

"Of course not, darling," she said softly. She left the dressing table and sat down on the side of the bed. She put her hand out and began to stroke his forehead. "Candy has gone to bed long ago. And why would Candy have a knife?"

"He's a Mex. They all have knives," Roger said in the same remote impersonal voice. "They like knives. And he doesn't like me."

"Nobody likes you," I said brutally.

She turned her head swiftly. "Please—please don't talk like that. He didn't know. He had a dream—"

"Where was the gun?" I growled, watching her, not paying any attention to him.

"Night table. In the drawer." He turned his head and met my stare. There hadn't been any gun in the drawer, and he knew I knew it. The pills had been in there and some odds and ends, but no gun.

"Or under the pillow," he added. "I'm vague about it. I shot once—" he lifted a heavy hand and pointed—"up there."

I looked up. There seemed to be a hole in the ceiling plaster all right. I went where I could look up at it. Yes. The kind of hole a bullet might make. From that gun it would go on through, into the attic. I went back close to the bed and stood looking down at him, giving him the hard eye.

"Nuts. You meant to kill yourself. You didn't have any nightmare. You were swimming in a sea of self-pity. You didn't have any gun in the drawer or under your pillow either. You got up and got the gun and got back into bed and there you were all ready to wipe out the whole messy business. But I don't think you had the nerve. You fired a shot not meant to hit anything. And your wife came running—that's what you wanted. Just pity and sympathy, pal. Nothing else. Even the struggle was mostly fake. She couldn't take a gun away from you if you didn't want her to."

"I'm sick," he said. "But you could be right. Does it matter?"

"It matters like this. They'd put you in the psycho ward, and believe me, the people who run that place are about as sympathetic as Georgia chain-gang guards."

Eileen stood up suddenly. "That's enough," she said sharply. "He *is* sick, and you know it."

"He wants to be sick. I'm just reminding him of what it would cost him."

"This is not the time to tell him."

"Go on back to your room."

Her blue eyes flashed. "How dare you—"

"Go on back to your room. Unless you want me to call the police. These things are supposed to be reported."

He almost grinned. "Yeah, call the police," he said, "like you did on Terry Lennox."

I didn't pay any attention to that. I was still watching her. She looked exhausted now, and frail, and very beautiful. The moment of flashing anger was gone. I put a hand out and touched her arm. "It's all right," I said. "He won't do it again. Go back to bed."

She gave him a long look and went out of the room. When the open door was empty of her I sat down on the side of the bed where she had been sitting.

"More pills?"

"No thanks. It doesn't matter whether I sleep. I feel a lot better."

"Did I hit right about that shot? It was just a crazy bit of acting?"

"More or less." He turned his head away. "I guess I was lightheaded."

"Nobody can stop you from killing yourself, if you really want to. I realize that. So do you."

"Yes." He was still looking away. "Did you do what I asked you—that stuff in the typewriter?"

"Uh huh. I'm surprised you remember. It's pretty crazy writing. Funny thing, it's clearly typed."

"I can always do that—drunk or sober—up to a point anyway."

"Don't worry about Candy," I said. "You're wrong about his not liking you. And I was wrong to say nobody did. I was trying to jar Eileen, make her mad."

"Why?"

"She pulled one faint already tonight."

He shook his head slightly. "Eileen never faints."

"Then it was a phony."

He didn't like that either.

"What did you mean—a good man died for you?" I asked.

He frowned, thinking about it. "Just rubbish. I told you I had a dream—"

"I'm talking about that guff you typed out."

He looked at me now, turning his head on the pillow as if it had enormous weight. "Another dream."

"I'll try again. What's Candy got on you?"

"Shove it, Jack," he said, and closed his eyes.

I got up and closed the door. "You can't run forever, Wade. Candy could be a blackmailer, sure. Easy. He could even be nice about it—like you and lift your dough at the same time. What is it—a woman?"

"You believe that fool, Loring," he said with his eyes closed.

"Not exactly. What about the sister—the one that's dead?"

It was a wild pitch in a sense but it happened to split the plate. His eyes snapped wide open. A bubble of saliva showed on his lips.

"Is that—why you're here?" he asked slowly, and in a whispering voice.

"You know better. I was invited. You invited me."

His head rolled back and forth on the pillow. In spite of the seconal he was eaten up by his nerves. His face was covered with sweat.

"I'm not the first loving husband who has been an adulterer. Leave me alone, damn you. Leave me alone."

I went into the bathroom and got a face towel and wiped his face off. I grinned at him sneeringly. I was the heel to end all heels. Wait until the man is down, then kick him and kick him again. He's weak. He can't resist or kick back.

"One of these days we'll get together on it," I said.

"I'm not crazy," he said.

"You just hope you're not crazy."

"I've been living in hell."

"Oh sure. That's obvious. The interesting point is why. Here—take this." I had another seconal out of the night table and another glass of water. He got up on one elbow and grabbed for the glass and missed it by a good four inches. I put it in his hand. He managed to drink and swallow his pill. Then he lay back flat and deflated, his face drained of emotion. His nose had that pinched look. He could almost have been a dead man. He wasn't throwing anybody down any stairs tonight. Most likely not any night.

When his eyelids got heavy I went out of the room. The

weight of the Webley was against my hip, dragging at my pocket. I started back downstairs again. Eileen's door was open. Her room was dark but there was enough light from the moon to frame her standing just inside the door. She called out something that sounded like a name, but it wasn't mine. I stepped close to her.

"Keep your voice down," I said. "He's gone back to sleep."

"I always knew you would come back," she said softly. "Even after ten years."

I peered at her. One of us was goofy.

"Shut the door," she said in the same caressing voice. "All these years I have kept myself for you."

I turned and shut the door. It seemed like a good idea at the moment. When I faced her she was already falling towards me. So I caught her. I damn well had to. She pressed herself hard against me and her hair brushed my face. Her mouth came up to be kissed. She was trembling. Her lips opened and her teeth opened and her tongue darted. Then her hands dropped and jerked at something and the robe she was wearing came open and underneath it she was as naked as September Morn but a darn sight less coy.

"Put me on the bed," she breathed.

I did that. Putting my arms around her I touched bare skin, soft skin, soft yielding flesh. I lifted her and carried her the few steps to the bed and lowered her. She kept her arms around my neck. She was making some kind of a whistling noise in her throat. Then she thrashed about and moaned. This was murder. I was as erotic as a stallion. I was losing control. You don't get that sort of invitation from that sort of woman very often anywhere.

Candy saved me. There was a thin squeak and I swung around to see the doorknob moving. I jerked loose and jumped for the door. I got it open and barged out through it and the Mex was tearing along the hall and down the stairs. Halfway down he stopped and turned and leered at me. Then he was gone.

I went back to the door and shut it—from the outside this time. Some kind of weird noises were coming from the woman on the bed, but that's all they were now. Weird noises. The spell was broken.

I went down the stairs fast and crossed into the study

and grabbed the bottle of Scotch and tilted it. When I couldn't swallow any more I leaned against the wall and panted and let the stuff burn in me until the fumes reached my brain.

It was a long time since dinner. It was a long time since anything that was normal. The whiskey hit me hard and fast and I kept guzzling it until the room started to get hazy and the furniture was all in the wrong places and the lamplight was like widlfire or summer lightning. Then I was flat out on the leather couch, trying to balance the bottle on my chest. It seemed to be empty. It rolled away and thumped on the floor.

That was the last incident of which I took any precise notice.

30

A SHAFT OF SUNLIGHT tickled one of my ankles. I opened my eyes and saw the crown of a tree moving gently against a hazed blue sky. I rolled over and leather touched my cheek. An axe split my head. I sat up. There was a rug over me. I threw that off and got my feet on the floor. I scowled at a clock. The clock said a minute short of six-thirty.

I got up on my feet and it took character. It took will power. It took a lot out of me, and there wasn't as much to spare as there once had been. The hard heavy years had worked me over.

I plowed across to the half bath and stripped off my tie and shirt and sloshed cold water in my face with both hands and sloshed it on my head. When I was dripping wet I toweled myself off savagely. I put my shirt and tie back on and reached for my jacket and the gun in the pocket banged against the wall. I took it out and swung the cylinder away from the frame and tipped the cartridges into my hand, five full, one just a blackened shell. Then I thought, what's the use, there are always more of them. So I put them back where they had been before and carried the gun into the study and put it away in one of the drawers of the desk.

When I looked up Candy was standing in the doorway, spick and span in his white coat, his hair brushed back and shining black, his eyes bitter.

"You want some coffee?"

"Thanks."

"I put the lamps out. The boss is okay. Asleep. I shut his door. Why you get drunk?"

"I had to."

He sneered at me. "Didn't make her, huh? Got tossed out on your can, shamus."

"Have it your own way."

"You ain't tough this morning, shamus. You ain't tough at all."

"Get the goddam coffee," I yelled at him.

"Hijo de la puta!"

In one jump I had him by the arm. He didn't move. He just looked at me contemptuously. I laughed and let go of his arm.

"You're right, Candy. I'm not tough at all."

He turned and went out. In no time at all he was back with a silver tray and a small silver pot of coffee on it and sugar and cream and a neat triangular napkin. He set it down on the cocktail table and removed the empty bottle and the rest of the drinking materials. He picked another bottle off the floor.

"Fresh. Just made," he said, and went out.

I drank two cups black. Then I tried a cigarette. It was all right. I still belonged to the human race. Then Candy was back in the room again.

"You want breakfast?" he asked morosely.

"No, thanks."

"Okay, scram out of here. We don't want you around."

"Who's we?"

He lifted the lid of a box and helped himself to a cigarette. He lit it and blew smoke at me insolently.

"I take care of the boss," he said.

"You making it pay?"

He frowned, then nodded. "Oh yes. Good money."

"How much on the side—for not spilling what you know?"

He went back to Spanish. "No entendido."

"You understand all right. How much you shake him for? I bet it's not more than a couple of yards."

"What's that? Couple of yards."

"Two hundred bucks."

He grinned. "You give me couple of yards, shamus. So I don't tell the boss you come out of her room last night."

"That would buy a whole busload of wetbacks like you."

He shrugged that off. "The boss gets pretty rough when he blows his top. Better pay up, shamus."

"Pachuco stuff," I said contemptuously. "All you're touching is the small money. Lots of men play around when they're lit. Anyhow she knows all about it. You don't have anything to sell."

There was a gleam in his eye. "Just don't come round any more, tough boy."

"I'm leaving."

I stood up and walked around the table. He moved enough to keep facing towards me. I watched his hand but he evidently wasn't wearing a knife this morning. When I was close enough I slapped a hand across his face.

"I don't get called a son of a whore by the help, greaseball. I've got business here and I come around whenever I feel like it. Watch your lip from now on. You might get pistol-whipped. That pretty face of yours would never look the same again."

He didn't react at all, not even to the slap. That and being called a greaseball must have been deadly insults to him. But this time he just stood there wooden-faced, motionless. Then without a word he picked up the coffee tray and carried it out.

"Thanks for the coffee," I said to his back.

He kept going. When he was gone I felt the bristles on my chin, shook myself, and decided to be on my way. I had had a skinful of the Wade family.

As I crossed the living room Eileen was coming down the stairs in white slacks and open-toed sandals and a pale blue shirt. She looked at me with complete surprise. "I didn't know you were here, Mr. Marlowe," she said, as though she hadn't seen me for a week and at that time I had just dropped in for tea.

"I put his gun in the desk," I said.

"Gun?" Then it seemed to dawn on her. "Oh, last night

was a little hectic, wasn't it? But I thought you had gone home."

I walked over closer to her. She had a thin gold chain around her neck and some kind of fancy pendant in gold and blue on white enamel. The blue enameled part looked like a pair of wings, but not spread out. Against these there was a broad white enamel and gold dagger that pierced a scroll. I couldn't read the words. It was some kind of military insigne.

"I got drunk," I said. "Deliberately and not elegantly. I was a little lonely."

"You didn't have to be," she said, and her eyes were as clear as water. There wasn't a trace of guile in them.

"A matter of opinion," I said. "I'm leaving now and I'm not sure I'll be back. You heard what I said about the gun?"

"You put it in his desk. It might be a good idea to put it somewhere else. But he didn't really mean to shoot himself, did he?"

"I can't answer that. But next time he might."

She shook her head. "I don't think so. I really don't. You were a wonderful help last night, Mr. Marlowe. I don't know how to thank you."

"You made a pretty good try."

She got pink. Then she laughed. "I had a very curious dream in the night," she said slowly, looking off over my shoulder. "Someone I used to know was here in the house. Someone who has been dead for ten years." Her fingers went up and touched the gold and enamel pendant. "That's why I am wearing this today. He gave it to me."

"I had a curious dream myself," I said. "But I'm not telling mine. Let me know how Roger gets on and if there is anything I can do."

She lowered her eyes and looked into mine. "You said you were not coming back."

"I said I wasn't sure. I may have to come back. I hope I won't. There is something very wrong in this house. And only part of it came out of a bottle."

She stared at me, frowning. "What does that mean?"

"I think you know what I'm talking about."

She thought it over carefully. Her fingers were still touching the pendant gently. She let out a slow patient sigh. "There's always another woman," she said quietly.

"At some time or other. It's not necessarily fatal. We're talking at cross purposes, aren't we? We are not even talking about the same thing, perhaps."

"Could be," I said. She was still standing on the steps, the third step from the bottom. She still had her fingers on the pendant. She still looked like a golden dream. "Especially if you have in mind that the other woman is Linda Loring."

She dropped her hand from the pendant and came down one more step of the stairs.

"Dr. Loring seems to agree with me," she said indifferently. "He must have some source of information."

"You said he had played that scene with half the males in the valley."

"Did I? Well—it was the conventional sort of thing to say at the time." She came down another step.

"I haven't shaved," I said.

That startled her. Then she laughed. "Oh, I wasn't expecting you to make love to me."

"Just what did you expect of me, Mrs. Wade—in the beginning, when you first persuaded me to go hunting? Why me—what have I got to offer?"

"You kept faith," she said quietly. "When it couldn't have been very easy."

"I'm touched. But I don't think that was the reason."

She came down the last step and then she was looking up at me. "Then what was the reason?"

"Or if it was—it was a damn poor reason. Just about the worst reason in the world."

She frowned a tiny frown. "Why?"

"Because what I did—this keeping faith—is something even a fool doesn't do twice."

"You know," she said lightly, "this is getting to be a very enigmatic conversation."

"You're a very enigmatic person, Mrs. Wade. So long and good luck and if you really care anything about Roger, you'd better find him the right kind of doctor—and quick."

She laughed again. "Oh, that was a mild attack last night. You ought to see him in a bad one. He'll be up and working by this afternoon."

"Like hell he will."

"But believe me he will. I know him so well."

I gave her the last shot right in the teeth and it sounded pretty nasty.

"You don't really want to save him, do you? You just want to look as if you are trying to save him."

"That," she said deliberately, "was a very beastly thing to say to me."

She stepped past me and walked through the dining room doors and then the big room was empty and I crossed to the front door and let myself out. It was a perfect summer morning in that bright secluded valley. It was too far from the city to get any smog and cut off by the low mountains from the dampness of the ocean. It was going to be hot later, but in a nice refined exclusive sort of way, nothing brutal like the heat of the desert, not sticky and rank like the heat of the city. Idle Valley was a perfect place to live. Perfect. Nice people with nice homes, nice cars, nice horses, nice dogs, possibly even nice children.

But all a man named Marlowe wanted from it was out. And fast.

31

I WENT HOME AND SHOWERED and shaved and changed clothes and began to feel clean again. I cooked some breakfast, ate it, washed up, swept the kitchen and the service porch, filled a pipe and called the phone answering service. I shot a blank. Why go to the office? There would be nothing there but another dead moth and another layer of dust. In the safe would be my portrait of Madison. I could go down and play with that, and with the five crisp hundred dollar bills that still smelled of coffee. I could do that, but I didn't want to. Something inside me had gone sour. None of it really belonged to me. What was it supposed to buy? How much loyalty can a dead man use? Phooey: I was looking at life through the mists of a hangover.

It was the kind of morning that seems to go on forever. I was flat and tired and dull and the passing minutes seemed to fall into a void, with a soft whirring sound, like spent rockets. Birds chirped in the shrubbery outside and the cars went up and down Laurel Canyon Boulevard endlessly. Usually I wouldn't even hear them. But I was brooding and irritable and mean and oversensitive. I decided to kill the hangover.

Ordinarily I was not a morning drinker. The Southern California climate is too soft for it. You don't metabolize fast enough. But I mixed a tall cold one this time and sat in an easy chair with my shirt open and pecked at a magazine, reading a crazy story about a guy that had two lives and two psychiatrists, one was human and one was some kind of insect in a hive. The guy kept going from one to the other and the whole thing was as crazy as a crumpet, but funny in an off-beat sort of way. I was handling the drink carefully, a sip at a time, watching myself.

It was about noon when the telephone rang and the voice said: "This is Linda Loring. I called your office and your phone service told me to try your home. I'd like to see you."

"Why?"

"I'd rather explain that in person. You go to your office from time to time, I suppose."

"Yeah. From time to time. Is there any money in it?"

"I hadn't thought of it that way. But I have no objection, if you want to be paid. I could be at your office in about an hour."

"Goody."

"What's the matter with you?" she asked sharply.

"Hangover. But I'm not paralyzed. I'll be there. Unless you'd rather come here."

"Your office would suit me better."

"I've got a nice quiet place here. Dead-end street, no near neighbors."

"The implication does not attract me—if I understand you."

"Nobody understands me, Mrs. Loring. I'm enigmatic. Okay, I'll struggle down to the coop."

"Thank you so much." She hung up.

I was slow getting down there because I stopped on the way for a sandwich. I aired out the office and switched on the buzzer and poked my head through the communicating door and she was there already, sitting in the same chair where Mendy Menendez had sat and looking through what could have been the same magazine. She had a tan gabardine suit on today and she looked pretty elegant. She put the magazine aside, gave me a serious look and said:

"Your Boston fern needs watering. I think it needs repotting too. Too many air roots."

I held the door open for her. The hell with the Boston fern. When she was inside and I had let the door swing shut I held the customer's chair for her and she gave the office the usual once-over. I got around to my side of the desk.

"You're establishment isn't exactly palatial," she said. "Don't you even have a secretary?"

"It's a sordid life, but I'm used to it."

"And I shouldn't think very lucrative," she said.

"Oh I don't know. Depends. Want to see a portrait of Madison?"

"A what?"

"A five-thousand-dollar bill. Retainer. I've got it in the safe." I got up and started over there. I spun the knob and opened it and unlocked a drawer inside, opened an envelope, and dropped it in front of her. She stared at it in something like amazement.

"Don't let the office fool you," I said. "I worked for an old boy one time that would cash in at about twenty millions. Even your old man would say hello to him. His office was no better than mine, except he was a bit deaf and had that soundproofing stuff on the ceiling. On the floor brown linoleum, no carpet."

She picked the portrait of Madison up and pulled it between her fingers and turned it over. She put it down again.

"You got this from Terry, didn't you?"

"Gosh, you know everything, don't you Mrs. Loring?"

She pushed the bill away from her, frowning. "He had one. He carried it on him ever since he and Sylvia were married the second time. He called it his mad money. It was not found on his body."

"There could be other reasons for that."

"I know. But how many people carry a five-thousand-dollar bill around with them? How many who could afford to give you that much money would give it to you in this form?"

It wasn't worth answering. I just nodded. She went on brusquely.

"And what were you supposed to do for it, Mr. Marlowe? Or would you tell me? On that last ride down to Tijuana he had plenty of time to talk. You made it very clear the other evening that you didn't believe his confession. Did he give you a list of his wife's lovers so that you might find a murderer among them?"

I didn't answer that either, but for different reasons.

"And would the name of Roger Wade appear on that list by any chance?" she asked harshly. "If Terry didn't kill his wife, the murderer would have to be some violent and irresponsible man, a lunatic or a savage drunk. Only that sort of man could, to use your own repulsive phrase, beat her face into a bloody sponge. Is that why you are making yourself so very useful to the Wades—a regular mother's helper who comes on call to nurse him when he is drunk, to find him when he is lost, to bring him home when he is helpless?"

"Let me set you right on a couple of points, Mrs. Loring. Terry may or may not have given me that beautiful piece of engraving. But he gave me no list and mentioned no names. There was nothing he asked me to do except what you seem to feel sure I did do, drive him to Tijuana. My getting involved with the Wades was the work of a New York publisher who is desperate to have Roger Wade finish his book, which involves keeping him fairly sober, which in turn involves finding out if there is any special trouble that makes him get drunk. If there is and it can be found out, then the next step would be an effort to remove it. I say effort, because the chances are you couldn't do it. But you could try."

"I could tell you in one simple sentence why he gets drunk," she said contemptuously. "That anemic blond show piece he's married to."

"Oh I don't know," I said. "I wouldn't call her anemic."

"Really? How interesting." Her eyes glittered.

I picked up my portrait of Madison. "Don't chew too long on that one, Mrs. Loring. I am not sleeping with the lady. Sorry to disappoint you."

I went over to the safe and put my money away in the locked compartment. I shut the safe and spun the dial.

"On second thought," she said to my back, "I doubt very much that anyone is sleeping with her."

I went back and sat on the corner of the desk. "You're getting bitchy, Mrs. Loring. Why? Are you carrying a torch for our alcoholic friend?"

"I hate remarks like that," she said bitingly. "I hate them. I suppose that idiotic scene my husband made makes you think you have the right to insult me. No, I am not carrying a torch for Roger Wade. I never did—even when he was a sober man who behaved himself. Still less now that he is what he is."

I flopped into my chair, reached for a matchbox, and stared at her. She looked at her watch.

"You people with a lot of money are really something," I said. "You think anything you choose to say, however nasty, is perfectly all right. You can make sneering remarks about Wade and his wife to a man you hardly know, but if I hand you back a little change, that's an insult. Okay, let's play it low down. Any drunk will eventually turn up with a loose woman. Wade is a drunk, but you're not a loose woman. That's just a casual suggestion your high-bred husband drops to brighten up a cocktail party. He doesn't mean it, he's just saying it for laughs. So we rule you out, and look for a loose woman elsewhere. How far do we have to look, Mrs. Loring—to find one that would involve you enough to bring you down here trading sneers with me? It has to be somebody rather special, doesn't it—otherwise why should you care?"

She sat perfectly silent, just looking. A long half minute went by. The corners of her mouth were white and her hands were rigid on her gabardine bag that matched her suit.

"You haven't exactly wasted your time, have you?" she said at last. "How convenient that this publisher should have thought of employing you! So Terry named no names to you! Not a name. But it really didn't matter, did it, Mr. Marlowe? Your instinct was unerring. May I ask what you propose to do next?"

"Nothing."

"Why, what a waste of talent! How can you reconcile it

with your obligation to your portrait of Madison? Surely there must be something you can do."

"Just between the two of us," I said, "you're getting pretty corny. So Wade knew your sister. Thanks for telling me, however indirectly. I already guessed it. So what? He's just one of what was most likely a fairly rich collection. Let's leave it there. And let's get around to why you wanted to see me. That kind of got lost in the shuffle didn't it?"

She stood up. She glanced at her watch once more. "I have a car downstairs. Could I prevail upon you to drive home with me and drink a cup of tea?"

"Go on," I said. "Let's have it."

"Do I sound so suspicious? I have a guest who would like to make your acquaintance."

"The old man?"

"I don't call him that," she said evenly.

I stood up and leaned across the desk. "Honey, you're awful cute sometimes. You really are. Is it all right if I carry a gun?"

"Surely you're not afraid of an old man." She wrinkled her lip at me.

"Why not? I'll bet you are—plenty."

She sighed. "Yes, I'm afraid I am. I always have been. He can be rather terrifying."

"Maybe I'd better take two guns," I said, then wished I hadn't.

32

IT WAS THE DAMNDEST-LOOKING HOUSE I ever saw. It was a square gray box three stories high, with a mansard roof, steeply sloped and broken by twenty or thirty double dormer windows with a lot of wedding cake decoration around them and between them. The entrance had double stone pillars on each side but the cream of the joint was an outside spiral staircase with a stone railing, topped by a tower room from which there must have been a view the whole length of the lake.

The motor yard was paved with stone. What the place really seemed to need was a half mile of poplar-lined driveway and a deer park and a wild garden and a terrace on three levels and a few hundred roses outside the library window and a long green vista from every window ending in forest and silence and quiet emptiness. What it had was a wall of fieldstone around a comfortable ten or fifteen acres, which is a fair hunk of real estate in our crowded little country. The driveway was lined with a cypress hedge trimmed round. There were all sorts of ornamental trees in clumps here and there and they didn't look like California trees. Imported stuff. Whoever built that place was trying to drag the Atlantic seaboard over the Rockies. He was trying hard, but he hadn't made it.

Amos, the middle-aged colored chauffeur, stopped the Caddy gently in front of the pillared entrance, hopped out, and came around to hold the open door for Mrs. Loring. I got out first and helped him hold it. I helped her get out. She had hardly spoken to me since we got into the car in front of my building. She looked tired and nervous. Maybe this idiotic hunk of architecture depressed her. It would have depressed a laughing jackass and made it coo like a mourning dove.

"Who built this place?" I asked her. "And who was he mad at?"

She finally smiled. "Hadn't you seen it before?"

"Never been this far into the valley."

She walked me over to the other side of the driveway and pointed up. "The man who built it jumped out of that tower room and landed about where you are standing. He was a French count named La Tourelle and unlike most French counts he had a lot of money. His wife was Ramona Desborough, who was not exactly threadbare herself. In the silent-picture days she made thirty thousand a week. La Tourelle built this place for their home. It's supposed to be a miniature of the Château de Blois. You know that, of course."

"Like the back of my hand," I said. "I remember now. It was one of those Sunday paper stories once. She left him and he killed himself. There was some kind of queer will too, wasn't there?"

She nodded. "He left his ex-wife a few millions for carfare and tied the rest up in a trust. The estate was to be kept on just as it was. Nothing was to be changed, the dining table was to be laid in style every night, and nobody was to be allowed inside the grounds except the servants and the lawyers. The will was broken, of course. Eventually the estate was carved up to some extent and when I married Dr. Loring my father gave it to me for a wedding present. It must have cost him a fortune merely to make it fit to live in again. I loathe it. I always have."

"You don't have to stay here, do you?"

She shrugged in a tired sort of way. "Part of the time, at least. One of his daughters has to show him some sign of stability. Dr. Loring likes it here."

"He would. Any guy who could make the kind of scene he made at Wade's house ought to wear spats with his pajamas."

She arched her eyebrows. "Why, thank you for taking such an interest, Mr. Marlowe. But I think enough has been said on that subject. Shall we go in? My father doesn't like to be kept waiting."

We crossed the driveway again and went up the stone steps and half of the big double doors swung open noiselessly and an expensive and very snooty looking character stood aside for us to enter. The hallway was bigger than all the floor space in the house I was living in. It had a tesselated floor and there seemed to be stained-glass windows at the back and if there had been any light coming through them I might have been able to see what else was there. From the hallway we went through some more double carved doors into a dim room that couldn't have been less than seventy feet long. A man was sitting there waiting, silent. He stared at us coldly.

"Am I late, Father?" Mrs. Loring asked hurriedly. "This is Mr. Philip Marlowe. Mr. Harlan Potter."

The man just looked at me and moved his chin down about half an inch.

"Ring for tea," he said. "Sit down, Mr. Marlowe."

I sat down and looked at him. He looked at me like an entomologist looking at a beetle. Nobody said anything. There was complete silence until the tea came. It was put down on a huge silver tray on a Chinese table. Linda sat at a table and poured.

"Two cups," Harlan Potter said. "You can have your tea in another room, Linda."

"Yes, Father. How do you like your tea, Mr. Marlowe?"

"Any way at all," I said. My voice seemed to echo off into the distance and get small and lonely.

She gave the old man a cup and then gave me a cup. Then she stood up silently and went out of the room. I watched her go. I took a sip of tea and got a cigarette out.

"Don't smoke, please. I am subject to asthma."

I put the cigarette back in the pack. I stared at him. I don't know how it feels to be worth a hundred million or so, but he didn't look as if he was having any fun. He was an enormous man, all of six feet five and built to scale. He wore a gray tweed suit with no padding. His shoulders didn't need any. He wore a white shirt and a dark tie and no display handkerchief. A spectacle case showed in the outside breast pocket. It was black, like his shoes. His hair was black too, no gray at all. It was brushed sideways across his skull in a MacArthur sweep. And I had a hunch there was nothing under it but bare skull. His eyebrows were thick and black. His voice seemed to come from a long way off. He drank his tea as if he hated it.

"It will save time, Mr. Marlowe, if I put my position before you. I believe you are interfering in my affairs. If I am correct, I propose to stop it."

"I don't know enough about your affairs to interfere in them, Mr. Potter."

"I disagree."

He drank some more tea and put the cup aside. He leaned back in the big chair he was sitting in and took me to pieces with his hard gray eyes.

"I know who you are, naturally. And how you make your living—if you make one—and how you became involved with Terry Lennox. It has been reported to me that you helped Terry get out of the country, that you have doubts about his guilt, and that you have since made contact with a man who was known to my dead daughter. For what purpose has not been explained to me. Explain it."

"If the man has a name," I said, "name it."

He smiled very slightly but not as if he was falling for me. "Wade. Roger Wade. Some sort of writer, I believe. A writer, they tell me, of rather prurient books which I should not be interested to read. I further understand that this man is a dangerous alcoholic. That may have given you a strange notion."

"Maybe you had better let me have my own notions, Mr. Potter. They are not important, naturally, but they're all I have. First, I do not believe Terry killed his wife, because of the way it was done and because I don't think he was that kind of man. Second, I didn't make contact with Wade. I was asked to live in his house and do what I could to keep him sober while he finished a job of writing. Third, if he is a dangerous alcoholic, I haven't seen any sign of it. Fourth, my first contact was at the request of his New York publisher and I didn't at that time have any idea that Roger Wade even knew your daughter. Fifth, I refused this offer of employment and then Mrs. Wade asked me to find her husband who was away somewhere taking a cure. I found him and took him home."

"Very methodical," he said dryly.

"I'm not finished being methodical, Mr. Potter. Sixth—you or someone on your instructions sent a lawyer named Sewell Endicott to get me out of jail. He didn't say who sent him, but there wasn't anyone else in the picture. Seventh, when I got out of jail a hoodlum named Mendy Menendez pushed me around and warned me to keep my nose clean and gave me a song and dance about how Terry had saved his life and the life of a gambler at Las Vegas named Randy Starr. The story could be true for all I know. Menendez pretended to be sore that Terry hadn't asked him for help getting to Mexico and had asked a punk like me instead. He, Menendez, could have done it two ways from the jack by lifting one finger, and done it much better."

"Surely," Harlan Potter said with a bleak smile, "you are not under the impression that I number Mr. Menendez and Mr. Starr among my acquaintances."

"I wouldn't know, Mr. Potter. A man doesn't make your kind of money in any way I can understand. The next person to warn me off the courthouse lawn was your daughter, Mrs. Loring. We met by accident at a bar and we spoke because we were both drinking gimlets, Terry's favorite drink, but an uncommon one around here. I didn't know who she was until she told me. I told her a little of how I felt about Terry and she gave me the idea that I would have a short unhappy career if I got you mad. Are you mad, Mr. Potter?"

"When I am," he said coldly, "you will not have to ask me. You will be in no uncertainty about it."

"What I thought. I've been kind of expecting the goon squad to drop around, but they haven't shown so far. I haven't been bothered by the cops either. I could have been. I could have been given a rough time. I think all you wanted, Mr. Potter, was quiet. Just what have I done to disturb you?"

He grinned. It was a sour kind of grin, but it was a grin. He put his long yellow fingers together and crossed a leg over his knee and leaned back comfortably.

"A pretty good pitch, Mr. Marlowe, and I have let you make it. Now listen to me. You are exactly right in thinking all I want is quiet. It's quite possible that your connection with the Wades may be incidental, accidental, and coincidental. Let it remain so. I am a family man in an age when it means almost nothing. One of my daughters married a Bostonian prig and the other made a number of foolish marriages, the last being with a complaisant pauper who allowed her to live a worthless and immoral life until he suddenly and for no good reason lost his self-control and murdered her. You think that impossible to accept because of the brutality with which it was done. You are wrong. He shot her with a Mauser automatic, the very gun he took with him to Mexico. And after he shot her he did what he did in order to cover the bullet wound. I admit the brutality of this, but remember the man had been in a war, had been badly wounded, had suffered a great deal and seen others suffer. He may not have intended to kill her. There may have been some sort of scuffle, since the gun belonged to my daughter. It was a small but powerful gun, 7.65 m/m caliber, a model called P.P.K. The bullet went completely through her head and lodged in the wall behind a chintz curtain. It was not found immediately and the fact was not published at all. Now let us consider the situation." He broke off and stared at me. "Are you very badly in need of a cigarette?"

"Sorry, Mr. Potter. I took it out without thinking. Force of habit." I put the cigarette back for the second time.

"Terry had just killed his wife. He had ample motive from the rather limited police point of view. But he also had an excellent defense—that it was her gun in her possession and that he tried to take it away from her and failed and she shot herself with it. A good trial lawyer could have done a lot with that. He would probably have been acquitted. If he had called me up then, I would have helped him. But by making the murder a brutal affair to cover the traces of the bullet, he made it impossible. He had to run away and even that he did clumsily."

"He certainly did, Mr. Potter. But he called you up in Pasadena first, didn't he? He told me he did."

The big man nodded. "I told him to disappear and I would still see what I could do. I didn't want to know where he was. That was imperative. I could not hide a criminal."

"Sounds good, Mr. Potter."

"Do I detect a note of sarcasm? No matter. When I learned the details there was nothing to be done. I could not permit the sort of trial that kind of killing would result in. To be frank, I was very glad when I learned that he had shot himself in Mexico and left a confession."

"I can understand that, Mr. Potter."

He beetled his eyebrows at me. "Be careful, young man. I don't like irony. Can you understand now that I cannot tolerate any further investigation of any sort by any person? And why I have used all my influence to make what investigation there was as brief as possible and as little publicized as possible?"

"Sure—if you're convinced he killed her."

"Of course he killed her. With what intent is another matter. It is no longer important. I am not a public character and I do not intend to be. I have always gone to a great deal of trouble to avoid any kind of publicity. I have influence but I don't abuse it. The District Attorney of Los Angeles County is an ambitious man who has too much good sense to wreck his career for the notoriety of the moment. I see a glint in your eye, Marlowe. Get rid of it. We live in what is called a democracy, rule by the majority of the people. A fine ideal if it could be made to work. The people elect, but the party machines nominate, and the party machines to be effective must spend a great deal of money. Somebody has to give it to them, and that somebody, whether it be an individual, a financial group, a trade union or what have you, expects some consideration in return. What I and people of my kind expect is to be allowed to live our lives in decent privacy. I own newspapers, but I don't like them. I regard them as a constant menace to whatever privacy we have left. Their constant yelping about a free press means, with a few honorable exceptions, freedom to peddle scandal, crime, sex, sensationalism, hate, innuendo, and the political and financial uses of propaganda. A newspaper is a business out to make money through advertising revenue. That is predicated on its circulation and you know what the circulation depends on."

I got up and walked around my chair. He eyed me with cold attention. I sat down again. I needed a little luck. Hell, I needed it in carload lots.

"Okay, Mr. Potter, what goes from here?"

He wasn't listening. He was frowning at his own thoughts. "There's a peculiar thing about money," he went on. "In large quantities it tends to have a life of its own, even a conscience of its own. The power of money becomes very difficult to control. Man has always been a venal animal. The growth of populations, the huge costs of wars, the incessant pressure of confiscatory taxation—all these things make him more and more venal. The average man is tired and scared, and a tired, scared man can't afford ideals. He has to buy food for his family. In our time we have seen a shocking decline in both public and private morals. You can't expect quality from people whose lives are a subjection to a lack of quality. You can't have quality with mass production. You don't want it because it lasts too long. So you substitute styling, which is a commercial swindle intended to produce artificial obsolescence. Mass production couldn't sell its goods next year unless it made what it sold this year look unfashionable a year from now. We have the whitest kitchens and the most shining bathrooms in the world. But in the lovely white kitchen the average American housewife can't produce a meal fit to eat, and the lovely shining bathroom is mostly a receptacle for deodorants, laxatives, sleeping pills, and the products of that confidence racket called the cosmetic industry. We make the finest packages in the world, Mr. Marlowe. The stuff inside is mostly junk."

He took out a large white handkerchief and touched his temples with it. I was sitting there with my mouth open, wondering what made the guy tick. He hated everything.

"It's a little too warm for me in these parts," he said. "I'm used to a cooler climate. I'm beginning to sound like an editorial that has forgotten the point it wanted to make."

"I got your point all right, Mr. Potter. You don't like the way the world is going so you use what power you have to close off a private corner to live in as near as possible to the way you remember people lived fifty years ago before the age of mass production. You've got a hundred million dollars and all it has bought you is a pain in the neck."

He pulled the handkerchief taut by two opposite corners, then crumpled it into a ball and stuffed it in a pocket.

"And then?" he asked shortly.

"That's all there is, there isn't any more. You don't care who murdered your daughter, Mr. Potter. You wrote her off as a bad job long ago. Even if Terry Lennox didn't kill her, and the real murderer is still walking around free, you don't care. You wouldn't want him caught, because that would revive the scandal and there would have to be a trial and his defense would blow your privacy as high as the Empire State Building. Unless, of course, he was obliging enough to commit suicide, before there was any trial. Preferably in Tahiti or Guatemala or the middle of the Sahara Desert. Anywhere where the County would hate the expense of sending a man to verify what had happened."

He smiled suddenly, a big rugged smile with a reasonable amount of friendliness in it.

"What do you want from me, Marlowe?"

"If you mean how much money, nothing. I didn't ask myself here. I was brought. I told the truth about how I met Roger Wade. But he did know your daughter and he does have a record of violence, although I haven't seen any of it. Last night the guy tried to shoot himself. He's a haunted man. He has a massive guilt complex. If I happened to be looking for a good suspect, he might do. I realize he's only one of many, but he happens to be the only one I've met."

He stood up and standing up he was really big. Tough too. He came over and stood in front of me.

"A telephone call, Mr. Marlowe, would deprive you of your license. Don't fence with me. I won't put up with it."

"Two telephone calls and I'd wake up kissing the gutter—with the back of my head missing."

He laughed harshly. "I don't operate that way. I suppose in your quaint line of business it is natural for you to think so. I've given you too much of my time. I'll ring for the butler to show you out."

"Not necessary," I said, and stood up myself. "I came here and got told. Thanks for the time."

He held his hand out. "Thank you for coming. I think you're a pretty honest sort of fellow. Don't be a hero, young man. There's no percentage in it."

I shook hands with him. He had a grip like a pipe wrench. He smiled at me benignantly now. He was Mr. Big, the winner, everything under control.

"One of these days I might be able to throw some business your way," he said. "And don't go away thinking that I buy politicians or law enforcement officers. I don't have to. Goodbye, Mr. Marlowe. And thank you again for coming."

He stood there and watched me out of the room. I had my hand on the front door when Linda Loring popped out of a shadow somewhere.

"Well?" she asked me quietly. "How did you get on with Father?"

"Fine. He explained civilization to me. I mean how it looks to him. He's going to let it go on for a little while longer. But it better be careful and not interfere with his private life. If it does, he's apt to make a phone call to God and cancel the order."

"You're hopeless," she said.

"Me? I'm hopeless? Lady, take a look at your old man. Compared with him I'm a blue-eyed baby with a brand new rattle."

I went on out and Amos had the Caddy there waiting. He drove me back to Hollywood. I offered him a buck but he wouldn't take it. I offered to buy him the poems of T. S. Eliot. He said he already had them.

33

A WEEK WENT BY and I heard nothing from the Wades. The weather was hot and sticky and the acid sting of the smog had crept as far west as Beverly Hills. From the top of Mulholland Drive you could see it leveled out all over the city like a ground mist. When you were in it you could taste it and smell it and it made your eyes smart. Everybody was griping about it. In Pasadena, where the stuffy millionaires holed up after Beverly Hills was spoiled for them by the movie crowd, the city fathers screamed with rage. Everything was the fault of the smog. If the canary wouldn't sing, if the milkman was late, if the Pekinese had fleas, if an old coot in a starched collar had a heart attack on the way to church, that was the smog. Where I lived it was usually clear in the early morning and nearly always at night. Once in a while a whole day would be clear, nobody quite knew why.

It was on a day like that—it happened to be a Thursday— that Roger Wade called me up. "How are you? This is Wade." He sounded fine.

"Fine, and you?"

"Sober, I'm afraid. Scratching a hard buck. We ought to have a talk. And I think I owe you some dough."

"Nope."

"Well, how about lunch today? Could you make it here somewhere around one?"

"I guess so. How's Candy?"

"Candy?" He sounded puzzled. He must have blacked out plenty that night. "Oh, he helped you put me to bed that night."

"Yeah. He's a helpful little guy—in spots. And Mrs. Wade?"

"She's fine too. She's in town shopping today."

We hung up and I sat and rocked in my swivel chair. I ought to have asked him how the book was going. Maybe you always ought to ask a writer how the book is going.

And then again maybe he gets damned tired of that question.

I had another call in a little while, a strange voice.

"This is Roy Ashterfelt. George Peters told me to call you up, Marlowe."

"Oh yes, thanks. You're the fellow that knew Terry Lennox in New York. Called himself Marston then."

"That's right. He was sure on the sauce. But it's the same guy all right. You couldn't very well mistake him. Out here I saw him in Chasen's one night with his wife. I was with a client. The client knew them. Can't tell you the client's name, I'm afraid."

"I understand. It's not very important now, I guess. What was his first name?"

"Wait a minute while I bite my thumb. Oh yeah, Paul. Paul Marston. And there was one thing more, if it interests you. He was wearing a British Army service badge. Their version of the ruptured duck."

"I see. What happened to him?"

"I don't know. I came west. Next time I saw him he was here too—married to Harlan Potter's somewhat wild daughter. But you know all that."

"They're both dead now. But thanks for telling me."

"Not at all. Glad to help. Does it mean anything to you?"

"Not a thing," I said, and I was a liar. "I never asked him about himself. He told me once he had been brought up in an orphanage. Isn't it just possible you made a mistake?"

"With that white hair and that scarred face, brother? Not a chance. I won't say I never forget a face, but not that one."

"Did he see you?"

"If he did, he didn't let on. Hardly expect him to in the circumstances. Anyhow he might not have remembered me. Like I said, he was always pretty well lit back in New York."

I thanked him some more and he said it was a pleasure and we hung up.

I thought about it for a while. The noise of the traffic outside the building on the boulevard made an unmusical obbligato to my thinking. It was too loud. In summer in hot weather everything is too loud. I got up and shut the lower part of the window and called Detective-Sergeant Green at Homicide. He was obliging enough to be in.

"Look," I said, after the preliminaries, "I heard something about Terry Lennox that puzzles me. A fellow I know used to know him in New York under another name. You check his war record?"

"You guys never learn," Green said harshly. "You just never learn to stay on your own side of the street. That matter is closed, locked up, weighted with lead and dropped in the ocean. Get it?"

"I spent part of an afternoon with Harlan Potter last week at his daughter's house in Idle Valley. Want to check?"

"Doing what?" he asked sourly. "Supposing I believe you."

"Talking things over. I was invited. He likes me. Incidentally, he told me the girl was shot with a Mauser P.P.K. 7.65 m/m. That news to you?"

"Go on."

"Her own gun, chum. Makes a little difference, maybe. But don't get me wrong. I'm not looking into any dark corners. This is a personal matter. Where did he get that wound?"

Green was silent. I heard a door close in the background. Then he said quietly, "Probably in a knife fight south of the border."

"Aw hell, Green, you had his prints. You sent them to Washington like always. You got a report back—like always. All I asked was something about his service record."

"Who said he had one,"

"Well, Mendy Menendez for one. Seems Lennox saved his life one time and that's how he got the wound. He was captured by the Germans and they gave him the face he had."

"Menendez, huh? You believe that son of a bitch? You got a hole in your own head. Lennox didn't have any war record. Didn't have any record of any kind under any name. You satisfied?"

"If you say so," I said. "But I don't see why Menendez would bother to come up here and tell me a yarn and warn me to keep my nose clean on account of Lennox was a pal of him and Randy Starr in Vegas and they didn't want anybody fooling around. After all Lennox was already dead."

"Who knows what a hoodlum figures?" Green asked bitterly. "Or why? Maybe Lennox was in a racket with them before he married all that money, and got respectable. He was a floor manager at Starr's place in Vegas for a while. That's where he met the girl. A smile and a bow and a dinner jacket. Keep the customers happy and keep an eye on the house players. I guess he had class for the job."

"He had charm," I said. "They don't use it in police business. Much obliged, Sergeant. How is Captain Gregorius these days?"

"Retirement leave. Don't you read the papers?"

"Not the crime news, Sergeant. Too sordid."

I started to say goodbye but he chopped me off. "What did Mr. Money want with you?"

"We just had a cup of tea together. A social call. He said he might put some business my way. He also hinted—just hinted, not in so many words—that any cop that looked cross-eyed at me would be facing a grimy future."

"He don't run the police department," Green said.

"He admits it. Doesn't even buy commissioners or D.A.'s, he said. They just kind of curl up in his lap when he's having a doze."

"Go to hell," Green said, and hung up in my ear.

A difficult thing, being a cop. You never know whose stomach it's safe to jump up and down on.

34

THE STRETCH OF BROKEN-PAVED ROAD from the highway to the curve of the hill was dancing in the noon heat and the scrub that dotted the parched land on both sides of it was flour-white with granite dust by this time. The weedy smell was almost nauseating. A thin hot acrid breeze was blowing. I had my coat off and my sleeves rolled up, but the door was too hot to rest an arm on. A tethered horse dozed wearily under a clump of live oaks. A brown Mexican sat on the ground and ate something out of a newspaper. A tumbleweed rolled lazily across the road and came to rest against a piece of granite outcrop, and a lizard that had been there an instant before disappeared without seeming to move at all.

Then I was around the hill on the blacktop and in another country. In five minutes I turned into the driveway of the Wades' house, parked and walked across the flagstones and rang the bell. Wade answered the door himself, in a brown and white checked shirt with short sleeves, pale blue denim slacks, and house slippers. He looked tanned and he looked good. There was an inkstain on his hand and a smear of cigarette ash on one side of his nose.

He led the way into his study and parked himself behind his desk. On it there was a thick pile of yellow typescript. I put my coat on a chair and sat on the couch.

"Thanks for coming, Marlowe. Drink?"

I got that look on my face you get when a drunk asks you to have a drink. I could feel it. He grinned.

"I'll have a coke," he said.

"You pick up fast," I said. "I don't think I want a drink right now. I'll take a coke with you."

He pressed something with his foot and after a while Candy came. He looked surly. He had a blue shirt on and an orange scarf and no white coat. Two-tone black and white shoes, elegant high-wasted gabardine pants.

Wade ordered the cokes. Candy gave me a hard stare and went away.

"Book?" I said, pointing to the stack of paper.

"Yeah. Stinks."

"I don't believe it. How far along?"

"About two thirds of the way—for what it's worth. Which is damn little. You know how a writer can tell when he's washed up?"

"Don't know anything about writers." I filled my pipe.

"When he starts reading his old stuff for inspiration. That's absolute. I've got five hundred pages of typescript here, well over a hundred thousand words. My books run long. The public likes long books. The damn fool public thinks if there's a lot of pages there must be a lot of gold. I don't dare read it over. And I can't remember half of what's in it. I'm just plain scared to look at my own work."

"You look good yourself," I said. "From the other night I wouldn't have believed it. You've got more guts than you think you have."

"What I need right now is more than guts. Something you don't get by wishing for it. A belief in yourself. I'm a spoiled writer who doesn't believe any more. I have a beautiful home, a beautiful wife, and a beautiful sales record. But all I really want is to get drunk and forget."

He leaned his chin in his cupped hands and stared across the desk.

"Eileen said I tried to shoot myself. Was it that bad?"

"You don't remember?"

He shook his head. "Not a damn thing except that I fell down and cut my head. And after a while I was in bed. And you were there. Did Eileen call you?"

"Yeah. Didn't she say?"

"She hasn't been talking to me very much this last week. I guess she's had it. Up to here." He put the edge of one hand against his neck just under his chin. "That show Loring put on here didn't help any."

"Mrs. Wade said it meant nothing."

"Well, she would, wouldn't she? It happened to be the truth, but I don't suppose she believed it when she said it. The guy is just abnormally jealous. You have a drink or two with his wife in the corner and laugh a little and kiss her goodbye and right off he assumes you are sleeping with her. One reason being that he isn't."

"What I like about Idle Valley," I said, "is that everybody is living just a comfortable normal life."

He frowned and then the door opened and Candy came in with two cokes and glasses and poured the cokes. He set one in front of me without looking at me.

"Lunch in half an hour," Wade said, "and where's the white coat?"

"This my day off," Candy said, deadpan. "I ain't the cook, boss."

"Cold cuts or sandwiches and beer will do," Wade said. "The cook's off today, Candy. I've got a friend to lunch."

"You think he is your friend?" Candy sneered. "Better ask your wife."

Wade leaned back in his chair and smiled at him. "Watch your lip, little man. You've got it soft here. I don't often ask a favor of you, do I?"

Candy looked down at the floor. After a moment he looked up and grinned. "Okay, boss. I put the white coat on. I get the lunch, I guess."

He turned softly and went out. Wade watched the door close. Then he shrugged and looked at me.

"We used to call them servants. Now we call them domestic help. I wonder how long it will be before we have to give them breakfast in bed. I'm paying the guy too much money. He's spoiled."

"Wages—or something on the side?"

"Such as what?" he asked sharply.

I got up and handed him some folded yellow sheets. "You'd better read it. Evidently you don't remember asking me to tear it up. It was in your typewriter, under the cover."

He unfolded the yellow pages and leaned back to read them. The glass of coke fizzed unnoticed on the desk in front of him. He read slowly, frowning. When he came to the end he refolded the sheets and ran a finger along the edge.

"Did Eileen see this?" he asked carefully.

"I wouldn't know. She might have."

"Pretty wild, isn't it?"

"I liked it. Especially the part about a good man dying for you."

He opened the paper again and tore it into long strips viciously and dumped the strips into his wastebasket.

"I suppose a drunk will write or say or do anything," he said slowly. "It's meaningless to me. Candy's not blackmailing me. He likes me."

"Maybe you'd better get drunk again. You might remember what you meant. You might remember a lot of things. We've been through this before—that night when the gun went off. I suppose the seconal blanked you out too. You sounded sober enough. But now you pretend not to remember writing that stuff I just gave you. No wonder you can't write your book, Wade. It's a wonder you can stay alive."

He reached sideways and opened a drawer of his desk. His hand fumbled in it and came up with a three-decker check book. He opened it and reached for a pen.

"I owe you a thousand dollars," he said quietly. He wrote in the book. Then on the counterfoil. He tore the check out, came around the desk with it, and dropped it in front of me. "Is that all right?"

I leaned back and looked up at him and didn't touch the check and didn't answer him. His face was tight and drawn. His eyes were deep and empty.

"I suppose you think I killed her and let Lennox take the rap," he said slowly. "She was a tramp all right. But you don't beat a woman's head in just because she's a tramp. Candy knows I went there sometimes. The funny part of it is I don't think he would tell. I could be wrong, but I don't think so."

"Wouldn't matter if he did," I said. "Harlan Potter's friends wouldn't listen to him. Also, she wasn't killed with that bronze thing. She was shot through the head with her own gun."

"She maybe had a gun," he said almost dreamily. "But I didn't know she had been shot. It wasn't published."

"Didn't know or didn't remember?" I asked him. "No, it wasn't published."

"What are you trying to do to me, Marlowe?" His voice was still dreamy, almost gentle. "What do you want me to do? Tell my wife? Tell the police? What good would it do?"

"You said a good man died for you."

"All I meant was that if there had been any real investigation I might have been identified as one—but only one—of the possible suspects. It would have finished me in several ways."

"I didn't come here to accuse you of a murder, Wade. What's eating you is that you're not sure yourself. You have a record of violence to your wife. You black out when you're drunk. It's no argument to say you don't beat a woman's head in just because she's a tramp. That is exactly what somebody did do. And the guy who got credit for the job seemed to me a lot less likely than you."

He walked to the open french windows and stood looking out at the shimmer of heat over the lake. He didn't answer me. He hadn't moved or spoken a couple of minutes later when there was a light knock at the door and Candy came in wheeling a tea wagon, with a crisp white cloth, silver-covered dishes, a pot of coffee, and two bottles of beer.

"Open the beer, boss?" he asked Wade's back.

"Bring me a bottle of whiskey." Wade didn't turn around.

"Sorry, boss. No whiskey."

Wade spun around and yelled at him, but Candy didn't budge. He looked down at the check lying on the cocktail table and his head twisted as he read it. Then he looked up at me and hissed something between his teeth. Then he looked at Wade.

"I go now. This my day off."

He turned and went. Wade laughed.

"So I get it myself," he said sharply, and went.

I lifted one of the covers and saw some neatly trimmed three-cornered sandwiches. I took one and poured some beer and ate the sandwich standing up. Wade came back with a bottle and a glass. He sat down on the couch and poured a stiff jolt and sucked it down. There was the sound of a car going away from the house, probably Candy leaving by the service driveway. I took another sandwich.

"Sit down and make yourself comfortable," Wade said. "We have all afternoon to kill." He had a glow on already. His voice was vibrant and cheerful. "You don't like me, do you, Marlowe?"

"That question has already been asked and answered."

"Know something? You're a pretty ruthless son of a bitch. You'd do anything to find what you want. You'd even make love to my wife while I was helpless drunk in the next room."

"You believe everything that knife thrower tells you?"

He poured some more whiskey into his glass and held it up against the light. "Not everything, no. A pretty color whiskey is, isn't it? To drown in a golden flood—that's not so bad. 'To cease upon the midnight with no pain.' How does that go on? Oh, sorry, you wouldn't know. Too literary. You're some kind of a dick, aren't you? Mind telling me why you're here."

He drank some more whiskey and grinned at me. Then he spotted the check lying on the table. He reached for it and read it over his glass.

"Seems to be made out to somebody named Marlowe. I wonder why, what for. Seems I signed it. Foolish of me. I'm a gullible chap."

"Stop acting," I said roughly. "Where's your wife?"

He looked up politely. "My wife will be home in due

course. No doubt by that time I shall be passed out and she can entertain you at her leisure. The house will be yours."

"Where's the gun?" I asked suddenly.

He looked blank. I told him I had put it in his desk. "Not there now, I'm sure," he said. "You may search if it pleases you. Just don't steal any rubber bands."

I went to the desk and frisked it. No gun. That was something. Probably Eileen had hidden it.

"Look, Wade, I asked you where your wife was. I think she ought to come home. Not for my benefit, friend, for yours. Somebody has to look out for you, and I'll be goddamned if it's going to be me."

He stared vaguely. He was still holding the check. He put his glass down and tore the check across, then again and again, and let the pieces fall to the floor.

"Evidently the amount was too small," he said. "Your services come very high. Even a thousand dollars *and* my wife fail to satisfy you. Too bad, but I can't go any higher. Except on this." He patted the bottle.

"I'm leaving," I said.

"But why? You wanted me to remember. Well—here in the bottle is my memory. Stick around, pal. When I get lit enough I'll tell you about all the women I have murdered."

"All right, Wade. I'll stick around for a while. But not in here. If you need me, just smash a chair against the wall."

I went out and left the door open. I walked across the big living room and out to the patio and pulled one of the chaises into the shadow of the overhang and stretched out on it. Across the lake there was a blue haze against the hills. The ocean breeze had begun to filter through the low mountains to the west. It wiped the air clean and it wiped away just enough of the heat. Idle Valley was having a perfect summer. Somebody had planned it that way. Paradise Incorporated, and also Highly Restricted. Only the nicest people. Absolutely no Central Europeans. Just the cream, the top drawer crowd, the lovely, lovely people. Like the Lorings and the Wades. Pure gold.

35

I LAY THERE FOR HALF AN HOUR trying to make up my mind
what to do. Part of me wanted to let him get good and
drunk and see if anything came out. I didn't think anything much would happen to him in his own study in his
own house. He might fall down again but it would be a
long time. The guy had capacity. And somehow a drunk
never hurts himself very badly. He might get back his
mood of guilt. More likely, this time he would just go
to sleep.

The other part of me wanted to get out and stay out,
but this was the part I never listened to. Because if I ever
had I would have stayed in the town where I was born and
worked in the hardware store and married the boss's
daughter and had five kids and read them the funny paper
on Sunday morning and smacked their heads when they got
out of line and squabbled with the wife about how much
spending money they were to get and what programs they
could have on the radio or TV set. I might even have got
rich—small-town rich, an eight-room house, two cars in the
garage, chicken every Sunday and the *Reader's Digest* on
the living room table, the wife with a cast iron permanent
and me with a brain like a sack of Portland cement. You
take it, friend. I'll take the big sordid dirty crooked city.

I got up and went back to the study. He was just sitting
there staring at nothing, the Scotch bottle more than half
empty, a loose frown on his face and a dull glitter in his
eyes. He looked at me like a horse looking over a fence.

"What d'you want?"

"Nothing. You all right?"

"Don't bother me. I have a little man on my shoulder
telling me stories."

I got another sandwich off the tea wagon and another
glass of beer. I munched the sandwich and drank the beer,
leaning against his desk.

"Know something?" he asked suddenly, and his voice

suddenly seemed much more clear. "I had a male secretary once. Used to dictate to him. Let him go. He bothered me sitting there waiting for me to create. Mistake. Ought to have kept him. Word would have got around I was a homo. The clever boys that write book reviews because they can't write anything else would have caught on and started giving me the buildup. Have to take care of their own, you know. They're all queers, every damn one of them. The queer is the artistic arbiter of our age, chum. The pervert is the top guy now."

"That so? Always been around, hasn't he?"

He wasn't looking at me. He was just talking. But he heard what I said.

"Sure, thousands of years. And especially in all the great ages of art. Athens, Rome, the Renaissance, the Elizabethan Age, the Romantic Movement in France—loaded with them. Queers all over the place. Ever read *The Golden Bough?* No, too long for you. Shorter version though. Ought to read it. Proves our sexual habits are pure conventions like—wearing a black tie with a dinner jacket. Me. I'm a sex writer, but with frills and straight."

He looked up at me and sneered. "You know something? I'm a liar. My heroes are eight feet tall and my heroines have callouses on their bottoms from lying in bed with their knees up. Lace and ruffles, swords and coaches, elegance and leisure, duels and gallant death. All lies. They used perfume instead of soap, their teeth rotted because they never cleaned them, their fingernails smelled of stale gravy. The nobility of France urinated against the walls in the marble corridors of Versailles, and when you finally got several sets of underclothes off the lovely marquise the first thing you noticed was that she needed a bath. I ought to write it that way."

"Why don't you?"

He chuckled. "Sure, and live in a five-room house in Compton—if I was that lucky." He reached down and patted the whiskey bottle. "You're lonely, pal. You need company."

He got up and walked fairly steadily out of the room. I waited, thinking about nothing. A speedboat came racketing down the lake. When it came in sight I could see that it was high out of the water on its step and towing a surfboard with a husky sunburned lad on it. I went over to the french windows and watched it make a sweeping turn. Too fast, the speedboat almost turned over. The surfboard rider danced on one foot trying to hold his balance, then went shooting off into the water. The speedboat drifted to a stop and the man in the water came up to it in a lazy crawl, then went back along the tow rope and rolled himself on to the surfboard.

Wade came back with another bottle of whiskey. The speedboat picked up and went off into the distance. Wade put his fresh bottle down beside the other. He sat down and brooded.

"Christ, you're not going to drink all that, are you?"

He squinted his eyes at me. "Take off, buster. Go on home and mop the kitchen floor or something. You're in my light." His voice was thick again. He had taken a couple in the kitchen, as usual.

"If you want me, holler."

"I couldn't get low enough to want you."

"Yeah, thanks. I'll be around until Mrs. Wade comes home. Ever hear of anybody named Paul Marston?"

His head came up slowly. His eyes focused, but with effort. I could see him fighting for control. He won the fight for the moment. His face became expressionless.

"Never did," he said carefully, speaking very slowly. "Who's he?"

The next time I looked in on him he was asleep, with his mouth open, his hair damp with sweat, and reeking of Scotch. His lips were pulled back from his teeth in a loose grimace and the furred surface of his tongue looked dry.

One of the whiskey bottles was empty. A glass on the table had about two inches in it and the other bottle was about three quarters full. I put the empty on the tea wagon and rolled it out of the room, then went back to close the french windows and turn the slats of the blinds. The speedboat might come back and wake him. I shut the study door.

I wheeled the tea wagon out to the kitchen, which was blue and white and large and airy and empty. I was still hungry. I ate another sandwich and drank what was left of the beer, then poured a cup of coffee and drank that. The beer was flat but the coffee was still hot. Then I went back to the patio. It was quite a long time before the speedboat came tearing down the lake again. It was almost four o'clock when I heard its distant roar swell into an ear-splitting howl of noise. There ought to be a law. Probably was and the guy in the speedboat didn't give a damn. He enjoyed making a nuisance of himself, like other people I was meeting. I walked down to the edge of the lake.

He made it this time. The driver slowed just enough on the turn and the brown lad on the surfboard leaned far out against the centrifugal pull. The surfboard was almost out of the water, but one edge stayed in and then the speedboat straightened out and the surfboard still had a rider and they went back the way they had come and that was that. The waves stirred up by the boat came charging in towards the shore of the lake at my feet. They slapped hard against the piles of the short landing and jumped the tied boat up and down. They were still slapping it around when I turned back to the house.

As I reached the patio I heard a bell chiming from the direction of the kitchen. When it sounded again I decided that only the front door would have chimes. I crossed to it and opened it.

Eileen Wade was standing there looking away from the house. As she turned she said: "I'm sorry, I forgot my key." Then she saw me. "Oh—I thought it was Roger or Candy."

"Candy isn't here. It's Thursday."

She came in and I shut the door. She put a bag down on the table between the two davenports. She looked cool and also distant. She pulled off a pair of white pigskin gloves.

"Is anything wrong?"

"Well, there's a little drinking being done. Not bad. He's asleep on the couch in his study."

"He called you?"

"Yes, but not for that. He asked me to lunch. I'm afraid he didn't have any himself."

"Oh." She sat down slowly on a davenport. "You know, I completely forgot it was Thursday. The cook's away too. How stupid."

"Candy got the lunch before he left. I guess I'll blow now. I hope my car wasn't in your way."

She smiled. "No. There was plenty of room. Won't you have some tea? I'm going to have some."

"All right." I didn't know why I said that. I didn't want any tea. I just said it.

She slipped off a linen jacket. She hadn't worn a hat. "I'll just look in and see if Roger is all right."

I watched her cross to the study door and open it. She stood there a moment and closed the door and came back.

"He's still asleep. Very soundly. I have to go upstairs for a moment. I'll be right down."

I watched her pick up her jacket and gloves and bag and go up the stairs and into her room. The door closed. I crossed to the study with the idea of removing the bottle of hooch. If he was still asleep, he wouldn't need it.

36

THE SHUTTING OF THE FRENCH WINDOWS had made the room stuffy and the turning of the venetian blinds had made it dim. There was an acrid smell on the air and there was too heavy a silence. It was not more than sixteen feet from the door to the couch and I didn't need more than half of that to know a dead man lay on that couch.

He was on his side with his face to the back of the couch, one arm crooked under him and the forearm of the other lying almost across his eyes. Between his chest and the back of the couch there was a pool of blood and in that pool lay the Webley Hammerless. The side of his face was a smeared mask.

I bent over him, peering at the edge of the wide open eye, the bare and gaudy arm, at the inner curve of which I could see the puffed and blackened hole in his head from which the blood oozed still.

I left him like that. His wrist was warm but there was no doubt he was quite dead. I looked around for some kind of note or scribble. There was nothing but the pile of script on the desk. They don't always leave notes. The typewriter was uncovered on its stand. There was nothing in that. Otherwise everything looked natural enough. Suicides prepare themselves in all sorts of ways, some with liquor, some with elaborate champagne dinners. Some in evening clothes, some in no clothes. People have killed themselves on the tops of walls, in ditches, in bathrooms, in the water, over the water, on the water. They have hanged themselves in bars and gassed themselves in garages. This one looked simple. I hadn't heard the shot but it must have gone off when I was down by the lake watching the surfboard rider make his turn. There was plenty of noise. Why that should have mattered to Roger Wade I didn't know. Perhaps it hadn't. The final impulse had coincided with the run of the speedboat. I didn't like it, but nobody cared what I liked.

The torn pieces of the check were still on the floor but I left them. The torn strips of that stuff he had written that other night were in the wastebasket. These I did not leave. I picked them out and made sure I had them all and stuffed them into my pocket. The basket was almost empty, which made it easy. No use wondering where the gun had been. There were too many places to hide it in. It could have been in a chair or in the couch, under one of the cushions. It could have been on the floor, behind the books, anywhere.

I went out and shut the door. I listened. From the kitchen, sounds. I went out there. Eileen had a blue apron on and the kettle was just beginning to whistle. She turned the flame down and gave me a brief impersonal glance.

"How do you like your tea, Mr. Marlowe?"

"Just out of the pot as it comes."

I leaned against the wall and got a cigarette out just to have something to do with my fingers. I pinched and squeezed it and broke it in half and threw one half on the floor. Her eyes followed it down. I bent and picked it up. I squeezed the two halves together into a little ball.

She made the tea. "I always take cream and sugar," she said over her shoulder. "Strange, when I drink my coffee black. I learned tea drinking in England. They were using saccharin instead of sugar. When the war came they had no cream, of course."

"You lived in England?"

"I worked there. I stayed all through the Blitz. I met a man—but I told you about that."

"Where did you meet Roger?"

"In New York."

"Married there?"

She swung around, frowning. "No, we were not married in New York. Why?"

"Just talking while the tea draws."

She looked out of the window over the sink. She could see down to the lake from there. She leaned against the edge of the drainboard and her fingers fiddled with a folded tea towel.

"It has to be stopped," she said, "and I don't know how. Perhaps he'll have to be committed to an institution. Somehow I can't quite see myself doing that. I'd have to sign something, wouldn't I?"

She turned around when she asked that.

"He could do it himself," I said. "That is, he could have up to now."

The tea timer rang its bell. She turned back to the sink and poured the tea from one pot into another. Then she put the fresh pot on the tray she had already fixed up with cups. I went over and got the tray and carried it to the table between the two davenports in the living room. She sat down opposite me and poured two cups. I reached for mine and set it down in front of me for it to cool. I watched her fix hers with two lumps of sugar and the cream. She tasted it.

"What did you mean by that last remark?" she asked suddenly. "That he could have up to now—committed himself to some institution, you meant, didn't you?"

"I guess it was a wild pitch. Did you hide the gun I told you about? You know, the morning after he made that play upstairs."

"Hide it?" she repeated frowning. "No. I never do anything like that. I don't believe in it. Why are you asking?"

"And you forgot your house keys today?"

"I told you I did."

"But not the garage key. Usually in this kind of house the outside keys are mastered."

"I don't need a key for the garage," she said sharply. "It opens by a switch. There's a relay switch inside the front door you push up as you go out. Then another switch beside the garage operates that door. Often we leave the garage open. Or Candy goes out and closes it."

"I see."

"You are making some rather strange remarks," she said with acid in her voice. "You did the other morning."

"I've had some rather strange experiences in this house. Guns going off in the night, drunks lying out on the front lawn and doctors coming that won't do anything. Lovely women wrapping their arms around me and talking as if they thought I was someone else, Mexican houseboys throwing knives. It's a pity about that gun. But you don't really love your husband, do you? I guess I said that before too."

She stood up slowly. She was as calm as a custard, but her violet eyes didn't seem quite the same color, nor of quite the same softness. Then her mouth began to tremble.

"Is—is something wrong in there?" she asked very slowly, and looked towards the study.

I barely had time to nod before she was running. She was at the door in a flash. She threw it open and darted in. If I expected a wild scream I was fooled. I didn't hear anything. I felt lousy. I ought to have kept her out and eased into that corny routine about bad news, prepare yourself, won't you sit down, I'm afraid something rather serious has happened. Blah, blah, blah. And when you have worked your way through it you haven't saved anybody a thing. Often enough you have made it worse.

I got up and followed her into the study. She was kneeling beside the couch with his head pulled against her breast, smearing herself with his blood. She wasn't making a sound of any kind. Her eyes were shut. She was rocking back and forth on her knees as far as she could, holding him tight.

I went back out and found a telephone and a book. I called the sheriff's substation that seemed to be nearest. Didn't matter, they'd relay it by radio in any case. Then I went out to the kitchen and turned the water on and fed the strips of yellow paper from my pocket down the electric garbage grinder. I dumped the tea leaves from the other pot after it. In a matter of seconds the stuff was gone. I shut off the water and switched off the motor. I went back to the living room and opened the front door and stepped outside.

There must have been a deputy cruising close by because he was there in about six minutes. When I took him into the study she was still kneeling by the couch. He went over to her at once.

"I'm sorry, ma'am. I understand how you must feel, but you shouldn't be touching anything."

She turned her head, then scrambled to her feet. "It's my husband. He's been shot."

He took his cap off and put it on the desk. He reached for the telephone.

"His name is Roger Wade," she said in a high brittle voice. "He's the famous novelist."

"I know who he is, ma'am," the deputy said, and dialed.

She looked down at the front of her blouse. "May I go upstairs and change this?"

"Sure." He nodded to her and spoke into the phone, then hung up and turned. "You say he's been shot. That mean somebody else shot him?"

"I think this man murdered him," she said without looking at me, and went quickly out of the room.

The deputy looked at me. He got a notebook out. He wrote something in it. "I better have your name," he said casually, "and address. You the one called in?"

"Yes." I told him my name and address.

"Just take it easy until Lieutenant Ohls gets here."

"Bernie Ohls?"

"Yeah. You know him?"

"Sure. I've known him a long time. He used to work out of the D.A.'s office."

"Not lately," the deputy said. "He's Assistant Chief of Homicide, working out of the L.A. Sheriff's office. You a friend of the family, Mr. Marlowe?"

"Mrs. Wade didn't make it sound that way."

He shrugged and half smiled. "Just take it easy, Mr. Marlowe. Not carrying a gun, are you?"

"Not today."

"I better make sure." He did. He looked towards the couch then. "In spots like this you can't expect the wife to make much sense. We better wait outside."

37

OHLS WAS A MEDIUM-SIZED THICK MAN with short-cropped faded blond hair and faded blue eyes. He had stiff white eyebrows and in the days before he stopped wearing a hat you were always a little surprised when he took it off—there was so much more head than you expected. He was a hard tough cop with a grim outlook on life but a very decent guy underneath. He ought to have made captain years ago. He had passed the examination among the top three half a dozen times. But the Sheriff didn't like him and he didn't like the Sheriff.

He came down the stairs rubbing the side of his jaw. Flashlights had been going off in the study for a long time. Men had gone in and out. I had just sat in the living room with a plain-clothes dick and waited.

Ohls sat down on the edge of a chair and dangled his hands. He was chewing on an unlit cigarette. He looked at me broodingly.

"Remember the old days when they had a gatehouse and a private police force in Idle Valley?"

I nodded. "And gambling also."

"Sure. You can't stop it. This whole valley is still private property. Like Arrowhead used to be, and Emerald Bay. Long time since I was on a case with no reporters jumping around. Somebody must have whispered in Sheriff Petersen's ear. They kept it off the teletype."

"Real considerate of them," I said. "How is Mrs. Wade?"

"Too relaxed. She must of grabbed some pills. There's a dozen kinds up there—even demerol. That's bad stuff. Your friends don't have a lot of luck lately, do they? They get dead."

I didn't have anything to say to that.

"Gunshot suicides always interest me," Ohls said loosely. "So easy to fake. The wife says you killed him. Why would she say that?"

"She doesn't mean it literally."

"Nobody else was here. She says you knew where the gun was, knew he was getting drunk, knew he had fired off the gun the other night when she had to fight with him to get the gun away from him. You were there that night too. Don't seem to help much, do you?"

"I searched his desk this afternoon. No gun. I'd told her where it was and to put it away. She says now she didn't believe in that sort of thing."

"Just when would 'now' be?" Ohls asked gruffly.

"After she came home and before I phoned the substation."

"You searched the desk. Why?" Ohls lifted his hands and put them on his knees. He was looking at me indifferently, as if he didn't care what I said.

"He was getting drunk. I thought it just as well to have the gun somewhere else. But he didn't try to kill himself the other night. It was just show-off."

Ohls nodded. He took the chewed cigarette out of his mouth, dropped it into a tray, and put a fresh one in place of it.

"I quit smoking," he said. "Got me coughing too much. But the goddam things still ride me. Can't feel right without one in my mouth. You supposed to watch the guy when he's alone?"

"Certainly not. He asked me to come out and have lunch. We talked and he was kind of depressed about his writing not going well. He decided to hit the bottle. Think I should have taken it away from him?"

"I'm not thinking yet. I'm just trying to get a picture. How much drinking did you do?"

"Beer."

"It's your tough luck you were here, Marlowe. What was the check for? The one he wrote and signed and tore up?"

"They all wanted me to come and live here and keep him in line. All means himself, his wife, and his publisher, a man named Howard Spencer. He's in New York, I guess. You can check with him. I turned it down. Afterwards she came to me and said her husband was off on a toot and she was worried and would I find him and bring him home. I did that. Next thing I knew I was carrying him in off his front lawn and putting him to bed. I didn't want any part of it, Bernie. It just kind of grew up around me."

"Nothing to do with the Lennox case, huh?"

"Aw, for Pete's sake. There isn't any Lennox case."

"How true," Ohls said dryly. He squeezed his kneecaps. A man came in at the front door and spoke to the other dick. Then came across to Ohls.

"There's a Dr. Loring outside, Lieutenant. Says he was called. He's the lady's doctor."

"Let him in."

The dick went back and Dr. Loring came in with his neat black bag. He was cool and elegant in a tropical worsted suit. He went past me without looking at me.

"Upstairs?" he asked Ohls.

"Yeah—in her room." Ohls stood up. "What you give her that demerol for, Doc?"

Dr. Loring frowned at him. "I prescribe for my patient as I think proper," he said coldly. "I am not required to explain why. Who says I gave Mrs. Wade demerol?"

"I do. The bottle's up there with your name on it. She's got a regular drugstore in her bathroom. Maybe you don't know it, Doc, but we have a pretty complete exhibit of the little pills downtown. Bluejays, redbirds, yellow jackets, goofballs, and all the rest of the list. Demerol's about the worst of the lot. That's the stuff Goering lived on, I heard somewhere. Took eighteen a day when they caught him. Took the army doctors three months to cut him down."

"I don't know what those words mean," Dr. Loring said frigidly.

"You don't? Pity. Bluejays are sodium amytal. Redbirds are seconal. Yellow jackets are nembutal. Goofballs are one of the barbiturates laced with benzedrine. Demerol is a synthetic narcotic that is very habit forming. You just hand 'em out, huh? Is the lady suffering from something serious?"

"A drunken husband can be a very serious complaint indeed for a sensitive woman," Dr. Loring said.

"You didn't get around to him, huh? Pity. Mrs. Wade's upstairs, Doc. Thanks for the time."

"You are impertinent, sir. I shall report you."

"Yeah, do that," Ohls said. "But before you report me, do something else. Keep the lady clear in her head. I've got questions to ask."

"I shall do exactly what I think best for her condition. Do you know who I am, by any chance? And just to make matters clear, Mr. Wade was not my patient. I don't treat alcoholics."

"Just their wives, huh?" Ohls snarled at him. "Yeah, I know who you are, Doc. I'm bleeding internally. My name is Ohls. Lieutenant Ohls."

Dr. Loring went on up the stairs. Ohls sat down again and grinned at me.

"You got to be diplomatic with this kind of people," he said.

A man came out of the study and came up to Ohls. A thin serious-looking man with glasses and a brainy forehead.

"Lieutenant."

"Shoot."

"The wound is contact, typically suicidal, with a good deal of distention from gas pressure. The eyes are exophthalmic from the same cause. I don't think there will be any prints on the outside of the gun. It's been bled on too freely."

"Could it be homicide if the guy was asleep or passed out drunk?" Ohls asked him.

"Of course, but there's no indication of it. The gun's a Webley Hammerless. Typically, this gun takes a very stiff pull to cock it, but a very light pull to discharge it. The recoil explains the position of the gun. I see nothing against suicide so far. I expect a high figure on alcoholic concentration. If it's high enough—" the man stopped and shrugged meaningly— "I might be inclined to doubt suicide."

"Thanks. Somebody call the coroner?"

The man nodded and went away. Ohls yawned and looked at his watch. Then he looked at me.

"You want to blow?"

"Sure, if you'll let me. I thought I was a suspect."

"We might oblige you later on. Stick around where you can be found, that's all. You were a dick once, you know how they go. Some you got to work fast before the evidence gets away from you. This one is just the opposite. If it was a homicide, who wanted him dead? His wife? She wasn't here. You? Fine, you had the house to yourself and knew where the gun was. A perfect setup. Everything but a motive, and we might perhaps give some weight to your experience. I figure if you wanted to kill a guy, you could maybe do it a little less obviously."

"Thanks, Bernie. I could at that."

"The help wasn't here. They're out. So it must have been somebody that just happened to drop by. That somebody had to know where Wade's gun was, had to find him drunk enough to be asleep or passed out, and had to pull the trigger when that speedboat was making enough noise to drown the shot, and had to get away before you came back into the house. That I don't buy on any knowledge I have now. The only person who had the means and opportunity was the one guy who wouldn't have used them—for the simple reason he *was* the one guy who had them."

I stood up to go. "Okay, Bernie. I'll be home all evening."

"There's just one thing," Ohls said musingly. "This man Wade was a big time writer. Lots of dough, lots of reputation. I don't go for his sort of crap myself. You might find nicer people than his characters in a whorehouse. That's a matter of taste and none of my business as a cop. With all this money he had a beautiful home in one of the best places to live in in the county. He had a beautiful wife, lots of friends, and no troubles at all. What I want to know is what made all that so tough that he had to pull a trigger? Sure as hell something did. If you know, you better get ready to lay it on the line. See you."

I went to the door. The man on the door looked back at Ohls, got the sign, and let me out. I got into my car and had to edge over on the lawn to get around the various official cars that jammed the driveway. At the gate another deputy looked me over but didn't say anything. I slipped my dark glasses on and drove back towards the main highway. The road was empty and peaceful. The afternoon sun beat down on the manicured lawns and the large roomy expensive houses behind them.

A man not unknown to the world had died in a pool of blood in a house in Idle Valley, but the lazy quiet had not been disturbed. So far as the newspapers were concerned it might have happened in Tibet.

At a turn of the road the walls of two estates came down to the shoulder and a dark green sheriff's car was parked there. A deputy got out and held up his hand. I stopped. He came to the window.

"May I see your driver's license, please?"

I took out my wallet and handed it to him open.

"Just the license, please. I'm not allowed to touch your wallet."

I took it out and gave it to him. "What's the trouble?"

He glanced into my car and handed me back my license.

"No trouble," he said. "Just a routine check. Sorry to have troubled you."

He waved me on and went back to the parked car. Just like a cop. They never tell you why they are doing anything. That way you don't find out they don't know themselves.

I drove home, bought myself a couple of cold drinks, went out to dinner, came back, opened the windows and my shirt and waited for something to happen. I waited a long time. It was nine o'clock when Bernie Ohls called up and told me to come in and not stop on the way to pick any flowers.

38

THEY HAD CANDY IN A HARD CHAIR against the wall of the Sheriff's anteroom. He hated me with his eyes as I went by him into the big square room where Sheriff Petersen held court in the middle of a collection of testimonials from a grateful public to his twenty years of faithful public service. The walls were loaded with photographs of horses and Sheriff Petersen made a personal appearance in every photograph. The corners of his carved desk were horses' heads. His inkwell was a mounted polished horse's hoof and his pens were planted in the mate to it filled with white sand. A gold plate on each of these said something or other about a date. In the middle of a spotless desk blotter lay a bag of Bull Durham and a pack of brown cigarette papers. Petersen rolled his own. He could roll one with one hand on horseback and often did, especially when leading a parade on a big white horse with a Mexican saddle loaded with beautiful Mexican silverwork. On horseback he wore a flat-crowned Mexican sombrero. He rode beautifully and his horse always knew exactly when to be quiet, when to act up so that the Sheriff with his calm inscrutable smile could bring the horse back under control with one hand. The Sheriff had a good act. He had a handsome hawklike profile, getting a little saggy under the chin by now, but he knew how to hold his head so it wouldn't show too much. He put a lot of hard work into having his picture taken. He was in his middle fifties and his father, a Dane, had left him a lot of money. The Sheriff didn't look like a Dane, because his hair was dark and his skin was brown and he had the impassive poise of a cigar store Indian and about the same kind of brains. But nobody had ever called him a crook. There had been crooks in his department and they had fooled him as well as they had fooled the public, but none of the crookedness rubbed off on Sheriff Petersen. He just went right on getting elected without even trying, riding white horses at the head of parades, and questioning suspects in front of cameras. That's what the captions said. As a matter of fact he never questioned anybody. He wouldn't have known how. He just sat at his desk looking sternly at the suspect, showing his profile to the camera. The flash bulbs would go off, the camera men would thank the Sheriff deferentially, and the suspect would be removed not having opened his mouth, and the Sheriff would go home to his ranch in the San Fernando Valley. There he could always be reached. If you couldn't reach him in person, you could talk to one of his horses.

Once in a while, come election time, some misguided politician would try to get Sheriff Petersen's job, and would be apt to call him things like The Guy With The Built-In Profile or The Ham That Smokes Itself, but it didn't get him anywhere. Sheriff Petersen just went right on getting re-elected, a living testimonial to the fact that you can hold an important public office forever in our country with no qualifications for it but a clean nose, a photogenic face, and a close mouth. If on top of that you look good on a horse, you are unbeatable.

As Ohls and I went in, Sheriff Petersen was standing behind his desk and the camera boys were filing out by another door. The Sheriff had his white stetson on. He was rolling a cigarette. He was all set to go home. He looked at me sternly.

"Who's this?" he asked in a rich baritone voice.

"Name's Philip Marlowe, Chief," Ohls said. "Only person in the house when Wade shot himself. You want a picture?"

The Sheriff studied me. "I don't think so," he said, and turned to a big tired-looking man with iron-gray hair. "If you need me, I'll be at the ranch, Captain Hernandez."

"Yes, sir."

Petersen lit his cigarette with a kitchen match. He lit it on his thumbnail. No lighters for Sheriff Petersen. He was strictly a roll-your-own-and-light-'em-with-one-hand type.

He said goodnight and went out. A deadpan character with hard black eyes went with him, his personal bodyguard. The door closed. When he was gone Captain Hernandez moved to the desk and sat in the Sheriff's enormous chair and a stenotype operator in the corner moved his stand out from the wall to get elbow room. Ohls sat at the end of the desk and looked amused.

"All right, Marlowe," Hernandez said briskly. "Let's have it."

"How come I don't get my photo taken?"

"You heard what the Sheriff said."

"Yeah, but why?" I whined.

Ohls laughed. "You know damn well why."

"You mean on account of I'm tall, dark, and handsome and somebody might look at me?"

"Cut it," Hernandez said coldly. "Let's get on with your statement. Start from the beginning."

I gave it to them from the beginning: my interview with Howard Spencer, my meeting with Eileen Wade, her asking me to find Roger, my finding him, her asking me to the house, what Wade asked me to do and how I found him passed out near the hibiscus bushes and the rest of it. The stenotype operator took it down. Nobody interrupted me. All of it was true. The truth and nothing but the truth. But not quite all the truth. What I left out was my business.

"Nice," Hernandez said at the end. "But not quite complete." This was a cool competent dangerous guy, this Hernandez. Somebody in the Sheriff's office had to be. "The night Wade shot off the gun in his bedroom you went into Mrs. Wade's room and were in there for some time with the door shut. What were you doing in there?"

"She called me in and asked me how he was."

"Why shut the door?"

"Wade was half asleep and I didn't want to make any noise. Also the houseboy was hanging around with his ear out. Also she asked me to shut the door. I didn't realize it was going to be important."

"How long were you in there?"

"I don't know. Three minutes maybe."

"I suggest you were in there a couple of hours," Hernandez said coldly. "Do I make myself clear?"

I looked at Ohls. Ohls didn't look at anything. He was chewing on an unlighted cigarette as usual.

"You are misinformed, Captain."

"We'll see. After you left the room you went downstairs to the study and spent the night on the couch. Perhaps I should say the rest of the night."

"It was ten minutes to eleven when he called me at home. It was long past two o'clock when I went into the study for the last time that night. Call it the rest of the night if you like."

"Get the houseboy in here," Hernandez said.

Ohls went out and came back with Candy. They put Candy in a chair. Hernandez asked him a few questions to establish who he was and so on. Then he said: "All right, Candy—we'll call you that for convenience—after you helped Marlowe put Roger Wade to bed, what happened?"

I knew what was coming more or less. Candy told his story in a quiet savage voice with very little accent. It seemed as if he could turn that on and off at will. His story was that he had hung around downstairs in case he was wanted again, part of the time in the kitchen where he got himself some food, part of the time in the living room. While in the living room sitting in a chair near the front door he had seen Eileen Wade standing in the door of her room and he had seen her take her clothes off. He had seen her put a robe on with nothing under it and he had seen me go into her room and I shut the door and stayed in there a long time, a couple of hours he thought. He had gone up the stairs and listened. He had heard the bedsprings making sounds. He had heard whispering. He made his meaning very obvious. When he had finished he gave me a corrosive look and his mouth was twisted tight with hatred.

"Take him out," Hernandez said.

"Just a minute," I said. "I want to question him."

"I ask the questions here," Hernandez said sharply.

"You don't know how, Captain. You weren't there. He's lying and he knows it and I know it."

Hernandez leaned back and picked up one of the Sheriff's pens. He bent the handle of the pen. It was long and pointed and made of stiffened horsehair. When he let go of the point it sprang back.

"Shoot," he said at last.

I faced Candy. "Where were you when you saw Mrs. Wade take her clothes off?"

"I was sitting down in a chair near the front door," he said in a surly tone.

"Between the front door and the two facing davenports?"

"What I said."

"Where was Mrs. Wade?"

"Just inside the door of her room. The door was open."

"What light was there in the living room?"

"One lamp. Tall lamp what they call a bridge lamp."

"What light was on the balcony?"

"No light. Light in her bedroom."

"What kind of light in her bedroom?"

"Not much light. Night table lamp, maybe."

"Not a ceiling light?"

"No."

"After she took her clothes off—standing just inside the door of her room, you said—she put on a robe. What kind of robe?"

"Blue robe. Long thing like a house coat. She tie it with a sash."

"So if you hadn't actually seen her take her clothes off you wouldn't know what she had on under the robe?"

He shrugged. He looked vaguely worried. "Sí. That's right. But I see her take her clothes off."

"You're a liar. There isn't any place in the living room from which you could see her take her clothes off right bang in her doorway, much less inside her room. She would have to come out to the edge of the balcony. If she had done that she would have seen you."

He just glared at me. I turned to Ohls. "You've seen the house. Captain Hernandez hasn't—or has he?"

Ohls shook his head slightly. Hernandez frowned and said nothing.

"There is no spot in that living room, Captain Hernandez, from which he could see even the top of Mrs. Wade's head—even if he was standing up—and he says he was sitting down—provided she was as far back as her own doorway or inside it. I'm four inches taller than he is and I could only see the top foot of an open door when I was standing just inside the front door of the house. She would have to come out to the edge of the balcony for him to see what he says he saw. Why would she do that? Why would she undress in her doorway even? There's no sense to it."

Hernandez just looked at me. Then he looked at Candy. "How about the time element?" he asked softly, speaking to me.

"That's his word against mine. I'm talking about what can be proved."

Hernandez spit Spanish at Candy too fast for me to understand. Candy just stared at him sulkily.

"Take him out," Hernandez said.

Ohls jerked a thumb and opened the door. Candy went out. Hernandez brought out a box of cigarettes, stuck one on his lip, and lit it with a gold lighter.

Ohls came back into the room. Hernandez said calmly: "I just told him that if there was an inquest and he told that story on the stand, he'd find himself doing a one-to-three up in Q for perjury. Didn't seem to impress him much. It's obvious what's eating him. An old-fashioned case of hot pants. If he'd been around and we had any reason to suspect murder, he'd make a pretty good pigeon —except that he would have used a knife. I got the impression earlier that he felt pretty bad about Wade's death. Any questions you want to ask, Ohls?"

Ohls shook his head. Hernandez looked at me and said: "Come back in the morning and sign your statement. We'll have it typed out by then. We ought to have a P.M. report by ten o'clock, preliminary anyway. Anything you don't like about this setup, Marlowe?"

"Would you mind rephrasing the question? The way you put it suggests there might be something I do like about it."

"Okay," he said wearily. "Take off. I'm going home."

I stood up.

"Of course I never did believe that stuff Candy pulled on us," he said. "Just used it for a corkscrew. No hard feelings, I hope."

"No feelings at all, Captain. No feelings at all."

They watched me go out and didn't say goodnight. I walked down the long corridor to the Hill Street entrance and got into my car and drove home.

No feelings at all was exactly right. I was as hollow and empty as the spaces between the stars. When I got home I mixed a stiff one and stood by the open window in the living room and sipped it and listened to the groundswell of the traffic on Laurel Canyon Boulevard and looked at the glare of the big angry city hanging over the shoulder of the hills through which the boulevard had been cut. Far off the banshee wail of police or fire sirens rose and fell, never for very long completely silent. Twenty-four hours a day somebody is running, somebody else is trying to catch him. Out there in the night of a thousand crimes people were dying, being maimed, cut by flying glass, crushed against steering wheels or under heavy tires. People were being beaten, robbed, strangled, raped, and murdered. People were hungry, sick; bored, desperate with loneliness or remorse or fear, angry, cruel, feverish, shaken by sobs. A city no worse than others, a city rich and vigorous and full of pride, a city lost and beaten and full of emptiness.

It all depends on where you sit and what your own private score is. I didn't have one. I didn't care.

I finished the drink and went to bed.

39

THE INQUEST WAS A FLOP. The coroner sailed into it before the medical evidence was complete, for fear the publicity would die on him. He needn't have worried. The death of a writer—even a loud writer—is not news for long, and that summer there was too much to compete. A king abdicated and another was assassinated. In one week three large passenger planes crashed. The head man of a big wire service was shot to pieces in Chicago in his own automobile. Twenty-four convicts were burned to death in a prison fire. The Coroner of Los Angeles County was out of luck. He was missing the good things in life.

As I left the stand I saw Candy. He had a bright malicious grin on his face—I had no idea why—and as usual he was dressed just a little too well, in a cocoa brown gabardine suit with a white nylon shirt and a midnight blue bow tie. On the witness stand he was quiet and made a good impression. Yes, the boss had been pretty drunk lately a lot of times. Yes, he had helped put him to bed the night the gun went off upstairs. Yes, the boss had demanded whiskey before he, Candy, left on the last day, but he had refused to get it. No, he didn't know anything about Mr. Wade's literary work, but he knew the boss had been discouraged. He kept throwing it away and then getting it out of the wastebasket again. No, he had never heard Mr. Wade quarreling with anyone. And so on. The coroner milked him but it was thin stuff. Somebody had done a good coaching job on Candy.

Eileen Wade wore black and white. She was pale and spoke in a low clear voice which even the amplifier could not spoil. The coroner handled her with two pairs of velvet gloves. He talked to her as if he had trouble keeping the sobs out of his voice. When she left the stand he stood up and bowed and she gave him a faint fugitive smile that nearly made him choke on his salvia.

She almost passed me without a glance on the way out, then at the last moment turned her head a couple of inches and nodded very slightly, as if I was somebody she must have met somewhere a long time ago, but couldn't quite place in her memory.

Outside on the steps when it was all over I ran into Ohls. He was watching the traffic down below, or pretending to.

"Nice job," he said without turning his head. "Congratulations."

"You did all right on Candy."

"Not me, kid. The D.A. decided the sexy stuff was irrelevant."

"What sexy stuff was that?"

He looked at me then. "Ha, ha, ha," he said. "And I don't mean you." Then his expression got remote. "I been looking at them for too many years. It wearies a man. This one came out of the special bottle. Old private stock. Strictly for the carriage trade. So long, sucker. Call me when you start wearing twenty-dollar shirts. I'll drop around and hold your coat for you."

People eddied around us going up and down the steps. We just stood there. Ohls took a cigarette out of his pocket and looked at it and dropped it on the concrete and ground it to nothing with his heel.

"Wasteful," I said.

"Only a cigarette, pal. It's not a life. After a while maybe you marry the girl, huh?"

"Shove it."

He laughed sourly. "I been talking to the right people about the wrong things," he said acidly. "Any objection?"

"No objection, Lieutenant," I said, and went on down the steps. He said something behind me but I kept going.

I went over to a corn-beef joint on Flower. It suited my mood. A rude sign over the entrance said: "Men Only. Dogs and Women Not Admitted." The service inside was equally polished. The waiter who tossed your food at you needed a shave and deducted his tip without being invited. The food was simple but very good and they had a brown Swedish beer which could hit as hard as a martini.

When I got back to the office the phone was ringing. Ohls said: "I'm coming by your place. I've got things to say."

He must have been at or near the Hollywood substation because he was in the office inside twenty minutes. He planted himself in the customer's chair and crossed his legs and growled:

"I was out of line. Sorry. Forget it."

"Why forget it? Let's open up the wound."

"Suits me. Under the hat, though. To some people you're a wrong gee. I never knew you to do anything too crooked."

"What was the crack about twenty-dollar shirts?"

"Aw hell, I was just sore," Ohls said. "I was thinking of old man Potter. Like he told a secretary to tell a lawyer to tell District Attorney Springer to tell Captain Hernandez you were a personal friend of his."

"He wouldn't take the trouble."

"You met him. He gave you time."

"I met him, period. I didn't like him, but perhaps it was only envy. He sent for me to give me some advice. He's big and he's tough and I don't know what else. I don't figure he's a crook."

"There ain't no clean way to make a hundred million bucks," Ohls said. "Maybe the head man thinks his hands are clean but somewhere along the line guys got pushed to the wall, nice little businesses got the ground cut from under them and had to sell out for nickels, decent people lost their jobs, stocks got rigged on the market, proxies got bought up like a pennyweight of old gold, and the five per centers and the big law firms got paid hundred-grand fees for beating some law the people wanted but the rich guys didn't, on account of it cut into their profits. Big money is big power and big power gets used wrong. It's the system. Maybe it's the best we can get, but it still ain't any Ivory Soap deal."

"You sound like a Red," I said, just to needle him.

"I wouldn't know," he said contemptuously. "I ain't been investigated yet. You liked the suicide verdict, didn't you?"

"What else could it be?"

"Nothing else, I guess." He put his hard blunt hands on the desk and looked at the big brown freckles on the backs of them. "I'm getting old. Keratosis, they call those brown spots. You don't get them until you're past fifty. I'm an old cop and an old cop is an old bastard. I don't like a few things about this Wade death."

"Such as?" I leaned back and watched the tight sun wrinkles around his eyes.

"You get so you can smell a wrong setup, even when you know you can't do a damn thing about it. Then you just sit and talk like now. I don't like that he left no note."

"He was drunk. Probably just a sudden crazy impulse."

Ohls lifted his pale eyes and dropped his hands off the desk. "I went through his desk. He wrote letters to himself. He wrote and wrote and wrote. Drunk or sober he hit that typewriter. Some of it is wild, some of it kind of funny, and some of it is sad. The guy had something on his mind.

He wrote all around it but he never quite touched it. That guy would have left a two-page letter if he knocked himself off."

"He was drunk," I said again.

"With him that didn't matter," Ohls said wearily. "The next thing I don't like is he did it there in that room and left his wife to find him. Okay, he was drunk. I still don't like it. The next thing I don't like is he pulled the trigger just when the noise of that speedboat could drown out the shot. What difference would it make to him? More coincidence, huh? More coincidence still that the wife forgot her door keys on the help's day off and had to ring the bell to get into the house."

"She could have walked around to the back," I said.

"Yeah, I know. What I'm talking about is a situation. Nobody to answer the door but you, and she said on the stand she didn't know you were there. Wade wouldn't have heard the bell if he had been alive and working in his study. His door is soundproofed. The help was away. That was Thursday. That she forgot. Like she forgot her keys."

"You're forgetting something yourself, Bernie. My car was in the driveway. So she knew I was there—or that somebody was there—before she rang the bell."

He grinned. "I forgot that, didn't I? All right, here's the picture. You were down at the lake, the speedboat was making all that racket—incidentally it was a couple of guys from Lake Arrowhead just visiting, had their boat on a trailer—Wade was asleep in his study or passed out, somebody took the gun out of his desk already, and she knew you had put it there because you told her that other time. Now suppose she didn't forget her keys, that she goes into the house, looks across and sees you down at the water, looks into the study and sees Wade asleep, knows where the gun is, gets it, waits for the right moment, plugs him, drops the gun where it was found, goes back outside the house, waits a little while for the speedboat to go away, and then rings the doorbell and waits for you to open it. Any objections?"

"With what motive?"

"Yeah," he said sourly. "That knocks it. If she wanted to slough the guy, it was easy. She had him over a barrel, habitual drunk, record of violence to her. Plenty alimony, nice fat property settlement. No motive at all. Anyhow the timing was too neat. Five minutes earlier and she couldn't have done it unless you were in on it."

I started to say something but he put his hand up. "Take it easy. I'm not accusing anybody, just speculating. Five minutes later and you get the same answer. She had ten minutes to pull it off."

"Ten minutes," I said irritably, "that couldn't possibly have been foreseen, much less planned."

He leaned back in the chair and sighed. "I know. You've got all the answers, I've got all the answers. And I still don't like it. What the hell were you doing with these people anyway? The guy writes you a check for a grand, then tears it up. Got mad at you, you say. You didn't want it anyway, wouldn't have taken it, you say. Maybe. Did he think you were sleeping with his wife?"

"Lay off, Bernie."

"I didn't ask were you, I asked did he think you were."

"Same answer."

"Okay, try this. What did the Mex have on him?"

"Nothing that I know of."

"The Mex has too much money. Over fifteen hundred in the bank, all kinds of clothes, a brand new Chevvy."

"Maybe he peddles dope," I said.

Ohls pushed himself up out of the chair and scowled down at me.

"You're an awful lucky boy, Marlowe. Twice you've slid out from under a heavy one. You could get overconfident. You were pretty helpful to those people and you didn't make a dime. You were pretty helpful to a guy named Lennox too, the way I hear it. And you didn't make a dime out of that one either. What do you do for eating money, pal? You got a lot saved so you don't have to work any more?"

I stood up and walked around the desk and faced him. "I'm a romantic, Bernie. I hear voices crying in the night and I go see what's the matter. You don't make a dime that way. You got sense, you shut your windows and turn up more sound on the TV set. Or you shove down on the gas and get far away from there. Stay out of other people's troubles. All it can get you is the smear. The last time I saw Terry Lennox we had a cup of coffee together that I made myself in my house, and we smoked a cigarette. So when I heard he was dead I went out to the kitchen and made some coffee and poured a cup for him and lit a cigarette for him and when the coffee was cold and the cigarette was burned down I said goodnight to him. You don't make a dime that way. *You* wouldn't do it. That's why you're a good cop and I'm a private eye. Eileen Wade is worried about her husband, so I go out and find him and bring him home. Another time he's in trouble and calls me up and I go out and carry him in off the lawn and put him to bed and I don't make a dime out of it. No percentage at all. No nothing, except sometimes I get my face pushed in or get tossed in the can or get threatened by some fast money boy like Mendy Menendez. But no money, not a dime. I've got a five-thousand-dollar bill in my safe but I'll never spend a nickel of it. Because there was something wrong with the way I got it. I played with it a little at first and I still get it out once in a while and look at it. But that's all—not a dime of spending money."

"Must be a phony," Ohls said dryly, "except they don't make them that big. So what's your point with all this yap?"

"No point. I told you I was a romantic."

"I heard you. And you don't make a dime at it. I heard that too."

"But I can always tell a cop to go to hell. Go to hell, Bernie."

"You wouldn't tell me to go to hell if I had you in the back room under the light, chum."

"Maybe we'll find out about that some day."

He walked to the door and yanked it open. "You know something, kid? You think you're cute but you're just stupid. You're a shadow on the wall. I've got twenty years on the cops without a mark against me. I know when I'm being kidded and I know when a guy is holding out on me. The wise guy never fools anybody but himself. Take it from me, chum. I know."

He pulled his head back out of the doorway and let the door close. His heels hammered down the corridor. I could still hear them when the phone on my desk started to sound. The voice said in that clear professional tone:

"New York is calling Mr. Philip Marlowe."

"I'm Philip Marlowe."

"Thank you. One moment, please, Mr. Marlowe. Here is your party."

The next voice I knew. "Howard Spencer, Mr. Marlowe. We've heard about Roger Wade. It was a pretty hard blow. We haven't the full details, but your name seems to be involved."

"I was there when it happened. He just got drunk and shot himself. Mrs. Wade came home a little later. The servants were away—Thursday's the day off."

"You were alone with him?"

"I wasn't with him. I was outside the house, just hanging around waiting for his wife to come home."

"I see. Well, I suppose there will be an inquest."

"It's all over, Mr. Spencer. Suicide. And remarkably little publicity."

"Really? That's curious." He didn't exactly sound disappointed—more like puzzled and surprised. "He was so well known. I should have thought—well, never mind what I thought. I guess I'd better fly out there, but I can't make it before the end of next week. I'll send a wire to Mrs. Wade. There may be something I could do for her—and also about the book. I mean there may be enough of it so that we could get someone to finish it. I assume you did take the job after all."

"No. Although he asked me to himself. I told him right out I couldn't stop him from drinking."

"Apparently you didn't even try."

"Look, Mr. Spencer, you don't know the first damn thing about this situation. Why not wait until you do before jumping to conclusions? Not that I don't blame myself a little. I guess that's inevitable when something like this happens, and you're the guy on the spot."

"Of course," he said. "I'm sorry I made that remark. Most uncalled for. Will Eileen Wade be at her home now—or wouldn't you know?"

"I wouldn't know, Mr. Spencer. Why don't you just call her up?"

"I hardly think she would want to speak to anyone yet," he said slowly.

"Why not? She talked to the Coroner and never batted an eye."

He cleared his throat. "You don't sound exactly sympathetic."

"Roger Wade is dead, Spencer. He was a bit of a bastard and maybe a bit of a genius too. That's over my head. He was an egotistical drunk and he hated his own guts. He made me a lot of trouble and in the end a lot of grief. Why the hell should I be sympathetic?"

"I was talking about Mrs. Wade," he said shortly.

"So was I."

"I'll call you when I get in," he said abruptly. "Goodbye."

He hung up. I hung up. I stared at the telephone for a couple of minutes without moving. Then I got the phone book up on the desk and looked for a number.

40

I CALLED SEWELL ENDICOTT'S OFFICE. Somebody said he was in court and would not be available until late in the afternoon. Would I care to leave my name? No.

I dialed the number of Mendy Menendez's joint on the Strip. It was called El Tapado this year, not a bad name either. In American Spanish that means buried treasure among other things. It had been called other names in the past, quite a few other names. One year it was just a blue neon number on a blank high wall facing south on the Strip, with its back against the hill and a driveway curving around one side out of sight of the street. Very exclusive. Nobody knew much about it except vice cops and mobsters and people who could afford thirty bucks for a good dinner and any amount up to fifty grand in the big quiet room upstairs.

I got a woman who didn't know from nothing. Then I got a captain with a Mex accent.

"You wish to speak with Mr. Menendez? Who is calling?"

"No names, amigo. Private matter."

"Un momento, por favor."

There was a longish wait. I got a hard boy this time. He

sounded as if he was talking through the slit in an armored car. It was probably just the slit in his face.

"Talk it up. Who wants him?"

"The name's Marlowe."

"Who's Marlowe?"

"This Chick Agostino?"

"No, this ain't Chick. Come on, let's have the password."

"Go fry your face."

There was a chuckle. "Hold the line."

Finally another voice said: "Hello, cheapie. What's the time by you?"

"You alone?"

"You can talk, cheapie. I been looking over some acts for the floor show."

"You could cut your throat for one."

"What would I do for an encore?"

I laughed. He laughed. "Been keeping your nose clean?" he asked.

"Haven't you heard? I got to be friends with another guy who suicided. They're going to call me the 'Kiss-of-Death Kid' from now on."

"That's funny, huh?"

"No, it isn't funny. Also the other afternoon I had tea with Harlan Potter."

"Nice going. I never drink the stuff myself."

"He said for you to be nice to me."

"I never met the guy and I don't figure to."

"He casts a long shadow. All I want is a little information, Mendy. Like about Paul Marston."

"Never heard of him."

"You said that too quick. Paul Marston was the name Terry Lennox used one time in New York before he came west."

"So?"

"His prints were checked through the F.B.I. files. No record. That means he never served in the Armed Forces."

"So?"

"Do I have to draw you a picture? Either that foxhole yarn of yours was all spaghetti or it happened somewhere else."

"I didn't say where it happened, cheapie. Take a kind word and forget the whole thing. You got told, you better stay told."

"Oh sure. I do something you don't like and I'm swimming to Catalina with a streetcar on my back. Don't try to scare me, Mendy. I've been up against the pros. You ever been in England?"

"Be smart, cheapie. Things can happen to a guy in this town. Things can happen to big strong boys like Big Willie Magoon. Take a look at the evening paper."

"I'll get one if you say so. It might even have my picture in it. What about Magoon?"

"Like I said—things can happen. I wouldn't know how except what I read. Seems Magoon tried to shake down four boys in a car with Nevada plates. Was parked right by his house. Nevada plates with big numbers like they don't have. Must have been some kind of a rib. Only Magoon ain't feeling funny, what with both arms in casts, and his jaw wired in three places, and one leg in high traction. Magoon ain't tough any more. It could happen to you."

"He bothered you, huh? I saw him bounce your boy Chick off the wall in front of Victor's. Should I ring up a friend in the Sheriff's office and tell him?"

"You do that, cheapie," he said very slowly. "You do that."

"And I'll mention that at the time I was just through having a drink with Harlan Potter's daughter. Corroborative evidence, in a sense, don't you think? You figure to smash her up too?"

"Listen to me careful, cheapie—"

"Were you ever in England, Mendy? You and Randy Starr and Paul Marston or Terry Lennox or whatever his name was? In the British Army perhaps? Had a little racket in Soho and got hot and figured the Army was a cooling-off spot?"

"Hold the line."

I held it. Nothing happened except that I waited and my arm got tired. I switched the receiver to the other side. Finally he came back.

"Now listen careful, Marlowe. You stir up that Lennox case and you're dead. Terry was a pal and I got feelings too. So you got feelings. I'll go along with you just this far. It was a Commando outfit. It was British. It happened in Norway, one of those islands off the coast. They got a million of them. November 1942. Now will you lie down and rest that tired brain of yours?"

"Thank you, Mendy. I will do that. Your secret is safe with me. I'm not telling it to anybody but the people I know."

"Buy yourself a paper, cheapie. Read and remember. Big tough Willie Magoon. Beat up in front of his own house. Boy, was he surprised when he come out of the ether!"

He hung up. I went downstairs and bought a paper and it was just as Menendez had said. There was a picture of Big Willie Magoon in his hospital bed. You could see half his face and one eye. The rest of him was bandages. Seriously but not critically injured. The boys had been very careful about that. They wanted him to live. After all he was a cop. In our town the mobs don't kill a cop. They leave that to the juveniles. And a live cop who has been put through the meat grinder is a much better advertisement. He gets well eventually and goes back to work. But from that time on something is missing—the last inch of steel that makes all the difference. He's a walking lesson that it is a mistake to push the racket boys too hard—especially if you are on the vice squad and eating at the best places and driving a Cadillac.

I sat there and brooded about it for a while and then I dialed the number of The Carne Organization and asked for George Peters. He was out. I left my name and said it was urgent. He was expected in about five-thirty.

I went over to the Hollywood Public Library and asked questions in the reference room, but couldn't find what I wanted. So I had to go back for my Olds and drive downtown to the Main Library. I found it there, in a smallish red-bound book published in England. I copied what I wanted from it and drove home. I called The Carne Organization again. Peters was still out, so I asked the girl to reroute the call to me at home.

I put the chessboard on the coffee table and set out a problem called The Sphynx. It is printed on the end papers of a book on chess by Blackburn, the English chess wizard, probably the most dynamic chess player who ever lived, although he wouldn't get to first base in the cold war type of chess they play nowadays. The Sphynx is an eleven-mover and it justifies its name. Chess problems seldom run to more than four or five moves. Beyond that the difficulty of solving them rises in almost geometrical progression. An eleven-mover is sheer unadulterated torture.

Once in a long while when I feel mean enough I set it out and look for a new way to solve it. It's a nice quiet way to go crazy. You don't even scream, but you come awfully close.

George Peters called me at five-forty. We exchanged pleasantries and condolences.

"You've got yourself in another jam, I see," he said cheerfully. "Why don't you try some quiet business like embalming?"

"Takes too long to learn. Listen, I want to become a client of your agency, if it doesn't cost too much."

"Depends what you want done, old boy. And you'd have to talk to Carne."

"No."

"Well, tell me."

"London is full of guys like me, but I wouldn't know one from the other. They call them private enquiry agents. Your outfit would have connections. I'd just have to pick a name at random and probably get hornswoggled. I want some information that should be easy enough to get, and I want it quick. Must have it before the end of next week."

"Spill."

"I want to know something about the war service of Terry Lennox or Paul Marston, whatever name he used. He was in the Commandos over there. He was captured wounded in November 1942 in a raid on some Norwegian island. I want to know what outfit he was posted from and what happened to him. The War Office will have all that. It's not secret information, or I wouldn't think so. Let's say a question of inheritance is involved."

"You don't need a P.I. for that. You could get it direct. Write them a letter."

"Shove it, George. I might get an answer in three months. I want one in five days."

"You have a thought there, pal. Anything else?"

"One thing more. They keep all their vital records over there in a place they call Somerset House. I want to know if he figures there in any connection—birth, marriage, naturalization, anything at all."

"Why?"

"What do you mean, why? Who's paying the bill?"

"Suppose the names don't show?"

"Then I'm stuck. If they do, I want certified copies of anything your man turns up. How much you soaking me?"

"I'll have to ask Carne. He may thumb it out altogether. We don't want the kind of publicity you get. If he lets me handle it, and you agree not to mention the connection, I'd say three hundred bucks. Those guys over there don't get much by dollar standards. He might hit us for ten guineas, less than thirty bucks. On top of that any expenses he might have. Say fifty bucks altogether and Carne wouldn't open a file for less than two-fifty."

"Professional rates."

"Ha, ha. He never heard of them."

"Call me, George. Want to eat dinner?"

"Romanoff's?"

"All right," I growled, "if they'll give me a reservation—which I doubt."

"We can have Carne's table. I happen to know he's dining privately. He's a regular at Romanoff's. It pays off in the upper brackets of the business. Carne is a pretty big boy in this town."

"Yeah, sure. I know somebody—and know him personally—who could lose Carne under his little fingernail."

"Good work, kid. I always knew you would come through in the clutch. See you about seven o'clock in the bar at Romanoff's. Tell the head thief you're waiting for Colonel Carne. He'll clear a space around you so you don't get elbowed by any riffraff like screenwriters or television actors."

"See you at seven," I said.

We hung up and I went back to the chess board. But The Sphynx didn't seem to interest me any more. In a little while Peters called me back and said it was all right with Carne provided the name of their agency was not connected with my problems. Peters said he would get a night letter off to London at once.

41

Howard Spencer called me on the following Friday morning. He was at the Ritz-Beverly and suggested I drop over for a drink in the bar.

"Better make it in your room," I said.

"Very well, if you prefer it. Room 828. I've just talked to Eileen Wade. She seems quite resigned. She has read the script Roger left and says she thinks it can be finished off very easily. It will be a good deal shorter than his other books, but that is balanced by the publicity value. I guess you think we publishers are a pretty callous bunch. Eileen will be home all afternoon. Naturally she wants to see me and I want to see her."

"I'll be over in half an hour, Mr. Spencer."

He had a nice roomy suite on the west side of the hotel. The living room had tall windows opening on a narrow iron-railed balcony. The furniture was upholstered in some candy-striped material and that with the heavily flowered design of the carpet gave it an old-fashioned air, except that everything you could put a drink down on had a plate glass top and there were nineteen ash trays spotted around. A hotel room is a pretty sharp indication of the manners of the guests. The Ritz-Beverly wasn't expecting them to have any.

Spencer shook hands. "Sit down," he said. "What will you drink?"

"Anything or nothing. I don't have to have a drink."

"I fancy a glass of Amontillado. California is poor drinking country in the summer. In New York you can handle four times as much for one half the hangover."

"I'll take a rye whiskey sour."

He went to the phone and ordered. Then he sat down on one of the candy-striped chairs and took off his rimless glasses to polish them on a handkerchief. He put them back on, adjusted them carefully, and looked at me.

238

"I take it you have something on your mind. That's why you wanted to see me up here rather than in the bar."

"I'll drive you out to Idle Valley. I'd like to see Mrs. Wade too."

He looked a little uncomfortable. "I'm not sure that she wants to see you," he said.

"I know she doesn't. I can get in on your ticket."

"That would not be very diplomatic of me, would it?"

"She tell you she didn't want to see me?"

"Not exactly, not in so many words." He cleared his throat. "I get the impression that she blames you for Roger's death."

"Yeah. She said that right out—to the deputy who came the afternoon he died. She probably said it to the Sheriff's homicide lieutenant that investigated the death. She didn't say it to the Coroner, however."

He leaned back and scratched the inside of his hand with a finger, slowly. It was just a sort of doodling gesture.

"What good would it do for you to see her, Marlowe? It was a pretty dreadful experience for her. I imagine her whole life had been pretty dreadful for some time. Why make her live it over? Do you expect to convince her that you didn't miss out a little?"

"She told the deputy I killed him."

"She couldn't have meant that literally. Otherwise—"

The door buzzer rang. He got up to go to the door and open it. The room service waiter came in with the drinks and put them down with as much flourish as if he was serving a seven course dinner. Spencer signed the check and gave him four bits. The guy went away. Spencer picked up his glass of sherry and walked away as if he didn't want to hand me my drink. I let it stay where it was.

"Otherwise what?" I asked him.

"Otherwise she *would* have said something to the Coroner, wouldn't she?" He frowned at me. "I think we are talking nonsense. Just what did you want to see me about?"

"You wanted to see me."

"Only," he said coldly, "because when I talked to you from New York you said I was jumping to conclusions. That implied to me that you had something to explain. Well, what is it?"

"I'd like to explain it in front of Mrs. Wade."

"I don't care for the idea. I think you had better make your own arrangements. I have a great regard for Eileen Wade. As a businessman I'd like to salvage Roger's work if it can be done. If Eileen feels about you as you suggest, I can't be the means of getting you into her house. Be reasonable."

"That's all right," I said. "Forget it. I can get to see her without any trouble. I just thought I'd like to have somebody along with me as a witness."

"Witness to what?" he almost snapped at me.

"You'll hear it in front of her or you won't hear it at all."

"Then I won't hear it at all."

I stood up. "You're probably doing the right thing, Spencer. You want that book of Wade's—if it can be used. And you want to be a nice guy. Both laudable ambitions. I don't share either of them. The best of luck to you and goodbye."

He stood up suddenly and started towards me. "Now just a minute, Marlowe. I don't know what's on your mind but you seem to take it hard. Is there some mystery about Roger Wade's death?"

"No mystery at all. He was shot through the head with a Webley Hammerless revolver. Didn't you see a report of the inquest?"

"Certainly." He was standing close to me now and he looked bothered. "That was in the eastern papers and a couple of days later a much fuller account in the Los Angeles papers. He was alone in the house, although you were not far away. The servants were away, Candy and the cook, and Eileen had been uptown shopping and arrived home just after it happened. At the moment it happened a very noisy motorboat on the lake drowned the sound of the shot, so that even you didn't hear it."

"That's correct," I said. "Then the motorboat went away, and I walked back from the lake edge and into the house, heard the doorbell ringing, and opened it to find Eileen Wade had forgotten her keys. Roger was already dead. She looked into the study from the doorway, thought he was asleep on the couch, went up to her room, then out to the kitchen to make some tea. A little later than she did I also looked into the study, noticed there was no sound of breathing, and found out why. In due course I called the law."

"I see no mystery," Spencer said quietly, all the sharpness gone from his voice. "It was Roger's own gun, and only the week before he had shot it off in his own room. You found Eileen struggling to get it away from him. His state of mind, his behavior, his depressions over his work—all that was brought out."

"She told you the stuff is good. Why should he be depressed over it?"

"That's just her opinion, you know. It may be very bad. Or he may have thought it worse than it was. Go on. I'm not a fool. I can see there is more."

"The homicide dick who investigated the case is an old friend of mine. He's a bulldog and a bloodhound and an old wise cop. He doesn't like a few things. Why did Roger leave no note—when he was a writing fool? Why did he shoot himself in such a way as to leave the shock of discovery to his wife? Why did he bother to pick the moment when I couldn't hear the gun go off? Why did she forget her house keys so that she had to be let in to the house? Why did she leave him alone on the day the help got off? Remember, she said she didn't know I would be there. If she did, those two cancel out."

"My God," Spencer bleated, "are you telling me the damn fool cop suspects Eileen?"

"He would if he could think of a motive."

"That's ridiculous. Why not suspect you? You had all afternoon. There could have been only a few minutes when she could have done it—and she had forgotten her house keys."

"What motive could I have?"

He reached back and grabbed my whiskey sour and swallowed it whole. He put the glass down carefully and got a handkerchief out and wiped his lips and his fingers where the chilled glass had moistened them. He put the handkerchief away. He stared at me.

"Is the investigation still going on?"

"Couldn't say. One thing is sure. They know by now whether he had drunk enough hooch to pass him out. If he had, there may still be trouble."

"And you want to talk to her," he said slowly, "in the presence of a witness."

"That's right."

"That means only one of two things to me, Marlowe. Either you are badly scared or you think she ought to be."

I nodded.

"Which one?" he asked grimly.

"I'm not scared."

He looked at his watch. "I hope to God you're crazy."

We looked at each other in silence.

42

NORTH THROUGH COLDWATER CANYON it began to get hot. When we topped the rise and started to wind down towards the San Fernando Valley it was breathless and blazing. I looked sideways at Spencer. He had a vest on, but the heat didn't seem to bother him. He had something else to bother him a lot more. He looked straight ahead through the windshield and said nothing. The valley had a thick layer of smog nuzzling down on it. From above it looked like a ground mist and then we were in it and it jerked Spencer out of his silence.

"My God, I thought Southern California had a climate," he said. "What are they doing—burning old truck tires?"

"It'll be all right in Idle Valley," I told him soothingly. "They get an ocean breeze in there."

"I'm glad they get something besides drunk," he said. "From what I've seen of the local crowd in the rich suburbs I think Roger made a tragic mistake in coming out here to live. A writer needs stimulation—and not the kind they bottle. There's nothing around here but one great big suntanned hangover. I'm referring to the upper crust people of course."

I turned off and slowed down for the dusty stretch to the entrance of Idle Valley, then hit the paving again and in a little while the ocean breeze made itself felt, drifting down through the gap in the hills at the far end of the lake. High sprinklers revolved over the big smooth lawns and the water made a swishing sound as it licked at the grass.

By this time most of the well-heeled people were away somewhere else. You could tell by the shuttered look of the houses and the way the gardener's truck was parked smack in the middle of the driveway. Then we reached the Wades' place and I swung through the gateposts and stopped behind Eileen's Jaguar. Spencer got out and marched stolidly across the flagstones to the portico of the house. He rang the bell and the door opened almost at once. Candy was there in the white jacket and the dark good-looking face and the sharp black eyes. Everything was in order.

Spencer went in. Candy gave me a brief look and nearly shut the door in my face. I waited and nothing happened. I leaned on the bell and heard the chimes. The door swung wide and Candy came out snarling.

"Beat it! Turn blue. You want a knife in the belly?"

"I came to see Mrs. Wade."

"She don't want any part of you."

"Out of my way, peasant. I got business here."

"Candy!" It was her voice, and it was sharp.

He gave me a final scowl and backed into the house. I went in and shut the door. She was standing at the end of one of the facing davenports, and Spencer was standing beside her. She looked like a million. She had white slacks on, very high-waisted, and a white sport shirt with half sleeves, and a lilac-colored handkerchief budding from the pocket over her left breast.

"Candy is getting rather dictatorial lately," she said to Spencer. "It's so good to see you, Howard. And so nice of you to come all this way. I didn't realize you were bringing someone with you."

"Marlowe drove me out," Spencer said. "Also he wanted to see you."

"I can't imagine why," she said coolly. Finally she looked at me, but not as if not seeing me for a week had left an emptiness in her life. "Well?"

"It's going to take a little time," I said.

She sat down slowly. I sat down on the other davenport. Spencer was frowning. He took his glasses off and polished them. That gave him a chance to frown more naturally. Then he sat on the other end of the davenport from me.

"I was sure you would come in time for lunch," she told him, smiling.

"Not today, thanks."

"No? Well, of course if you are too busy. Then you just want to see that script."

"If I may."

"Of course. Candy! Oh, he's gone. It's on the desk in Roger's study. I'll get it."

Spencer stood up. "May I get it?"

Without waiting for an answer he started across the room. Ten feet behind her he stopped and gave me a strained look. Then he went on. I just sat there and waited until her head came around and her eyes gave me a cool impersonal stare.

"What was it you wanted to see me about?" she asked curtly.

"This and that. I see you are wearing that pendant again."

"I often wear it. It was given to me by a very dear friend a long time ago."

"Yeah. You told me. It's a British military badge of some sort, isn't it?"

She held it out at the end of the thin chain. "It's a jeweler's reproduction of one. Smaller than the original and in gold and enamel."

Spencer came back across the room and sat down again and put a thick pile of yellow paper on the corner of the cocktail table in front of him. He glanced at it idly, then his eyes were watching Eileen.

"Could I look at it a little closer?" I asked her.

She pulled the chain around until she could unfasten the clasp. She handed the pendant to me, or rather she dropped it in my hand. Then she folded her hands in her lap and just looked curious. "Why are you so interested? It's the badge of a regiment called the Artists Rifles, a Territorial regiment. The man who gave it to me was lost soon afterwards. At Andalsnes in Norway, in the spring of that terrible year—1940." She smiled and made a brief gesture with one hand. "He was in love with me."

"Eileen was in London all through the Blitz," Spencer said in an empty voice. "She couldn't get away."

We both ignored Spencer. "And you were in love with him," I said.

She looked down and then raised her head and our

glances locked. "It was a long time ago," she said. "And there was a war. Strange things happen."

"There was a little more to it than that, Mrs. Wade. I guess you forget how much you opened up about him. 'The wild mysterious improbable kind of love that never comes but once.' I'm quoting you. In a way you're still in love with him. It's darn nice of me to have the same initials. I suppose that had something to do with your picking me out."

"His name was nothing like yours," she said coldly. "And he is dead, dead, dead."

I held the gold and enamel pendant out to Spencer. He took it reluctantly. "I've seen it before," he muttered.

"Check me on the design," I said. "It consists of a broad dagger in white enamel with a gold edge. The dagger points downwards and the flat of the blade crosses in front of a pair of upward-curling pale blue enamel wings. Then it crosses in back of a scroll. On the scroll are the words: WHO DARES WINS."

"That seems to be correct," he said. "What makes it important?"

"She says it's a badge of the Artists Rifles, a Territorial outfit. She says it was given to her by a man who was in that outfit and was lost in the Norwegian campaign with the British Army in the spring of 1940 at Andalsnes."

I had their attention. Spencer watched me steadily. I wasn't talking to the birds and he knew it. Eileen knew it too. Her tawny eyebrows were crimped in a puzzled frown which could have been genuine. It was also unfriendly.

"This is a sleeve badge," I said. "It came into existence because the Artists Rifles were made over or attached or seconded or whatever the correct term is into a Special Air Service Outfit. They had originally been a Territorial Regiment of infantry. This badge didn't even exist until 1947. Therefore nobody gave it to Mrs. Wade in 1940. Also, no Artists Rifles were landed at Andalsnes in Norway in 1940. Sherwood Foresters and Leicestershires, yes. Both Territorial. Artists Rifles, no. Am I being nasty?"

Spencer put the pendant down on the coffee table and pushed it slowly across until it was in front of Eileen. He said nothing.

"Do you think I wouldn't know?" Eileen asked me contemptuously.

"Do you think the British War Office wouldn't know?" I asked her right back.

"Obviously there must be some mistake," Spencer said mildly.

I swung around and gave him a hard stare. "That's one way of putting it."

"Another way of putting it is that I am a liar," Eileen said icily. "I never knew anyone named Paul Marston, never loved him or he me. He never gave me a reproduction of his regimental badge, he was never missing in action, he never existed. I bought this badge myself in a shop in New York where they specialize in imported British luxuries, things like leather goods, hand-made brogues, regimental and school ties and cricket blazers, knickknacks with coats of arms on them and so on. Would an explanation like that satisfy you, Mr. Marlowe?"

"The last part would. Not the first. No doubt somebody told you it was an Artists Rifles badge and forgot to mention what kind, or didn't know. But you did know Paul Marston and he did serve in that outfit, and he was missing in action in Norway. But it didn't happen in 1940, Mrs. Wade. It happened in 1942 and he was in the Commandos then, and it wasn't at Andalsnes, but on a little island off the coast where the Commando boys pulled a fast raid."

"I see no need to be so hostile about it," Spencer said in an executive sort of voice. He was fooling with the yellow sheets in front of him now. I didn't know whether he was trying to stooge for me or was just sore. He picked up a slab of yellow script and weighed it on his hand.

"You going to buy that stuff by the pound?" I asked him.

He looked startled, then he smiled a small difficult smile.

"Eileen had a pretty rough time in London," he said. "Things get confused in one's memory."

I took a folded paper out of my pocket. "Sure," I said. "Like who you got married to. This is a certified copy of a marriage certificate. The original came from Caxton Hall Registry Office. The date of the marriage is August 1942. The parties named are Paul Edward Marston and Eileen Victoria Sampsell. In a sense Mrs. Wade is right. There was no such person as Paul Edward Marston. It was a fake name because in the army you have to get permission to get married. The man faked an identity. In the army he had another name. I have his whole army history. It's a wonder to me that people never seem to realize that all you have to do is ask."

Spencer was very quiet now. He leaned back and stared. But not at me. He stared at Eileen. She looked back at him with one of those faint half deprecatory, half seductive smiles women are so good at.

"But he was dead, Howard. Long before I met Roger. What could it possibly matter? Roger knew all about it. I never stopped using my unmarried name. In the circumstances I had to. It was on my passport. Then after he was killed in action—" She stopped and drew a slow breath and let her hand fall slowly and softly to her knee. "All finished, all done for, all lost."

"You're sure Roger knew?" he asked her slowly.

"He knew something," I said. "The name Paul Marston had a meaning for him. I asked him once and he got a funny look in his eyes. But he didn't tell me why."

She ignored that and spoke to Spencer.

"Why, of course Roger knew all about it." Now she was smiling at Spencer patiently as if he was being a little slow on the take. The tricks they have.

"Then why lie about the dates?" Spencer asked dryly. "Why say the man was lost in 1940 when he was lost in 1942? Why wear a badge that he couldn't have given you and make a point of saying that he did give it to you?"

"Perhaps I was lost in a dream," she said softly. "Or a nightmare, more accurately. A lot of my friends were killed in the bombing. When you said goodnight in those days you tried not to make it sound like goodbye. But that's what it often was. And when you said goodbye to a soldier—it was worse. It's always the kind and gentle ones that get killed."

He didn't say anything. I didn't say anything. She looked down at the pendant lying on the table in front of her. She picked it up and fitted it to the chain around her neck again and leaned back composedly.

"I know I haven't any right to cross-examine you, Eileen," Spencer said slowly. "Let's forget it. Marlowe made a big thing out of the badge and the marriage certificate and so on. Just for a moment I guess he had me wondering."

"Mr. Marlowe," she told him quietly, "makes a big thing

out of trifles. But when it comes to a really big thing—like saving a man's life—he is out by the lake watching a silly speedboat."

"And you never saw Paul Marston again," I said.

"How could I when he was dead?"

"You didn't know he was dead. There was no report of his death from the Red Cross. He might have been taken prisoner."

She shuddered suddenly. "In October 1942," she said slowly, "Hitler issued an order that all Commando prisoners were to be turned over to the Gestapo. I think we all know what that meant. Torture and a nameless death in some Gestapo dungeon." She shuddered again. Then she blazed at me: "You're a horrible man. You want me to live that over again, to punish me for a trivial lie. Suppose someone you loved had been caught by those people and you knew what had happened, what must have happend to him or her? Is it so strange that I tried to build another kind of memory—even a false one?"

"I need a drink," Spencer said. "I need a drink badly. May I have one?"

She clapped her hands and Candy drifted up from nowhere as he always did. He bowed to Spencer.

"What you like to drink, Señor Spencer?"

"Straight Scotch, and plenty of it," Spencer said.

Candy went over in the corner and pulled the bar out from the wall. He got a bottle up on it and poured a stiff jolt into a glass. He came back and set it down in front of Spencer. He started to leave again.

"Perhaps, Candy," Eileen said quietly, "Mr. Marlowe would like a drink too."

He stopped and looked at her, his face dark and stubborn.

"No, thanks," I said. "No drink for me."

Candy made a snorting sound and walked off. There was another silence. Spencer put down half of his drink. He lit a cigarette. He spoke to me without looking at me.

"I'm sure Mrs. Wade or Candy could drive me back to Beverly Hills. Or I can get a cab. I take it you've said your piece."

I refolded the certified copy of the marriage license. I put it back in my pocket.

"Sure that's the way you want it?" I asked him.

"That's the way everybody wants it."

"Good." I stood up. "I guess I was a fool to try to play it this way. Being a big time publisher and having the brains to go with it—if it takes any—you might have assumed I didn't come out here just to play the heavy. I didn't revive ancient history or spend my own money to get the facts just to twist them around somebody's neck. I didn't investigate Paul Marston because the Gestapo murdered him, because Mrs. Wade was wearing the wrong badge, because she got mixed up on her dates, because she married him in one of those quickie wartime marriages. When I started investigating him I didn't know any of those things. All I knew was his name. Now how do you suppose I knew that?"

"No doubt somebody told you," Spencer said curtly.

"Correct, Mr. Spencer. Somebody who knew him in New York after the war and later on saw him out here in Chasen's with his wife."

"Marston is a pretty common name," Spencer said, and sipped his whiskey. He turned his head sideways and his right eyelid drooped a fraction of an inch. So I sat down again. "Even Paul Marstons could hardly be unique. There are nineteen Howard Spencers in the Greater New York area telephone directories, for instance. And four of them are just plain Howard Spencer with no middle initial."

"Yeah. How many Paul Marstons would you say had had one side of their faces smashed by a delayed-action mortar shell and showed the scars and marks of the plastic surgery that repaired the damage?"

Spencer's mouth fell open. He made some kind of heavy breathing sound. He got out a handkerchief and tapped his temples with it.

"How many Paul Marstons would you say had saved the lives of a couple of tough gamblers named Mendy Menendez and Randy Starr on that same occasion? They're still around, they've got good memories. They can talk when it suits them. Why ham it up any more, Spencer? Paul Marston and Terry Lennox were the same man. It can be proved beyond any shadow of a doubt."

I didn't expect anyone to jump six feet into the air and scream and nobody did. But there is a kind of silence that is almost as loud as a shout. I had it. I had it all around me, thick and hard. In the kitchen I could hear water run.

Outside on the road I could hear the dull thump of a folded newspaper hit the driveway, then the light inaccurate whistling of a boy wheeling away on his bicycle.

I felt a tiny sting on the back of my neck. I jerked away from it and swung around. Candy was standing there with his knife in his hand. His dark face was wooden but there was something in his eyes I hadn't seen before.

"You are tired, amigo," he said softly. "I fix you a drink, no?"

"Bourbon on the rocks, thanks," I said.

"De pronto, señor."

He snapped the knife shut, dropped it into the side pocket of his white jacket and went softly away.

Then at last I looked at Eileen. She sat leaning forward, her hands clasped tightly. The downward tilt of her face hid her expression if she had any. And when she spoke her voice had the lucid emptiness of that mechanical voice on the telephone that tells you the time and if you keep on listening, which people don't because they have no reason to, it will keep on telling you the passing seconds forever, without the slightest change of inflection.

"I saw him once, Howard. Just once. I didn't speak to him at all. Nor he to me. He was terribly changed. His hair was white and his face—it wasn't quite the same face. But of course I knew him, and of course he knew me. We looked at each other. That was all. Then he was gone out of the room and the next day he was gone from her house. It was at the Lorings' I saw him—and her. One afternoon late. You were there, Howard. And Roger was there. I suppose you saw him too."

"We were introduced," Spencer said. "I knew who he was married to."

"Linda Loring told me he just disappeared. He gave no reason. There was no quarrel. Then after a while that woman divorced him. And still later I heard she found him again. He was down and out. And they were married again. Heaven knows why. I suppose he had no money and it didn't matter to him any more. He knew that I was married to Roger. We were lost to each other."

"Why?" Spencer asked.

Candy put my drink in front of me without a word. He looked at Spencer and Spencer shook his head. Candy drifted away. Nobody paid any attention to him. He was like the prop man in a Chinese play, the fellow that moves things around on the stage and the actors and audience alike behave as if he wasn't there.

"Why?" she repeated. "Oh, you wouldn't understand. What we had was lost. It could never be recovered. The Gestapo didn't get him after all. There must have been *some* decent Nazis who didn't obey Hitler's order about the Commandos. So he survived, he came back. I used to pretend to myself that I would find him again, but as he had been, eager and young and unspoiled. But to find him married to that redheaded whore—that was disgusting. I already knew about her and Roger. I have no doubt Paul did too. So did Linda Loring, who is a bit of a tramp herself, but not completely so. They all are in that set. You ask me why I didn't leave Roger and go back to Paul. After he had been in her arms and Roger had been in those same willing arms? No thank you. I need a little more inspiration than that. Roger I could forgive. He drank, he didn't know what he was doing. He worried about his work and he hated himself because he was just a mercenary hack. He was a weak man, unreconciled, frustrated, but understandable. He was just a husband. Paul was either much more or he was nothing. In the end he was nothing."

I took a swig of my drink. Spencer had finished his. He was scratching at the material of the davenport. He had forgotten the pile of paper in front of him, the unfinished novel of the very much finished popular author.

"I wouldn't say he was nothing," I said.

She lifted her eyes and looked at me vaguely and dropped them again.

"Less than nothing," she said, with a new note of sarcasm in her voice. "He knew what she was, he married her. Then because she was what he knew she was, he killed her. And then ran away and killed himself."

"He didn't kill her," I said, "and you know it."

She came upright with a smooth motion and stared at me blankly. Spencer let out a noise of some kind.

"Roger killed her," I said, "and you also know that."

"Did he tell you?" she asked quietly.

"He didn't have to. He did give me a couple of hints. He would have told me or someone in time. It was tearing him to pieces not to."

She shook her head slightly. "No, Mr. Marlowe. That was not why he was tearing himself to pieces. Roger didn't know he had killed her. He had blacked out completely. He knew something was wrong and he tried to bring it to the surface, but he couldn't. The shock had destroyed his memory of it. Perhaps it would have come back and perhaps in the last moments of his life it did come back. But not until then. Not until then."

Spencer said in a sort of growl: "That sort of thing just doesn't happen, Eileen."

"Oh yes, it does," I said. "I know of two well established instances. One was a blackout drunk who killed a woman he picked up in a bar. He strangled her with a scarf she was wearing fastened with a fancy clasp. She went home with him and what went on then is not known except that she got dead and when the law caught up with him he was wearing the fancy clasp on his own tie and he didn't have the faintest idea where he got it."

"Never?" Spencer asked. "Or just at the time?"

"He never admitted it. And he's not around any more to be asked. They gassed him. The other case was a head wound. He was living with a rich pervert, the kind that collects first editions and does fancy cooking and has a very expensive secret library behind a panel in the wall. The two of them had a fight. They fought all over the house, from room to room, the place was a shambles and the rich guy eventually got the low score. The killer, when they caught him, had dozens of bruises on him and a broken finger. All he knew for sure was that he had a headache and he couldn't find his way back to Pasadena. He kept circling around and stopping to ask directions at the same service station. The guy at the service station decided he was nuts and called the cops. Next time around they were waiting for him."

"I don't believe that about Roger," Spencer said. "He was no more psycho than I am."

"He blacked out when he was drunk," I said.

"I was there. I *saw* him do it," Eileen said calmly.

I grinned at Spencer. It was some kind of grin, not the cheery kind probably, but I could feel my face doing its best.

"She's going to tell us about it," I told him. "Just listen. She's going to tell us. She can't help herself now."

"Yes, that is true," she said gravely. "There are things no one likes to tell about an enemy, much less about one's own husband. And if I have to tell them publicly on a witness stand, you are not going to enjoy it, Howard. Your fine, talented, ever so popular and lucrative author is going to look pretty cheap. Sexy as all get out, wasn't he? On paper, that is. And how the poor fool tried to live up to it! All that woman was to him was a trophy. I spied on them. I should be ashamed of that. One has to say these things. I am ashamed of nothing. I saw the whole nasty scene. The guest house she used for her amours happens to be a nice secluded affair with its own garage and entrance on a side street, a dead end, shaded by big trees. The time came, as it must to people like Roger, when he was no longer a satisfactory lover. Just a little too drunk. He tried to leave but she came out after him screaming and stark naked, waving some kind of small statuette. She used language of a depth of filth and depravity I couldn't attempt to describe. Then she tried to hit him with the statuette. You are both men and you must know that nothing shocks a man quite so much as to hear a supposedly refined woman use the language of the gutter and the public urinal. He was drunk, he had had sudden spells of violence, and he had one then. He tore the statuette out of her hand. You can guess the rest."

"There must have been a lot of blood," I said.

"Blood?" She laughed bitterly. "You should have seen him when he got home. When I ran for my car to get away he was just standing there looking down at her. Then he bent and picked her up in his arms and carried her into the guest house. I knew then that the shock had partially sobered him. He got home in about an hour. He was very quiet. It shook him when he saw me waiting. But he wasn't drunk then. He was dazed. There was blood on his face, on his hair, all over the front of his coat. I got him into the lavatory off the study and got him stripped and cleaned off enough to get him upstairs into the shower. I put him to bed. I got an old suitcase and went downstairs and gathered up the bloody clothes and put them in the suitcase. I cleaned the basin and the floor and then I took a wet towel out and made sure his car was clean. I put it away and got mine out. I drove to the Chatsworth

Reservoir and you can guess what I did with the suitcase full of bloody clothes and towels."

She stopped. Spencer was scratching at the palm of his left hand. She gave him a quick glance and went on.

"While I was away he got up and drank a lot of whiskey. And the next morning he didn't remember a single thing. That is, he didn't say a word about it or behave as if he had anything on his mind but a hangover. And I said nothing."

"He must have missed the clothes," I said.

She nodded. "I think he did eventually—but he didn't say so. Everything seemed to happen at once about that time. The papers were full of it, then Paul was missing, and then he was dead in Mexico. How was I to know that would happen? Roger was my husband. He had done an awful thing, but she was an awful woman. And he hadn't known what he was doing. Then almost as suddenly as it began the papers dropped it. Linda's father must have had something to do with that. Roger read the papers, of course, and he made just the sort of comments one would expect from an innocent bystander who had just happened to know the people involved."

"Weren't you afraid?" Spencer asked her quietly.

"I was sick with fear, Howard. If he remembered, he would probably kill me. He was a good actor—most writers are—and perhaps he already knew and was just waiting for a chance. But I couldn't be sure. He might—just might—have forgotten the whole thing permanently. And Paul was dead."

"If he never mentioned the clothes that you had dumped in the reservoir, that proved he suspected something," I said. "And remember, in that stuff he left in the typewriter the other time—the time he shot the gun off upstairs and I found you trying to get it away from him—he said a good man had died for him."

"He said that?" Her eyes widened just the right amount.

"He wrote it—on the typewriter. I destroyed it, he asked me to. I supposed you had already seen it."

"I never read anything he wrote in his study."

"You read the note he left the time Verringer took him away. You even dug something out of the wastebasket."

"That was different," she said coolly. "I was looking for a clue to where he might have gone."

"Okay," I said, and leaned back. "Is there any more?"

She shook her head slowly, with a deep sadness. "I suppose not. At the very last, the afternoon he killed himself, he may have remembered. We'll never know. Do we want to know?"

Spencer cleared his throat. "What was Marlowe supposed to do in all this? It was your idea to get him here. You talked me into that, you know."

"I was terribly afraid. I was afraid of Roger and I was afraid *for* him. Mr. Marlowe was Paul's friend, almost the last person to see him who knew him. Paul might have told him something. I had to be sure. If he was dangerous, I wanted him on my side. If he found out the truth, there might still be some way to save Roger."

Suddenly and for no reason that I could see, Spencer got tough. He leaned forward and pushed his jaw out.

"Let me get this straight, Eileen. Here was a private detective who was already in bad with the police. They'd had him in jail. He was supposed to have helped Paul—I call him that because you do—jump the country to Mexico. That's a felony, if Paul was a murderer. So if he found out the truth and could clear himself, he would just sit on his hands and do nothing. Was that your idea?"

"I was afraid, Howard. Can't you understand that? I was living in the house with a murderer who might be a maniac. I was alone with him a large part of the time."

"I understand that," Spencer said, still tough. "But Marlowe didn't take it on, and you were still alone. Then Roger fired the gun off and for a week after that you were alone. Then Roger killed himself and very conveniently it was Marlowe who was alone that time."

"That is true," she said. "What of it? Could I help it?"

"All right," Spencer said. "Is it just possible you thought Marlowe might find the truth and with the background of the gun going off once already, just kind of hand it to Roger and say something like, 'Look, old man, you're a murderer and I know it and your wife knows it. She's a fine woman. She has suffered enough. Not to mention Sylvia Lennox's husband. Why not do the decent thing and pull the trigger and everybody will assume it was just a case of too much wild drinking? So I'll stroll down by the lake and smoke a cigarette, old man. Good luck and goodbye. Oh, here's the gun. It's loaded and it's all yours.' "

"You're getting horrible, Howard. I didn't think anything of the sort."

"You told the deputy Marlowe had killed Roger. What was that supposed to mean?"

She looked at me briefly, almost shyly. "I was very wrong to say that. I didn't know what I was saying."

"Maybe you thought Marlowe had shot him," Spencer suggested calmly.

Her eyes narrowed. "Oh no, Howard. Why? Why would he do that? That's an abominable suggestion."

"Why?" Spencer wanted to know. "What's abominable about it? The police had the same idea. And Candy gave them a motive. He said Marlowe was in your room for two hours the night Roger shot a hole in his ceiling—after Roger had been put to sleep with pills."

She flushed to the roots of her hair. She stared at him dumbly.

"And you didn't have any clothes on," Spencer said brutally. "That's what Candy told them."

"But at the inqest—" she began to say in a shattered kind of voice. Spencer cut her off.

"The police didn't believe Candy. So he didn't tell it at the inquest."

"Oh." It was a sigh of relief.

"Also," Spencer went on coldly, "the police suspected you. They still do. All they need is a motive. Looks to me like they might be able to put one together now."

She was on her feet. "I think you had both better leave my house," she said angrily. "The sooner the better."

"Well, did you or didn't you?" Spencer asked calmly, not moving except to reach for his glass and find it empty.

"Did I or didn't I what?"

"Shoot Roger?"

She was standing there staring at him. The flush had gone. Her face was white and tight and angry.

"I'm just giving you the sort of thing you'd get in court."

"I was out. I had forgotten my keys. I had to ring to get into the house. He was dead when I got home. All that is known. What has got into you, for God's sake?"

He took a handkerchief out and wiped his lips. "Eileen,

I've stayed in this house twenty times. I've never known that front door to be locked during the daytime. I don't say you shot him. I just asked you. And don't tell me it was impossible. The way things worked out it was easy."

"I shot my own husband?" she asked slowly and wonderingly.

"Assuming," Spencer said in the same indifferent voice, "that he *was* your husband. You had another when you married him."

"Thank you, Howard. Thank you very much. Roger's last book, his swan song, is there in front of you. Take it and go. And I think you had better call the police and tell them what you think. It will be a charming ending to our friendship. Most charming. Goodbye, Howard. I am very tired and I have a headache. I'm going to my room and lie down. As for Mr. Marlowe—and I suppose he put you up to all this—I can only say to him that if he didn't kill Roger in a literal sense, he certainly drove him to his death."

She turned to walk away. I said sharply: "Mrs. Wade, just a moment. Let's finish the job. No sense in being bitter. We are all trying to do the right thing. That suitcase you threw into the Chatsworth Reservoir—was it heavy?"

She turned and stared at me. "It was an old one, I said. Yes, it was very heavy."

"How did you get it over the high wire fence around the reservoir?"

"What? The fence?" She made a helpless gesture. "I suppose in emergencies one has an abnormal strength to do what has to be done. Somehow or other I did it. That's all."

"There isn't any fence," I said.

"Isn't any fence?" She repeated it dully, as if it didn't mean anything."

"And there was no blood on Roger's clothes. And Sylvia Lennox wasn't killed outside the guest house, but inside it on the bed. And there was practically no blood, because she was already dead—shot dead with a gun—and when the statuette was used to beat her face to a pulp, it was beating a dead woman. And the dead, Mrs. Wade, bleed very little."

She curled her lip at me contemptuously. "I suppose you were there," she said scornfully.

Then she went away from us.

We watched her go. She went up the stairs slowly, moving with calm elegance. She disappeared into her room and the door closed softly but firmly behind her. Silence.

"What was that about the wire fence?" Spencer asked me vaguely. He was moving his head back and forth. He was flushed and sweating. He was taking it gamely but it wasn't easy for him to take.

"Just a gag," I said. "I've never been close enough to the Chatsworth Reservoir to know what it looks like. Maybe it has a fence around it, maybe not."

"I see," he said unhappily. "But the point is she didn't know either."

"Of course not. She killed both of them."

43

THEN SOMETHING MOVED softly and Candy was standing at the end of the couch looking at me. He had his switch knife in his hand. He pressed the button and the blade shot out. He pressed the button and the blade went back into the handle. There was a sleek glitter in his eye.

"Million de pardones, señor," he said. "I was wrong about you. She killed the boss. I think I—" He stopped and the blade shot out again.

"No." I stood up and held my hand out. "Give me the knife, Candy. You're just a nice Mexican houseboy. They'd hang it onto you and love it. Just the kind of smoke screen that would make them grin with delight. You don't know what I'm talking about. But I do. They fouled it up so bad that they couldn't straighten it out now if they wanted to. And they don't want to. They'd blast a confession out of you so quickly you wouldn't even have time to tell them your full name. And you'd be sitting on your fanny up in San Quentin with a life sentence three weeks from Tuesday."

"I tell you before I am not a Mexican. I am Chileno from Viña del Mar near Valparaíso."

"The knife, Candy. I know all that. You're free. You've got money saved. You've probably got eight brothers and sisters back home. Be smart and go back where you came from. This job here is dead."

"Lots of jobs," he said quietly. Then he reached out and dropped the knife into my hand. "For you I do this."

I dropped the knife into my pocket. He glanced up towards the balcony. "La señora—what do we do now?"

"Nothing. We do nothing at all. The señora is very tired. She has been living under a great strain. She doesn't want to be disturbed."

"We've got to call the police," Spencer said grittily.

"Why?"

"Oh my God, Marlowe—we have to."

"Tomorrow. Pick up your pile of unfinished novel and let's go."

"We've got to call the police. There is such a thing as law."

"We don't have to do anything of the sort. We haven't enough evidence to swat a fly with. Let the law enforcement people do their own dirty work. Let the lawyers work it out. They write the laws for other lawyers to dissect in front of other lawyers called judges so that other judges can say the first judges were wrong and the Supreme Court can say the second lot were wrong. Sure there's such a thing as law. We're up to our necks in it. About all it does is make business for lawyers. How long do you think the big-shot mobsters would last if the lawyers didn't show them how to operate?"

Spencer said angrily: "That has nothing to do with it. A man was killed in this house. He happened to be an author and a very successful and important one, but that has nothing to do with it either. He was a man and you and I know who killed him. There's such a thing as justice."

"Tomorrow."

"You're just as bad as she is if you let her get away with it. I'm beginning to wonder about you a little, Marlowe. You could have saved his life if you had been on your toes. In a sense you let her get away with it. And for all I know this whole performance this afternoon has been just that—a performance."

"That's right. A disguised love scene. You could see Eileen is crazy about me. When things quiet down we may get married. She ought to be pretty well fixed. I haven't made a buck out of the Wade family yet. I'm getting impatient."

He took his glasses off and polished them. He wiped perspiration from the hollows under his eyes, replaced the glasses and looked at the floor.

"I'm sorry," he said. "I've taken a pretty stiff punch this afternoon. It was bad enough to know Roger had killed himself. But this other version makes me feel degraded— just knowing about it." He looked up at me. "Can I trust you?"

"To do what?"

"The right thing—whatever it is." He reached down and picked up the pile of yellow script and tucked it under his arm. "No, forget it. I guess you know what you are doing. I'm a pretty good publisher but this is out of my line. I guess what I really am is just a goddam stuffed shirt."

He walked past me and Candy stepped out of his way, then went quickly to the front door and held it open. Spencer went out past him with a brief nod. I followed. I stopped beside Candy and looked into his dark shining eyes.

"No tricks, amigo," I said.

"The señora is very tired," he said quietly. "She has gone to her room. She will not be disturbed. I know nothing, señor. No me acuerdo de nada . . . A sus órdenes, señor."

I took the knife out of my pocket and held it out to him. He smiled.

"Nobody trusts me, but I trust you, Candy."

"Lo mismo, señor. Muchas gracias."

Spencer was already in the car. I got in and started it and backed down the driveway and drove him back to Beverly Hills. I let him out at the side entrance of the hotel.

"I've been thinking all the way back," he said as he got out. "She must be a little insane. I guess they'd never convict her."

"They won't even try," I said. "But she doesn't know that."

He struggled with the batch of yellow paper under his arm, got it straightened out, and nodded to me. I watched him heave open the door and go on in. I eased up on the brake and the Olds slid out from the white curb, and that was the last I saw of Howard Spencer.

I got home late and tired and depressed. It was one of those nights when the air is heavy and the night noises seem muffled and far away. There was a high misty indifferent moon. I walked the floor, played a few records, and hardly heard them. I seemed to hear a steady ticking somewhere, but there wasn't anything in the house to tick. The ticking was in my head. I was a one-man death watch.

I thought of the first time I had seen Eileen Wade and the second and the third and the fourth. But after that something in her got out of drawing. She no longer seemed quite real. A murderer is always unreal once you know he is a murderer. There are people who kill out of hate or fear or greed. There are the cunning killers who plan and expect to get away with it. There are the angry killers who do not think at all. And there are the killers who are in love with death, to whom murder is a remote kind of suicide. In a sense they are all insane, but not in the way Spencer meant it.

It was almost daylight when I finally went to bed.

The jangle of the telephone dragged me up out of a black well of sleep. I rolled over on the bed, fumbled for slippers, and realized that I hadn't been asleep for more than a couple of hours. I felt like a half-digested meal eaten in a greasy-spoon joint. My eyes were stuck together and my mouth was full of sand. I heaved up on the feet and lumbered into the living room and pulled the phone off the cradle and said into it: "Hold the line."

I put the phone down and went into the bathroom and hit myself in the face with some cold water. Outside the window something went snip, snip, snip. I looked out vaguely and saw a brown expressionless face. It was the once-a-week Jap gardener I called Hardhearted Harry. He was trimming the tecoma—the way a Japanese gardener trims your tecoma. You ask him four times and he says, "next week," and then he comes by at six o'clock in the morning and trims it outside your bedroom window.

I rubbed my face dry and went back to the telephone.

"Yeah?"

"This is Candy, señor."

"Good morning, Candy."

"La señora es muerta."

Dead. What a cold black noiseless word it is in any language. The lady is dead.

"Nothing you did, I hope."

"I think the medicine. It is called demerol. I think forty, fifty in the bottle. Empty now. No dinner last night. This morning I climb up on the ladder and look in the window. Dressed just like yesterday afternoon. I break the screen open. La señora es muerta. Frio como agua de nieve."

Cold as icewater. "You call anybody?"

"Sí. El Doctor Loring. He call the cops. Not here yet."

"Dr. Loring, huh? Just the man to come too late."

"I don't show him the letter," Candy said.

"Letter to who?"

"Señor Spencer."

"Give it to the police, Candy. Don't let Dr. Loring have it. Just the police. And one more thing, Candy. Don't hide anything, don't tell them any lies. We were there. Tell the truth. This time the truth and all the truth."

There was a little pause. Then he said: "Sí. I catch. Hasta la vista, amigo." He hung up.

I dialed the Ritz-Beverly and asked for Howard Spencer.

"One moment, please. I'll give you the desk."

A man's voice said: "Desk speaking. May I help you?"

"I asked for Howard Spencer. I know it's early, but it's urgent."

"Mr. Spencer checked out last evening. He took the eight o'clock plane to New York."

"Oh, sorry. I didn't know."

I went out to the kitchen to make coffee—yards of coffee. Rich, strong, bitter, boiling hot, ruthless, depraved. The lifeblood of tired men.

It was a couple of hours later that Bernie Ohls called me.

"Okay, wise guy," he said. "Get down here and suffer."

44

It was like the other time except that it was day and we were in Captain Hernandez's office and the Sheriff was up in Santa Barbara opening Fiesta Week. Captain Hernandez was there and Bernie Ohls and a man from the coroner's office and Dr. Loring, who looked as if he had been caught performing an abortion, and a man named Lawford, a deputy from the D.A.'s office, a tall gaunt expressionless man whose brother was vaguely rumored to be a boss of the numbers racket in the Central Avenue district.

Hernandez had some handwritten sheets of note paper in front of him, flesh-pink paper, deckle-edged, and written on with green ink.

"This is informal," Hernandez said, when everybody was as comfortable as you can get in hard chairs. "No stenotype or recording equipment. Say what you like. Dr. Weiss represents the coroner who will decide whether an inquest is necessary. Dr. Weiss?"

He was fat, cheerful, and looked competent. "I think no inquest," he said. "There is every surface indication of narcotic poisoning. When the ambulance arrived the woman was still breathing very faintly and she was in a deep coma and all the reflexes were negative. At that stage you don't save one in a hundred. Her skin was cold and respiration would not be noticed without close examination. The houseboy thought she was dead. She died approximately an hour after that. I understand the lady was subject to occasional violent attacks of bronchial asthma. The demerol was prescribed by Dr. Loring as an emergency measure."

"Any information or deduction about the amount of demerol taken, Dr. Weiss?"

"A fatal dose," he said, smiling faintly. "There is no quick way of determining that without knowing the medical history, the acquired or natural tolerance. According to her confession she took twenty-three hundred milligrams, four or five times the minimal lethal dose for a non-addict." He looked questioningly at Dr. Loring.

"Mrs. Wade was not an addict," Dr. Loring said coldly. "The prescribed dose would be one or two fifty-milligram tablets. Three or four during a twenty-four-hour period would be the most I'd permit."

"But you gave her fifty at a whack," Captain Hernandez said. "A pretty dangerous drug to have around in that quantity, don't you think? How bad was this bronchial asthma, Doctor?"

Dr. Loring smiled contemptuously. "It was intermittent, like all asthma. It never amounted to what we term *status asthmaticus*, an attack so severe that the patient seems in danger of suffocating."

"Any comment, Dr. Weiss?"

"Well," Dr. Weiss said slowly, "assuming the note didn't exist and assuming we had no other evidence of how much of the stuff she took, it could be an accidental overdose. The safey margin isn't very wide. We'll know for sure tomorrow. You don't want to suppress the note, Hernandez, for Pete's sake?"

Hernandez scowled down at his desk. "I was just wondering. I didn't know narcotics were standard treatment for asthma. Guy learns something every day."

Loring flushed. "An emergency measure, I said, Captain. A doctor can't be everywhere at once. The onset of an asthmatic flareup can be very sudden."

Hernandez gave him a brief glance and turned to Lawford. "What happens to your office, if I give this letter to the press?"

The D.A.'s deputy glanced at me emptily. "What's this guy doing here, Hernandez?"

"I invited him."

"How do I know he won't repeat everything said in here to some reporter?"

"Yeah, he's a great talker. You found that out. The time you had him pinched."

Lawford grinned, then cleared his throat. "I've read that purported confession," he said carefully. "And I don't believe a word of it. You've got a background of emotional exhaustion, bereavement, some use of drugs, the strain of wartime life in England under bombing, this clandestine marriage, the man coming back here, and so on. Undoubtedly she developed a feeling of guilt and tried to purge herself of it by a sort of transference."

He stopped and looked around, but all he saw was faces with no expression. "I can't speak for the D.A. but my own feeling is that your confession would be no grounds to seek an indictment even if the woman had lived."

"And having already believed one confession you wouldn't care to believe another that contradicted the first one," Hernandez said caustically.

"Take it easy, Hernandez. Any law enforcement agency has to consider public relations. If the papers printed that confession we'd be in trouble. That's for sure. We've got enough eager beaver reformer groups around just waiting for that kind of chance to stick a knife into us. We've got a grand jury that's already jittery about the working-over your vice squad lieutenant got last week—it's about ten days."

Hernandez said: "Okay, it's your baby. Sign the receipt for me."

He shuffled the pink deckle-edged pages together and Lawford leaned down to sign a form. He picked up the pink pages, folded them, put them in his breast pocket and walked out.

Dr. Weiss stood up. He was tough, good-natured, unimpressed. "We had the last inquest on the Wade family too quick," he said. "I guess we won't bother to have this one at all."

He nodded to Ohls and Hernandez, shook hands formally with Loring, and went out. Loring stood up to go, then hesitated.

"I take it that I may inform a certain interested party that there will be no further investigation of this matter?" he said stiffly.

"Sorry to have kept you away from your patients so long, Doctor."

"You haven't answered my question," Loring said sharply. "I'd better warn you—"

"Get lost, Jack," Hernandez said.

Dr. Loring almost staggered with shock. Then he turned and fumbled his way rapidly out of the room. The door closed and it was a half minute before anybody said anything. Hernandez shook himself and lit a cigarette. Then he looked at me.

"Well?" he said.

"Well what?"

"What are you waiting for?"

"This is the end, then? Finished? Kaput."

"Tell him, Bernie."

"Yeah, sure it's the end," Ohls said. "I was all set to pull her in for questioning. Wade didn't shoot himself. Too much alcohol in his brain. But like I told you, where was the motive? Her confession could be wrong in details, but it proves she spied on him. She knew the layout of the guest house in Encino. The Lennox frail had taken both her men from her. What happened in the guest house is just what you want to imagine. One question you forgot to ask Spencer. Did Wade own a Mauser P.P.K.? Yeah, he owned a small Mauser automatic. We talked to Spencer already today on the phone. Wade was a blackout drunk. The poor unfortunate bastard either thought he had killed Sylvia Lennox or he actually had killed her or else he had some reason to know his wife had. Either way he was going to lay it on the line eventually. Sure, he'd been hitting the hooch long before, but he was a guy married to a beautiful nothing. The Mex knows all about it. The little bastard knows damn near everything. That was a dream girl. Some of her was here and now, but a lot of her was there and then. If she ever got hot pants, it wasn't for her husband. Get what I'm talking about?"

I didn't answer him.

"Damn near made her yourself, didn't you?"

I gave him the same no answer.

Ohls and Hernandez both grinned sourly. "Us guys aren't exactly brainless," Ohls said. "We knew there was something in that story about her taking her clothes off. You outtalked him and he let you. He was hurt and confused and he liked Wade and he wanted to be sure. When he got sure he'd have used his knife. This was a personal matter with him. He never snitched on Wade. Wade's wife did, and she deliberately fouled up the issue just to confuse Wade. It all adds. In the end I guess she was scared of him. And Wade never threw her down any stairs. That was an accident. She tripped and the guy tried to catch her. Candy saw that too."

"None of it explains why she wanted me around."

"I could think of reasons. One of them is old stuff. Every

cop has run into it a hundred times. You were the loose end, the guy that helped Lennox escape, his friend, and probably to some extent his confidant. What did he know and what did he tell you? He took the gun that had killed her and he knew it had been fired. She could have thought he did it for her. That made her think he knew she had used it. When he killed himself she was sure. But what about you? You were still the loose end. She wanted to milk you, and she had the charm to use, and a situation ready-made for an excuse to get next to you. And if she needed a fall guy, you were it. You might say she was collecting fall guys."

"You're imputing too much knowledge to her," I said.

Ohls broke a cigarette in half and started chewing on one half. The other half he stuck behind his ear.

"Another reason is she wanted a man, a big, strong guy that could crush her in his arms and make her dream again."

"She hated me," I said. "I don't buy that one."

"Of course," Hernandez put in dryly. "You turned her down. But she would have got over that. And then you blew the whole thing up in her face with Spencer listening in."

"You two characters been seeing any psychiatrists lately?"

"Jesus," Ohls said, "hadn't you heard? We got them in our hair all the time these days. We've got two of them on the staff. This ain't police business any more. It's getting to be a branch of the medical racket. They're in and out of jail, the courts, the interrogation rooms. They write reports fifteen pages long on why some punk of a juvenile held up a liquor store or raped a schoolgirl or peddled tea to the senior class. Ten years from now guys like Hernandez and me will be doing Rohrschach tests and word associations instead of chin-ups and target practice. When we go out on a case we'll carry little black bags with portable lie detectors and bottles of truth serum. Too bad we didn't grab the four hard monkeys that poured it on Big Willie Magoon. We might have been able to unmaladjust them and make them love their mothers."

"Okay for me to blow?"

"What are you not convinced about?" Hernandez asked, snapping a rubber band.

"I'm convinced. The case is dead. She's dead, they're all dead. A nice smooth routine all around. Nothing to do but go home and forget it ever happened. So I'll do that."

Ohls reached the half cigarette from behind his ear, looked at it as if wondering how it got there, and tossed it over his shoulder.

"What are you crying about?" Hernandez said. "If she hadn't been fresh out of guns she might have made it a perfect score."

"Also," Ohls said grimly, "the telephone was working yesterday."

"Oh sure," I said. "You'd have come running and what you would have found would have been a mixed up story that admitted nothing but a few silly lies. This morning you have what I suppose is a full confession. You haven't let me read it, but you wouldn't have called in the D.A. if it was just a love note. If any real solid work had been done on the Lennox case at the time, somebody would have dug up his war record and where he got wounded and all the rest of it. Somewhere along the line a connection with the Wades would have turned up. Roger Wade knew who Paul Marston was. So did another P.I. I happened to get in touch with."

"It's possible," Hernandez admitted, "but that isn't how police investigations work. You don't fool around with an open-shut case, even if there's no heat on to get it finalized and forgotten. I've investigated hundreds of homicides. Some are all of a piece, neat, tidy, and according to the book. Most of them make sense here, don't make sense there. But when you get motive, means, opportunity, flight, a written confession, and a suicide immediately afterwards, you leave it lay. No police department in the world has the men or the time to question the obvious. The only thing against Lennox being a killer was that somebody thought he was a nice guy who wouldn't have done it and that there were others who could equally well have done it. But the others didn't take it on the lam, didn't confess, didn't blow their brains out. He did. And as for being a nice guy I figure sixty to seventy percent of all the killers that end up in the gas chamber or the hot seat or on the end of a rope are people the neighbors thought were just as harmless as a Fuller Brush salesman. Just as harmless and quiet and well bred as Mrs. Roger Wade. You want to read what she wrote in that letter? Okay, read it. I've got to go down the hall."

He stood up and pulled a drawer open and put a folder on the top of the desk. "There are five photostats in here, Marlowe. Don't let me catch you looking at them."

He started for the door and then turned his head and said to Ohls: "You want to talk to Peshorek with me?"

Ohls nodded and followed him out. When I was alone in the office I lifted the cover of the file folder and looked at the white-on-black photostats. Then touching only the edges I counted them. There were six, each of several pages clipped together. I took one and rolled it up and slipped it into my pocket. Then I read over the next one in the pile. When I had finished I sat down and waited. In about ten minutes Hernandez came back alone. He sat down behind his desk again, tallied the photostats in the file folder, and put the file back in his desk.

He raised his eyes and looked at me without any expression. "Satisfied?"

"Lawford know you have those?"

"Not from me. Not from Bernie. Bernie made them himself. Why?"

"What would happen if one got loose?"

He smiled unpleasantly. "It won't. But if it did, it wouldn't be anybody in the Sheriff's office. The D.A. has photostat equipment too."

"You don't like District Attorney Springer too well, do you, Captain?"

He looked surprised. "Me? I like everybody, even you. Get the hell out of here. I've got work to do."

I stood up to go. He said suddenly: "You carry a gun these days?"

"Part of the time."

"Big Willie Magoon carried two. I wonder why he didn't use them."

"I guess he figured he had everybody scared."

"That could be it," Hernandez said casually. He picked up a rubber band and stretched it between his thumbs. He stretched it farther and farther. Finally with a snap it broke. He rubbed his thumb where the loose end had snapped back against it. "Anybody can be stretched too far," he said. "No matter how tough he looks. See you around."

I went out of the door and got out of the building fast. Once a patsy, always a patsy.

45

BACK IN MY DOG HOUSE on the sixth floor of the Cahuenga Building I went through my regular double play with the morning mail. Mail slot to desk to wastebasket, Tinker to Evers to Chance. I blew a clear space on the top of the desk and unrolled the photostat on it. I had rolled it so as not to make creases.

I read it over again. It was detailed enough and reasonable enough to satisfy any open mind. Eileen Wade had killed Terry's wife in a fit of jealous fury and later when the opportunity was set up she had killed Roger because she was sure he knew. The gun fired into the ceiling of his room that night had been part of the setup. The unanswered and forever unanswerable question was why Roger Wade had stood still and let her put it over. He must have known how it would end. So he had written himself off and didn't care. Words were his business, he had words for almost everything, but none for this.

"I have forty-six demerol tablets left from my last prescription," she wrote. "I now intend to take them all and lie down on the bed. The door is locked. In a very short time I shall be beyond saving. This, Howard, is to be understood. What I write is in the presence of death. Every word is true. I have no regrets—except possibly that I could not have found them together and killed them together. I have no regrets for Paul whom you have heard called Terry Lennox. He was the empty shell of the man I loved and married. He meant nothing to me. When I saw him that afternoon for the only time after he came back from the war—at first I didn't know him. Then I did and he knew me at once. He should have died young in the snow of Norway, my lover that I gave to death. He came back a friend of gamblers, the husband of a rich whore, a spoiled and ruined man, and probably some kind of crook in his past life. Time makes everything mean and shabby and wrinkled. The tragedy of life, Howard, is not that the beautiful things die young, but that they grow old and mean. It will not happen to me. Goodbye, Howard."

I put the photostat in the desk and locked it up. It was time for lucnch but I wasn't in the mood. I got the office bottle out of the deep drawer and poured a slug and then got the phone book off the hook at the desk and looked up the number of the *Journal*. I dialed it and asked the girl for Lonnie Morgan.

"Mr. Morgan doesn't come in until around four o'clock. You might try the press room at the City Hall."

I called that. And I got him. He remembered me well enough. "You've been a pretty busy guy, I heard."

"I've got something for you, if you want it. I don't think you want it."

"Yeah? Such as?"

"A photostat of a confession to two murders."

"Where are you?"

I told him. He wanted more information. I wouldn't give him any over the phone. He said he wasn't on a crime beat. I said he was still a newspaperman and on the only independent paper in the city. He still wanted to argue.

"Where did you get this whatever it is? How do I know it's worth my time?"

"The D.A.'s office has the original. They won't release it. It breaks open a couple of things they hid behind the icebox."

"I'll call you. I have to check with the brass."

We hung up. I went to the drugstore and ate a chicken salad sandwich and drank some coffee. The coffee was overtrained and the sandwich was as full of rich flavor as a piece torn off an old shirt. Americans will eat anything if it is toasted and held together with a couple of toothpicks and has lettuce sticking out of the sides, preferably a little wilted.

At three-thirty or so Lonnie Morgan came in to see me. He was the same long thin wiry piece of tired and expressionless humanity as he had been the night he drove me home from the jailhouse. He shook hands listlessly and rooted in a crumpled pack of cigarettes.

"Mr. Sherman—that's the M.E.—said I could look you up and see what you have."

"It's off the record unless you agree to my terms." I unlocked the desk and handed him the photostat. He read the four pages rapidly and then again more slowly. He looked very excited—about as excited as a mortician at a cheap funeral.

"Gimme the phone."

I pushed it across the desk. He dialed, waited, and said: "This is Morgan. Let me talk to Mr. Sherman." He waited and got some other female and then got his party and asked him to ring back on another line.

He hung up and sat holding the telephone in his lap with the forefinger pressing the button down. It rang again and he lifted the receiver to his ear.

"Here it is, Mr. Sherman."

He read slowly and distinctly. At the end there was a pause. Then, "One moment, sir." He lowered the phone and glanced across the desk. "He wants to know how you got hold of this."

I reached across the desk and took the photostat away from him. "Tell him it's none of his goddam business how I got hold of it. Where is something else. The stamp on the back of the pages show that."

"Mr. Sherman, it's apparently an official document of the Los Angeles Sheriff's office. I guess we could check its authenticity easy enough. Also there's a price."

He listened some more and then said;: "Yes, sir. Right here." He pushed the phone across the desk. "Wants to talk to you."

It was a brusque authoritative voice. "Mr. Marlowe, what are your terms? And remember the *Journal* is the only paper in Los Angeles which would even consider touching this matter."

"You didn't do much on the Lennox case, Mr. Sherman."

"I realize that. But at that time it was purely a question of scandal for scandal's sake. There was no question of who was guilty. What we have now, if your document is genuine, is something quite different. What are your terms?"

"You print the confession in full in the form of a photographic reproduction. Or you don't print it at all."

The Long Goodbye / 273

"It will be verified. You understand that?"

"I don't see how, Mr. Sherman. If you ask the D.A. he will either deny it or give it to every paper in town. He'd have to. If you ask the Sheriff's office they will put it up to the D.A."

"Don't worry about that, Mr. Marlowe. We have ways. How about your terms?"

"I just told you."

"Oh. You don't expect to be paid?"

"Not with money."

"Well, you know your own business, I suppose. May I have Morgan again?"

I gave the phone back to Lonnie Morgan.

He spoke briefly and hung up. "He agrees," he said. "I take that photostat and he checks it. He'll do what you say. Reduced to half size it will take about half of page 1A."

I gave him back the photostat. He held it and pulled at the tip of his long nose. "Mind my saying I think you're a damn fool?"

"I agree with you."

"You can still change your mind."

"Nope. Remember that night you drove me home from the City Bastille? You said I had a friend to say goodbye to. I've never really said goodbye to him. If you publish this photostat, that will be it. It's been a long time—a long, long time."

"Okay, chum." He grinned crookedly. "But I still think you're a damn fool. Do I have to tell you why?"

"Tell me anyway."

"I know more about you than you think. That's the frustrating part of newspaper work. You always know so many things you can't use. You get cynical. If this confession is printed in the *Journal*, a lot of people will be sore. The D.A., the coroner, the Sheriff's crowd, an influential and powerful private citizen named Potter, and a couple of toughies called Menendez and Starr. You'll probably end up in the hospital or in jail again."

"I don't think so."

"Think what you like, pal. I'm telling you what *I* think. The D.A. will be sore because he dropped a blanket on the Lennox case. Even if the suicide and confession of Lennox made him look justified, a lot of people will want to know how Lennox, an innocent man, came to make a confession, how he got dead, did he really commit suicide or was he helped, why was there no investigation into the circumstances, and how come the whole thing died so fast. Also, if he has the original of this photostat he will think he has been double-crossed by the Sheriff's people."

"You don't have to print the identifying stamp on the back."

"We won't. We're pals with the Sheriff. We think he's a straight guy. We don't blame him because he can't stop guys like Menendez. Nobody can stop gambling as long as it's legal in all forms in some places and legal in some forms in all places. You stole this from the Sheriff's office. I don't know how you got away with it. Want to tell me?"

"No."

"Okay. The coroner will be sore because he buggered up the Wade suicide. The D.A. helped him with that too. Harlan Potter will be sore because something is reopened that he used a lot of power to close up. Menendez and Starr will be sore for reasons I'm not sure of, but I know you got warned off. And when those boys get sore at somebody he gets hurt. You're apt to get the treatment Big Willie Magoon got."

"Magoon was probably getting too heavy for his job."

"Why?" Morgan drawled. "Because those boys have to make it stick. If they take the trouble to tell you to lay off, you lay off. I you don't and they let you get away with it they look weak. The hard boys that run the business, the big wheels, the board of directors, don't have any use for weak people. They're dangerous. And then there's Chris Mady."

"He just about runs Nevada, I heard."

"You heard right, chum. Mady is a nice guy but he knows what's right for Nevada. The rich hoodlums that operate in Reno and Vegas are very careful not to annoy Mr. Mady. If they did, their taxes would go up fast and their police co-operation would go down the same way. Then the top guys back East would decide some changes were necessary. An operator who can't get along with Chris Mady ain't operating correctly. Get him the hell out of there and put somebody else in. Getting him out of there means only one thing to them. Out in a wooden box."

"They never heard of me," I said.

Morgan frowned and whipped an arm up and down in a

meaningless gesture. "They don't have to. Mady's estate on the Nevada side of Tahoe is right next to Harlan Potter's estate. Could be they say hello once in a while. Could be some character that is on Mady's payroll hears from another guy on Potter's payroll that a punk named Marlowe is buzzing too loud about things that are not any of his business. Could be that this passing remark gets passed on down to where the phone rings in some apartment in L.A. and a guy with large muscles gets a hint to go out and exercise himself and two or three of his friends. If somebody wants you knocked off or smashed, the muscle men don't have to have it explained why. It's mere routine to them. No hard feelings at all. Just sit still while we break your arm. You want this back?"

He held out the photostat.

"You know what I want," I said.

Morgan stood up slowly and put the photostat in his inside pocket. "I could be wrong," he said. "You may know more about it than I do. I wouldn't know how a man like Harlan Potter looks at things."

"With a scowl," I said. "I've met him. But he wouldn't operate with a goon squad. He couldn't reconcile it with his opinion of how he wants to live."

"For my money," Morgan said sharply, "stopping a murder investigation with a phone call and stopping it by knocking off the witnesses is just a question of method. See you around—I hope."

He drifted out of the office like something blown by the wind.

46

I DROVE OUT TO VICTOR'S with the idea of drinking a gimlet and sitting around until the evening edition of the morning papers was on the street. But the bar was crowded and it wasn't any fun. When the barkeep I knew got around to me he called me by name.

"You like a dash of bitters in it, don't you?"

"Not usually. Just for tonight two dashes of bitters."

"I haven't seen your friend lately. The one with the green ice."

"Neither have I."

He went away and came back with the drink. I pecked at it to make it last, because I didn't feel like getting a glow on. Either I would get really stiff or stay sober. After a while I had another of the same. It was just past six when the kid with the papers came into the bar. One of the barkeeps yelled at him to beat it, but he managed one quick round of the customers before a waiter got hold of him and threw him out. I was one of the customers. I opened up the *Journal* and glanced at page 1A. They had made it. It was all there. They had reversed the photostat by making it black on white and by reducing it in size they had fitted it into the top half of the page. There was a short brusque editorial on another page. There was a half column by Lonnie Morgan with a by-line, on still another page.

I finished my drink and left and went to another place to eat dinner and then drove home.

Lonnie Morgan's piece was a straightforward factual recapitulation of the facts and happenings involved in the Lennox case and the "suicide" of Roger Wade—the facts as they had been published. It added nothing, deduced nothing, imputed nothing. It was clear concise businesslike reporting. The editorial was something else. It asked questions—the kind a newspaper asks of public officials when they are caught with jam on their faces.

About nine-thirty the telephone rang and Bernie Ohls said he would drop by on his way home.

"Seen the *Journal?*" he asked coyly, and hung up without waiting for an answer.

When he got there he grunted about the steps and said he would drink a cup of coffee if I had one. I said I would make some. While I made it he wandered around the house and made himself very much at home.

"You live pretty lonely for a guy that could get himself disliked," he said. "What's over the hill in back?"

"Another street. Why?"

"Just asking. Your shrubbery needs pruning."

I carried some coffee into the living room and he parked himself and sipped it. He lit one of my cigarettes and puffed at it for a minute or two, then put it out. "Getting so I don't care for the stuff," he said. "Maybe it's the TV commercials. They make you hate everything they try to sell. God, they must think the public is a halfwit. Every time some jerk in a white coat with a stethoscope hanging around his neck holds up some toothpaste or a pack of cigarettes or a bottle of beer or a mouthwash or a jar of shampoo or a little box of something that makes a fat wrestler smell like mountain lilac I always make a note never to buy any. Hell, I wouldn't buy the product even if I liked it. You read the *Journal,* huh?"

"A friend of mine tipped me off. A reporter."

"You got friends?" he asked wonderingly. "Didn't tell you how they got hold of the material, did he?"

"No. And in this state he doesn't have to tell you."

"Springer is hopping mad. Lawford, the deputy D.A. that got the letter this morning, claims he took it straight to his boss, but it makes a guy wonder. What the *Journal* printed looks like a straight reproduction from the original."

I sipped coffee and said nothing.

"Serves him right," Ohls went on. "Springer ought to have handled it himself. Personally I don't figure it was Lawford that leaked. He's a politician too." He stared at me woodenly.

"What are you here for, Bernie? You don't like me. We used to be friends—as much as anybody can be friends with a tough cop. But it soured a little."

He leaned forward and smiled—a little wolfishly. "No cop likes it when a private citizen does police work behind his back. If you had connected up Wade and the Lennox frail for me the time Wade got dead I'd have made out. If you had connected up Mrs. Wade and this Terry Lennox I'd have had her in the palm of my hand—alive. If you had come clean from the start Wade might be still alive. Not to mention Lennox. You figure you're a pretty smart monkey, don't you?"

"What would you like me to say?"

"Nothing. It's too late. I told you a wise guy never fools anybody but himself. I told you straight and clear. So it didn't take. Right now it might be smart for you to leave town. Nobody likes you and a couple of guys that don't like people do something about it. I had the word from a stoolie."

"I'm not that important, Bernie. Let's stop snarling at each other. Until Wade was dead you didn't even enter the case. After that it didn't seem to matter to you and to the coroner or to the D.A. or to anybody. Maybe I did some things wrong. But the truth came out. You could have had her yesterday afternoon—with what?"

"With what you had to tell us about her."

"Me? With the police work I did behind your back?"

He stood up abruptly. His face was red. "Okay, wise guy. She'd have been alive. We could have booked her on suspicion. You *wanted* her dead, you punk, and you know it."

"I wanted her to take a good long quiet look at herself. What she did about it was her business. I wanted to clear an innocent man. I didn't give a good goddam how I did it and I don't now. I'll be around when you feel like doing something about me."

"The hard boys will take care of you, buster. I won't have to bother. You think you're not important enough to bother them. As a P.I. named Marlowe, check. You're not. As a guy who was told where to get off and blew a raspberry in their faces publicly in a newspaper, that's different. That hurts their pride."

"That's pitiful," I said, "Just thinking about it makes me bleed internally, to use your own expression."

He went across to the door and opened it. He stood looking down the redwood steps and at the trees on the hill across the way and up the slope at the end of the street.

"Nice and quiet here," he said. "Just quiet enough."

He went on down the steps and got into his car and left. Cops never say goodbye. They're always hoping to see you again in the line-up.

47

For a short time the next day things looked like getting lively. District Attorney Springer called an early press conference and delivered a statement. He was the big florid black-browed prematurely gray-haired type that always does so well in politics.

"I have read the document which purports to be a confession by the unfortunate and unhappy woman who recently took her life, a document which may or may not be genuine, but which, if genuine, is obviously the product of a disordered mind. I am willing to assume that the *Journal* published this document in good faith, in spite of its many absurdities and inconsistencies, and these I shall not bore you with enumerating. If Eileen Wade wrote these words, and my office in conjunction with the staff of my respected coadjutor, Sheriff Petersen, will soon determine whether or no she did, then I say to you that she did not write them with a clear head, nor with a steady hand. It is only a matter of weeks since the unfortunate lady found her husband wallowing in his own blood, spilled by his own hand. Imagine the shock, the despair, the utter loneliness which must have followed so sharp a disaster! And now she has joined him in the bitterness of death. Is anything to be gained by disturbing the ashes of the dead? Anything, my friends, beyond the sale of a few copies of a newspaper which is badly in need of circulation? Nothing, my friends, nothing. Let us leave it at that. Like Ophelia in that great dramatic masterpiece called *Hamlet*, by the immortal William Shakespeare, Eileen Wade wore her rue with a difference. My political enemies would like to make much of that difference, but my friends and fellow voters will not be deceived. They know that this office has long stood for wise and mature law enforcement, for justice tempered with mercy, for solid, stable, and conservative government. The *Journal* stands for I know not what, and for what it stands I do not much or greatly care. Let the enlightened public judge for itself."

The *Journal* printed this guff in its early edition (it was a round-the-clock newspaper) and Henry Sherman, the Managing Editor, came right back at Springer with a signed comment.

Mr. District-Attorney Springer was in good form this morning. He is a fine figure of a man and he speaks with a rich baritone voice that is a pleasure to listen to. He did not bore us with any facts. Any time Mr.

Springer cares to have the authenticity of the document in question proved to him, the *Journal* will be most happy to oblige. We do not expect Mr. Springer to take any action to reopen cases which had been officially closed with his sanction or under his direction, just as we do not expect Mr. Springer to stand on his head on the tower of the City Hall. As Mr. Springer so aptly phrases it, is anything to be gained by disturbing the ashes of the dead? Or, as the *Journal* would prefer to phrase it less elegantly, is anything to be gained by finding out who committed a murder when the murderee is already dead? Nothing, of course, but justice and truth.

On behalf of the late William Shakespeare, the *Journal* wishes to thank Mr. Springer for his favorable mention of *Hamlet,* and for his substantially, although not exactly, correct allusion to Ophelia. 'You must wear your rue with a difference' was not said of Ophelia but by her, and just what she meant has never been very clear to our less erudite minds. But let that pass. It sounds well and helps to confuse the issue. Perhaps we may be permitted to quote, also from that officially approved dramatic production known as *Hamlet,* a good thing that happened to be said by a bad man: "And where the offence is let the great axe fall."

Lonnie Morgan called me up about noon and asked me how I liked it. I told him I didn't think it would do Springer any harm.

"Only with the eggheads," Lonnie Morgan said, "and they already had his number. I meant what about you?"

"Nothing about me. I'm just sitting here waiting for a soft buck to rub itself against my cheek."

"That wasn't exactly what I meant."

"I'm still healthy. Quit trying to scare me. I got what I wanted. If Lennox was still alive he could walk right up to Springer and spit in his eye."

"You did it for him. And by this time Springer knows that. They got a hundred ways to frame a guy they don't like. I don't figure what made it worth your time. Lennox wasn't that much man."

"What's that got to do with it?"

He was silent for a moment. Then he said: "Sorry, Marlowe. Shut my big mouth. Good luck."

We hung up after the usual goodbyes.

About two in the afternoon Linda Loring called me. "No names, please," she said. "I've just flown in from that big lake up north. Somebody up there is boiling over something that was in the *Journal* last night. My almost ex-husband got it right between the eyes. The poor man was weeping when I left. He flew up to report."

"What do you mean, almost ex-husband?"

"Don't be stupid. For once Father approves. Paris is an excellent place to get a quiet divorce. So I shall soon be leaving to go there. And if you have any sense left you could do worse than spend a little of that fancy engraving you showed me going a long way off yourself."

"What's it got to do with me?"

"That's the second stupid question you've asked. You're not fooling anyone but yourself, Marlowe. Do you know how they shoot tigers?"

"How would I?"

"They tie a goat to a stake and then hide out in a blind. It's apt to be rough on the goat. I like you. I'm sure I don't know why, but I do. I hate the idea of your being the goat. You tried so hard to do the right thing—as you saw it."

"Nice of you," I said. "If I stick my neck out and it gets chopped, it's still my neck."

"Don't be a hero, you fool," she said sharply. "Just because someone we knew chose to be a fall guy, you don't have to imitate him."

"I'll buy you a drink if you're ging to be around long enough."

"Buy me one in Paris. Paris is lovely in the fall."

"I'd like to do that too. I hear it was even better in the spring. Never having been there I wouldn't know."

"The way you're going you never will."

"Goodbye, Linda. I hope you find what you want."

"Goodbye," she said coldly. "I always find what I want. But when I find it, I don't want it any more."

She hung up. The rest of the day was a blank. I ate dinner and left the Olds at an all night garage to have the brake linings checked. I took a cab home. The street was as empty as usual. In the wooden mailbox was a free soap coupon. I went up the steps slowly. It was a soft night with a little haze in the air. The trees on the hill hardly moved. No breeze. I unlocked the door and pushed it part way open and then stopped. The door was about ten inches open from the frame. It was dark inside, there was no sound. But I had the feeling that the room beyond was not empty. Perhaps a spring squeaked faintly or I caught the gleam of a white jacket across the room. Perhaps on a warm still night like this one the room beyond the door was not warm enough, not still enough. Perhaps there was a drifting smell of man on the air. And perhaps I was just on edge.

I stepped sideways off the porch on to the ground and leaned down against the shrubbery. Nothing happened. No light went on inside, there was no movement anywhere that I heard, I had a gun in a belt holster on the left side, butt forward, a short-barreled Police 38. I jerked it out and it got me nowhere. The silence continued. I decided I was a damn fool. I straightened up and lifted a foot to go back to the front door, and then a car turned the corner and came fast up the hill and stopped almost without sound at the foot of my steps. It was a big black sedan with the lines of a Cadillac. It could have been Linda Loring's car, except for two things. Nobody opened a door and the windows on my side were all shut tight. I waited and listened, crouched against the bush, and there was nothing to listen to and nothing to wait for. Just a dark car motionless at the foot of my redwood steps, with the windows closed. If its motor was still running I couldn't hear it. Then a big red spotlight clicked on and the beam struck twenty feet beyond the corner of the house. And then very slowly the big car backed until the spotlight could swing across the front of the house, across the hood and up.

Policemen don't drive Cadillacs. Cadillacs with red spotlights belong to the big boys, mayors and police commissioners, perhaps District Attorneys. Perhaps hoodlums.

The spotlight traversed. I went down flat, but it found me just the same. It held on me. Nothing else. Still the car door didn't open, still the house was silent and without light.

Then a siren growled in low pitch just for a second or

two and stopped. And then at last the house was full of lights and a man in a white dinner jacket came out to the head of the steps and looked sideways along the wall and the shrubbery.

"Come on in, cheapie," Menendez said with a chuckle. "You've got company."

I could have shot him with no trouble at all. Then he stepped back and it was too late—even if I could have done it. Then a window went down at the back of the car and I could hear the thud as it opened. Then a machine pistol went off and fired a short burst into the slope of the bank thirty feet away from me.

"Come on in, cheapie," Menendez said again from the doorway. "There just ain't anywhere else to go."

So I straightened up and went and the spotlight followed me accurately. I put the gun back in the hoslter on my belt. I stepped up onto the small redwood landing and went in through the door and stopped just inside. A man was sitting across the room with his legs crossed and a gun resting sideways on his thigh. He looked rangy and tough and his skin had that dried-out look of people who live in sun-bleached cilmates. He was wearing a dark brown gabardine-type windbreaker and the zipper was open almost to his waist. He was looking at me and neither his eyes nor the gun moved. He was as calm as an adobe wall in the moonlight.

48

I LOOKED AT HIM TOO LONG. There was a brief half-seen move at my side and a numbing pain in the point of my shoulder. My whole arm went dead to the fingertips. I turned and looked at a big mean-looking Mexican. He wasn't grinning, he was just watching me. The .45 in his brown hand dropped to his side. He had a mustache and his head bulged with oily black hair brushed up and back and over and down. There was a dirty sombrero on the back of his head and the leather chin strap hung loose in two strands down the front of a stitched shirt that smelled of sweat. There is nothing tougher than a tough Mexican, just as there is nothing gentler than a gentle Mexican, nothing more honest than an honest Mexican, and above all nothing sadder than a sad Mexican. This guy was one of the hard boys. They don't come any harder anywhere.

I rubbed my arm. It tingled a little but the ache was still there and the numbness. If I had tried to pull a gun I should probably have dropped it.

Menendez held his hand out towards the slugger. Without seeming to look he tossed the gun and Menendez caught it. He stood in front of me now and his face glistened. "Where would you like it, cheapie?" His black eyes danced.

I just looked at him. There is no answer to a question like that.

"I asked you a question, cheapie."

I wet my lips and asked one back. "What happened to Agostino? I thought he was your gun handler."

"Chick went soft," he said gently.

"He was always soft—like his boss."

The man in the chair flicked his eyes. He almost but not quite smiled. The tough boy who had paralyzed my arm neither moved nor spoke. I knew he was breathing. I could smell that.

"Somebody bump into your arm, cheapie?"

"I tripped over an enchilada."

Negligently, not quite looking at me even, he slashed me across the face with the gun barrel.

"Don't get gay with me, cheapie. You're out of time for all that. You got told and you got told nice. When I take the trouble to call around personally and tell a character to lay off—he lays off. Or else he lays down and don't get up."

I could feel a trickle of blood down my cheek. I could feel the full numbing ache of the blow in my cheekbone. It spread until my whole head ached. It hadn't been a hard blow, but the thing he used was hard. I could still talk and nobody tried to stop me.

"How come you do your own slugging, Mendy? I thought that was coolie labor for the sort of boys that beat up Big Willie Magoon."

"It's the personal touch," he said softly, "on account of I

had personal reasons for telling you. The Magoon job was strictly business. He got to thinking he could push me around—me that bought his clothes and his cars and stocked his safe deposit box and paid off the trust deed on his house. These vice squad babies are all the same. I even paid school bills for his kid. You'd think the bastard would have some gratitude. So what does he do? He walks into my private office and slaps me around in front of the help."

"On account of why?" I asked him, in the vague hope of getting him mad at somebody else.

"On account of some lacquered chippie said we used loaded dice. Seems like the bim was one of his sleepy-time gals. I had her put out of the club—with every dime she brought in with her."

"Seems understandable," I said. "Magoon ought to know no professional gambler plays crooked games. He doesn't have to. But what have I done to you?"

He hit me again, thoughtfully. "You made me look bad. In my racket you don't tell a guy twice. Not even a hard number. He goes out and does it, or you ain't got control. You ain't got control, you ain't in business."

"I've got a hunch that there's a little more to it than that," I said. "Excuse me if I reach for a handkerchief."

The gun watched me while I got one out and touched the blood on my face.

"A two-bit peeper," Menendez said slowly, "figures he can make a monkey out of Mendy Menendez. He can get me laughed at. He can get me the big razzoo—me, Menendez. I ought to use a knife on you, cheapie. I ought to cut you into slices of raw meat."

"Lennox was your pal," I said, and watched his eyes. "He got dead. He got buried like a dog without even a name over the dirt where they put his body. And I had a little something to do with proving him innocent. So that makes you look bad, huh? He saved your life and he lost his, and that didn't mean a thing to you. All that means anything to you is playing the big shot. You didn't give a hoot in hell for anybody but yourself. You're not big, you're just loud."

His face froze and he swung his arm back to slug me a third time and this time with the power behind it. His arm was still going back when I took a half step forward and kicked him in the pit of the stomach.

I didn't think, I didn't plan, I didn't figure my chances or whether I had any. I just got enough of his yap and I ached and bled and maybe I was just a little punch drunk by this time.

He jackknifed, gasping, and the gun fell out of his hand. He groped for it wildly making strained sounds deep in his throat. I put a knee into his face. He screeched.

The man in the chair laughed. That staggered me. Then he stood up and the gun in his hand came up with him.

"Don't kill him," he said mildly. "We want to use him for live bait."

Then there was movement in the shadows of the hall and Ohls came through the door, blank-eyed, expressionless and utterly calm. He looked down at Menendez. Menendez was kneeling with his head on the floor.

"Soft," Ohls said. "Soft as mush."

"He's not soft," I said. "He's hurt. Any man can be hurt. Was Big Willie Magoon soft?"

Ohls looked at me. The other man looked at me. The tough Mex at the door hadn't made a sound.

"Take that goddam cigarette out of your face," I snarled at Ohls. "Either smoke it or leave it alone. I'm sick of watching you. I'm sick of you, period. I'm sick of cops."

He looked surprised. Then he grinned.

"That was a plant, kiddo," he said cheerfully. "You hurt bad? Did the nasty mans hit your facey-wacey? Well for my money you had it coming and it was damn useful that you had." He looked down at Mendy. Mendy had his knees under him. He was climbing out of a well, a few inches at a time. He breathed gaspingly.

"What a talkative lad he is," Ohls said, "when he doesn't have three shysters with him to button his lip."

He jerked Menendez to his feet. Mendy's nose was bleeding. He fumbled the handkerchief out of his white dinner jacket and held it to his nose. He said no word.

"You got crossed up, sweetheart," Ohls told him carefully. "I ain't grieving a whole lot over Magoon. He had it coming. But he was a cop and punks like you lay off cops—always and forever."

Menendez lowered the handkerchief and looked at Ohls. He looked at me. He looked at the man who had been sitting in the chair. He turned slowly and looked at the tough Mex by the door. They all looked at him. There was nothing in their faces. Then a knife shot into view from nowhere and Mendy lunged for Ohls. Ohls side-stepped and took him by the throat with one hand and chopped the knife out of his hand with ease, almost indifferently. Ohls spread his feet and straightened his back and bent his legs slightly and lifted Menendez clear off the floor with one hand holding his neck. He walked him across the floor and pinned him against the wall. He let him down, but didn't let go of his throat.

"Touch me with one finger and I'll kill you," Ohls said. "One finger." Then he dropped his hands.

Mendy smiled at him scornfully, looked at his handkerchief, and refolded it to hide the blood. He held it to his nose again. He looked down at the gun he had used to hit me. The man from the chair said loosely: "Not loaded, even if you could grab it."

"A cross," Mendy said to Ohls. "I heard you the first time."

"You ordered three muscles," Ohls said. "What you got was three deputies from Nevada. Somebody in Vegas don't like the way you forget to clear with them. The somebody wants to talk to you. You can go along with the deputies or you can go downtown with me and get hung on the back of the door by a pair of handcuffs. There's a couple of boys down there would like to see you close up."

"God help Nevada," Mendy said quietly, looking around again at the tough Mex by the door. Then he crossed himself quickly and walked out of the front door. The tough Mex followed him. Then the other one, the dried out desert type, picked up the gun and the knife and went out too. He shut the door. Ohls waited motionless. There was a sound of doors banging shut, then a car wnet off into the night.

"You sure those mugs were deputies?" I asked Ohls.

He turned as if surprised to see me there. "They had stars," he said shortly.

"Nice work, Bernie. Very nice. Think he'll get to Vegas alive, you coldhearted son of a bitch?"

I went to the bathroom and ran cold water and held a soaked towel against my throbbing cheek. I looked at myself in the glass. The cheek was puffed out of shape and bluish and there were jagged wounds on it from the force of the gun barrel hitting against the cheekbone. There was a discoloration under my left eye too. I wasn't going to be beautiful for a few days.

Then Ohls' reflection showed behind me in the mirror. He was rolling his damn unlighted cigarette along his lips, like a cat teasing a half-dead mouse, trying to get it to run away just once more.

"Next time don't try to outguess the cops," he said gruffly. "You think we let you steal that photostat just for laughs? We had a hunch Mendy would come gunning for you. We put it up to Starr cold. We told him we couldn't stop gambling in the county, but we could make it tough enough to cut way into the take. No mobster beats up a cop, not even a bad cop, and gets away with it in our territory. Starr convinced us he had nothing to do with it, that the outfit was sore about it and Menendez was going to get told. So when Mendy called for a squad of out-of-town hard boys to come and give you the treatment, Starr sent him three guys he knew, in one of his own cars, at his own expense. Starr is a police commissioner in Vegas."

I turned around and looked at Ohls. "The coyotes out in the desert will get fed tonight. Congratulations. Cop business is wonderful uplifting idealistic work, Bernie. The only thing wrong with cop business is the cops that are in it."

"Too bad for you, hero," he said with a sudden cold savagery. "I could hardly help laughing when you walked into your own parlor to take your beating. I got a rise out of that, kiddo. It was a dirty job and it had to be done dirty. To make these characters talk you got to give them a sense of power. You ain't hurt bad, but we had to let them hurt you some."

"So sorry," I said. "So very sorry you had to suffer like that."

He shoved his taut face at me. "I hate gamblers," he said in a rough voice. "I hate them the way I hate dope pushers. They pander to a disease that is every bit as corrupting as dope. You think those palaces in Reno and Vegas are just for harmless fun? Nuts, they're there for the little guy, the something-for-nothing sucker, the lad that stops off with his pay envelope in his pocket and loses the week-end grocery money. The rich gambler loses forty grand and laughs it off and comes back for more. But the rich gambler don't make the big racket, pal. The big steal is in dimes and quarters and half dollars and once in a while a buck or even a five-spot. The big racket money comes in like water from the pipe in your bathroom, a steady stream that never stops flowing. Any time anybody wants to knock off a professional gambler, that's for me. I like it. And any time a state government takes money from gambling and calls it taxes, that government is helping to keep the mobs in business. The barber or the beauty parlor girl puts two bucks on the nose. That's for the Syndicate, that's what really makes the profits. The people want an honest police force, do they? What for? To protect the guys with courtesy cards? We got legal horse tracks in this state, we got them all year round. They operate honest and the state gets its cut, and for every dollar laid at the track there's fifty laid with the bookies. There's eight or nine races on a card and in half of them, the little ones nobody notices, the fix can be in any time somebody says so. There's only one way a jock can win a race, but there's twenty ways he can lose one, with a steward at every eighth pole watching, and not able to do a damn thing about it if the jock knows his stuff. That's legal gambling, pal, clean honest business, state approved. So it's right, is it? Not by my book, it ain't. Because it's gambling and it breeds gamblers and when you add it up there's one kind of gambling—the wrong kind."

"Feel better?" I asked him, putting some white iodine on my wounds.

"I'm an old tired beat-up cop. All I feel is sore."

I turned around and stared at him. "You're a damn good cop, Bernie, but just the same you're all wet. In one way cops are all the same. They all blame the wrong things. If a guy loses his pay check at a crap table, stop gambling. If he gets drunk, stop liquor. If he kills somebody in a car crash, stop making automobiles. If he gets pinched with a girl in a hotel room, stop sexual intercourse. If he falls downstairs, stop building houses."

"Aw shut up!"

"Sure, shut me up. I'm just a private citizen. Get off it, Bernie. We don't have mobs and crime syndicates and goon squads because we have crooked politicians and their stooges in the City Hall and the legislatures. Crime isn't a disease, it's a symptom. Cops are like a doctor that gives you aspirin for a brain tumor, except that the cop would rather cure it with a blackjack. We're a big rough rich wild people and crime is the price we pay for it, and organized crime is the price we pay for organization. We'll have it with us a long time. Organized crime is just the dirty side of the sharp dollar."

"What's the clean side?"

"I never saw it. Maybe Harlan Potter could tell you. Let's have a drink."

"You looked pretty good walking in that door," Ohls said.

"You looked better when Mendy pulled the knife on you."

"Shake," he said, and put his hand out.

We had the drink and he left by the back door, which he had jimmied to get in, having dropped by the night before for scouting purposes. Back doors are a soft touch if they open out and are old enough for the wood to have dried and shrunk. You knock the pins out of the hinges and the rest is easy. Ohls showed me a dent in the frame when he left to go back over the hill to where he had left his car on the next street. He could have opened the front door almost as easily but that would have broken the lock. It would have showed up too much.

I watched him climb through the trees with the beam of a torch in front of him and disappear over the rise. I locked the door and mixed another mild drink and went back to the living room and sat down. I looked at my watch. It was still early. It only seemed a long time since I had come home.

I went to the phone and dialed the operator and gave her the Lorings' phone number. The butler asked who was calling, then went to see if Mrs. Loring was in. She was.

"I was the goat all right," I said, "but they caught the tiger alive. I'm bruised up a little."

"You must tell me about it sometime." She sounded about as far away as if she had got to Paris already.

"I could tell you over a drink—if you had time."

"Tonight? Oh, I'm packing my things to move out. I'm afraid that would be impossible."

"Yes, I can see that. Well, I just thought you might like

to know. It was kind of you to warn me. It had nothing at all to do with your old man."

"Are you sure?"

"Positive."

"Oh. Just a minute." She was gone for a time, then she came back and sounded warmer. "Perhaps I could fit a drink in. Where?"

"Anywhere you say. I haven't a car tonight, but I can get a cab."

"Nonsense, I'll pick you up, but it will be an hour or longer. What is the address there?"

I told her and she hung up and I put the porch light on and then stood in the open door inhaling the night. It had got much cooler.

I went back in and tried to phone Lonnie Morgan but couldn't reach him. Then just for the hell of it I put a call in to the Terrapin Club at Las Vegas, Mr. Randy Starr. He probably wouldn't take it. But he did. He had a quiet, competent, man-of-affairs voice.

"Nice to hear from you, Marlowe. Any friend of Terry's is a friend of mine. What can I do for you?"

"Mendy is on his way."

"On his way where?"

"To Vegas, with the three goons you sent after him in a big black Caddy with a red spotlight and siren. Yours, I presume?"

He laughed. "In Vegas, as some newspaper guy said, we use Cadillacs for trailers. What's this all about?"

"Mendy staked out here in my house with a couple of hard boys. His idea was to beat me up—putting it low—for a piece in the paper he seemed to think was my fault."

"Was it your fault?"

"I don't own any newspapers, Mr. Starr."

"I don't own any hard boys in Cadillacs, Mr. Marlowe."

"They were deputies maybe."

"I couldn't say. Anything else?"

"He pistol-whipped me. I kicked him in the stomach and used my knee on his nose. He seemed dissatisfied. All the same I hope he gets to Vegas alive."

"I'm sure he will, if he started this way. I'm afraid I'll have to cut this conversation short now."

"Just a second, Starr. Were you in on that caper at Otatoclán—or did Mendy work it alone?"

"Come again?"

"Don't kid, Starr. Mendy wasn't sore at me for why he said—not to the point of staking out in my house and giving me the treatment he gave Big Willie Magoon. Not enough motive. He warned me to keep my nose clean and not to dig into the Lennox case. But I did, because it just happened to work out that way. So he did what I've just told you. So there was a better reason."

"I see," he said slowly and still mildly and quietly. "You think there was something not quite kosher about how Terry got dead? That he didn't shoot himself, for instance, but someone else did?"

"I think the details would help. He wrote a confession which was false. He wrote a letter to me which got mailed. A waiter or hop in the hotel was going to sneak it out and mail it for him. He was holed up in the hotel and couldn't get out. There was a big bill in the letter and the letter was finished just as a knock came at his door. I'd like to know who came into the room."

"Why?"

"If it had been a bellhop or a waiter, Terry would have added a line to the letter and said so. If it was a cop, the letter wouldn't have been mailed. So who was it—and why did Terry write that confession?"

"No idea, Marlowe. No idea at all."

"Sorry I bothered you, Mr. Starr."

"No bother, glad to hear from you. I'll ask Mendy if he has any ideas."

"Yeah—if you ever see him again—alive. If you don't— find out anyway. Or somebody else will."

"You?" His voice hardened now, but it was still quiet.

"No, Mr. Starr. Not me. Somebody that could blow you out of Vegas without taking a long breath. Believe me, Mr. Starr. Just believe me. This is strictly on the level."

"I'll see Mendy alive. Don't worry about that, Marlowe."

"I figured you knew all about that. Goodnight, Mr. Starr."

49

WHEN THE CAR STOPPED out front and the door opened I went out and stood at the top of the steps to call down. But the middle-aged colored driver was holding the door for her to get out. Then he followed her up the steps carrying a small overnight case. So I just waited.

She reached the top and turned to the driver: "Mr. Marlowe will drive me to my hotel, Amos. Thank you for everything. I'll call you in the morning."

"Yes, Mrs. Loring. May I ask Mr. Marlowe a question?"

"Certainly, Amos."

He put the overnight case down inside the door and she went in past me and left us.

" 'I grow old . . . I grow old . . . I shall wear the bottoms of my trousers rolled.' What does that mean, Mr. Marlowe?"

"Not a bloody thing. It just sounds good."

He smiled. "That is from the 'Love Song of J. Alfred Prufrock.' Here's another one. 'In the room the women come and go/Talking of Michael Angelo.' Does that suggest anything to you, sir?"

"Yeah—it suggests to me that the guy didn't know very much about women."

"My sentiments exactly, sir. Nonetheless I admire T. S. Eliot very much."

"Did you say 'nonetheless'?"

"Why, yes I did. Mr. Marlowe. Is that incorrect?"

"No, but don't say it in front of a millionaire. He might think you were giving him the hotfoot."

He smiled sadly. "I shouldn't dream of it. Have you had an accident, sir?"

"Nope. It was planned that way. Goodnight, Amos."

"Goodnight, sir."

He went back down the steps and I went back into the house. Linda Loring was standing in the middle of the living room looking around her.

"Amos is a graduate of Howard University," she said. "You don't live in a very safe place—for such an unsafe man, do you?"

"There aren't any safe places."

"Your poor face. Who did that to you?"

"Mendy Menendez."

"What did you do to him?"

"Nothing much. Kicked him a time or two. He walked into a trap. He's on his way to Nevada in the company of three or four tough Nevada deputies. Forget him."

She sat down on the davenport.

"What would you like to drink?" I asked. I got a cigarette box and held it out to her. She said she didn't want to smoke. She said anything would do to drink.

"I thought of champagne," I said. "I haven't any ice bucket, but it's cold. I've been saving it for years. Two bottles. Cordon Rouge. I guess it's good. I'm no judge."

"Saving it for what?" she asked.

"For you."

She smiled, but she was still staring at my face. "You're all cut." She reached her fingers up and touched my cheek lightly. "Saving it for me? That's not very likely. It's only a couple of months since we met."

"Then I was saving it until we met. I'll go get it." I picked up her overnight bag and started across the room with it.

"Just where are you going with that?" she asked sharply.

"It's an overnight bag, isn't it?"

"Put it down and come back here."

I did that. Her eyes were bright and at the same time they were sleepy.

"This is something new," she said slowly. "Something quite new."

"In what way?"

"You've never laid a finger on me. No passes, no suggestive remarks, no pawing, no nothing. I thought you were tough, sarcastic, mean, and cold."

"I guess I am—at times."

"Now I'm here and I suppose without preamble, after we have had a reasonable quantity of champagne you plan to grab me and throw me on the bed. Is that it?"

"Frankly," I said, "some such idea did stir at the back of my mind."

"I'm flattered, but suppose I don't want it that way? I like you. I like you very much. But it doesn't follow that I want to go to bed with you. Aren't you rather jumping at conclusions—just because I happen to bring an overnight bag with me?"

"Could be I made an error," I said. I went and got her overnight bag and put it back by the front door. "I'll get the champagne."

"I didn't mean to hurt your feelings. Perhaps you would rather save the champagne for some more auspicious occasion."

"It's only two bottles," I said. "A really auspicious occasion would call for a dozen."

"Oh, I see," she said, suddenly angry. "I'm just to be a fill-in until someone more beautiful and attractive comes along. Thank you so very much. Now you've hurt my feelings, but I suppose it's something to know that I'm safe here. If you think a bottle of champagne will make a loose woman out of me, I can assure you that you are very much mistaken."

"I admitted the mistake already."

"The fact that I told you I was going to divorce my husband and that I had Amos drop me by here with an overnight bag doesn't make me as easy as all that," she said, still angry.

"Damn the overnight bag!" I growled. "The hell with the overnight bag! Mention it again and I'll throw the damn thing down the front steps. I asked you to have a drink. I'm going out to the kitchen to get the drink. That's all. I hadn't the least idea of getting you drunk. You don't want to go to bed with me. I understand perfectly. No reason why you should. But we can still have a glass or two of champagne, can't we? This doesn't have to be a wrangle about who is going to get seduced and when and where and on how much champagne."

"You don't have to lose your temper," she said, flushing.

"That's just another gambit," I snarled. "I know fifty of them and I hate them all. They're all phony and they all have a sort of leer at the edges."

She got up and came over close to me and ran the tips of her fingers gently over the cuts and swollen places on my face. "I'm sorry. I'm a tired and disappointed woman. Please be kind to me. I'm no bargain to anyone."

"You're not tired and you're no more disappointed than most people are. By all the rules you ought to be the same sort of shallow spoiled promiscuous brat your sister was. By some miracle you're not. You've got all the honesty and a large part of the guts in your family. You don't need anyone to be kind to you."

I turned and walked out of the room down the hall to the kitchen and got one of the bottles of champagne out of the icebox and popped the cork and filled a couple of shallow goblets quickly and drank one down. The sting of it brought tears to my eyes, but I emptied the glass. I filled it again. Then I put the whole works on a tray and carted it into the living room.

She wasn't there. The overnight bag wasn't there. I put the tray down and opened the front door. I hadn't heard any sound of its opening and she had no car. I hadn't heard any sound at all.

Then she spoke from behind me. "Idiot, did you think I was going to run away?"

I shut the door and turned. She had loosened her hair and she had tufted slippers on her bare feet and a silk robe the color of a sunset in a Japanese print. She came towards me slowly with a sort of unexpectedly shy smile. I held a glass out to her. She took it, took a couple of sips of the champagne, and handed it back.

"It's very nice," she said. Then very quietly and without a trace of acting or affectation she came into my arms and pressed her mouth against mine and opened her lips and her teeth. The tip of her tongue touched mine. After a long time she pulled her head back but kept her arms around my neck. She was starry-eyed.

"I meant to all the time," she said. "I just had to be difficult. I don't know why. Just nerves perhaps. I'm not really a loose woman at all. Is that a pity?"

"If I had thought you were I'd have made a pass at you the first time I met you in the bar at Victor's."

She shook her head slowly and smiled. "I don't think so. That's why I am here."

"Perhaps not that night," I said. "That night belonged to something else."

"Perhaps you don't ever make passes at women in bars."

"Not often. The light's too dim."

"But a lot of women go to bars just to have passes made at them."

"A lot of women get up in the morning with the same idea."

"But liquor is an aphrodisiac—up to a point."

"Doctors recommend it."

"Who said anything about doctors? I want my champagne."

I kissed her some more. It was light, pleasant work.

"I want to kiss your poor cheek," she said, and did. "It's burning hot," she said.

"The rest of me is freezing."

"It is not. I want my champagne."

"Why?"

"It'll get flat if we don't drink it. Besides I like the taste of it."

"All right."

"Do you love me very much? Or will you if I go to bed with you?"

"Possibly."

"You don't have to go to bed with me, you know. I don't absolutely insist on it."

"Thank you."

"I want my champagne."

"How much money have you got?"

"Altogether? How would I know? About eight million dollars."

"I've decided to go to bed with you."

"Mercenary," she said.

"I paid for the champagne."

"The hell with the champagne," she said.

50

An hour later she stretched out a bare arm and tickled my ear and said: "Would you consider marrying me?"

"It wouldn't last six months."

"Well, for God's sake," she said, "suppose it didn't. Wouldn't it be worth it? What do you expect from life—full coverage against all possible risks?"

"I'm forty-two years old. I'm spoiled by independence. You're spoiled a little—not too much—by money."

"I'm thirty-six. It's no disgrace to have money and no disgrace to marry it. Most of those who have it don't deserve it and don't know how to behave with it. But it won't be long. We'll have another war and at the end of that nobody will have any money—except the crooks and the chiselers. We'll all be taxed to nothing, the rest of us."

I stroked her hair and wound some of it around my finger. "You may be right."

"We could fly to Paris and have a wonderful time." She raised herself on an elbow and looked down at me. I could see the shine of her eyes but I couldn't read her expression. "Do you have something against marriage?"

"For two people in a hundred it's wonderful. The rest just work at it. After twenty years all the guy has left is a work bench in the garage. American girls are terrific. American wives take in too damn much territory. Besides—"

"I want some champagne."

"Besides," I said, "it would be just an incident to you. The first divorce is the only tough one. After that its merely a problem in economics. No problem to you. Ten years from now you might pass me on the street and wonder where the hell you had seen me before. If you noticed me at all."

"You self-sufficient, self-satisfied, self-confident, untouchable bastard. I want some champagne."

"This way you will remember me."

"Conceited too. A mass of conceit. Slightly bruised at the moment. You think I'll remember you? No matter how many men I marry or sleep with, you think I'll remember you? Why should I?"

"Sorry. I overstated my case. I'll get you some champagne."

"Aren't we sweet and reasonable?" she said sarcastically. "I'm a rich woman, darling, and I shall be infinitely richer. I could buy you the world if it were worth buying. What have you now? An empty house to come home to, with not even a dog or cat, a small stuffy office to sit in and wait. Even if I divorced you I'd never let you go back to that."

"How would you stop me? I'm no Terry Lennox."

"Please. Don't let's talk about him. Nor about that golden icicle, the Wade woman. Nor about her poor drunken sunken husband. Do you want to be the only man who turned me down? What kind of pride is that? I've paid you the greatest compliment I know how to pay. I've asked you to marry me."

"You paid me a greater compliment."

She began to cry. "You fool, you utter fool!" Her cheeks were wet. I could feel the tears on them. "Suppose it lasted six months or a year or two years. What would you have lost except the dust on your office desk and the dirt on your venetian blinds and the loneliness of a pretty empty kind of life?"

"You still want some champagne?"

"All right."

I pulled her close and she cried against my shoulder. She wasn't in love with me and we both knew it. She wasn't crying over me. It was just time for her to shed a few tears.

Then she pulled away and I got out of bed and she went into the bathroom to fix her face. I got the champagne. When she came back she was smiling.

"I'm sorry I blubbered," she said. "In six months from now I won't even remember your name. Bring it into the living room. I want to see lights."

I did what she said. She sat on the davenport as before. I put the champagne in front of her. She looked at the glass but didn't touch it.

"I'll introduce myself," I said. "We'll have a drink together."

"Like tonight?"

"It won't ever be like tonight again."

She raised her glass of champagne, drank a little of it slowly, turned her body on the davenport and threw the rest in my face. Then she began to cry again. I got a handkerchief out and wiped my face off and wiped hers for her.

"I don't know why I did that," she said. "But for God's sake don't say I'm a woman and a woman never knows why she does anything."

I poured some more champagne into her glass and laughed at her. She drank it slowly and then turned the other way and fell across my knees.

"I'm tired," she said. "You'll have to carry me this time." After a while she went to sleep.

In the morning she was still asleep when I got up and made coffee. I showered and shaved and dressed. She woke up then. We had breakfast together. I called a cab and carried her overnight case down the steps.

We said goodbye. I watched the cab out of sight. I went back up the steps and into the bedroom and pulled the bed to pieces and remade it. There was a long dark hair on one of the pillows. There was a lump of lead at the pit of my stomach.

The French have a phrase for it. The bastards have a phrase for everything and they are always right.

To say goodbye is to die a little.

51

SEWELL ENDICOTT said he was working late and I could drop around in the evening about seven-thirty.

He had a corner office with a blue carpet, a red mahogany desk with carved corners, very old and obviously very valuable, the usual glass-front bookshelves of mustard-yellow legal books, the usual cartoons by Spy of famous English judges, and a large portrait of Justice Oliver Wendell Holmes on the south wall, alone. Endicott's chair was quilted in black leather. Near him was an open rolltop desk jammed with papers. It was an office no decorator had had a chance to pansy up.

He was in his shirtsleeves and he looked tired, but he had that kind of face. He was smoking one of his tasteless cigarettes. Ashes from it had fallen on his loosened tie. His limp black hair was all over the place.

He stared at me silently after I sat down. Then he said: "You're a stubborn son of a bitch, if ever I met one. Don't tell me you're still digging into that mess."

"Something worries me a little. Would it be all right now if I assumed you were representing Mr. Harlan Potter when you came to see me in the birdcage?"

He nodded. I touched the side of my face gently with my fingertips. It was all healed up and the swelling was gone, but one of the blows must have damaged a nerve. Part of the cheek was still numb. I couldn't let it alone. It would get all right in time.

"And that when you went to Otatoclán you were temporarily deputized as a member of the D.A.'s staff?"

"Yes, but don't rub it in, Marlowe. It was a valuable connection. Perhaps I gave it too much weight."

"Still is, I hope."

He shook his head. "No. That's finished. Mr. Potter does his legal business through San Francisco, New York, and Washington firms."

"I guess he hates my guts—if he thinks about it."

Endicott smiled. "Curiously enough, he put all the blame on his son-in-law, Dr. Loring. A man like Harlan Potter has to blame somebody. He couldn't possibly be wrong himself. He felt that if Loring hadn't been feeding the woman dangerous drugs, none of it would have happened."

"He's wrong. You saw Terry Lennox's body in Otatoclán, didn't you?"

"I did indeed. In the back of a cabinet maker's shop. They have no proper mortuary there. He was making the coffin too. The body was ice-cold. I saw the wound in the temple. There's no question of identity, if you had any ideas along those lines."

"No, Mr. Endicott, I didn't, because in his case it could hardly be possible. He was disguised a little though, wasn't he?"

"Face and hands darkened, hair dyed black. But the scars were still obvious. And the fingerprints, of course, were easily checked from things he had handled at home."

"What kind of police force do they have down there?"

"Primitive. The jefe could just about read and write. But he knew about fingerprints. It was hot weather, you know. Quite hot." He frowned and took his cigarette out of his mouth and dropped it negligently into an enormous black basalt sort of receptacle. "They had to get ice from the hotel," he added. "Plenty of ice." He looked at me again. "No embalming there. Things have to move fast."

"You speak Spanish, Mr. Endicott?"

"Only a few words. The hotel manager interpreted." He smiled. "A well-dressed smoothie, that fellow. Looked tough, but he was very polite and helpful. It was all over in no time."

"I had a letter from Terry. I guess Mr. Potter would know about it. I told his daughter, Mrs. Loring. I showed it to her. There was a portrait of Madison in it."

"A what?"

"Five-thousand-dollar bill."

He raised his eyebrows. "Really. Well, he could certainly afford it. His wife gave him a cool quarter of a million the second time they were married. I've an idea he meant to go to Mexico to live anyhow—quite apart from what happened. I don't know what happened to the money. I wasn't in on that."

"Here's the letter, Mr. Endicott, if you care to read it."

I took it out and gave it to him. He read it carefully, the way lawyers read everything. He put it down on the desk and leaned back and stared at nothing.

"A little literary, isn't it?" he said quietly. "I wonder why he did it."

"Killed himself, confessed, or wrote me the letter?"

"Confessed and killed himself, of course," Endicott said sharply. "The letter is understandable. At least you got a reasonable recompense for what you did for him—and since."

"The mailbox bothers me," I said. "Where he says there was a mailbox on the street under his window and the hotel waiter was going to hold his letter up before he mailed it, so Terry could see that it was mailed."

Something in Endicott's eyes went to sleep. "Why?" he asked indifferently. He picked another of his filtered cigarettes out of a square box. I held my lighter across the desk for him.

"They wouldn't have one in a place like Otatoclán," I said.

"Go on."

"I didn't get it at first. Then I looked the place up. It's a mere village. Population say ten or twelve thousand.

One street partly paved. The jefe has a Model A Ford as an official car. The post office is in the corner of a store, the chanceria, the butcher shop. One hotel, a couple of cantinas, no good roads, a small airfield. There's hunting around there in the mountains—lots of it. Hence the airfield. Only decent way to get there."

"Go on. I know about the hunting."

"So there's a mailbox on the street. Like there's a race course and a dog track and a golf course and a jai alai frontón and park with a colored fountain and a bandstand."

"Then he made a mistake," Endicott said coldly. "Perhaps it was something that looked like a mailbox to him—say a trash receptacle."

I stood up. I reached for the letter and refolded it and put it back in my pocket.

"A trash receptacle," I said. "Sure, that's it. Painted with the Mexican colors, green, white, red, and a sign on it stenciled in large clear print: KEEP OUR CITY CLEAN. In Spanish, of course. And lying around it seven mangy dogs."

"Don't get cute, Marlowe."

"Sorry if I let my brains show. Another small point I have already raised with Randy Starr. How come the letter got mailed at all? According to the letter the method was prearranged. So somebody told him about the mailbox. So somebody lied. So somebody mailed the letter with five grand in it just the same. Intriguing, don't you agree?"

He puffed smoke and watched it float away.

"What's your conclusion—and why ring Starr in on it?"

"Starr and a heel named Menendez, now removed from our midst, were pals of Terry's in the British Army. They are wrong gees in a way—I should say in almost every way—but they still have room for personal pride and so on. There was a cover-up here engineered for obvious reasons. There was another sort of cover-up in Otatoclán, for entirely different reasons."

"What's your conclusion?" he asked me again and much more sharply.

"What's yours?"

He didn't answer me. So I thanked him for his time and left.

He was frowning as I opened the door, but I thought it was an honest frown of puzzlement. Or maybe he was trying to remember how it looked outside the hotel and whether there was a mailbox there.

It was another wheel to start turning—no more. It turned for a solid month before anything came up.

Then on a certain Friday morning I found a stranger waiting for me in my office. He was a well-dressed Mexican or Suramericano of some sort. He sat by the open window smoking a brown cigarette that smelled strong. He was tall and very slender and very elegant, with a neat dark mustache and dark hair, rather longer than we wear it, and a fawn-colored suit of some loosely woven material. He wore those green sunglasses. He stood up politely.

"Señor Marlowe?"

"What can I do for you?"

He handed me a folded paper. "Un aviso de parte del Señor Starr en Las Vegas, señor. Habla Usted Español?"

"Yeah, but not fast. English would be better."

"English then," he said. "It is all the same to me."

I took the paper and read it. "This introduces Cisco Maioranos, a friend of mine. I think he can fix you up. S."

"Let's go inside, Señor Maioranos," I said.

I held the door open for him. He smelled of perfume as he went by. His eyebrows were awfully damned dainty too. But he probably wasn't as dainty as he looked because there were knife scars on both sides of his face.

52

HE SAT DOWN in the customer's chair and crossed his knees. "You wish certain information about Señor Lennox, I am told."

"The last scene only."

"I was there at the time, señor. I had a position in the hotel." He shrugged. "Unimportant and of course temporary. I was the day clerk." He spoke perfect English but with a Spanish rhythm. Spanish—American Spanish that is—has a definite rise and fall which to an American ear seems to have nothing to do with the meaning. It's like the swell of the ocean.

"You don't look the type," I said.

"One has difficulties."

"Who mailed the letter to me?"

He held out a box of cigarettes. "Try one of these."

I shook my head. "Too strong for me. Colombian cigarettes I like. Cuban cigarettes are murder."

He smiled faintly, lit another pill himself, and blew smoke. The guy was so goddam elegant he was beginning to annoy me.

"I know about the letter, señor. The mozo was afraid to go up to the room of this Señor Lennox after the guarda was posted. The cop or dick, as you say. So I myself took the letter to the correo. After the shooting, you understand."

"You ought to have looked inside. It had a large piece of money in it."

"The letter was sealed," he said coldly. "El honor no se mueve de lado como los congrejos. That is, honor does not move sidewise like a crab, señor."

"My apologies. Please continue."

"Señor Lennox had a hundred-peso note in his left hand when I went into the room and shut the door in the face of the guarda. In his right hand was a pistol. On the table before him was the letter. Also another paper which I did not read. I refused the note."

"Too much money," I said, but he didn't react to the sarcasm.

"He insisted. So I took the note finally and gave it to the mozo later. I took the letter out under the napkin on the tray from the previous service of coffee. The dick looked hard at me. But he said nothing. I was halfway down the stairs when I heard the shot. Very quickly I hid the letter and ran back upstairs. The dick was trying to kick the door open. I used my key. Señor Lennox was dead."

He moved his fingertips gently along the edge of the desk and sighed. "The rest no doubt you know."

"Was the hotel full?"

"Not full, no. There were half a dozen guests."

"Americans?"

"Two Americanos del Norte. Hunters."

"Real Gringos or just transplanted Mexicans?"

He drew a fingertip slowly along the fawn-colored cloth above his knee. "I think one of them could well have been of Spanish origin. He spoke border Spanish. Very inelegant."

"They go near Lennox's room at all?"

He lifted his head sharply but the green cheaters didn't do a thing for me. "Why should they, señor?"

I nodded. "Well, it was damn nice of you to come in here and tell me about it, Señor Maioranos. Tell Randy I'm ever so grateful, will you?"

"No hay de que, señor. It is nothing."

"And later on, if he has time, he could send me somebody who knows what he is talking about."

"Señor?" His voice was soft, but icy. "You doubt my word?"

"You guys are always talking about honor. Honor is the cloak of thieves—sometimes. Don't get mad. Sit quiet and let me tell it another way."

He leaned back superciliously.

"I'm only guessing, mind. I could be wrong. But I could be right too. These two Americanos were there for a purpose. They came in on a plane. They pretended to be hunters. One of them was named Menendez, a gambler. He registered under some other name or not. I wouldn't know. Lennox knew they were there. He knew why. He wrote me that letter because he had a guilty conscience. He had played me for a sucker and he was too nice a guy for that to rest easy on him. He put the bill—five thousand dollars it was—in the letter because he had a lot of money and he knew I hadn't. He also put in a little off-beat hint which might or might not register. He was the kind of guy who always wants to do the right thing but somehow winds up doing something else. You say you took the letter to the correo. Why didn't you mail it in the box in front of the hotel?"

"The box, señor?"

"The mailbox. The cajón cartero, you call it, I think."

He smiled. "Otatoclán is not Mexico City, señor. It is a very primitive place. A street mailbox in Otatoclán? No one there would understand what it was for. No one would collect letters from it."

I said: "Oh. Well, skip it. You did not take any coffee on any tray up to Señor Lennox's room, Señor Maioranos. You did not go into the room past the dick. But the two Americanos did go in. The dick was fixed, of course. So were several other people. One of the Americanos slugged Lennox from behind. Then he took the Mauser pistol and opened up one of the cartridges and took out the bullet and put the cartridge back in the breech. Then he put this gun to Lennox's temple and pulled the trigger. It made a nasty-looking wound, but it did not kill him. Then he was carried out on a stretcher covered up and well hidden. Then when the American lawyer arrived, Lennox was doped and packed in ice and kept in a dark corner of the carpintería where the man was making a coffin. The American lawyer saw Lennox there, he was ice-cold, in a deep stupor, and there was a bloody blackened wound in his temple. He looked plenty dead. The next day the coffin was buried with stones in it. The American lawyer went home with the fingerprints and some kind of document which was a piece of cheese. How do you like that, Señor Maioranos?"

He shrugged. "It would be possible, señor. It would require money and influence. It would be possible, perhaps, if this Señor Menendez was closely related to important people in Otatoclán, the alcalde, the hotel proprietor and so on."

"Well, that's possible to. It's a good idea. It would explain why they picked a remote little place like Otatoclán."

He smiled quickly. "Then Señor Lennox may still be alive, no?"

"Sure. The suicide had to be some kind of fake to back up the confession. It had to be good enough to fool a lawyer who had been a district attorney, but it would make a very sick monkey out of the current D.A. if it backfired. This Menendez is not as tough as he thinks he is, but he was tough enough to pistol-whip me for not keeping my nose clean. So he had to have reasons. If the fake got exposed, Menendez would be right in the middle of an international stink. The Mexicans don't like crooked police work any more than we do."

"All that is possible, señor, as I very well know. But you accused me of lying. You said I did not go into the room where Señor Lennox was and get his letter."

"You were already in there, chum—writing the letter."

He reached up and took the dark glasses off. Nobody can change the color of a man's eyes.

"I suppose it's a bit too early for a gimlet," he said.

53

THEY HAD DONE A WONDERFUL JOB on him in Mexico City, but why not? Their doctors, technicians, hospitals, painters, architects are as good as ours. Sometimes a little better. A Mexican cop invented the paraffin test for powder nitrates. They couldn't make Terry's face perfect, but they had done plenty. They had even changed his nose, taken out some bone and made it look flatter, less Nordic. They couldn't eliminate every trace of a scar, so they had put a couple on the other side of his face too. Knife scars are not uncommon in Latin countries.

"They even did a nerve graft up here," he said, and touched what had been the bad side of his face.

"How close did I come?"

"Close enough. A few details wrong, but they are not important. It was a quick deal and some of it was improvised and I didn't know myself just what was going to happen. I was told to do certain things and to leave a clear trail. Mendy didn't like my writing to you, but I held out for that. He undersold you a little. He never noticed the bit about the mailbox."

"You know who killed Sylvia?"

He didn't answer me directly. "It's pretty tough to turn a woman in for murder—even if she never meant much to you."

"It's a tough world. Was Harlan Potter in on all this?"

He smiled again. "Would he be likely to let anyone

know that? My guess is not. My guess is he thinks I am dead. Who would tell him otherwise—unless you did?"

"What I'd tell him you could fold into a blade of grass. How's Mendy these days—or is he?"

"He's doing all right. In Acapulco. He slipped by because of Randy. But the boys don't go for rough work on cops. Mendy's not as bad as you think. He has a heart."

"So has a snake."

"Well, what about that gimlet?"

I got up without answering him and went to the safe. I spun the knob and got out the envelope with the portrait of Madison on it and the five C notes that smelled of coffee. I dumped the lot out on the desk and then picked up the five C notes.

"These I keep. I spent almost all of it on expenses and research. The portrait of Madison I enjoyed playing with. It's all yours now."

I spread it on the edge of the desk in front of him. He looked at it but didn't touch it.

"It's yours to keep," he said. "I've got plenty. You could have let things lie."

"I know. After she killed her husband and got away with it she might have gone on to better things. He was of no real importance, of course. Just a human being with blood and a brain and emotions. He knew what happened too and he tried pretty hard to live with it. He wrote books. You may have heard of him."

"Look, I couldn't very well help what I did," he said slowly. "I didn't want anyone to get hurt. I wouldn't have had a dog's chance up here. A man can't figure every angle that quick. I was scared and I ran. What should I have done?"

"I don't know."

"She had a mad streak. She might have killed him anyway."

"Yeah, she might."

"Well, thaw out a little. Let's go have a drink somewhere where it's cool and quiet."

"No time right now, Señor Maioranos."

"We were pretty good friends once," he said unhappily.

"Were we? I forget. That was two other fellows, seems to me. You permanently in Mexico?"

"Oh yes. I'm not here legally even. I never was. I told you I was born in Salt Lake City. I was born in Montreal. I'll be a Mexican national pretty soon now. All it takes is a good lawyer. I've always liked Mexico. It wouldn't be much risk going to Victor's for that gimlet."

"Pick up your money, Señor Maioranos. It has too much blood on it."

"You're a poor man."

"How would you know?"

He picked the bill up and stretched it between his thin fingers and slipped it casually into an inside pocket. He bit his lip with the very white teeth you can have when you have a brown skin.

"I couldn't tell you any more than I did that morning you drove me to Tijuana. I gave you a chance to call the law and turn me in."

"I'm not sore at you. You're just that kind of guy. For a long time I couldn't figure you at all. You had nice ways and nice qualities, but there was something wrong. You had standards and you lived up to them, but they were personal. They had no relation to any kind of ethics or scruples. You were a nice guy because you had a nice nature. But you were just as happy with mugs or hoodlums as with honest men. Provided the hoodlums spoke fairly good English and had fairly acceptable table manners. You're a moral defeatist. I think maybe the war did it and again I think maybe you were born that way."

"I don't get it," he said. "I really don't. I'm trying to pay you back and you won't let me. I couldn't have told you any more than I did. You wouldn't have stood for it."

"That's as nice a thing as was ever said to me."

"I'm glad you like something about me. I got in a bad jam. I happened to know the sort of people who know how to deal with bad jams. They owed me for an incident that happened long ago in the war. Probably the only time in my life I ever did the right thing quick like a mouse. And when I needed them, they delivered. And for free. You're not the only guy in the world that has no price tag, Marlowe."

He leaned across the desk and snapped at one of my cigarettes. There was an uneven flush on his face under the deep tan. The scars showed up against it. I watched him spring a fancy gas cartridge lighter loose from a pocket and light the cigarette. I got a whiff of perfume from him.

"You bought a lot of me, Terry. For a smile and a nod and a wave of the hand and a few quiet drinks in a quiet bar here and there. It was nice while it lasted. So long, amigo. I won't say goodbye. I said it to you when it meant something. I said it when it was sad and lonely and final."

"I came back too late," he said. "These plastic jobs take time."

"You wouldn't have come at all if I hadn't smoked you out."

There was suddenly a glint of tears in his eyes. He put his dark glasses back on quickly.

"I wasn't sure about it," he said. "I hadn't made up my mind. They didn't want me to tell you anything. I just hadn't made up my mind."

"Don't worry about it, Terry. There's always somebody around to do it for you."

"I was in the Commandos, bud. They don't take you if you're just a piece of fluff. I got badly hurt and it wasn't any fun with those Nazi doctors. It did something to me."

"I know all that, Terry. You're a very sweet guy in a lot of ways. I'm not judging you. I never did. It's just that you're not here any more. You're long gone. You've got nice clothes and perfume and you're as elegant as a fifty-dollar whore."

"That's just an act," he said almost desperately.

"You get a kick out of it, don't you?"

His mouth dropped in a sour smile. He shrugged an expressive energetic Latin shrug.

"Of course. An act is all there is. There isn't anything else. In here—" he tapped his chest with the lighter—"there isn't anything. I've had it, Marlowe. I had it long ago. Well—I gues that winds things up."

He stood up. I stood up. He put out a lean hand. I shook it.

"So long, Señor Maioranos. Nice to have known you—however briefly."

"Goodbye."

He turned and walked across the floor and out. I watched the door close. I listened to his steps going away down the imitation marble corridor. After a while they got faint, then they got silent. I kept on listening anyway.

What for? Did I want him to stop suddenly and turn and come back and talk me out of the way I felt? Well, he didn't. That was the last I saw of him.

I never saw any of them again—except the cops. No way has yet been invented to say goodbye to them.